A Storybook Wedding

KJ MICCICHE

Published by Sourcebooks Casablanca, an imprint of Sourcebooks
P.O. Box 4410, Naperville, Illinois 6056-74410
(630) 961-3900
sourcebooks.com

Cataloging-in-Publication Data is on file with the Library of Congress.

Printed and bound in the United States of America.
LSC 10 9 8 7 6 5 4 3 2 1

PROLOGUE

Cecily

"And they lived happily ever after."

I close the storybook, satisfied at the sound of the hardcover as it claps shut. From my itty-bitty plastic purple chair, I look up and meet the eyes of the dozen children and single dog who are seated on the fluffy round area rug before me in the laps of tired mommies and weary caregivers. Earlier, I was informed by my director that the canine companion—a low to the ground but otherwise charming young beagle named Tinkerbell—is allowed to be here in spite of the library's strict *no pets* policy, since she is technically an emotional support animal for Joshie, a rambunctious toddler who's currently trying to shove one of our rice shakers into his mouth. More accurately, I suspect, Tinkerbell is here to support Joshie's mother, a grade-A Karen best known for complaining about everything from our restroom-key policies to the timing of our parent-child yoga class, from which she absolutely could benefit.

Despite my aggravation at having to monitor the noticeably squirmy pup, I cannot help but be transported by the story—or, more specifically, the line, its syllables exploding with the lofty weight of *expectation*. The very same words were the theme song of my childhood. Such an innocent phrase. Blissful, ignorant optimism.

Happily ever after.

My memory, clear as day, brings me back to the high school classroom where it all began—or ended, I suppose one could argue—with those same words printed on page 73 of the crisp May issue of *Seventeen* magazine nestled in the lap of Ms. Brown, my beloved English teacher. She was careful not to fold down the binding or crease the thin pages with her fingers by accident, as it was my personal copy, mailed directly from the Hearst Corporation in a large yellow envelope. Ms. Brown knew its value far surpassed the newsstand price on the cover. She gingerly set it down on her desk and looked right at me.

Her smile conveyed more joy than any words my young mind could think of.

"You did it," she said, beaming. Her teeth were so white, they illuminated the space between us, like a flashlight under the covers lights up a hidden paperback after bedtime. "You, my dear, are officially a published author."

Pride made my heart swell up like an allergic reaction to a bee sting.

The short story, titled "Malled," was a modern-day fairy-tale retelling of what happened when Rapunzel, struck with agoraphobia from being locked up her whole life, escaped her tower and got lost in a shopping center. Not only did it win me bragging rights in my ninth grade advanced English class, but it also came with the handsome prize of $500. Yet the real excitement was in this moment, lodged in my mind eternally—the moment that produced the next six words uttered from Ms. Brown's mouth.

"I'm so proud of you, Cecily."

I basked in the blinding glow of her praise. Ms. Brown was an *author*. She minimized it, calling it her "side hustle," but she'd privately divulged to a select few students—me included—that her dream was to write middle-grade fiction for a living. She shared all kinds of interesting stories about "the industry" with us—*publishing*—throwing around words like *agent*, *editor*, and *release*, words that intoxicated my wildly ambitious adolescent psyche. And in my memory, hearing her use my name in the same breath as the phrase *published author*, well. I was…dumbfounded. Until the next six words came.

"So what did your parents say?"

I could feel my cheeks drop from their rounded positions flanking my grin. Gravity tugged them back into place, reminding me that despite our life in New York City—the metropolis of the *world*—I was silently expected to walk a different path. Never mind the fact that even Alicia Keys promised my hometown to be a "concrete jungle where dreams are made of." Well, okay, *fine*, maybe not my exact suburban outer-borough neighborhood of Bayside, Queens, but you get what I'm saying. People with aspirations like mine *came* here to grow, to learn, to immerse themselves in the culture and the thrumming rhythm of constant striving that exists around every corner. (Again, not so much in Bayside, where around the corner sat a squat sushi take-out joint and a wash-n-fold, but just a quick thirty-five-minute ride on the Long Island Railroad could transport one to the mecca of inspired, metamorphosis-inducing, glorious *Manhattan*, the publishing capital of the world.)

"Um," I stammered. "They're happy for me."

"This is a *huge* deal," she exclaimed.

I forced my cheeks to stay where they were, fake smiling my way around the truth, which was that my news was promptly overshadowed by a phone call from my aunt announcing that she was going to become a grandmother (again—her fourth grandchild in as many years). Not to say that I wasn't excited to hear that my cousin's womb was as fertile as the soil on an organic sustainable farm. I was.

I am.

"That's really something." My mom regarded my big news with a nod. The response notably lacked the squealing she emitted when my sister Melanie found the perfect prom dress, or the clapping that accompanied Jamie's first boy-girl dance invitation, or the happy tears that ensued immediately following Anna's engagement announcement. I quietly measured it against the screeching joy she doused me with when I was invited out for pizza with a boy from the tutoring center just weeks prior. Being published was, sadly, in a far distant second place. Still, I imagined my mother was proud of me in her own way, even if she lacked the gushing enthusiasm that Ms. Brown generously showered me with in my memory.

Ironically, it is a different type of shower that yanks me from this private moment in the recesses of my mind.

I feel it first, the sudden splash of something warm that dots, then soaks the ankle of my khaki pants.

I smell it next, wafting up from the new puddle that grazes against my fluffy story time slippers.

Then I hear it, the "Oh my God, I'm *so* sorry!" that erupts at the exact same time as my own gasp.

Fucking Tinkerbell peed on my foot.

"She gets excited," the suddenly flustered Karen explains, "and sometimes, she piddles when that happens." Karen collects Joshie, who is laughing maniacally at the scene unfolding, up into her free arm and goes on. "I better take her outside, you know, so it doesn't happen again." She blushes, grabs her coat off a chairback, and hustles Tinkerbell out of the children's section, leaving me aghast, a human toilet amid eleven remaining bite-size sets of gigantic, curious eyes.

"Welp," I finally say, "I'm sorry, friends. I'm afraid we'll have to save the remainder of story time for next week."

Understanding if sad maternal nods bob up and down, and parents yearning for just a few more minutes of somebody *else* entertaining their kids begin gathering jackets, hats, and other assorted winter items to head back out and brave the cold January morning. I, meanwhile, kick off my slippers, remove my ankle socks, and begin to roll up the fluffy area rug from the far edge. As the patrons walk out, Ramona walks in.

"What happened in here?" she wonders.

"Don't ask."

"What is that smell?"

I look up from the ground. "You know Joshie? The blondie with the beagle?"

"Did he pee himself?"

"Worse. His puppy mistook me for a fire hydrant."

"Oh my God, seriously? Someone's having a Monday," Ramona giggles.

"And, to add insult to injury, I'm pretty sure he stole one of my brand-new rice shakers."

"Aggravated assault *and* robbery?"

I drop the rug, having rolled up most of it, and grab the hand sanitizer off the shelf behind me. "You have no idea what it's like over here. It's pure mayhem."

"Please. Plenty of nonsense goes on in the adult section. Remember, I had to deal with the flasher?"

"Ew, yes. But you had actual police assistance. This is not a real 911 kind of emergency."

"True. My point is you're not the only one," she says. Then she extends her hand to offer me an envelope. "Anyway, this came for you."

I take it from her.

"I'll go ask Jeff to bring you a mop and a garbage bag. But that looks important," she continues. "Maybe like something you've been waiting for," she sings.

Ramona winks at me and hightails it out of there. I examine the business-size envelope. It's from the Northeast Library Association. I set the rug down so I have two free hands available to open it.

Dear Ms. Allerton, it reads. Congratulations! After careful consideration, your application has been selected to receive an award from the Northeast Library Association's Future Leaders Scholarship Fund. We are pleased to offer you a one-time grant of $20,000 toward your pursuit of an MFA in Creative Writing.

Holy shit.

I got the scholarship.

I look around. Shelves of colorful children's books smile at me, delivering silent praise. After all these years, laden with scores of weddings and babies and more weddings and more babies, I know better than to expect that my parents will get excited at the prospect of me going back to school. I sometimes imagine the utter chagrin my poor family must face on a daily basis, knowing that I have grown into a twenty-nine-year-old spinster who reads storybooks aloud to neighborhood kiddos on Monday mornings at the Forest Hills branch of the Queens Public Library. Month after month, I recklessly allow my menstrual cycle to fall short of my mother's aspirations for my womb. Surely, a scholarship for $20,000 as I approach my thirtieth birthday will mean just as little to her as the $500 prize I won half a lifetime ago.

I force myself to ignore my knee-jerk reaction to call her and share this exciting news.

After all, this is the beginning of *my* happily-ever-after, not hers.

CHAPTER 1

Cecily

It wasn't supposed to be like this.

I came here toting a backpack filled with hopes, dreams, and Sharpie highlighters. Like a true first-day-of-school experience, I laid out my outfit the day before and tossed and turned all night from the eager anticipation. I was going to get to be around *authors*—real authors who've published some of the very books we carry in our library! I would meet other writers striving toward publication. Lovers of literature! People like me!

Kindred spirits.

Unfortunately, I'm beginning to think I may have misjudged this whole experience based on the promotional materials. In fact, it's possible that I may have inadvertently broken cardinal rule number one: *Don't judge a book by its cover.*

"I appreciate the attempt to create a world fraught with emotion, but the drama seems a little thin overall. I mean, I get the whole 'what's at stake' for the narrator—sure, high school is hard and she wants to be accepted—but it's not quite hitting home for me. This story, in my opinion, just feels trite."

Whoa. Ouch.

As I listen to the criticism, tears spring to my eyes. I blink them back, busying myself by frantically scribbling notes onto the first page in my brand-new mint-colored spiral notebook, now sullied by the word *trite* written under the heading *Workshop with Nate Ellis—Day One*. I read online that MFA workshops can be brutal, but jeez. I wasn't expecting to hear a nasty word like *trite* in my first moment out of the gate.

Breathe, Cecily. It's not like this random guy is your target audience.

"Please, Tim, let's follow the standard workshop rules. We need to be sensitive to the writer, although in this case, I tend to agree that the need for acceptance as a theme is falling a bit short in terms of depth." These words come from the mouth of my teacher, a PEN Award winner who is disturbingly (1) young and (2) handsome. I guess his novel must have ranked pretty high on the *depth* scale to earn him such a prestigious literary accolade, but if I'm being entirely truthful, I rode the struggle bus big time in my attempt to read it. Which sort of makes me wonder, does this guy work here just so people buy his book, since it's required reading for the program?

"May I—" I begin to ask, hoping to defend my work.

"Hang on, Cecily. For now, let's hear what else folks have to say."

I clamp my mouth shut and resume staring down at my notebook.

"Harold, how about you?"

Across from me, a middle-aged man with a round face, brown bangs, and circular glasses who is wearing (I cannot make this up) a *cape* strokes an invisible goatee, staring out the window as if searching for the perfect words to use to describe my life's work. Perhaps this Hogwarts doppelganger is precisely what our workshop needs: an intelligent soul who can remind the group that I worked hard on this piece, and even if it's not perfect, I am here to learn, and I have tremendous potential.

"Overall?" he begins, and I wait optimistically for him to find the appropriate commendation. "I thought it was good. But—"

"Remember," Professor PEN Award says, "we're not looking for subjective opinions on the readability of the work. We're looking for *constructive* criticism here. What can Cecily do to improve this piece?"

Ugh. Why'd you have to interrupt him? Didn't you hear him use the word good? *He thought it was good! Just leave it alone!*

My heart's pumping hard, as if I just finished an hour on the treadmill, minus the endorphins and the feeling of satisfaction one can get from a good sweat. It's more akin to the thumping of a young deer's pulse after hearing gunshots in the tranquil forest. *Run. Hide, Bambi. You're under siege by a literary elitist hunter who undoubtedly reads Faulkner, Proust, and Dostoyevsky for fun. No Emily Henry novels to be found here. Just the author of some critically acclaimed* New York Times *bestselling debut author parading around like a professor whose sole mission is, apparently, to get people to trash talk your work.* My feet are anchored to the ground, and I absently pick at my thumbnail cuticle. I will not allow the words to sting me. Sticks and stones and all that. I will just breathe, and the fresh ocean air will infuse clarity through my veins, cleansing my mind and (more importantly) my heart from the toxic highbrow remarks in this workshop. Inhale. Exhale. Let the words float out to sea.

I am an island.

"Well," Harry Potter replies, "in my opinion, the narrator, Daisy, lacked a character arc. She felt more like a grumbly teenager than a stoic ingenue."

"Can you give us an example?"

"Hm," Harold replies, furrowing his brow. He uses his pointer finger to scroll on his tablet screen. "Here. On page sixteen. Third paragraph down." He clears his throat.

"'Tony was sitting with Veronica in the cafeteria, only seventy-two hours after sliding his tongue down my throat. How could this be, after I told him how she tried to ruin my life in middle school? A slick of bile threatened regurgitation as I considered my options. I could slash his bicycle tires, of course, although that might look fairly obvious. I could throw my lunch tray in his face, but I'd never been one for theatrics. What else was there? Pull the fire alarm? Feed arsenic to his dog? I stood there for a moment, staring at them from behind the trash can, when it hit me. The sweetest revenge is indifference. I held my chin high and strode easily past them.'"

He looks up. "I don't know. I get that she's trying to work through this big moment or whatever, but I just feel like it lacks interiority."

Remain calm, I tell myself. I try to hear the comments as if they're not about my work. *Lacks interiority,* I write down.

"Thank you," Tim says, gesturing at Harold and nodding vehemently. "That's exactly what I'm talking about. Like, okay, so Tony is sitting with Veronica. And yes, we know that Veronica spread rumors about Daisy and that they hate each other, but how is Daisy not more impacted by this moment of betrayal in the lunchroom? I think that's my issue with the story."

"So it's not the plotline," Professor PEN Award says.

"No," Tim replies. "It's the character development."

"This is YA, obviously," another voice says. This time, it's the pretty woman to my left with twin purple braids cascading down her back and bright red lipstick accentuating her high cheekbones. Her name is Andrea, but she pronounces it *Ahn-dray-uh,* all fancy-like. My hope is that she's about to come to my rescue, that her comments will be as lovely as the tattoo of angel wings adorning her bare shoulder. In fact, I direct what remaining strength I have to the task of forgetting that her workshop submission, titled "Lotus Blossom Soup," was so abstract it was nearly unintelligible. But when she opens her mouth, I am met with my own personal horror once again. "I think you're creating false expectations for genre fiction," she says, and the words turn her braids into horns. My mind twists her angled face into *Sleeping Beauty's* Maleficent;

the angel wings morph into those of a black dragon as my breath catches in my throat. *Seriously?* This from a woman whose piece opened with the following line: *To find the soul of one's ethereal depth, one must look no further than the spoon of life.* Which made me wonder if I was reading a bad fortune cookie, or if the line had been written while the author was extremely high.

"How do you mean?" PEN Award asks.

She purses her chapped lips. "It's commercial," Maleficent explains. "Surface. Character arc not required." She waves her hand, as if shooing an illiterate mosquito out of the space immediately in front of her right boob.

The realization hits me like a stack of hardcovers.

I am the illiterate mosquito.

No, no. Stop it, Cecily! You are above this! You are transcendent in this maelstrom of negativity. I write the words *character arc* on the college-ruled page before me.

"I disagree," Trite Tim rebuts.

This goes on for several minutes, and I will myself not to listen to any of it. I work on intentional breathing. In, two three, four. Out, two, three, four.

To be fair, none of this was on the website. Or in the welcome folder. Or even discussed at orientation yesterday! In fact, when I got my acceptance letter from Matthias University, the director of the program—a novelist and poet laureate named Dillon Norway—actually *complimented* my ability to write about young people with depth and verve. He also said that my work had *resounding acoustic density* and *emotional complexity.*

Those phrases were the reason I chose this school. Well, that and the low-residency model. When I began applying, my director at the library told me she wouldn't be able to change my work schedule to accommodate regularly scheduled grad classes all year long. However, she told me to look into low-res programs, since she could convince the board to approve me taking a short stint away twice a year. That's the model. You come away for an eight-day intensive in the summer and an eight-day intensive in the winter, and you're paired with a mentor for the in-between time, which is technically considered independent study. You write and submit twenty-five pages a month to your mentor, who meets with you virtually to discuss the work you've produced. You're also responsible for reading ten books per semester and writing craft essays on them. Lather, rinse, repeat four times for two years, and then come back for the fifth residency, where you'll graduate with an MFA.

Sure, this might seem like a heavy lift on top of an already busy day job, but keep in mind that minus a relationship status, I've got more than enough time to tackle these assignments. Also, my acceptance kind of felt like a dream come true. This was due in large part to the glossy catalog photographs, because the residencies at Matthias College take place on beautiful, remote Block Island at a retreat center called New Beginnings. I mean, really—does it get more perfect than that? You get to write and be amid breathtaking scenery, and the website features New England clambake dinners at sunset with people laughing and wearing lobster bibs. My library scholarship covered half the cost of my tuition, and I had enough in my savings account to cover the other half without having to dip into my rainy-day fund. But more than all that, the chance to become an *author*—to write a novel, send it out in search of a literary agent, submit it to publishing houses, and ultimately see it on the shelf in my own library—now *that* would be a real-life happy ending.

I packed like a madwoman for this first residency. Between Amazon and Staples, I purchased every school supply one could imagine. Unsure of what the ever-fluctuating evening temperatures on Block Island would bring, I brought sweatshirts and leggings along with business-casual-type outfits for daytime workshops and seminars. I hugged my colleague Ramona and made her promise to feed Blinky, the betta fish I keep at the circulation desk, and at sunrise the next morning, I drove my car a hundred miles from Little Neck, Queens, out to Montauk to catch myself a ferry to Block Island. My large suitcase sported a duffel on top, and I awkwardly carried a backpack filled with books, binders, and my laptop strapped to my torso like a bulletproof vest. In my free hand, I clutched the folder of information regarding travel and lodging at the retreat house, flyers advertising open mic readings, talent night, and more, sandwiched in between the collage of professional pictures boasting serenity along the coastline.

Let the record show that Trite Tim, Harry Potter, and Maleficent did *not* appear in any of these promotional materials. Nor did the model students adequately express in their motivational quotes throughout these brochures the emotional tug-of-war that could develop in one's psyche as a result of participating in *workshop,* the only part of residency that was unequivocally mandatory.

I arrived on the island with my heavy luggage and, at the ferry terminal, was greeted by a shuttle van that had been arranged by the school. The driver, a woman wearing a surprisingly tight, low-cut T-shirt for the occupation of van driving, greeted me with a toothy smile. "Heading to Matthias?" she asked.

I nodded, noticing upon closer inspection that her shirt had a picture of Frog and Toad on it. *A soul mate,* I thought excitedly. Someone who appreciated classic children's stories as much as me. I mean, what are the odds? But just as I was about to comment on Arnold Lobel's brand of kid lit genius, I adjusted my glasses and read the caption beneath the screen print. *Reading makes me horny,* it announced, which certainly expressed a very different vibe than one might expect from a picture of a Caldecott Honor Award–winning book cover. I guess the shirt was youth-size on purpose to allow her ample bosom to present itself to anyone with eyes. I suppose that's in the vein of the old adage, *If you've got it, flaunt it.* Just not the look of a typical livery driver is all I'm saying. "I'm Cecily," I offered, holding out my hand to shake hers.

"Nice to meet you," she replied. "I'm Maggie. Hop on in and buckle up. I'll put your things in the back."

I climbed in and sat on a bench seat, veins pumping with adrenaline, despite the attempted sedation of an earlier dose of Dramamine coursing through my blood. Maggie's driving was as unexpected as her bookish thirst trap of a T-shirt. She sped up and down rolling hills flanked with kelly-green grass, around curves, hugging the edges of shoulder-less windy roads and making my stomach do flip-flops. Flocks of bicycles hogged the single-lane road close to the public beaches, but as we drove farther away from the center of the island, the bikes were replaced by mopeds with solo riders and the occasional compact car. I tried extremely hard not to toss my cookies everywhere and realized that had it not been for the Dramamine, this ride might have taken a real turn for the worse.

Maggie, I learned, was quite the Chatty Cathy. She disclosed that she was an employee of the retreat center who lived on Block Island all year round, she was a transplant from the West Coast, and that she once drove Nelson DeMille to Matthias to do a guest lecture. "I tried to get him to meet up with me for drinks after," she smirked, "because I could tell he liked what he saw, you know?"

I nodded politely as her lips formed a pout. "But he said some nonsense about being *married*." Maggie rolled her eyes. "He couldn't handle all this anyway."

We almost settled into a quiet lull after that, but Maggie decided to appoint herself my unofficial tour guide, telling me about the Mohegan Bluffs, the Great Salt Pond, and Dead Eye Dick's, all must-dos on her list. She recommended renting a bike to get around. "You don't realize how far three miles is until you have to walk it round trip with a bag of groceries in tow," she explained. "There's no delivery here either."

I made a mental note of that as I took in the briny salt air. The luscious view permeated my senses. We turned into New Beginnings and bounced up the cobblestone road leading to the main house.

"You're one of the first ones here, I think," she informed me. "Lunch won't be served until one. But if you go right in those big doors, I'm sure you'll find someone who can get you all checked in."

"Thanks for the ride," I said as she retrieved my bags from the back of the van.

"My pleasure," she replied. "I'm hoping my next fare will be that hottie, Nate Ellis."

Nate Ellis, as in the PEN Award winner who would become my teacher in a few hours. *Noted,* I thought. *I guess literary groupies are a thing here.*

Inside the main house, an older, brusque lady with wispy, thin bangs covering half of her line of sight scurried over to me with a clipboard. She introduced herself as Lucy (no last name or title) and gave me a name badge with a lanyard to wear around my neck all week, a packet of information, and a room key. She explained that there would be a whiteboard in the lobby of the North Wind building that would have all of the important information for each day's activities. "Any questions you have," she shared, "will likely be addressed on the whiteboard. The whiteboard is how we keep everyone organized."

The Whiteboard, I repeated over and over in my head, as if it was its own character in the Matthias University MFA story. I arrived at my room—a tiny little bedroom on the second floor of the residence hall fit for a Polly Pocket if she were entering a serious nunnery phase. Bare walls surrounded two twin beds, each home to a single folded threadbare towel and accompanying washcloth. A small closet featured exactly two old wire hangers and nothing else, no extra blankets or towels or anything personifying the notion of a warm welcome. A random bathroom sink, replete with greenish-teal stains around the drain and a fluorescent pull-string light topping the mirror above it, looked very out of place tucked into the corner, but alas, I came here to learn, and if my first lesson was that a low-res MFA and a high-security prison were cut from the same cloth on the accommodations scale, well, consider me schooled.

I set about unpacking my wardrobe into the miniature chest of drawers, placing my toothbrush, face wash, and other toiletry items over on the shelf by the sink, and putting my TBR stack of novels on the nightstand that lived between the twin beds. All of a sudden, the door handle jerked, and the plank of wood disguising itself as a privacy barrier flew open.

In walked a *woman*. Let me be clear: this was not a girl in her twenties or thirties; this person could easily have been my mother's age. Possibly older. I'm not an ageist, though, so I perked up at the thought of this lost soul accidentally stumbling into my room and being offered not only directions to her own dormitory assignment but also a warm welcome from a potential new friend. Unfortunately, this particular woman had a rolling suitcase and a large yellow purse, cropped white hair, glasses, the pointiest canine tooth I'd ever seen on a human, and a chip. On. Her. Shoulder.

"Is this room two twelve?" she asked.

I nodded and gave her my best photo-day grin. "Sure is!" I said.

"Who are you then?" she demanded. A wily chin hair wriggled at me as she spoke, threatening my smile with its ferocity.

"I'm Cecily." I reached onto the spare bed—the one I was using to house my luggage and my welcome folder—and showed her the page with my room assignment. "This is my room." I pointed to the sheet of paper. *212,* it read. "But I would be more than happy to help you find yours."

"No need."

I felt my smile fade as fear bubbled up in my belly to replace it. She sized me up and down with a death stare, as if she was considering her options with regard to how she might dispose of my body and make it look like an accident. "Looks like we're sharing," the obviously formerly incarcerated woman decided. "I requested a single," she grumbled to herself.

We had to request a single? They actually expected two people to fit in each of these tiny rooms?

I didn't know how to properly respond, so I tried on a fresh smile and went the route of *If you have nothing nice to say, don't say anything at all,* which somehow immediately made things worse.

"Perhaps you'd like to remove your *items* from *my* quarters," Sergeant Snaggletooth declared.

"Um, sure," I replied, quickly gathering up my things and dumping them onto what had now become my side of the room.

As my life was rapidly deteriorating into a bad episode of *Orange Is the New Black,* I tried to find the humor in the situation. Of course I should imagine that this older woman might be a seasoned writing pro who could guide and coach me as we become unlikely friends, like Matilda and Miss Honey in Roald Dahl's classic of the same name. But instead she quickly morphed into an R. L. Stine–esque haggard creature of my nightmares. *It's okay,* I told myself. *All potential fodder for future stories I could write.* Still, I'm the type of person who tries to see the rainbow beyond the thunderstorm, the glass as half-full, so I tried to engage her in more conversation.

"I'm sorry," I said. "I didn't catch your name."

"You can call me Gert."

"Gert? That's a nice name. Is it short for something? Gertrude?"

"No." She glared at me. I saw that indeed, her name was Gurt, as per the thick piece of masking tape across the side of her hard-bodied suitcase that read GURT LAWRENCE.

"Is that how you spell it?" I asked, pointing to the tape.

"Do you always ask so many questions?" she snapped.

I'm sure it's a sensitive thing when your parents inadvertently give you a name that results in you spending your entire childhood being called "Yogurt," but I was not even conceived when she carried that weighty cross, and I had been nothing but nice to her thus far, so I did not appreciate being spoken to with such a sharp tone.

"Well, it's nice to meet you," I tried.

At this, Gurt coughed—not a dainty little *let me clear my throat* cough but more of a full *rabid raccoon with a garbage hair ball* cough.

I checked my watch, and seeing as how there were only twenty uncomfortable minutes with Gurt standing between me and my orientation lunch, and she was making it extremely clear that friendship of any sort was not in the cards for us, I decided to leave her to unpacking. Figured I could check out the makeshift "Matthias Bookstore" downstairs (which is essentially a hallway lined with books for sale that were written by faculty members) and maybe meet a person who wouldn't have their sights set on killing me in my sleep. Donning my all-important name tag lanyard, I slid my room key into my pocket and bid my adieu to Gurt.

Now that it was early afternoon, students were beginning to arrive en masse, and the dormitory hallway was pulsating with energy. I tried to look casual as people walked by in groups of two and three as if they'd known each other forever. I passed a casual smile at some of them, but seeing as how my cheer tank was all spent on Gurt, I immediately felt foolish and decided no more of that would be necessary for right now. The "bookstore" was in such a narrow space that my presence in front of it created a physical barrier between incoming students and their room assignments, so I moved myself down the hall to a larger space in the lobby of the North Wind.

Ah, there it was. *The Whiteboard.*

It was the size of a small house and contained enough information that one could stand there for quite some time and never appear foolish. It listed the date at the top, exclaimed *Welcome Students!* and had a detailed account of the events for the remainder of the day. I breathed a deep sigh of relief as I could easily stand in front of it and be overwhelmed by its majesty, its neat handwriting in red Expo marker, its plethora of intel, and most importantly, its lack of judgment.

Thank you, beautiful Whiteboard, I thought, *for spending these few peaceful moments with me.*

My pleasure, Cecily, I imagined it responding in much the same voice as Shel Silverstein's *The Giving Tree. Come, look at my many offerings. After your orientation lunch, there is some time to unpack and settle in. Then, at three p.m., there is a mixer for everyone on the lawn. At five p.m., dinner will be served. Tonight you may choose from a bounty of options, as it is Taco Night. I will list every ingredient selection here in this fun little corner, titled* Fiesta! *But wait, there's more! After dinner, at seven p.m., you can attend a reading in the Spiritual Sanctuary, led by Professor Dillon Norway, director of the MFA, and after that, there will be an informal gathering in North Wind Room B.*

Ka-chick.

I looked next to me and found an annoyingly good-looking man snapping a photo of the whiteboard with his cell phone. His facial hair was the first thing I noticed about him. It wasn't a full beard, far from it. Just scruff, as if he opted not to shave for the last few days. Under the fluorescent lighting, it looked almost auburn. But his hair was brown. Or maybe chestnut. Hard to define in that weird light. I tried to place the color—sort of like hot cocoa with a cinnamon stick in it—when he asked me, "You good?"

"Um. Yeah," I replied.

"You were staring," he noted.

"Was I?" My face flushed, and I could feel my neck turning red and splotchy as if just speaking to another human person could result in a fresh case of contact dermatitis.

"You were."

"Oh. Sorry." *Was I staring?* I didn't think so.

"I think you're just supposed to take a picture and move on."

"Excuse me?" I asked. My eyebrows knit together. *The nerve of this one.*

He pointed at the whiteboard. "It's too much to remember. So you just take a picture and then you'll have it with you on your phone."

"Oh my God. You meant that I was staring at the board."

He nodded.

"I thought you meant that I was staring—" I began. "Forget it." My cheeks became engulfed in flames of self-inflicted arson.

"I'm Nate," he said, shifting the messenger bag draped across his chest. I looked at his lanyard. *Nate Ellis,* it read.

"*You're* Nate Ellis?" I asked. He looked nothing like his author photos, where he was clean shaven, hair parted neatly to the side, and wearing a shirt and tie. *This* guy did not resemble an award-winning supernova of the literati. He looked...hot-guy normal.

I cleared my throat and stood up a little taller, trying to compose myself. "Cecily Jane Allerton," I said. "I'm in your workshop."

He smiled and reached out his hand. I gripped it hard and gave him the firmest handshake possible. *Here is a career author, Cecily. Big leagues. Act like you belong.*

"Ow," he said, pulling back reflexively. "You've got some grip."

"Sorry." I ran the offending fingers through my hair in a poor attempt to illustrate how soft and gentle they could be, or perhaps how skilled with a pen and words and such.

He shrugged, rubbing his hand on his thigh. "Anyway, nice to meet you. I'll see you around."

With that, Nate Ellis walked away. It was at this moment that I realized he was wearing a T-shirt and khaki cargo shorts, low white socks, and sneakers. Like a typical person my age who was going out on a Saturday for, I don't know, groceries or something.

I looked down, considering my own outfit: a wrap dress and a chunky statement necklace paired with gladiator sandals. I looked classy, I decided. Very business casual. Appropriate. *This is higher education, not Stop & Shop,* I told myself. I flipped my cell phone over in my hand and checked the time, then begrudgingly snapped a photo of my one friend so far, *the Whiteboard,* and left for the orientation lunch.

As I walked to the entrance of the dining hall, located on the side of the adjacent main house, I could smell burgers and hot dogs being grilled and saw smoke off in the distance. There were two lunches, separate and distinct from one another, for this day. The outdoor offering, overlooking the beautiful blue-gray Atlantic, was being prepared around back and was for faculty and returning students to partake in. My lunch—the indoor one—was for the incoming class. Professor Dillon Norway, the fine gentleman who wrote about my submission with such generous praise, would be in attendance, along with eight other new students, plus me.

The room itself was set up with round tables, each seating ten people, with a buffet-style line running through the center of the room. Sandwiches, several salads, and a soup tureen labeled *tomato basil* were all displayed down the buffet in a sightly exhibit of culinary art. The tables were dressed in burgundy cloths, a fine match for the cedar-planked walls of the room. Sconces lit up the space and made it feel like a New England tavern on a brisk autumn day. Truly, it was lovely, a stark contrast to the holding cell I was sharing with Gurt.

I positioned myself at the one table set with cutlery, facing the door so that I could see people as they entered the space. Students trickled in. The first one was a girl younger than me, probably fresh out of undergrad. She wore short shorts, high-top Chuck Taylors, and a T-shirt with a picture of Harry Styles on the front. She gave me an awkward half smile and sat down several seats away from me. "This is the orientation thing, right?" she asked.

I pushed my glasses up on the bridge of my nose and nodded. "I'm Cecily. What's your name?"

"Ashlyn," she said, taking out her phone and swiping at it.

"Pretty name," I replied. When she didn't respond, I didn't want to repeat myself and seem weird. Instead, I figured I'd speak a little louder to make sure she could hear me. "So you a big 1D fan?" I asked at a significantly elevated decibel.

She startled. *Too loud,* I noted. *My bad.*

"1D hasn't been a thing since 2015," Ashlyn said, setting her eyes back on her cell phone screen and keeping them there.

"Right." I laughed awkwardly as another girl about Ashlyn's age entered and sat down right next to her.

"Orientation?" the new girl asked.

"Yeah," Ashlyn said. "I'm Ashlyn."

"Kelsey," the girl replied. "Cool tat." Kelsey looked at Ashlyn's wrist.

"Aw, thanks. I just had it done, like, a month ago."

"Oh yeah? Let me see," I said, trying to remain involved in the conversation.

Ashlyn rolled her eyes and reluctantly showed me her wrist. On it, there were four small black birds flying in no particular formation. "That's wicked dope," I followed up in an attempt not to seem like an old lady who still equated Harry Styles with One Direction.

Evidently, *wicked dope* is not trending, because the girls just sneered at me. A third girl came in and sat beside them, and the three began chattering away about where they were from and some show that's all the rage on MTV.

"Is that like the *Jersey Shore?*" I asked, feigning interest.

Again, they snickered, but neither Ashlyn nor Kelsey even bothered to answer the question. The newest of the three, who introduced herself as Trix (*Like the cereal?* I wondered), just said, "*Jersey Shore?* I don't know. I think my parents used to watch that show."

"Yeah, for sure. Mine too," I replied, faking a laugh, even though my parents only watch *Jeopardy* and *Law and Order: SVU*.

I'm twenty-nine years old. I'm not a dinosaur, but I began to feel like these girls were working hard to make me feel like one, so I kept quiet as the remaining members of our cohort trickled in. I was confident I would be among the older students in the group but was surprised to learn that more than half (count: five) of the students in my cohort were entering straight out of undergrad. The Gen Z trio began giggling with each other as they discovered their shared love of Post Malone over pasta salad and turkey clubs. One young man had AirPods in throughout the entire meal, signaling (at least to me) that he would prefer not to speak at all, and the other younger man spoke in short, one-word answers. In addition to those five, there was an older man with a handlebar mustache, like the kind you might see at a three-ring circus in the 1940s. Sandwich crumbs crept into his pubic upper lip and nested there, and I tried not to look so as not to upset my (sometimes sensitive) gag reflexes. The last two people at the table were a real feast for the eyes: a set of middle-aged women, possibly about fifty years old, who were identical twins. All the way down to their outfits, like schoolchildren. They wore matching purple sleeveless mock turtlenecks and knee-length denim skirts. Their synchronized hairstyles were coiffed in tufted layers, like a halo of dirty-blond feathers reaching up toward the sky on top, out to the east and west on the sides, and limply falling in the back, just grazing their shoulders, with enough Aqua Net holding it all in place to power a small blowtorch for days. And their makeup. All I can say is turquoise eye shadow.

Cat and Pat.

Yes, I am serious.

Needless to say, it took a laborious amount of conscious effort not to stare.

That woman from before (Lucy, I remembered) was at the table as well, seated alongside the one and only Dillon Norway. The MFA gatekeeper. The admission decider. He personally chose these individuals to be in this program along with me, so who was I to judge their makeup or their choice of facial hair? *Artists come in all shapes and sizes,* I reminded myself. Dillon Norway himself was about five feet, eight inches tall, with thick, gray, wavy hair and wire-rimmed glasses thoughtfully perched along the bridge of his long nose. He wore a hunter-green polo shirt tucked into tan pants with a classic leather belt and brown shoes. He could have been a walking advertisement for Banana Republic if he was about thirty years younger and Banana Republic was still a thing. (Is it? I have no idea.)

He gently tapped the end of his soupspoon on the side of his water glass, quieting the small group of diners. When he spoke, his voice was soft. "Hi, there," he said, immediately channeling his inner Mr. Rogers. He should have been wearing a cardigan, removing his shoes while "Won't You Be My Neighbor?" played in the background. "I'm delighted to welcome you to Matthias University's MFA program, and thank you for joining us at this little introductory lunch."

Simultaneous nods permeated the space, along with polite half smiles.

"I'm Dillon Norway, and I'm happy to see each of you. Hope you all had safe travels to the island and have had a chance to settle in a bit."

More head bobs.

"My role here is technically MFA director, but I really prefer to think of myself as the conductor of a symphony. You all represent the instruments, and with the help of my colleagues, our goal is to turn your work into beautiful music."

Ah. Such a gorgeous metaphor. I love you already, Dillon Norway, I thought.

He gestured at Lucy, who was seated to his right. "I'm happy to introduce Lucy Jones, my assistant. She's responsible for all the meticulous items in your welcome packets, the surveys, the room assignments, basically everything that makes our world go round here on the island. She's your point person for questions about anything in the weeds, anything specific."

The woman beside him, who was collating and clipping stacks of paper (instead of eating lunch), raised up a hand as if in solidarity but failed to give any further introduction.

"I'm good for your global issues," Dillon Norway continued. "I'll help assign you to a mentor who you'll work with for the semester. I'm here if you feel yourself gravitating toward a specific concentration, like poetry, perhaps to your own surprise or even chagrin," he chuckled. "I keep office hours, which are on your schedule, and so does Lucy, so you can check your folder to know where and when to find us should you need to." He paused to take a sip of water. "Now, I'm not great at this part, but we should really all take a turn to properly introduce ourselves. Maybe just share your name, where you come from, what you do there, and a goal or two that you have for the program. Who would like to start us off?"

Sudden, deafening silence swept the room. Not wanting to disappoint Dillon Norway, the only breathing soul in this entire program with whom I felt a kinship, I raised my hand.

"Sure. You." He pointed at me and offered a friendly nod, then sat down and took a spoonful of tomato soup.

I stood up and smoothed out my dress.

"Oh, you don't have to stand," he said. "I mean, you can if you want to, but this is, like, informal."

Heart pounding, I sat back down. "Sorry," I began. "I'm Cecily Jane Allerton. I write fiction, and I'm a children's librarian in Queens, New York, which is where I'm from. This is my second master's degree. The first is in library sciences. I'd say my goal here is pretty simple. I want to become an agented, published author of commercial novels with strong heroines." I smiled my best *just passed my road test* driver's-license smile and added, "Thank you for giving me the opportunity to be here."

I thought I heard a sidebar comment at the table, but I ignored it. Dillon Norway thanked me, and Mustache Man went next. The salutations continued until everyone had a turn. Despite my determined efforts to be nonjudgmental, I unfortunately did not leave that particular exercise feeling the potential for kinship with any of my cohort members. None of the rest of them shared goals that seemed like goals to me. Mustache Man said his goal was to "harness his inner power," and one of the Post Malone fangirls said she wanted to "just, um, figure out my life." I had to physically restrain myself from shaking my head. And I have to be honest—it made me wonder a little about Dillon Norway's sense of good reasoning as a gatekeeper, but that sounded rude, even locked up in my own brain, so I admonished myself by pinching my thigh and continued smiling courteously at the group. After everyone had a turn, Lucy took over the meeting. She gave us the rundown on what to expect for the next nine days, explained the importance of the whiteboard, and shared how to submit surveys at the conclusion of each seminar, disseminating a packet of them to each of us.

The rest of the day continued as per the schedule. There was far more free time than I was comfortable with, so I grabbed one of the new YA novels I'd brought along and made my way down to a quiet bench overlooking the water until the 3:00 p.m. mixer, which I could easily have done without. I decided to stay on that bench (a safe haven, seeing as how my bedroom had been invaded by Gurt) until the very last minute when the mixer began, and as a result, I arrived with my book in tow. My paperback became its own sort of icebreaker.

"*Pep Rally Pretender?*" an older man asked. "What's that about?"

"Oh! It's a story about a dead girl whose ghost disguises itself as a high school student and becomes really popular. It's super interesting."

He stroked his beard while I spoke—a fully-grown-in-mountain-man situation, mind you—and then replied, "That sounds like a children's story."

"Well, it is. I mean, it's YA, actually. It's trending on TikTok though, so…"

"I'm reading *Perimeter Spaces* by Ulto Blankin. It's an allegory about the machination of our borders by the man."

I coughed. *The fuck?* "That's nice," I said. "Did you say the author's name was Ulta? Like the cosmetics store?"

Scruffleupagus dug his fingers deep into his beard and gave a hearty tug. *What is it with men and their chin hair?* I wondered. "No," he said. "I'm not familiar with that store."

I nodded. "Well, it's nice to meet you. I'm just going to go grab another drink."

Another dude, this one a giant at easily six feet five inches, completely bald (a welcome change), and thin as a rail, opened with a similar line. "Whatcha got there?" he said in an unexpectedly thick Irish brogue.

I had to stop myself from laughing because my immediate thought was, *You'll never get your hands on me Lucky Charms!* Instead, I remained silent in an attempt to keep my face from exploding and simply held up my book so he could see its cover. "Ah, *Pep Rally Pretender* then. Is that the one where the woman goes on a journey of self-discovery after a divorce?"

At this, I couldn't help but giggle. "I think you're thinking of *Eat, Pray, Love.*"

I think I embarrassed him though, because he side-shuffled his way into a conversation with a person to my left almost immediately after I laughed at him.

My bad.

From what I've heard, most writers aren't natural extroverts, and I'm no exception. So the fact that this wasn't going well for me was kind of to be expected. Dillon Norway was in a circle with several very comfortable-looking people, so I thought perhaps it would be wise to veer in that general direction. Only I had no idea how to insert myself into their conversation (read: *mingle*), so I sort of maneuvered my way next to them, pretending to study the back cover of my book while technically just eavesdropping on the conversations around me.

Norway was listening to another faculty member discuss a recent stint at Yaddo as a few others looked on in awe. Only when I heard a lady behind me comment under her breath, "I guess they're just accepting *anyone* at Yaddo these days," did I realize the speaker in Dillon Norway's group was that Nate Ellis guy again. I turned around to check out the hater and glimpsed her name tag: ALICE DEVEREAUX, FACULTY. She was maybe a hundred years old (fine, seventy) and was sharing this particular opinion with another similarly bouffanted fossil in orthopedic shoes whose name tag I couldn't see and Lucy, who surprised me by nodding in agreement. That struck me as being off-brand for her. One would think that a prerequisite skill of the assistant to the director of this program would be the capacity for professionalism and the ability to keep her opinions to herself. I made a mental note of the observation and filed it away into my cranial *Haters Gonna Hate* folder.

Did Nate Ellis deserve such a scathing sidebar commentary? I didn't know, seeing as how our only interaction up until that point had been a brief moment of confusion at the whiteboard.

But now, in his workshop, while these three demon writers try to terrorize me, I suspect that yes, perhaps he is just another highbrow literary snob, and perhaps Alice Devereaux and her centenarian cronies would like to partake in a Mike's Hard Lemonade with me later on this evening.

I shall ask, I decide, as Trite Tim continues to wax academic about all the things that are wrong with my submission.

It's as I am daydreaming about my imminent future befriending Alice Devereaux's mah-jongg group that I am interrupted by Professor PEN Award himself. "Cecily? Do you have any questions for the group?"

I shake my head no. Of course, I am awash with questions, from *How dare you all?* to *What the actual fuck?* but for now, it just seems wiser to let sleeping dogs lie, as they say.

"Are you sure?" he prods. "Earlier, you wanted to say something."

I nod primly. "I'm sure."

He emits what might be a sigh, but it's clipped, so I can't be sure. "Well, everyone, please make sure you submit your responses to Cecily so she can review them. Also, it's required that your signature be on your critique letter. Okay, guys. Let's take a ten-minute break, and then we'll dive into a lecture on setting. Go ahead and grab some coffee or a snack, and I'll catch you back here in ten."

Three loose pieces of paper slide my way from the offending parties in my group, letters that will undoubtedly *not* make my "instrument sing," or whatever Dillon Norway's exquisite metaphor was. I place them in a pocket folder that I've strategically hole-punched and added to the back of my binder for handouts and such as my colleagues stand, stretch, and leave the West Room in the annex, where we are gathered.

Before I can escape to the restroom, Nate Ellis hands me a letter. His, I'm guessing. He looks around before speaking and lowers his voice when he does.

"I'm sorry, Cecily. That wasn't supposed to go down quite the way it did. Are you okay?"

This, I think. *This whatever-this-is pretending to be kindness. This will be my undoing.* Tears well up in my eyes. *Stop it, stop it! Don't even think about getting upset in front of this man.* I gulp, eyes fixated on my binder in all its organized glory. A drop splashes against a divider tab, but I ignore it. Instead, I nod silently, swallowing my humiliation in much the same way that I have learned to swallow my optimism and hopefulness over the past thirty-six hours.

"You sure?"

I nod again, harder this time, willing him to leave.

When he does, I exhale and cautiously look up. I'm alone. I can breathe. *You're fine. You've got this,* I tell myself. I put away Professor PEN Award's letter of defamation in my pocket folder without allowing myself to read any of its words. Then I duck into the ladies' room and dab at my tears. I check myself in the mirror.

Okay, so it's not exactly what you thought it would be. But it's a learning experience.

You will *become a published author.*

The girl in the mirror doesn't look so sure.

You. Can. Do. This, I tell her.

CHAPTER 2

Nate

They say, "Those who can, do. Those who can't, teach."

Well, whoever wrote that dumbass quote clearly never taught in an MFA program.

First of all, these *people*. What is it about adult students? They're all either trying way too hard or have given up trying altogether. Absolutely zero middle ground.

They're nasty to each other too. Grown-ass people who've completely lost their manners.

I mean, you had to be in there to see it. They just ripped this poor girl to shreds. Her work was decent too. Not my speed, but her piece was written for teenagers, so I'm not the intended audience. I'll tell you this: it was a fuck ton better than that "Lotus Blossom Soup" nonsense that other one wrote.

They made her *cry.*

Then me? I just sort of panicked and left her there. I didn't want to embarrass her. Figured I would give her some space.

I chose her piece to go first because I thought it would cause the *least* amount of drama. I know we're not supposed to quantifiably judge art, but between us, it was the *best* submission of the four. By a *lot*. Yes, she's obviously writing commercial genre stuff, but so what? Good, effective storytelling isn't only bound to literary fiction. I thought Cecily was digging into a story with tons of potential. And it just so happened her last name starts with *A*, so I was able to make like it was an alphabetical order thing.

Get it together, dude. She's a grown-up. She'll be fine.

I splash some water on my face and grab a paper towel to dry myself off.

This was supposed to be my easy distraction. Not *another* heavy lift. I'll tell you what though. When I interviewed for the job, Dillon didn't mention anything about students crying in workshop on the first day. Or about the fact that I would have to keep a straight face around the absolutely ludicrous dress code in the room. No one said anything about grown men wearing cloaks to class as if we were all going to some Dungeons and Dragons convention instead of sitting at a table talking about writing.

I check the time. Gotta keep it moving. I take a breath and head back into the room. With a flip chart and my notes, I manage to get through my lecture pretty smoothly. Cecily acts fine, like nothing ever happened, God bless her. I teach them how to draw a map of their scene, and she draws the cafeteria where her conflict is set. It's good. They all stay engaged, minus a couple of asinine comments from Tim and a solitary eye roll from Andrea. I give them a standard read-and-respond assignment for homework, and then we disperse, and I head to the dining room to grab something for lunch. It's a sad attempt at pizza—small, round thin-crust concoctions of sauce and cheese on what feels like a burned-up burrito skin. Worlds apart from Ray's on Columbus and West 82nd, but hey, we're not in Kansas anymore, Toto.

At least I don't have to give my seminar today. That's tomorrow's albatross. It weighs heavy though, burrowing under my skin all through lunch and through the seminars of my colleagues, which I attend in the afternoon because that is the expectation. I try to remain focused, but my brain is like scrambled eggs. This happens now, whenever I feel pressure, and I can't figure out how to make it stop.

You'd think all this salt air would help. The open space and isolation. I tried that at Yaddo too though, to no avail.

What's Yaddo, you ask? Sorry. I just assume everyone knows. Yaddo is an artists' retreat house in upstate New York. It's beautiful and peaceful and pretty exclusive. Big application process to get in, and if you do get accepted, they sponsor the cost of you being there.

I thought going there for four weeks would help me write my second book.

I was wrong then, so it's no surprise that I should be wrong now—assuming that being here to dance around *other* people's writing like some kind of great literary shepherd would be of any real use to me. Nope, instead, I'm just the moderator who made the overprepared student with the giant binder cry on day one.

Jesus.

I know what you're thinking. *He's a has-been. A one-hit wonder.* Well, who knows? You might be right. My debut novel, *Work*, came out of my own personal *Tuesdays with Morrie* kind of situation. My grandfather was in an assisted-living facility in Midtown, overlooking the East River. He had been diagnosed with dementia so my parents set him up there, only they live in Florida and couldn't visit him often, so I went to see him twice a week, every week, for almost a year. He was a lifelong employee of the New York State Department of Labor in his former life, and as he started to deteriorate, I recorded our conversations. He talked about the declining state of work in our country, and I wove some of his ramblings into a story. Before I knew it, I was writing a full-length novel, my first ever. He passed away, and I finished the novel as an homage to him.

It only took me three months.

I queried ten agents. Got seven full requests. Four offers of rep. They all said the same thing. *Genre-bending. A story that lives at the crossroads where speculative and literary fiction meet.* I didn't know what the hell they were talking about. I just wrote a story about a man living in New York City who works for the State Department of Labor when a pandemic shuts down the country.

In 2018.

My agent sold the book for a decent advance to a Big Five house in the first round of submissions. No huge hoopla or anything. They thought it was an interesting premise. High concept, they said.

It released the first week of January 2020.

Who fucking knew, right?

People magazine called me the "Literary Nostradamus," a nickname that took off with the same speed as the toilet paper flying off the shelves at Costco.

You can imagine what happened next. The rights all sold—and fast—as the world basically crumbled around us. My editor suggested we submit the book for a PEN America Award. It won. I quit my day job as a copy editor for *Men's Health*. I had money coming in. Surprising amounts of money.

Game-changing money.

And so, fast forward. My publisher wants to continue riding the "Nate Ellis wave of predictions," my agent is excited about another big fat paycheck, and like an idiot, I'm like, "Sure. I'll write another book."

As if it's just that easy. No pressure, right? *The whole world is watching. They all want to hear what you have to say, Nate.*

My agent sells the new book, an untitled void of emptiness with exactly zero pages written, to my publisher for a *lot* of money.

They set up a schedule for me.

I try to write. I really do. I start a few different stories, but I can't quite figure out what I even *want* to write. I figure that I'll practice by composing short stories in an attempt to test the waters in a few different genres. I write a thriller-esque thing that's basically unreadable, a nonfiction essay about my time as a copy editor (boring as hell), and finally, a sci-fi story about humankind struggling to survive after global warming all but destroys our planet. This one, I think, has chops, but it's in a different wheelhouse than the first book, so I submit it to a variety of magazines under a pseudonym to see if it garners the same kind of excitement.

It gets no takers.

The New Yorker and the *Atlantic* don't even bother to respond. The *Kenyon Review* says thanks but no thanks, and *McSweeney's* says it's not for them. *Harper's* and *Zoetrope* offer comments in response, but they're all negative. One even goes so far as to suggest several titles of books I should read to improve my craft. I'm tempted to write back, *I'm Nate Ellis, goddammit!* but all that would do is make me feel even more like an idiot. Everything just feels, I don't know, *wrong*. Like, who the hell am I? I had one story, and it wasn't even really *mine*. I ask my agent for help, but I'm dismissed. "You're the creative genius," I'm told. "Just breathe, and let it flow."

I try. I even sign up for a yoga class, once I realize that "just breathing" is evidently something I am not very good at.

Eventually, the first deadline comes. I request an extension. *Granted.*

Then, in what seems like the blink of an eye, the next deadline approaches. I explain that I just need a few more months. "I applied to Yaddo and got accepted," I tell my editor. "That'll help."

"Sure, Nate, but we should really get a move on. Strike while the iron's still hot and all that."

The iron is in the back of the damn freezer as far as I'm concerned.

I get back from Yaddo. I'm working on something now, but I hate it. There's no passion there. It's just words on a screen. Like fifty thousand of them, but it's shapeless. Makes no sense. I could care less about the protagonist. It's going nowhere.

Another deadline creeps up. "This is the last time, I promise," I tell my editor.

"It has to be," he says. "They're pushing back at me from the top. I've done everything I can to stave them off, dude."

"I get it," I say. "I just got a job working at an MFA program. It's exactly what I need to cross the finish line. I've got to be around other writers."

"Whatever you need to do, Nate. Just get it done."

Now, here we are. Tomorrow afternoon, I'm leading a seminar about character development, and holy hell, the impostor syndrome is eating me alive from the inside out. Today, I let a bunch of adult bullies make a student cry. I've written about twelve words since I got here yesterday, and now I have to go to *lobster night,* which should be great but is actually just a social experiment where just shy of a hundred people don plastic bibs and rip apart sea creatures that look like giant red cockroaches in some display of—I don't know—New England opulence? Everyone keeps staring at me like I'm some kind of celebrity, which did *not* happen at Yaddo, and I don't feel like I can talk to anyone except for Dillon Norway, the guy who hired me and who is actually really chill but is busy, you know, *leading the whole residency,* so it's not like he's available to just hang out and talk shop with me until I get inspired. The other faculty members look at me like I'm some sort of science experiment they're trying to figure out, except this one old lady who glared at me as if I stabbed her cat with a screwdriver when Dillon introduced me. *Ann? Agnes?*

Alice. With a French last name beginning with D—Deville, perhaps, like Cruella. *C'est une chienne,* in my humble opinion. And I'm half Canadian, so I'm allowed to say that.

Just calm down, man, I tell myself. *Bitching about eating lobster. You've got some real first-world problems, huh?*

So I do. I take a breath. I sit at a picnic table. I put on the white bib. The lady with the too-tight-T-shirt who drove me here in the school van serves me a lobster. I smile, because I'm polite. The faculty and students around me chitchat about something or other. Then I crack the stupid red shell open, dip the meat in some hot butter, and eat it.

Never for a second thinking that I'm about to look death in the face.

When I wake up, I'm in a hospital bed, in some sort of—I don't know—hallway, maybe? There's an IV in my arm. And I'm definitely hallucinating, because I look to my left and see the girl from my workshop— Cecily—on the opposite side of the hallway, dry heaving into a bucket in a bed just like mine.

I mumble something incoherent.

She looks over at me, appearing oddly reminiscent of an owl. All I see is a pair of blue glasses over big brown eyes, the rest of her face covered by the rim of the oversize orange Home Depot bucket. White stenciled block words on the side of the bucket read, *You can do it. We can help.*

I'm in the fucking twilight zone. This is one hundred percent not real.

Except when she stops retching, she says, "Huh?"

I try to move, but my middle cramps up and sends a sharp wave of nausea over my body. "Oh, shit," I say. At least I think those are the words that come out of my mouth. The pain is blinding.

"You okay?" she asks weakly.

My eyes are squeezed shut, and I am rendered mute, afraid that if I open my mouth again, I'm going to puke all over the place. I shake my head no. Definitely no. I am not okay. I am the opposite of okay.

I hear her shift in the loud-as-fuck bed she's in, and there's some kind of sound, like a buzz or something. Within seconds, I can sense a third person in our general vicinity.

"You rang?" an unfamiliar female voice says.

"For him," Cecily replies. Her voice sounds hoarse.

"Ah, he's awake. Well, good morning, Mr. Ellis," the voice croons. Yes, *croons,* like as if she is trying to sing me a lullaby. "And how are we feeling?"

I try to open my eyes, but my intestines are waging full war with my colon, and something is about to happen that I most definitely cannot watch. My body lurches forward involuntarily, and then, there it is. An overwhelming amount of vomit comes out of me, caught miraculously by the unnamed lady who I cannot look at. A hand appears on my back, making gentle circles that do nothing to soothe me as the contents of my entire gastrointestinal system unleash themselves into—I peek—another orange Home Depot bucket.

Are we at the Home Depot right now? I wonder.

Once a few waves of sickness pass over me, I somehow feel momentarily a little better, and I push the bucket away, unable to view its contents. I have a real thing about puke. Not a fan. I'm one of those *if I see you vomit, then I'm going to vomit* people. So you can imagine the gravity of a moment like this—where I'm not only sick but sick in mixed company, in front of a *student,* of all people. And in *public.* Like, are there no rooms here in this long-ass hallway?

The hand moves from my back to the front pocket of her nurse-uniform shirt, where it procures a pocket pack of tissues, which the lady (who looks a lot like my aunt Rose: tall and skinny with pockmarked skin, a winning combination if there ever was one) hands to me. "That's it, Mr. Ellis. Get it all out," she encourages me. "You all done for now?"

I nod, and the small movement sends a fresh wave of nausea over me. "Where are we?"

Aunt Rose's doppelganger smiles. "You're at the Block Island Medical Center."

"A hospital?"

She shakes her head. "No, my friend. This is actually a very modest primary care facility, but with the absence of a hospital on the island, we also offer urgent care as needed."

I look at Cecily. "What happened?"

Aunt Rose goes on. "It appears that you and quite a few others from your program suffered from paralytic shellfish poisoning. Happens every now and again in this area, unfortunately."

"What is that?" I ask.

"It's caused by a marine biotoxin. Essentially, you ate a lobster that ate some toxic microscopic algae. But don't worry, Mr. Ellis. You'll be okay. You were brought here for monitoring because you passed out."

"Really?"

"Yes. It appears you may have had a panic attack. We gave you some Klonopin, and now that you're awake, I'm happy to give you some anti-nausea medication."

"Please," I say weakly.

"Sure thing," she agrees. "Be right back."

"Wait," I manage. "Can I be moved into, like, a *room*? Please?"

"I'm sorry, but we only have three private rooms, and they're all at capacity. You were asleep, so we placed you out here in the hallway instead," Aunt Rose explains. "We're not really set up for this many visitors, you understand." She smiles, and I cannot discern whether it's intended to be sweet or condescending. "Several others in your program ate the bad lobster as well. In fact, had there been any additional, we would have had to airlift some of you back to the mainland."

Still, three rooms? For an entire island of people? I wonder. *Really?*

"What about her?" I ask, gesturing in the general direction of Cecily.

"She was willing to stay out here as well," I am told. "And thank you again, dear, for being so accommodating." Aunt Rose pats Cecily on the hand before turning back to face me. "Now, let me go grab those meds for you before you get hit with another wave of nausea." She winks at me, as if we are both in on a little secret.

I look across the hall at Cecily, who has pushed her bucket to the far edge of her bed. Her knees are bent, and her forehead rests on them. Her eyes are closed; her glasses press into the thin skin of her kneecaps, leaving a mark. There's no room in our shared area to pretend like she's not there, but I swear, if she starts crying again, I won't know what to do with myself, and the position she's in certainly feels reminiscent of one a person might choose when they're about to begin sobbing.

Try a little small talk, I decide. I clear my throat. "Bad day, huh?"

She turns her head sideways, still resting on her knees, and pushes her glasses up on the bridge of her nose with her pointer finger. *I must be drugged,* I think, *because that little thing she just did there was surprisingly really cute.*

"This wasn't in the brochure," she says. It strikes me as funny, but when I chuckle, my stomach squeezes so hard I feel like I might black out from the pressure.

I wince, and she gives me a sympathetic half smile.

The nurse who looks like Aunt Rose returns and adds something to my IV—the anti-nausea meds, God willing. We sit quietly after she leaves, and yes, by some saving grace, I manage to start feeling a little less disgusting.

"Did they give you this stuff too?" I ask, gesturing at the IV.

She nods gently. "A while ago. You were asleep."

"Then how come you were still getting sick?"

She shrugs. "Aftershocks, I guess. I feel better than before, by a lot. Just exhausted."

"What time is it? Any idea?"

Cecily is wearing a watch—an actual analog silver bracelet thing that ticks. She checks it. "Almost midnight," she says.

"Damn it," I mutter.

"What?"

"Nothing," I reply. "It's just—I've got this presentation tomorrow."

"I know. Character development. Three o'clock in the North Wind building."

"And we have workshop."

She groans and buries her face back in her knees. "Don't remind me."

I swallow back a burp. "Did you read my feedback letter?"

"No," she admits. "I was giving myself some space for the dust to settle, but then I ate deadly microscopic algae and, well, you know the rest."

Surprised by her snarky response, I shake my head and almost grin.

"Please don't rehash it though. I'm still in a pretty fragile state, and I have to be honest, just the thought of your workshop is already doing things to my stomach that I'm trying to consciously ignore. I don't think I can handle your verbal venom at this particular moment." Her glasses make her look like she's a terrified woodland creature, some small animal with big, curious, wounded eyes.

I'm struck by it, rendered unable to return the conversation volley.

"I'm sorry," Cecily continues. "I'm not a rude person, and that sounded rude." She sighs. "I just wasn't expecting this all to suck so bad."

My brow furrows.

"Ugh. Now I sound like I'm complaining." She shoots me a glance. "I'm just going to stop talking. Hope you feel better." She sets her bucket on the ground between us, puts her knees down, and lies back onto the standard-issue flat pillow at the head of her hospital bed. Then she rolls to the left so that when I look over at her, I'm faced with the entire length of her back.

One would expect that I'd feel relieved at the break in conversation, but I'm bothered by it. I get that she's not a big fan of me or my workshop. Fine, that's fair. But we can't be stuck in this remarkably small hallway area mimicking an urgent care facility and *not* speak to each other. That's just awkward. And it'll only get worse when I inevitably need to use this bucket again.

"I won't force you to talk to me, Cecily. But I think you should know that your writing has a lot of potential."

"Huh?" she asks, still facing the wall.

"That's what I said in my letter."

Nothing.

"I believe I wrote that even if it wasn't a workshop piece, I would be happy to read on and see where you take the story and how you connect the dots."

"Really?" She stays put, but single-word answers are better than nothing.

"You juggled all the pieces well without dropping the topic," I continue. *Please turn around.*

"I thought you said it was shallow," she replies. I strain to decipher the words because she says them not to me but to the wall.

"I said you could have done more to develop the theme. Have you read *The Hate U Give* by Angie Thomas?"

"Of course." Her knees bend in again, up toward her chest.

"You know how, in the book, Starr struggles to find her voice? How the whole book is like an internal dichotomy?"

"Yeah."

"I think you need more of that."

She swings her knees in a rainbow, up toward the ceiling and back to face me. "*The Hate U Give* is a masterpiece though. It's a powerful statement about our society. It's literally about life or death."

"That's true. But you see your reaction to it?"

"What? You mean, right now?"

"Yes. Right now. You need to bring that kind of intentionality to your own work. That kind of urgency."

"I am not Angie Thomas," she says.

"No, you're not. But you're Cecily Joan Allerton, and if you don't believe that your characters are the most important thing in the world, then nobody will."

"It's Jane."

"What?"

"Cecily *Jane* Allerton."

"Oh. My bad. How about if I just call you CJ?"

"I would prefer if you called me Cecily."

"Too late. It's already done. You're CJ now."

She knits her eyebrows together. "You're maddening," she mutters.

"Fight me on it then," I say.

"I have no energy for that. I've been puking for the past five hours, thank you very much."

"Fine. You get a pass for illness. A proverbial doctor's note, if you will. But you're missing my point."

"Which is?"

"You need to live so deeply inside your character's head that you share her spirit. You feel her passion. If she's hurt, you're hurt, and it spills out onto the page like an overflowing bathtub. Go deep. Like, so deep that you can't even find your way back out again. That's where the *best* writing lives."

She cocks her head quizzically but stays silent. The uncomfortable beat lasts a moment too long.

"What?" I ask. "Why are you looking at me like that?"

"Is that what you did?"

"What do you mean?"

"Well, you won a PEN Award for your novel. So I'm asking if that's what you did when you wrote it."

"I guess, yeah."

"How?"

"How what?"

"How did you do it?" she wonders aloud.

I take a deep breath. "The story was inspired by my grandfather. He had just died when I really took up the task of writing it. I don't know, I felt some sort of way about that and wanted to pay tribute to him."

"I'm sorry," she says. "For your loss."

"It was a long time ago," I reply. "But thank you."

She nods quietly.

"But that had nothing to do with the award I got," I add.

"Hm?"

"That part was really just luck."

"What? That's insane. How can you say that?"

"It was all timing. The stars aligned."

She squints at me as if I just shone a flashlight in her eyes.

"You didn't hear about the nickname they gave me?"

"Literary Nostradamus?" she asks. "I heard it. Certainly beats CJ."

I smile. "I think CJ's a perfectly acceptable moniker."

"Focus up, Professor PEN Award," she says. "Finish your thought."

"Now *that's* a nickname," I say.

"I can be surprisingly clever," she retorts. "But I'm honestly trying to understand the point you're trying to make. So"—she waves her hand—"on with it, please."

I nod. "My book released the same week as the coronavirus made its first appearance in Washington. Do you remember that?"

"Uh-huh."

"And it was about a guy who worked for the Department of Labor who watched the state of work in America unravel as a result of a pandemic. Early reviews were like, *It's an interesting social commentary*, but then it all started to come true. It brought the notion of 'Life imitates art' to a whole new level."

"So you think if there hadn't been a pandemic at that moment that you wouldn't be famous?"

"Exactly," I say. "And I'm not famous. In fact, I'm weeks away from being dropped by my editor."

"Excuse my language, but I call bullshit—to all of that," she says.

"I mean it. I can't get it together to write my second novel."

"Really?"

"Yes, really. I've pushed back the deadline a bunch of times."

"Why?"

"Because lightning doesn't strike twice. Nothing I write will be able to compare with the first book, and that had nothing to do with me. It was all a huge coincidence."

"You really think that?"

"100%."

"But you won a PEN Award."

"So what?"

"You're a big deal." She blinks those giant night-bird eyes at me.

"Listen, CJ. I'm just a regular guy. You know I don't even have an MFA, right?"

"Seriously?"

"I was a copy editor before the book took off. I've got a bachelor's in English and a subscription to Grammarly. That's about it," I admit. "In fact, our workshop? It's the first fiction workshop I've ever been in."

"How is that possible?"

I shrug. "I don't know. It just is?"

"They hired you for star power?" she asks.

"I guess. I don't know. I just took the job so that I could be around other writers. I thought that would help me get my flow going."

"And has it?"

I shake my head. "Nope. So far, all I've gotten is food poisoning."

She exhales. "Wow."

"My point is I'm sorry about the workshop. But don't let those other guys get you down. It's easy to be critical of other people when you're feeling insecure about your own stuff. Takes the spotlight off you."

"I suppose."

"And listen, I may have just confessed to you that I'm not the best writer, but I'm a damn good reader, and as a reader, I'm here to tell you that your work is solid."

She nods.

"I mean it. You've got tremendous potential, CJ." I shift in my bed. "Can I ask you something?"

"Sure."

"Why do you want this?"

She scrunches up her nose. "An MFA, you mean?"

I shake my head. "No. A degree's a degree. I'm talking about the big picture. Why do you want to be a writer?"

"Hm." The faintest hint of a smile turns the corners of her mouth up, and she looks off into the distance, awash in some kind of memory. "Well," she begins. "Ever since I can remember, I've found myself in books. I don't know if that sounds weird, but it's true. I set the house on fire when I was in the second grade—"

"Wait. What?" I interrupt.

"It's a funny story—well, kind of," she chuckles. "I was little, and I wanted to light a scented candle that sat on our kitchen counter, so I took a box of matches from the drawer, struck one, and touched it to the wick of the candle. It took a few seconds to catch. As the match flickered, it got close to my fingers, and I was scared I'd get burned, so out of instinct, I dropped it and accidentally set the dish towel on fire. I didn't know what to do with the flaming dish towel, so I picked it up and shoved it in the food pantry. I shut the door and pretended I had no knowledge of where the smoke was coming from. But I'm sure you can imagine what happened next."

"All out mayhem?"

"Yeah. The smoke alarm went off. My father rushed in and grabbed the fire extinguisher, and my mom screamed bloody murder and called 911. She got my sisters and me out of the house, and somehow, my dad was able to put out the blaze, but the smoke was nuts, and a big red hook and ladder truck showed up, and it was just really, really bad. I was extremely shook. Like, I had nightmares for months afterward. And my mother gave me the spanking of a lifetime once my dad got out okay."

"Yikes," I say, waiting for her to connect the dots and tell me what on earth this story has to do with writing.

"Anyway, I never let my budding curiosity get the better of me again. First of all, I was grounded. No TV or anything like that for a month. So all I had left was books. And I was lucky enough to be a good reader, so I just started vicariously living through the pages of other children's rule-breaking adventures."

"You really don't strike me as the type to get in trouble."

"I'm *not. That's* the thing! I've always been a nerd," she says matter-of-factly.

"Don't say that," I rebut.

"It's true," she declares. "And the fire thing scared the crap out of me, to be honest."

"I'm sure."

"But even before the kitchen incident, I was always different. I have three sisters, and I'm nothing like them."

"They're not pyromaniacs?"

"Ha, ha," she deadpans, a cute smirk playing on her lips. "No, even worse. They're 'cool girls.'" Here, she throws up air quotes before continuing. "They all developed an early love of makeup and clothing and unnecessary trips to the Queens Center mall. The older ones—Anna and Melanie—shared a bedroom, and my little sister, Jamie, was stuck with me. She was the top bunk to my bottom bunk, the wild and crazy to my quiet and shy, the yin to my yang. I would read books by flashlight, while she'd watch music videos and pose in front of the full-length mirror in one of Anna's training bras."

"Wow," I respond, careful not to say anything that could be misconstrued as inappropriate or disrespectful.

"Yeah, well, they say that when you come from a big family, the younger children are way less disciplined because the parents are outnumbered. In my opinion, that tracks, minus incidents of accidental arson."

"I don't know. I'm a younger sibling, and I think I was pretty tame."

"I'm sure you're just an anomaly in all sorts of ways," she retorts.

"Doubtful. But what I'm hearing you say is that you want to be a writer so that you can stop lighting things on fire."

"No," she laughs, but something in her eyes changes. "Obviously, my storytelling needs work. I want to be a writer because…" There's a long pause during which Aunt Rose rounds the corner and reenters our section of the hall.

"How nice. You're both looking a little better." She grins. "Scale of one to ten, how's everyone feeling?" She hands each of us a miniature can of ginger ale and a package of individually wrapped saltines, like you might get at a diner with your soup if you were over eighty and meeting your bridge club for an early bird special. "Ten being the best you've ever felt."

Cecily accepts the snack and sets it on the nightstand beside her. "Thank you," she says. "And I don't know. Maybe like a five?"

"Nausea gone?"

"Not all the way," she admits. "But I think I got most of it out." She opens her mouth in a yawn, covering it with her hand.

"Tired?" Aunt Rose asks.

Cecily nods.

"How about you?" she asks me.

I think about it. The room's not spinning, so that's good. Talking to Cecily has been a good distraction. "Probably about the same. Like a five."

"Okay. Well, like I mentioned, there are others from your school here, and the doctor wants to keep all of you overnight for observations. Give you a chance to rest, and if you feel closer to a seven or an eight in the morning, we'll let you go."

"How will we get back?" Cecily wonders.

"Oh, don't worry. They'll come get you."

"Will it cost a lot more if we stay? My co-pay for an ER visit is fifty bucks, but an overnight is a lot more. I think I'm okay enough to go back now." She sits up a little straighter.

"Nope. There's no cost to you at all. Matthias is footing the bill. It's included with your residency."

"Oh," she replies.

"So make yourself comfortable—I mean, as comfortable as you can, and definitely get some sleep. I'll bring you both some fresh buckets, and I'll dim the lights as much as I can out here. Bathroom's straight down on the right there, so help yourself. I'll be in the office, but you can just buzz for me if you need anything."

"Okay," Cecily says. "Thank you."

"Thanks," I echo.

Aunt Rose leaves, and Cecily breaks into her crackers. "In the absence of a much-needed toothbrush," she shares, crunching, "I'm hoping this will make me a little less offensive in the morning." Crumbs cascade down her shirt. She wipes them away.

"I'm not worried about you," I say. "I can't even look at food right now though. So if you want mine"—I hold up the flimsy package—"have at it."

"I'm good, thanks." She sets the wrapper on the tiny tray table attached to the side of the bed and scoots down under the thin white blanket, pulling it up to her neck.

"I guess the rest of the story will have to wait?" I ask.

Cecily sighs. "Yeah. I guess." She rolls to face me. "Long story short, books can't hurt you."

"That's a loaded sentence," I reply. "You mean books can't hurt you like fire can?"

"Well, that's certainly true. But I was thinking more like books can't hurt you like people can."

I swallow. "Wow."

"Well, it's true, don't you think?"

I stifle a yawn, feeling exhaustion settle on top of me like a weight. "Honestly? I think that's true if you're a reader. You'd be surprised at what books can do when you're on the other side of the page." I catch myself, surprised at my own words.

"Hm," she mumbles into the darkness.

I close my eyes. For some reason, I don't want to see her reaction to my admission. It feels...vulnerable. Or like I'm some kind of fraud. In the silence, I notice the gurgling in my stomach is gone. I hear the whir of an exhaust fan and the slow drip of my IV.

"Hey, Professor," she whispers.

I smile at the ceiling. "Just call me Nate, please."

"Okay. Nate," she repeats.

"Yes, CJ, how can I help you?"

"You want to know something funny?"

"Sure."

"This is actually a way better sleeping situation than the one I'm in currently."

"In the middle of a pocket-size health facility?"

"Sadly, yes."

"How's that?"

"Well, at school, they've got me rooming with an elderly woman who I think is plotting to kill me. In fact, if it hadn't been for the fact that other people got sick too, I would have guessed that she was the one who poisoned my lobster."

"Who is it?"

"Her name's Gurt."

"Haven't met her yet."

"Better for you. I'm sure she's thrilled I'm gone."

"I'm sorry."

"Don't be," she says, yawning.

Several beats of calm pass, and I feel myself drifting in and out of sleep. "You know what?" Cecily whispers.

"Mm?" I reply.

"You're not so bad after all."

"Thanks?"

She lets out a sound that's like a half stretch, half moan. It's reminiscent of the muted soundtrack of a cat curling up for a nap in the afternoon sun. Cecily carefully removes her glasses, folds them, and sets them on the tray table beside her ginger ale. "You're welcome," she says. "Good night, Nate."

"'Night, CJ," I say, my heavy-lidded eyes closing involuntarily.

For the first time in as long as I can remember, I fall asleep smiling.

CHAPTER 3

Cecily

Returning to campus the next morning feels like a weird van ride of shame. I think it has something to do with Maggie. Today, she's wearing a neon purple tank top that claims *I Love Me Some WAP* with a picture of Tolstoy's *War and Peace* below it. (One really has to wonder if she knows what WAP stands for or if this is just a fluke.) She smiles at all of us as we file into the van, and when it's Nate's turn to climb inside, she touches his arm and says, "Come, love. Sit shotgun next to me." He politely declines with a shake of his head, and Maggie shrugs, walks around to the driver's side, and sulks in her seat until everyone is safely on board. Meanwhile, all of the not-quite-one-hundred-percent-better-yet passengers had to endure many rounds of puking last night without brushing our teeth afterward, so I can't speak for the others, but I opt to keep my mouth shut so nobody is subjected to my rank morning breath.

Thankfully, Maggie doesn't drive like a maniac this time. She does, however, seem much quieter than the last time we were here together. To fill the void, she puts on the radio, and suddenly the van is overcome with the Jamaican dancehall stylings of one Mad Cobra circa 1992, whose one-hit wonder is marked by the refrain, "Gyal, flex. Time to have sex." As if we were in need of a reggae-based alarm clock. Perhaps it's not exactly what you or I might select at 7:30 in the morning after a stay in an infirmary, but I'm starting to think that this is definitely an on-brand move for Maggie.

Physically, I feel about eighty-five percent better, but emotionally, I somehow feel significantly lighter this morning, like the heavy weight of loneliness and feeling like I don't belong that was crushing my shoulders is noticeably absent today. I woke up before Profes—um, Nate, and I worried for a split second that he would regret talking to me last night, like when you meet a guy when you're tipsy in a dark bar and then see him sober in the light of day and you're like, *Wow...no.*

But that's not how it goes down at all. When we woke up, he smiled at me, his hair all askew, and we exchanged very few words other than his "How are you feeling?" and my "A little better. You?" which was followed by a nod, a grunt, and the word "Same." We're side by side in the back of the van, but I'm staring out the back window at the scenery, which I must admit is quite bucolic, especially in the early morning peachy glow of the sun. He's checking his phone. If we were friends, I would say, "Look! You're missing it." But we're just—I don't know. Teacher and student, I guess.

When we arrive at the retreat center, I wave goodbye to Nate and to Maggie and immediately head to the shower. I stave off a warm welcome from Gurt, who is thankfully absent from our room when I arrive, and who (by some miracle of God) has not removed all of my personal belongings and changed the locks while I was gone. I luxuriate in one of the vertical coffins masquerading as a shower in the communal restroom, scrub the enamel off my teeth over the sink for a solid five minutes, and slip on a sundress with a light cardigan over it. I tie my wet hair in a topknot and decide to skip the makeup for today, seeing as how there's no way I could look more haggard than I did last night. *Clean is the goal,* I decide. *Just be clean and healthy, and keep all your food down.*

With my backpack in tow, I head to the dining hall and make myself a toasted English muffin for breakfast. Dry. It's about all my stomach can handle. I sit through Nate's workshop. Today, we are reviewing Trite Tim's work: the first eighteen pages of a novel that is supposed to be a modern-day take on George Orwell's *Animal Farm*, only in his version, a hamster and a guinea pig try to take over a Petco, and there's nothing to be found but entirely unrealistic action scenes that Tim *insists* are allegorical. I'm reminded of Humphrey, the hamster from the series by the same name that is quite popular with the third and fourth graders at the library, and even though I say very little out loud in our workshop together, I laugh as I remember the fact that I offered this up as a book recommendation in my feedback letter to Tim.

It's so tempting to cut him down, but I'm exhausted, and I remind myself that's not what I came here for anyway. Nate manages to give him a good dose of thoughtful feedback, Harold persists with the stroking of his imperceivable facial hair (the cape is blessedly absent from his outfit today), and Maleficent expresses her discontent for stories in which humans are not the main characters. We break for a snack, and while Tim is clearly pissed, at least he's not crying, so I'm pretty sure Nate sees that as a win.

Later that afternoon, I'm settling into a chair in Room B of the North Wind building, readying myself for Nate's seminar. I feel a little bit better, although the occasional errant burp reminds me of last night's debacle and the fact that I will never eat shellfish again. The room is packed. Apparently, everyone's really excited to hear Nate speak.

I wouldn't have classified Nate Ellis as a nervous sort of person prior to my conversation with him last night. Descriptors for him might have included words like *egotistical, narcissistic,* or perhaps even *holier-than-thou.* Now, I feel like he's a lot more regular that I previously realized; he's maybe just a little better at navigating social situations that I am. (Fine, *significantly* better.) There's something about accolades in the literary world that create unfair assumptions. I mean, between his prestigious award and his Yaddo stint, he's an easy person to be jealous of. And to be fair, his writing isn't half-bad. His book just struck me as a little bit reminiscent of *Death of a Salesman,* if it was set in the aftermath of a pandemic and Willy Loman was replaced by a Department of Labor employee. It wasn't bad. I just wouldn't choose it off a shelf in Barnes & Noble is all I'm saying.

I'm not *rude* about it though. I'm not shouting from the rooftops that I wouldn't curl up with *Work* on a Saturday night.

But apparently, I'm very naïve. I've brought an expectation with me to this school that faculty members will be collegial toward one another and that they are as invested in each other's success as they are in their students' learning. So forgive me for not expecting what happens next.

"Good afternoon, everyone," Nate begins. "We're here today to discuss the way in which plot affects character development in literature." He starts up a PowerPoint presentation using the clicker that Lucy has provided him with. The first few slides offer examples, along with references to short stories that we were expected to read in advance of the seminar. All of these items are neatly printed out in my binder, and I follow along with the *Nate Ellis Show* without concern.

Until.

"I'd like us to take a few moments here to do a generative exercise. Everyone, please take out a notebook or an iPad. Whatever you've got." He switches the slide and begins to read the assignment aloud. "This exercise is called 'Put Yourself in the Story.' Essentially, I want you to think of yourself as the main character in a novel or piece of short fiction. Think of a moment—a real moment from your own personal biography—that you feel shifted your outlook on life or on the world around you. Write that moment for us. And when we're done, I'll take a few minutes and give people a chance to share."

I begin to ruminate on the question, knowing full well exactly which moment it was that altered the trajectory of my life—but my train of thought is interrupted by someone.

"Excuse me, Mr. Ellis. What makes you think that this exercise is *relevant?* I can think of a number of famous stories where the plot has nothing to do with the character's internal arc. In fact, the arc happens *despite* the plot. I'd say we can all agree that this is a critical element of what sets literary fiction apart from genre fiction, hm?"

I swivel around to see that the demeaning voice belongs to that woman from the mixer the other day, the one who made the comment about Nate and Yaddo. Alice Some-French-Last-Name-That-Probably-Means-Fuck-Tart.

"I'm sorry?" he asks.

She clears her throat and repeats her insult using a different set of SAT prep words.

"Well, if we disregard plot as an essential element of storytelling, we're left with very little, Professor Devereaux," he rebuts. "And I happen to have it on good authority that not every student in our program is writing literary fiction."

She harrumphs, openly sneering at him. "*You* certainly weren't."

He laughs off the obvious insult, but I can feel the tension mounting. "You're right. Like many of the artists here, I came to the page without a clear plan for what I was going to write. I think you're missing the point of the exercise though. The point of the exercise is to take a deeper look at plot as a device to create change and move the needle for a protagonist. They say, 'Write what you know,' so I'm here offering our students that opportunity."

Dillon Norway stands up. "It's an interesting conversation, one that often persists in the MFA world: literary versus commercial fiction. There's no right or wrong though. There's plenty of space for both. So let's get on with the exercise then. What'd you say, Nate? Ten minutes? Fifteen?"

"Fifteen minutes should work," he agrees and then turns to shuffle some handouts as the room goes quiet with the white noise of pens scribbling on paper and tablet screens.

I can't help but notice the slump in Nate's shoulders as he busies himself with anything to keep his back turned to the audience. Alice Douchebag Devereaux receives a silent tap on the shoulder from Dillon Norway, who juts out his chin toward the door, mutely requesting that she follow him outside, which she does, but not without a puss on her face.

Thoughts of Alice Devereaux's obvious frigidity sadly translate into the story I'm about to jot down about myself, causing me no small amount of panic at the thought of a sexless, judgmental future not unlike the one she must be experiencing presently. *But I am not a bitter person,* I remind myself. *In fact, my story is actually quite hopeful.*

So I write.

You know the whole *Always a bridesmaid, never a bride* thing? Well, that's kind of been my personal tagline for the past nine years. I've been in thirteen weddings. That's thirteen bridal showers I've had to help plan, thirteen bachelorette parties I've tried (and failed) to enjoy, thirteen awkward nights out in uncomfortable shoes doing the Cha Cha Slide with my nieces while my adoring aunts drink themselves giggly and post wastey-pants videos of their synchronized dance attempts on TikTok. Now I'm sure you're thinking that the reason I've been involved in so many weddings must be on account of my sparkling personality. (*She's awash with friends!* you presume. *Ha,* I respond; if only that were the case.) I actually come from a gigantic family. Three sisters. Twelve cousins. All girls. All of whom I love dearly! And all of prime childbearing age, raised by a quartet of women from the easternmost New York City outer borough.

The estrogen in our bloodline is next level.

We must put out some serious pheromones too, because all thirteen of the weddings in question happened before the brides turned thirty. We're not living in *Little House on the Prairie* times either, where girls had kids by eighteen and were dead by fifty. This story takes place now, not hundreds of years ago.

My younger sister, Jamie (bride number thirteen), was going for her master's degree at Merrimack College in Massachusetts, studying to become a certified athletic trainer, when she got a job working for the New Hampshire Fisher Cats, a double-A affiliate of the Toronto Blue Jays.

In professional baseball, guys move up and down the minor league ladder, all hoping for a shot to play in the majors. It's a real grind too. Players have to work out every day, and they have to report to games six days a week with an off day on Monday. They live in obscure towns across the country—or even in Canada, if you happen to play for the Blue Jays—and as they move up and down the ladder, they can be plucked up out of one of those areas and sent to another team within the franchise in a totally different time zone overnight. I happen to know this information courtesy of Bryce Archer, my first and only long-term boyfriend ever. We met in homeroom at Cardozo High School in Queens, New York. Like people used to—none of this online business you see happening these days. Things were good until they weren't, and then we broke up. There were no new verbs aligned with our time together, no gaslighting or catfishing. He was not sus, and neither of us were woke. In fact, our relationship read a lot more like a traditional teen romance movie than the current online dumpster fire of my social life. Bryce was cute and popular. I was shy and awkward. It was very *Twilight* minus the vampires, *The Fault in Our Stars* minus the terminal illness. Cool guy plus nerdy girl equals happy ending, which sounds a lot like common core math to me in that it makes no logical sense whatsoever. Still, we stayed together for six years, which is a long time for any relationship, I know now. We even stuck it out through college, both of us moving to the wilds of Rhode Island. He played baseball for Bryant University, and I went to Brown University to study literature, so we were twenty minutes away from each other in the Dunkin' drinking Ocean State. Until he got drafted by the Toronto Blue Jays his junior year of college and poof! Within days, he was gone, suddenly living in Vancouver, Canada, on a work visa playing minor league baseball for a Blue Jays farm team. Bryce left me behind to handle the *ring by spring* expectation of my mother, who would not stop begging me to make it work long distance while I succumbed to the quiet understanding that he was out there chasing his dreams, just like all of my overachieving friends at Brown.

I was chasing mine too—or, at the very least, I was figuring out exactly what mine were while immersing myself in the written word: classics, contemporaries, and everything in between. I could lose myself in a book just as easily as I could find myself in one, and I knew that I yearned for a future where I could be surrounded by stories. I loved words like Bryce loved baseball.

So when he left, it hurt, but it wasn't a shock, and I certainly wasn't about to force a round peg into a square hole just to appease my mother. Besides, our relationship had devolved into a ticking clock. Waiting for the draft. Waiting for the call. Scoping out teams, locations. I would have been really stupid if I thought he'd quit all that so he could stay in Rhode Island with me, especially when the whole reason he'd gone there in the first place was so that he could get noticed by scouts, chase opportunities, and find a way into a world he'd wanted to be part of since he was a little kid. We'd stay friends, we decided. You know, the kind of friends who barely ever speak to each other because of time zones, practices, games, and all that.

It was fine. There were other fish in the sea.

Besides, I had my books. My books would never leave. They'd see me through the pain of a breakup. Books could see me through anything. Plus, the leading men in books were a whole lot more interesting and desirable than the ones I knew in real life. Mr. Darcy never talked about anal during Mexican night at the dining hall the way Todd did. Marc Antony didn't ask Cleopatra if she wanted to have a threesome with her roommate. (Vinny sure did though.)

In the years following graduation, I dated Les, who was conveniently "between jobs" and made me pay for our dinner; Devin, who had a legit toe fetish; and Jared, who was kind enough to inform me that the thing on his lip was not a pimple but a herpes sore (as I'd suspected). Anyway, all of that was a far cry from my most recent relationship, which took place last year and lasted exactly one evening, ending with me climbing out of the bathroom window of a restaurant after being informed that my date, Adrian, "occasionally dabbled" in methamphetamines.

And no, that was not a fact that he listed on his Tinder profile.

But (and my apologies for the digression, but we're back to minor league baseball here) I now know that the minors are kind of like the military, minus the weapons training and risking-your-life-for-freedom thing. The guys often get lonely, and many look for the companionship of a wife at a relatively early age. How did I learn this tidbit of intel, you wonder? Well, courtesy of Bryce, of course.

And my sister.

Lucky wedding number thirteen, a.k.a. the day my ex-boyfriend became my brother-in-law, was fraught with pitiful looks from my huge extended family. Exuberance for my baby sister was marred by mumbled sidebar concerns for my mental health as my chronological age was nearing twenty-nine and my ovaries had zero prospects in sight.

Please allow me to remind you that this is a work of nonfiction, so yes, your knee-jerk response of *"You're kidding, right?"* is fully warranted.

Jamie called me when Bryce showed up on her team, fresh off a stint with the Buffalo Bisons. He was bummed to be climbing down the ladder after a not-so-hot season, demoted from triple-A to double-A, and was grateful for the surprise of Jamie's familiar face. She asked me if it was okay to go out with him for a drink a week or two later, and what was I going to say? No?

I *couldn't* say no. She's my *sister*, and I love her! Bryce was just a guy from my past. And so what if he took my virginity?

Okay, fine. In retrospect, maybe I should have said no.

Jamie's wedding day should have been a sad day for me, walking down the aisle toward my Bryce plus seven years of muscle decked out in a tuxedo. To be fair, I'll admit that it was hard not to be reminded of our prom night, seeing him standing there dressed like that. Yet as I arrived just steps shy of his position at the altar, I veered to the left to line up alongside my relatives, a lopsided smile plastered to my face, making space for his bride, my sister, whose fidget spinner collection he used to make fun of back when we were dating. And I was...fine. Not angry, not sad. Bryce was a minor-league baseball player who dropped out of college, and Jamie was content to toss aside her expensive private school education and interest in science and biology to accompany him up and down the MLB flowchart, living in crappy rental apartments paid for by the team and going to six baseball games a week with no end in sight.

If that was the journey she wanted to have, more power to her.

One thing bears mentioning though. I had an epiphany during that wedding. So this is the "character arc" part of the story, if you will. As I shifted from left foot to right foot in my painful sparkly shoes, there was a moment when I realized I wasn't like the rest of my female family members. For them, the idea of being married and procreating was some sort of apex to aspire to. But I never really saw marriage that way. My dad was always busy working; my mom was busy feeding everyone and running us all over the city to our various activities and playdates. My parents never got all fancy and went out together unless they had to. There were no Broadway shows or date nights. Dad only dressed up for work, for weddings, or for Nana's funeral. Life was just always super *busy*.

Well, I mean, for the rest of us. (Rest in peace, Nana.)

Meanwhile, I grew up hiding from the ever-present noise in my childhood home by burying my nose in a book, wearing oversize, unsightly red headphones to mute the constant drama that comes with a house full of girls. I immersed myself in stories about strong women, books like *The Poisonwood Bible* and *The Handmaid's Tale*—narratives that reinforced the notion that there was more to life than just the search for a man. Then I'd pen short stories or fanfic, mostly coming-of-age YA stuff, in an attempt to fill a void that I felt existed for young girls like me in bookstores and libraries. The classics portray male protagonists going on great adventures; think Huckleberry Finn or

Odysseus. Even Holden Caulfield was going on his own kind of journey. But female protagonists of the past—much like my sisters and cousins—journeyed only toward marriage and childbirth, leaving careers and other meaningful life goals on the wayside in pursuit of that sperm.

So as I stood there at Jamie's wedding, hiding behind my robin's-egg-blue glasses, I received those pathetic looks from my family members and found myself awash with resolve. No more of this *always a bridesmaid* bullshit. No more being defined by my lack of a plus-one at family functions.

No more of me just being a *reader*, a sideline participant, a children's librarian swimming in an endless sea of other people's stories.

Why waste my time on dating apps when I could spend it pursuing my dreams? And maybe, I figured, if my family could see how fulfilling my life was as a solo act, they'd leave me alone about having babies and actually be proud of my *professional* accomplishments.

Yes, as my baby sister took her vows to love, honor, and cherish Bryce Archer, so too did I take a vow, to love, honor, and cherish myself! *This* was the moment I decided I would pursue my childhood dream of becoming a published author. I would write books and people would buy them, and I would be Cecily Jane Allerton, the self-fulfilled author whose family was proud of her, not Cecily Jane Allerton, the poor soul whose prom date married her sister.

That counts as a character arc, right?

I scribble away, recounting the story that has shaped my adult life most to date, until Nate informs us that it's time to be done. "That'll do it, folks. Anyone want to share what they wrote?"

Overzealous students raise their hands, eager to hop on board the Nate Ellis express train to success, but all I keep thinking about is what he told me last night at the medical center. *He thinks he's just a fluke.* Maleficent attempts to share her pearls of wisdom with the group, only she doesn't really answer the question and instead talks about Hemingway's alcoholism, which seems irrelevant but is in much the same vein as Professor Douchebag Devereaux's previous comment. I turn around to see if the douchebag herself has reentered the room, and not a moment too soon, as it appears she is not only back but has something new to say.

"I agree with Andrea," she pontificates. "Real character arcs develop due to more than just circumstances. For example," she goes on, "if we were to take your success as an author, we would see that you went from a no-name copywriter to a big-name *somebody* in the time it took for a pop-up animal market to go batty in Wuhan."

Oh, damn.

"Which is not exactly the same as a character arc, now is it?" she goes on.

Nate pauses, takes a breath, and puts on the fakest smile I have ever seen on a man in my life. "Well, since this is intended to be a personal activity, I would be happy to share that my success as an author has definitely *contributed* to the development of my character over time, but I don't think it's the sole factor."

"Then what is?" she counters.

Nate shrugs. "It's not just one thing. It's been a series of events."

"Okay, Mr. Ellis. Riddle me this. How can you ask our fledgling writers here to choose just one moment and characterize it as *the* moment that defines their personal arc? How can you expect them to do something that you yourself are unable to do?"

"This is just an exercise, Alice. Real character arc doesn't happen in a vacuum."

I'm not sure what possesses me at this exact moment, but before I can stop myself, I am raising my hand. Nate looks at me and nods his head.

"I'd like to share," I say in a voice bolder than one who spent six of the past twenty-four hours puking her guts out should have.

His face shifts the tiniest bit from exasperation to relief, like he's narrowly avoiding heart palpitations.

"My ex-boyfriend married my sister," I overshare loudly. "And as I was walking down the aisle as her bridesmaid, I realized I wanted to pursue my dream of becoming a published author instead of pursuing my family's dream of me becoming a wife and popping out a bunch of kids. It was a single moment, and I think it resulted in a huge character arc," I say in a moment of verbal vomit (a welcome contrast from my earlier bout of *real* vomit).

In response to this information, I hear some very low murmuring from the audience, but I choose to ignore it. Nate Ellis eyeballs me curiously. Then Dillon Norway pipes up. "That would make a great novel," he says.

That would *make a great novel,* I realize.

Dillon Norway continues. "I also think it's an excellent example of how there's not one single right answer. Still, I appreciate the heated discussion. Who else would like to share?"

Others tentatively raise their hands, and once it's clear that there are plenty of people who believe that character arc *can* be borne from a solitary plot twist, Douchebag Devereaux quietly leaves the room. I only know this because I can see Nate's face change. Students engage in meaningful discussions, he offers a few more examples, and the session comes to a close.

Afterward, some students linger, and some try to approach him for sidebar conversations. I pack up my backpack and hoist it onto my shoulders.

"CJ!" I hear as I walk toward the exit. "Cecily!" the voice says again.

I turn around. Nate is waving me over.

"Stick around for a sec, please?"

I try to make a smooth about-face, but the tortoise shell on my back bonks into a few fellow MFAers. I work my way back to the front of the room, and the Nate Ellis fan club begrudgingly dissipates.

He lowers his voice when he speaks to me. "Thank you for doing that," he says.

"Doing what?"

"Shutting her down like that with your god-awful story."

I shrug. "No worries. I was just trying to save you from the same humiliation I went through."

"Huh?"

"In workshop. When they all ripped me to shreds," I explain. "I don't know. I don't like watching nice people be attacked for no good reason."

He nods. "Well, really, thank you. I appreciate what you did."

"My pleasure."

"Did that really happen to you? That thing with your sister?"

"It did."

"Wow. I'm sorry. I guess that was what you meant."

"Huh?"

"When you said that books can't hurt you like people can."

"Oh. That." I shuffle my feet. "Yeah. But it's all good. Remember? I said it was a glass-half-full situation."

"You did say that."

The conversation fades out, and I'm met with an awkward pause. "Well, I'm going to head out," I say. "Good seminar, by the way."

"Thank you," he says.

I walk toward the exit, and just before I cross the threshold, I turn around and hold up my hand in a little wave, surprised to see that he's still looking at me. An unexpected warmth fills my belly, but I quickly ignore it.

I'm sure it's just the bad fish, I tell myself.

CHAPTER 4

Nate

Something happens in the days that follow. I'm not sure how to pinpoint the shift, but all of a sudden, I'm able to write. It's like a door that was jammed is busted open, and words rush through it like a biblical flood.

I get up early and walk out to a picnic table overlooking the water, the glow of my laptop illuminating the space around me like a force field until the sun comes up. I get into this very calm, zen space in the solitude of the morning. The crickets in the grass arrange a private symphony for me with the waves that crash against the rocks along the perimeter of the retreat center. I do this every day for the five remaining days of the residency. With the stress of my seminar gone and the four days of workshop over, I am merely a participant here, and somehow this unlocks my creative juices. I write for three hours each morning, from 4:30 until 7:30, when the scent of bacon wafts out of the kitchen and mixes with salt air in the atmosphere of my outdoor office. I pack up my things and drop them in my room, then head out for a run to digest the morning's work. Come back, shower, grab breakfast, and because I only have to lead a workshop for the first half of the residency (after which point, the students are placed in a second workshop with a different faculty member), I find myself free for another three hours from 9:00 a.m. to noon.

So I write some more.

I manage to cram almost fifteen thousand words into five days of writing, and I realize, Alice Devereaux be damned, I *love* this place.

In the afternoons, I host an office hour so that I can be interviewed by students as a possible mentor choice for the semester. It feels a little bit like what I would imagine speed dating to be like. They come in, sit down, ask me a bunch of questions off a list, and decide whether we would "be a good fit," which is funny to me in that it should really be mutual, but evidently I am just the writing equivalent of a piece of meat at the butcher shop.

On the last day of the residency, a hilarious if tragic thing happens. Mentor choices, which have the entire student body in a tizzy, are posted on the whiteboard during breakfast, so as soon as the clock strikes 9:30 a.m., students and faculty are welcome to go and check out who they've been assigned to. The expectation is that once you know who your mentor is, you'll seek them out prior to the end of the day (which is abbreviated so that folks have time to ferry over to the mainland to catch connecting flights or pick up their cars and drive to wherever they hail from). Students are to, at the very least, exchange personal contact info with their mentors or—best-case scenario—they should come up with a semester plan.

So I'm walking to the North Wind building at around 9:15 a.m. on this final day, as faculty are allowed fifteen minutes of whiteboard time prior to it being available for students, and who's barreling down the hall toward me but my favorite student, CJ. (She hates that I've persisted with this nickname, but it suits her and makes her laugh, and she's the only person besides Dillon who I actually like here, so CJ it is.) Lucy has just finished writing out all the mentor pairings—a lofty assignment as there are seventy-four students to match—and is en route to the dining room to inform folks that the board is available for viewing. This leaves me standing there, alone, with a bewildered and frazzled CJ.

"I overslept," she whines. "I never oversleep." There's panic in her eyes as she searches the board. Her full name is written under Dillon Norway. "Oh my gosh!" she exclaims. "I got paired with Dillon Norway!"

"That's great," I say. "He's awesome. I think he'll be a really good mentor for you."

"He was my top choice," she confesses. "No offense."

"None taken."

"Who'd you get?" she asks, scanning. "Oof." Her face drops. "I don't know these two"—she points—"but you got Tim and Gurt." Her face turns solemn. "You're going to learn a lot about hamsters and passive-aggressive behavior this semester, I guess."

I grin. "Yup. I'm actually eager to hear about what an awful roommate you are. I have no doubt that Gurt will provide me with endless stories about you."

She swats my arm. "You stop that," she chides me. "Listen, I've got to get something in my stomach before workshop. I'll catch you in a little bit."

"You got it," I say.

Then CJ spins around so quickly that her massive backpack sweeps against the whiteboard, taking at least a third of the names with it. She looks over her shoulder in horror. "Oh, *shit*," she seethes.

I die laughing. I can't help it. "Go," I tell her in an exaggerated whisper. "Hurry—before anyone sees!"

"Everyone's going to be so mad at me," she cries.

"Nobody has to know," I insist. "Just go. Your secret's safe with me. You go to the dining hall, and I'll go out the other door. It'll be fine. But get a move on!" I shoo her out the door, tears forming in my eyes from giggling like a child.

Poor CJ leaves, her small frame speed waddling like a third-trimester penguin under the weight of her gargantuan pack, now marred with the scandalous evidence of red dry-erase ink that will hopefully go unnoticed.

Like a salmon swimming upstream, I watch her enter the dining hall just as the rest of the student body spills out onto the walkway to come find out who they're assigned to work with for the semester.

I duck into Room B to hide and hold in my hysterical guffaws as I listen to the wails of students who cannot locate their names in the red-streaked mess.

For some reason, this lunacy is a major highlight of the whole residency for me.

Later on, after the whiteboard is corrected and I've had the distinct displeasure of meeting with Gurt (who looks like she could beat me in an arm wrestle), I board one of three vans headed to the 3:00 p.m. Block Island ferry. Of course, I'm stuck with Maggie, who's inappropriate undersized T-shirt boasts the line *Books make me touch my shelf*. She gives me her phone number as I unload my bag at the dock, and I'm so caught off guard by it that I ask, "Do you give rides on the mainland as well?"

"Sugar," she replies. "I'll give you a ride wherever you like."

My face turns beet red, and I shove the slip of paper with her phone number on it deep into the pocket of my jeans. "Um, 'kay. Thanks," I say and promptly hightail it onto the ferry.

The boat ride is a bit surreal, as the small interior cabin is jam-packed with students and faculty, many of whom are napping, some who are quietly chatting in pairs, and others, like me, who've tuned out the noise with AirPods. I see CJ reading a book several rows to my right, and when she looks over and smiles at me, I shoot her a wink and try not to chuckle at the memory of her whiteboard mishap from this morning.

The ferry is not quite as nice as the one that I've taken out of Orient Point, on the northern tip of Long Island, across the sound to Connecticut, with connecting buses to the casinos there. That ferry accepted cars and was a nice way to avoid all of the I-95 traffic if one was trying to escape the city for a weekend. I don't have a car (don't need one in Manhattan), but the Hampton Jitney offered a nice straight run from Midtown out to the ferry on Friday afternoons and back home again on Sundays.

That ferry was Avery's favorite. I used to tease her that she had a gambling problem, but really she only played the penny slots at Mohegan Sun (although she could sit there for hours if I let her). We only did that trip twice in our two and a half years together. The first trip was good, but the second one catapulted us toward our inevitable demise.

Avery and I met back in my old copyediting days. We worked together at the magazine; she was the assistant to the editor in chief, and our paths crossed weekly during Friday staff meetings. We caught eyes once, and she asked me what my favorite kind of breakfast pastry was as I was doctoring my coffee. Bear claws magically appeared on the danish tray the following week, and when I asked her out, she said yes.

Our relationship was fun at first. I mean, all relationships are usually pretty fun at the beginning, right? I'd say it became a little strained at about the one-year mark. Two things happened then: (1) I started the visits with my grandfather, as he was on the decline, and (2) we celebrated our one-year anniversary, and she began throwing out hints about wanting a ring. I was twenty-seven at the time though, and an engagement was the furthest thing from my radar.

I'd spend my days at work, and we fell into a pretty comfortable routine—we'd have lunch together in the break room on Tuesdays and Thursdays, and she'd stay at my place on Friday and Saturday nights. On Wednesdays, we would grab dinner somewhere near her apartment on the West Side (which she shared with two roommates, thus, we never spent the night there), and on Tuesday and Thursday evenings, I would fly solo to visit with my grandfather. I liked our routine. I'm a fan of schedules. But after that one-year mark, she wanted to switch it up and be together more often, and there just wasn't a whole lot of extra time. I used Monday nights to write, since at the time I was beginning to take the stories my grandpa would share with me and build them into a novel, and the deeper he descended into oblivion, the more important and sacred our time together felt. So I certainly wasn't willing to give up my Tuesdays or Thursdays.

Avery called me a workaholic; she said I didn't know how to let loose and have fun. I told her I wanted to find a literary agent because my novel was really shaping up to be interesting, and I wanted to see if I could sell it. She said I was too ambitious. She was the maid of honor in her older sister's wedding and recounted every single detail to me, swooning over nonsense like party favors or seven different blue fabric swatches. ("Who cares about the difference between teal, aqua, and turquoise?" I made the mistake of asking. In response, she didn't speak to me for two days.) On more than one occasion after sex, she snuggled up to my chest and whispered her ring size in my ear.

Her birthday came, and I took her to Mohegan Sun for the weekend. She had a blast: we went out to a fancy steak house where the waiters sang "Happy Birthday" while a sparkler spit out tiny bits of fire over her molten lava cake, I sent her to the spa for a facial and a pedicure, and she spent upward of four hours and $300 playing slots. Yet somehow, at the end of the weekend, she was pissed at me because nowhere in there did a diamond ring present itself.

I finished my novel after my grandfather passed away and began to submit it to literary agents. Avery felt like I was wasting precious time writing query letters and researching agency trends on Query Tracker when I could have been spending what little savings I had on our future together. I got some full-manuscript requests, and every time I'd share my excitement with her, she'd respond by reminding me that most authors can't make a living writing without a solid day job and that being so busy would really cut into my ability to be a good father to our potential 2.5 children. (To which I responded with silence, because by this point, it just made more sense to stay quiet than to argue with her. Plus, I could tell that our days were numbered, even if I didn't necessarily want to admit it.)

When I got signed by Trina Richards from Table of Contents Literary Agency, I was over-the-moon excited. To celebrate, I booked a surprise trip for Avery and me to go back to Mohegan Sun. I thought it would be fun. I planned us a big night at that same steak house that she liked so much, and between the main course and dessert, I told her I had big news. Her eyes got wide, and she gazed at me with weighty anticipation.

I should have seen it coming.

I should have known she was expecting a proposal.

I shouldn't have been shocked when, after sharing my big news, she got up and left the table to cry in the ladies' room after screeching, "*That's what you wanted to tell me?*"

The ferry ride home that weekend was awkward, to say the least.

Even more uncomfortable was the email she sent me almost two years later, a few months into the pandemic, once news of my book was all over Yahoo and my name was in everyone's mouth.

Hi Nate! it read. I know it's been a long time, but I just wanted to check in with you and tell you how totally psyched I am for you about your book. I always knew you'd be a big deal. Xoxo, Avery

PS—We should get together sometime. You're welcome in my pod if you want. 😉

Hard not to remember that story anytime I get on a ferry now. She was my last girlfriend—and that was over five years ago. It's not that I haven't been with anyone since then; I've just been a lot more careful not to inadvertently lead anyone on. Plus, I started to find that the more people learned about me, the more attractive I became to women, especially when it came to the dollars attached to my film option and subsequent second book deal. To be clear, I'm not saying that all women are gold diggers. I've just been a little hard-pressed to find a woman who *isn't* asking about my net worth by the third date.

When I look over at CJ, with her nose buried in that thick YA paperback, I consider what she shared in my seminar. I haven't met many women who put their professional ambitions ahead of their relationships. I wonder if she would feel the same way if her ex-boyfriend *hadn't* married her sister. I feel something tug at me, annoying me in the same way a tiny piece of gravel might if it landed inside my shoe during a hike.

Dillon's lucky he gets to work with her this semester.

When the boat docks, I see the jitney parked in a bus lane. We line up to disembark from the ferry, and I pop out an earbud as I move next to CJ. "What's the next leg of your journey?" I ask.

She nods at the long-term parking lot. "Just a drive. It's only about two hours, so it's not that bad."

"You live on Long Island?" I ask.

She shakes her head. "Queens."

"Cool. I'm on the jitney back to the city," I reply. "You should come in for one of my events sometime."

CJ smiles. "Maybe."

"Are you on social media?"

"Nope. That's a time suck," she says as the crowd inches forward.

"True," I agree. "Well, I can have my publicist add you to my mailing list if you want. I have your email from workshop."

She shrugs. "Sure."

"So then maybe I'll see you before the next residency."

CJ grins, and her nose wriggles, showcasing a sprinkle of freckles. "Perhaps. But if not, I wish you a happy Halloween, happy Thanksgiving, happy Hanukkah, merry Christmas, and happy Kwanzaa. And anything else you might celebrate."

"Thanks. And yes, all of those things to you as well."

She reaches out to shake my hand, like she did when we first met. "Don't worry. I won't hurt you," she offers.

I slide my hand around hers, noticing its dry warmth. "It was great meeting you this week," I say, meaning it.

"You too," she replies. "Have a great semester."

Then she whacks me in the stomach with her backpack as she turns to leave the boat, and all I can do is laugh.

CHAPTER 5

Cecily

As the summer drips away and the brisk air of fall settles in, I experience my own kind of quiet rebirth. Energized by the time away at Block Island, I come back to my basement apartment in Little Neck with renewed purpose. I will write a novel this semester, I decide. I will be the hardest-working student that Dillon Norway has ever had the pleasure of mentoring, and I will take every suggestion and critique and shape it into something acquirable by a Big Five publisher. I will learn everything I can about the industry, and I will find an agent by the time I graduate. I will read all the craft books, subscribe to all the magazines, comb through all the databases.

This program is a gift, and I will squander none of it.

In residency, there was a lot of talk about the "writer's life." People are always quick to ask authors *how* they write—like, the mechanics. I took a lot of notes so that I could compare what worked for the faculty members who mentioned it. One teacher, a screenwriter from California, said that she writes in the middle of the night from about 2 a.m. until 5 a.m. She called it "the witching hour." Another one said she wrote in a home office with headphones on and music blaring. I do not have a writing practice, so I decide that developing one will be a fun challenge.

I start by taking a trip to Bay Terrace Shopping Center, where I visit

Bath & Body Works and discover a scent simply called Leaves; I buy a three-wick candle to satisfy my olfactory needs. At Staples, I purchase a wrist-protecting mouse pad, since many of my professors complained of carpal tunnel, and I buy a few new spiral notebooks and good clicky pens. I clear off my kitchen table and conclude that it will work better than my little computer desk. I feel like I need open space around me. And who are we kidding? I always eat dinner on the couch anyway, so the table doesn't get much use, outside of being a landing zone for bills and assorted papers that I'm too lazy to file.

In late August, after devouring several craft books, I begin to write. I carve out three-hour time increments for this. I try doing it after work, but I find that I'm exhausted by about an hour in and am in no way producing anything readable, much less sellable. So I try the whole 5 a.m. thing. This is not without its issues. First of all, I typically wake up at 6 a.m. and exercise for an hour before getting ready for work. Second, I'm not vain, but I have a lot of hair, and I usually take time to blow-dry and style it in the morning. Third, I enjoy breakfast—so I tend to sit down (yes, on the couch) and have a cup of coffee and some prepared meal: oatmeal, bacon and eggs, a toasted bagel with cream cheese, an acai bowl. But when I get up at 5 a.m. to write and commit three hours to it, that leaves me with a single remaining hour to shower, do something to my wet hair (forget makeup, no time for that), pour the coffee in a Yeti, and grab a muffin and eat it in the car on the twenty-minute drive to the library. There's no time to work out, and I arrive at my place of business looking frazzled and praying there are no blueberry stains on my shirt. But this is a small trade-off for all the progress I'm experiencing.

Yes, this is my life now. I've switched the workouts to after work (which is its own kind of challenge), and I'm asleep by 8:30 every night.

It's a good thing I'm not trying to date anymore, because my whole vibe screams *future crazy cat lady*.

You know what though? I'm happy, and the pages are coming. By the end of September, I've got fifty pages of a new novel written. I tell Dillon Norway that I wrote fifty pages, but since we are only supposed to send in twenty-five pages per month, I ask him if he would rather I submit the first twenty-five pages or the later ones as well. He surprises me by asking for the whole thing, which makes me equal parts nervous, excited, and grateful.

The story is about a young woman whose sister marries her ex-boyfriend.

Yes, I realize it's kind of an obvious move, but hey, *Write what you know*, right? And Dillon Norway himself said he thought it would make a great story!

Plus, the words come so naturally, since I already know the characters pretty intimately. Yes, yes, I know what you're thinking. Of *course* I changed the names of all the real-life characters, and it's not *exactly* the story of what happened. It's fiction. Lots of space for creative license.

So he reads the fifty pages, and we get on our very first Zoom call the first week of October. He tells me the opening is pitch-perfect: I drop the reader right into the wedding and work backward from there; he believes this is the right move. He says the work is laced with humor, which makes the narrative voice a pleasure to experience. These are his actual words. I scribble them down so they are preserved forever in my notes. He asks me what the plan is for this piece—will I be attempting to extend it into a novel? I say yes, and he seems pleased. He offers suggestions, but they are minimal, because he wants to see how the story unfolds. There might be some pacing issues with the flashbacks, but it's too soon to tell.

It's not all roses and sunshine. Dillon Norway is honest. There are moments where my dialogue needs work; there are occasional inconsistencies in my timeline. Still, he treats me like someone whose writing is worth something, which is more than I can say for Tim, Harry Potter, and Maleficent. I email him craft essays, which prompt dialogue unlike any I've ever had before. We discuss elements of storytelling using my current manuscript, comparing it to similar texts in the same genre, using other stories and books to identify what works and what doesn't. Dillon Norway recommends that I read specific, wedding-themed books by Emily Giffin, Helen Hoang, Jojo Moyes, and Jasmine Guillory. He explains that he's asked his wife's book club to help him identify these— which means that he's talking about me to his wife, to people in his circle. I am a real person with writing potential—not just some item on the to-do list of a low-paying adjunct faculty member's job. *This*—this being treated like an artist worthy of respect—this is a high that I cannot get enough of.

My hair is always curly now, left wet in the morning and held up by a giant claw clip. I've lost five pounds because I'm skipping breakfast, as I've found that by doing so, I can squeeze in an extra fifteen minutes of writing time. I'm brainstorming during my lunch break. One time, over lunch, Ramona says I talk about my characters as if they're real people. Another time, she comments that I am starting to look like someone an anthropologist might study. I'm not sure if she means it as a compliment, but she still eats with me, so it can't be that bad.

By the time I submit my second packet at the end of October, I've written a total of 125 pages. Dillon Norway is impressed. He says I've caught the bug, and best not to let go of it. He allows me to submit the new seventy pages, even though the university expectation still remains that he only has to read a third of that per month. A week after submitting, we Zoom again, and this time he says he thinks we've got a novel on our hands. It's not perfect, of course, and he recommends more craft books, including Anne Lamott's *Bird by Bird*, in which she talks about "shitty first drafts" and many other anti-perfectionism ideas that encourage me to give myself grace without enabling me to be lazy. It is the exact book I need to read at this moment in my young writing life, and I eagerly write my craft essay on it via a voice note on my phone while on a power walk one evening.

I learn that November is something called NaNoWriMo, which stands for National Novel Writing Month, and that writers across the globe come together to try and pen fifty thousand words in just one month. There's a huge community for this online, but I am not interested in social media, so I participate from the fringes, keeping an old-school log of my daily word count on a magnetized pad on my fridge that is supposed to be for my grocery list. Fifty thousand words seems achievable, seeing as how I've already written thirty-five thousand in such a short time. In order to accomplish this new goal, I begin writing on the weekends for eight hours a day. It's a lot, but I take the writing with me to the laundromat on Saturdays and make sure I still show up for Sunday dinner at my parents' house. Jamie and Bryce are almost always there during the offseason months of October through January, since they come down to long-term visit in my parents' basement. Just looking at them gives me new ideas and fuel for the week to come.

The story ends on November 20, all by itself. It's shorter than I thought it would be at 278 pages and seventy-six thousand words. But it's done.

I have completed my first manuscript.

I email Dillon Norway to share the good news. I also tell him I've been researching potential agents and that I want to spend the rest of the semester revising and polishing this first draft so that I can begin the querying process in January. It is my New Year's resolution, I explain proudly. I am grateful when he doesn't laugh at me. Instead, he gives me the green light to send along the manuscript in its entirety and suggests that I begin to venture out into the literary scene. He says there are a lot of areas where I'm still super green. For example, I've never read my work aloud to an audience. In fact, I've never even been to a reading, outside of the few mandatory ones I attended at the residency.

Now that I have some breathing room, I take Dillon Norway's suggestion, because any and all words that he says are gospel truth that fill my soul with hope and possibility.

A Google search of "NYC literary scene" pulls up some events that are contenders. I ask Ramona if she'd be willing to come with me into the city. There's a thing on Wednesday night, I say. She points out that it's the day before Thanksgiving, but neither one of us is hosting or cooking, so it's fine. It'll feel sort of like a Friday night.

And I already know the talent.

Nate Ellis, as it turns out, will be reading selections from his *New York Times* bestselling debut, *Work*, along with selections from his current project. This is taking place at the Book Club Bar in downtown Manhattan, 8 p.m. on Wednesday. "An Evening with Nate," it's called.

I check the Book Club Bar's website though, and the event is sold out.

No sweat, I tell myself.

An email ensues. Dear Nate, I hope this note finds you well! I am writing because you mentioned on board the SS Titanic that you'd be happy to see me at an event over the course of the semester. Wondering if that offer still stands? I am interested in attending your thing at the Book Club Bar, but tickets are sold out. I would need two—one for me and one for a friend. Any chance you can help? Please let me know. Warmly, Cecily Jane Allerton

A few minutes later, a response lights up my inbox.

CJ! It's great to hear from you. Unfortunately, I can't distribute extra tickets because there's a very limited capacity at the venue. However, I have a ticket for myself (that they never use/scan) so you're welcome to it if you want. It's only one though. Sorry I can't be of more help. Let me know if you're still interested.—Nate

I am, I reply. Please send it—that would be great! I'll see you Wednesday!

I text Ramona to cancel with her, and she's great about it; she was just trying to be a supportive friend, she says, but is happy to return to her regularly scheduled programming of bingeing *Never Have I Ever* on Netflix in her sweatpants.

And that is what brings me here, standing at the doorway to the Book Club Bar in Alphabet City, a half hour shy of what has become my bedtime.

I'm dressed like a person this evening, in faux leather pants that I bought off Poshmark last year but never had the guts to wear, a drapey gray sweater, low platform boots, and a long black winter coat with a fur-trimmed hood. My glasses don't match my ensemble, but I don't care enough to break into my box of disposable contact lenses, and plus, glasses give you character—at least that's what my mom always told me. *I look city-ish,* I decide. A couple pushes past me into the space: the man's jeans are so tight they look like they've been painted on his legs, and the woman has pink dreadlocks that almost reach her ankles. *My pants sound a little like a fart if I move the wrong way, so yeah. I totally blend,* I tell myself.

I take a breath and follow them in, scanning the ticket on my phone at the door. I'm nervous, but it's a bar, so there is a remedy. I shall have a drink.

The space is cool; in fact, this might be one of the most interesting bookstores I've ever been inside of. The punched-tin ceiling gives off a very Brooklyn-meets-Savannah-Georgia vibe, and the chairs set up for the event point toward a red brick wall. It's warm and cozy, kind of like what I'd imagine F. Scott Fitzgerald's living room to feel like, as if perhaps one should sit down in an overstuffed leather chair and smoke a pipe and sip scotch from a lowball glass. There's wine and craft beer available at the bar, but sadly I drink neither of these, as beer smells like subway urine (in my humble opinion) and wine reminds me of the gaggle of moms on Halloween who gulp from red Solo cups while their children trick-or-treat on my block.

When the bartender asks me what I'll be having, I pick up the wine list and point to the second most expensive thing on the list, hoping that it won't taste like pure swill. "Would you like a glass or a bottle?" the bartender asks me.

"Just a glass, thank you," I reply.

I sip from my stemless glass and find myself a seat. The wine tastes kind of like medicine, but it works quickly, and seeing as how I am in a rush to take the edge off being in this kind of situation alone, I drink it much like I do all other things lately: with purpose.

Before too long, Nate Ellis is on the stage in front of me, and when they call his name, I foolishly applaud, only to immediately learn that this is not what one does at a bookstore reading. The girl to my right glares at me through her extremely cool vintage-sixties-vibe glasses, which make me feel as though my spectacles are best suited for a fifth grader. But alas! Nothing another sip can't cure, am I right?

Nate spots me in the crowd and smiles before getting started. He begins with a selection from his new piece, explaining that the inspiration for the setting came from a new school he's working at that offered him the good fortune of spending eight days this summer on Block Island. *Yes!* I cheer, but inwardly, now that I know that public readings are not unlike visiting a monastery. The tone of the narrative is different from his first book, lighter and maybe a little bit more playful. *It's surprisingly enjoyable,* I think. Although it could just be the wine talking.

Anyway, after that selection, he moves on to a piece of what's being referred to as "bonus material" from *Work*—essentially, we're looking at deleted scenes here. I drain my wine and laugh at my own thought that the glass is neither half-full nor half-empty but quite literally fully empty, and this earns me another snarky scowl from the thrift shop model next to me. By the time Nate's done, I'm feeling a little floaty, and I can't help but think that was seventeen dollars well spent.

People around me stand, and one of the Book Club's owners pulls Nate to the side for a chat, leaving me to return to the bar for a refill. Dillon Norway's words fill my brain: *Immerse yourself in the culture,* he said. *See how it makes you feel.*

So far, it makes me feel like I've been giving wine a bad rap for years and that compared to High Noon, this stuff is pretty legit.

I wish I brought a notebook to write that gem down in.

Upon receipt of glass number two, I take a hearty sip and fearlessly approach the area where Nate Ellis is holding court. He excuses himself from the small crowd around him and waves me over, into his personal bubble. "CJ!" he exclaims. "So happy you made it."

"Thanks for the ticket," I reply.

"Of course," he says. "Sorry again about your plus-one."

"No worries," I say. "Ramona's into mysteries and thrillers anyway. She would have thought this was a big snoozefest." I realize what I've said, and it makes me giggle. "Not that this is a snoozefest, obviously. I mean, this was great. *Is* great. Did you try the wine?" I ask, holding up my glass.

He gives me a sidelong glance. "You good?" he asks.

"Oh, yeah," I say, swinging my hand to wave away his comment but failing to realize that this hand holds the wine in it. My fancy juice almost spills. "Whoa," I say, taking another sip.

"How's your semester going?" he asks.

"Oh my God, *so* good. Dillon Norway is *life*. I finished a whole manuscript already."

"Wait. What? Really?"

"Yes! I started it at the end of the summer."

"How long is it?"

"Seventy-six thousand words."

"Wow," he says. "Good for you. That's a huge accomplishment. Was this the same story we looked at in workshop?"

"Nope," I say. "It's a new one."

"That's awesome, CJ. I'm proud of you."

"Ugh," I groan. "I can't get you to reconsider about this nickname, huh?"

He beams, teeth and all, and it makes him look very young.

"I think you need one too then." I take a sip of my wine and smirk at him while I consider my options. "From this moment forward, I shall call you Pen." I giggle. "Get it? Because of your award?"

"I get it," he says. "And sure. Call me whatever you want. I'm just glad to see a familiar face here." He lowers his voice and leans in toward my ear. "I hate these things."

The scent of clean man fresh out of the shower fills my nose. "Ooh. You smell good," I reply.

"Excuse me?" Now it's his turn to smirk.

Shit! "Sorry. That was an inside-my-head thought."

"I think this drink might be messing up your filter."

"Well, if we're telling secrets, I'll have you know that this is my first time drinking wine."

"Really? How old are you?"

"I turn thirty on New Year's Day," I say.

"Not much of a drinker then, I'm guessing."

I shake my head.

"Well, maybe you'd like to come with me and go grab a cup of coffee. We can sober you up a little bit before you head home."

"I am here to immerse myself in the literary scene," I declare.

"Yes. I can see that," he says. He looks amused.

"This is serious business," I add.

"Oh, I know. But us literary folks are *really* into our coffee."

"Why do you want me to leave? Am I *embarrassing* you?"

"Not at all. I don't want *you* to leave," he corrects me. "I want *us* to leave. And hey, I *am* the literary scene, am I not?"

"Wowwww," I say. "I hope you have extra space in your pockets for all that ego."

"No ego here at all. I'm just saying. You came here to see me, and here I am. Now I'm basically begging you to come have coffee with me so we can talk about all the ins and outs of the publishing industry, and you're going to leave me hanging?"

I consider this offer. It's not every day a *New York Times* bestselling author asks me to have coffee, so I concede. "Fine," I say. "Are you just yanking my chain though? You're not trying to kidnap me?"

"*Kidnap* you? You're a grown woman. And no, this is not some kind of trap, CJ." He leans in toward my ear, and I can feel his breath on me. "I told you, I don't like events. You'd really be doing me a favor if you let me take you to Starbucks. Please?"

I get chills, starting from my ear and running down my neck. I'm not expecting them, and combined with the scent of this man's body, well, let's just say it's reminding my lady parts that it's been a while. "Fine. Let's go."

"Okay," he replies. "Hang tight for just a minute. I pre-signed copies of the book for the store, so I just want to make sure that they don't need anything else from me before we take off."

"Okay, Pen. Do you. I'm going to peruse these fine books over here,"

I say, pointing at the wall, which results in my body shifting in the direction of the wall as if I was on ice skates.

Nate places his hand on my lower back to stop me from spinning all the way around, and a surge of heat radiates from his hand down to my ass. "Easy, killer. Stay right here."

I watch him carefully remove his palm from my spine as if he is concerned that I might fall down (*Pish! I am sturdy as a tree!*) and then he walks away from me.

Well. I did not expect to notice this, but Professor Nate Ellis has a mighty fine posterior.

He speaks to a group of city folk, and I stand very still, like a statue. It is a game I am playing with myself. *How still can a statue stand?* This is a tongue twister, and everything I say is brilliant, I decide.

I pause my game to take another sip from my glass, which I realize is almost empty. Upon this discovery, I become sad. *I should get more of the yum drink,* I tell myself. I move from side to side, almost as if I am gently dancing, creating a beautiful, soft zigzag from the giant bookshelf over to the bar.

The bartender approaches. "Hey," he says. "What can I get you?"

"You, kind sir, have a ring in your lip."

"I do," he says. And now he is smiling. *I make people smile. Literary people are happy, smiley people, and I am—*

"Okay, I'm back." Nate has returned to my side.

"I was just about to order a refill of this," I tell him, holding up my empty goblet of deliciousness.

"But we're going, remember?" he asks. "For coffee?"

"We have coffee here," Mr. Lip Ring shares.

"Did you see his lip?" I whisper to Nate.

"Yeah, thanks, bro," Nate says. "But we're going to head out."

They exchange a fist bump. "See you soon, man," Mr. Lip Ring says.

I offer my fist to Mr. Lip Ring. "Yeah, bro dude," I say. His expression is now entertained. "Don't leave me hangin' here, Broseph." He laughs and gives me a pound, and I have done it. *This outing has been a success. I am now an official member of the literary community.*

Nate offers me his arm, and I link mine through it. "Chivalry," I say. We walk outside together. It is colder than I expect.

"So there's a Starbucks on First Avenue," he says.

"What time is it?" I wonder aloud.

"Like nine thirty."

"I like the city at night," I say.

"Yeah, it's not bad. This is a good time of year too."

"Tomorrow is Thanksgiving."

"So I've heard."

"You got big plans?"

"Not really. My sister's hosting. She lives in Jersey."

"Ewwww. Jersey."

He laughs. "What about you?"

"My parents." I nod. "They still do all our holidays."

"Do you come from a big family?"

"Huge," I say. "The ladies of my tribe are extremely fertile."

"Is that so?" he asks.

It's rhetorical, I know, but I feel the need to continue. We walk across Avenue A. "Yes. That's why I'm the black sheep." Nate glances at me, but I stop dead in my tracks once we reach the corner. "Do you hear that?"

"Huh?"

"Shh," I say. "Listen. There's music."

He says nothing for a moment. "I hear it."

"It's this way." I pull his arm and walk toward East 4th Street.

"Do you always get this excited over music?" he asks.

"It's *old* music!" I exclaim.

"Not really," he says, jogging next to me. We cross the street. "It sounds like Camila Cabello."

I locate the source of the music. I have discovered a wild party that has spilled out onto the sidewalk. And yes, Nate is correct, it *is* Camila Cabello's "Havana" on full blast, with accompaniment from over a dozen people who must have had their own fancy juice because they are *so* happy. But I am also correct because "Havana" is over five years old.

"What *is* this place?" I ask Nate.

He looks up. "It's Sing Sing," he says. "It's a karaoke bar."

"Pen! We have to go in there!"

"No," he says. "I think we're good. I think coffee is what we need."

"*One* song. Please? I promise if we can just sing one song, then we can go." I give him my best puppy dog eyes.

"What is this *we* business? You want *me* to sing a song with you?"

"Yes! I have to! Dillon Norway said I must immerse myself in the literary community. He said that I haven't even read my stuff out loud. *This* will prepare me! Don't you see? This is research!"

"I'm going to be honest. I don't think that you even know what karaoke is, based on what you just said."

"Just come," I insist. I approach the door, and the bouncer there insists we sign some piece of paper attached to a clipboard in order to go in. I have no idea what it is but it's the only thing keeping me from the stage, so I scribble my name and look at Nate. He's trying to read the thing, but I tug at his sleeve and put my face up to his ear. "Come on," I whine.

"Should I call my agent before I sign this?" he asks, confused.

"What are you even *talking* about? My God, Pen, listen to yourself! *Do I need my* agent *to let me sing karaoke?* It's. One. Song." I cock my hip and give him a face of pure exasperation. He shakes his head, but I can see a smile playing on his lips as he hurriedly signs on the dotted line.

"Finally!" I clap. I take him by the hand and pull him inside, through a crowd of singers and dancers, directly into a sauna. Not kidding. It's balls hot in this place. The venue is deceptively large, with multiple rooms inside. In the corner of the first room, which is where "Havana" is coming from, I see a pair of DJs. I make a beeline through the crowd for them, almost losing Nate in the process. A beautiful drag queen decked out in glitter is the soulful voice behind Camila's ode to Cuba.

I wave one of the DJs down to me. I fish through my pocket and place some bills in his hand. "Can I please go next?" I beg.

He eyeballs the money in his palm. I'm not sure how much I gave him, but it must be enough, because he nods and hands me a Post-it note and a pen. "Write your name and your song here," he hollers in my ear.

I scribble on the yellow sticky and hand it to the DJ before looking back at Nate, raising my eyebrows. "So fun!" I yell. He's looking at me like I've lost my mind. *Maybe I have,* I think. *Maybe this is what happens when you discover your true passion.*

The singer finishes up, and the DJ waves to let me know it's my turn. He reads my chicken scratch through his microphone, and I am empowered. "Next up, we've got CJ and Pen with their rendition of this Ne-Yo classic. Where all my independent ladies at?"

The crowd roars, estrogen pulsing through the throngs of bodies undulating on the dance floor. Gripping Nate's hand, I use superhuman strength to pull him up onto the stage, where I see a screen toward the floor with a fuchsia background and white words scrolling. The stage is completely empty except for a random drum set, and *Holy cow, that's a lot of lights.* I squint while grabbing the microphone out of its little cradle holder, and I stretch my arm out to position it between me and Nate. The music begins, and I'm off to the races. *Look at all these people!* I think as I begin to wave my free hand back and forth while two-stepping for the first set of eight counts. Nate stands to the side of me, his hands deep in the pockets of his jeans. His formerly bemused expression has developed into one of complete bewilderment—as in, *What the fuck is happening right now and how did it come to this?* Yet before I can orchestrate a presentation about the effects of high-quality alcohol on an extreme lightweight who indulges maybe once a year, my mouth takes off on a journey all its own. "Ooh it's somethin' about, just somethin' about the way she moves," I sing. "I can't figure it out. It's somethin' about her." *You got this, Cecily. Work those pipes.*

Nate studies my face as if he's surprised that I can sing. He's smiling at me but is silent, so I keep the mic in my hand and begin to work the stage around him as if he is my prop.

"Said, ooh, it's somethin' about the kind of woman that want you but don't need you," I croon, doing my best to walk sexy in a circle around Nate, the heat of the lights making me squint and throwing me a bit off-kilter. "I can't figure it out; it's somethin' about her," I go on. The crowd is happy with my music selection—everyone loves "Miss Independent"—and I give exactly zero fucks about what I look like or whether I am city-ish enough because really, I am a writer now, and writers don't do stage fright. The song is my story now. The lyrics are my prose. I give Nate Ellis my best *come hither* look and I. Sing. It. My hips pop out: first the left, then the right, and I boldly run my forefinger down Nate's body from his chest to his navel as I continue. "'Cause she walk like a boss, talk like a boss, manicured nails to set the pedicure off. She's fly effortlessly…" I close my eyes, feeling the moment, singing the rest of the lyric by heart. I don't need a prompter; this was one of my favorite songs growing up. It's like Ne-Yo's silky smooth voice is one with my soul, and I dig deep to channel his cute-hat-wearing hotness and spin it into my own personal brand of swagger.

At the split second of anticipation before the chorus sets in, with my eyes still closed, I prepare my body to use my diaphragm to belt out the words that come next. The crowd must be with me because all of a sudden, there is cheering—like *real* loud cheering and what sounds like the rushed movement of bodies on the dance floor before me. I inhale all of their energy deep into my soul and expunge it into the microphone: "She's got her own thing, that's why I love her. Miss Independent, won't you come and spend a little time?" The crowd is going absolutely wild. I mean, I know I can carry a tune, but it's not exactly *American Idol* up here, and it's in this moment that I realize there are some new sounds harmonizing with me.

The *drums,* for one thing.

And *What the hell? What is that other sound? It sounds like a buzzing nasal sound, reminiscent of one of my musical toys from the library. It's almost like a—*

I open my eyes and turn to look at Nate, but he's still standing to the side, only now his hand is actually covering his mouth in what looks like very real shock.

So I look behind us to the drum set.

I must be drunk, because I'm definitely hallucinating.

Is that Questlove? As in, the *Questlove from The Roots crew on* The Tonight Show Starring Jimmy Fallon? *The producer—the DJ—the famous author Questlove?*

Is he backing me up on drums? Is this real? *Is that a fucking kazoo in his mouth?*

My eyes do this thing where they threaten to excuse themselves from my face permanently—like they bug out so far that I am very likely straining my ocular muscles, and my jaw drops to my chest.

"Miss Independent, ooh the way we shine," I sing off key, stupefied by this new development.

In pure confusion, I turn back to look at Nate, whose face (which I can only describe as *terrorized if gleeful*) confirms that *yes,* that is Ahmir fucking Questlove Thompson, and he is smoothly grooving on the drum set behind me.

Kazooing.

I am going to die.

There's a man with a camera in the audience directly in line with Questlove—like, a *real* camera, none of this iPhone bullshit—although it stands to mention that there are also now literally *hundreds* of iPhones being hastily taken out and held up by the crowd in front of us. I have the world's fastest come-to-Jesus moment. *This is happening. Questlove and I are performing this karaoke number together.*

But wait. This isn't okay. I can't leave Nate just standing there looking like he drank a bottle of lamesauce. He *has* to join me! As the second verse begins, I sexy-walk-dance over to him with a look on my face that lets him know yes, this is *very much a situation,* and we are here for *all* of it, whether he likes it or not. I plunge the microphone at him with determination, and he takes it from me, possibly because my forceful handoff looks a bit like I might be readying myself to punch him in the mouth. Nate remains mute, limply holding the microphone as I rip off my jacket and toss it to the back of the stage, and now the crowd cheers because they undoubtedly think that the nerdy girl hanging out with Questlove from the Roots is about to embark on a wintertime striptease.

"C'mon!" I say to Nate with a hysterical grin. I grab the mic back with one hand and pull him up to the front of the stage with the other. We've somehow only missed two lines of the song, but Quest has carried our team like an ace with his kazoo. Nate almost trips over his own feet, but by the time we rejoin Questlove, we are both upright, bouncing to the beat of this glorious feminist anthem. At the next chorus, Nate and I dance into each other (naturally, I choose this exact moment to try twerking for the very first time) while we cry out together, "She's got her own thing, that's why I love her!" and it is next-level magic with Quest on percussion and killing it with that damn kazoo. A Thanksgiving miracle. Take a picture, folks. Cecily Jane Allerton is winning at life.

Adrenaline and alcohol swirl like dreams down the toilet as I hit every note of Ne-Yo's bridge. Alongside these two fantasy men (*What? I'm still human. I can have sexual fantasies about whoever I want, thank you very much!*), I crescendo through the peak of the song and back into the last set of choruses, and I am overcome. *This is my best day ever. I am a writer with a completed manuscript who immersed herself so deeply in the literary world today that she got rewarded like a boss with a karaoke number featuring not one but* two New York Times *bestselling authors.*

I manifest success all around me.

I am the shit!

The final lines of the song are muffled by the screams of the crowd in front of us, and in a moment of delirium, I turn toward Nate. He's laughing—open, hearty laughs that feel like the warm welcome of an old friend. His smile is incredulous. I can't imagine that this is the same guy from my workshop, the same guy who had to defend his own seminar in the throes of Alice Devereaux's attempted humiliation, the same guy who puked in a bucket in the bed across from mine only months ago. I've seen him brooding, busy, thoughtful, and even sick, but this is the first time I've ever seen him really happy.

It's because of me! Look at all that I am capable of!

I throw my arms around Nate's neck and plant a giant kiss right on his mouth. The crowd cheers even louder.

"That's right!" Questlove spits out his kazoo and yells into the mic that extends from his earpiece down his jawline. "Y'all just been hit by a Questlove Kazoo Karaoke Bomb!"

They continue to cheer, and I grab Nate's hand and raise it high into the sky as if we are champions who've just crossed a finish line or won a competition. He is still smiling, but now he's watching me with an expression of confusion? Concern? Consternation? Words befuddle me.

Quest gets up and walks over to us, still talking into the wireless mic affixed to his beautiful bearded face. "Thanksgiving Eve! Biggest party night of the year! Much gratitude to Sing Sing for having us! And to these two lovebirds. Let me get your names!"

I lift the microphone to my face. "Cecily," I say. *Holy shit, now Questlove is talking to me!* "And this is Nate!" I am unhinged, so I just start screeching. "Woo! We love you, Questlove!" with my fist punched into the air like the Statue of Liberty.

Quest talks a little bit more, sounding like a PSA for karaoke everywhere, until finally his cameraman shuts off the camera and the DJ pumps up some new music and switches the lights so that there's no spotlight on the stage anymore. We're escorted offstage by a gigantic man dressed all in black who is holding my coat and whom I hadn't noticed previously. He looks at me sternly as he hands me my outerwear. Then Quest shakes our hands and says, "Thanks for being good sports about it!" The cameraman hands each of us an extra-large shirt that says, *I was Kazoo Karaoke Bombed by Questlove and all I got was this lousy T-shirt.* Quest grins at us and says, "Happy Thanksgiving," with a nod, and then the two of them turn around. The larger-than-life bodyguard parts the crowd like Moses and the Red Sea, allowing Questlove and his cameraman to leave Sing Sing safely.

Nate turns to me, still cheesing, his new shirt slung over his shoulder. He leans in to my ear. "One song," he reminds me.

I frown dramatically, and he nods his head toward the exit.

"You promised," he says.

"Fine," I agree, rolling my eyes. I'm giddy though. This night has been incredible. Maybe the best night of my life. Easily top three.

Once we get outside, words pour out of me into the darkness. "Can you believe that? Can you believe we just *sang* with Ahmir Questlove Thompson? Like, whatevs, no big deal. I just hang out with famous people all day long. Can you even?"

Nate shakes his head. "Nope. Never in a million years would I have thought that this was where the night would take me. Is this your brand of antics, CJ? I would never have pegged you as a party girl."

"What are you talking about? I'm fun," I insist.

"You've got a backpack the size of Montana," he laughs.

"Wow," I say. "Way to bring a girl down."

"I'm serious! Your binder has more pages in it than the Bible."

"Work hard, play hard," I retort.

His smile. It's like a drug. You would think I never saw a man's teeth before.

"You definitely know how to play hard, that's for damn sure," he says.

We walk then. Up the block and around the corner. Somehow, with the adrenaline draining from my system and the chill of the air mixed with the exercise, I'm sobering up. I can feel it. It's almost as if I am remembering that this cool thing happened to me but it feels far away, as if it was a long time ago instead of only a few minutes earlier.

Suddenly, I become extremely self-conscious. I can smell Nate's cologne faintly. Our strides match: left foot, right foot, left foot. I don't know what to say. Evidently, Nate has lost his capacity for small talk also, because it's just step after step after step in the twilight.

Until we get to Starbucks. He holds the door open for me. "Thank you," I say.

He orders a grande honey citrus mint tea for himself, and I get a vanilla latte. He pays for the drinks, waving away my credit card.

We sit in a pair of comfortable chairs while the baristas do their thing. I try really hard to think of something to say. "So what would you have been doing if you weren't here with me right now?"

Nate shrugs. "I would probably have stayed at the Book Club a little longer. Then I would have headed home."

"Oh. I hope I didn't steal you away from, like, work," I say, just now realizing that this was an event that he was probably paid to do.

"No. It's fine. I told you, I don't like that kind of stuff. It's just an occupational hazard. I'm sure I wouldn't have stayed that long. What about you?" he asks. "Is this just your typical Wednesday night?"

"Ha," I say. "Far from it. Contrary to my performance this evening, I don't go out all that much."

"Really?" he says. "Because you made it seem like you're a wild animal." He raises an eyebrow.

"Far from it. I'm a children's librarian, actually."

"Really? That's what you do?"

"Yeah. Why?"

He eyeballs me. "No, I see it. I'd say that suits you."

"Did you think I was just coasting through life with no day job?"

"No. I figured you did *something*. Just didn't know what. Honestly, you give off a bit of a kindergarten teacher vibe, so this development is quite on-brand for you. I think I know the answer to this, but I'll ask anyway. What made you choose that career path?"

"I mean, all the obvious reasons. I love books; I'm passionate about literacy; I think a good story can heal a broken child in very much the same way as the right medicine can. I grew up in a house full of people, hiding from the noise with my nose in a book. And I like kids. Although I'm not sure that I want any."

"Really?"

"Yeah. It's kind of funny, actually. My family is very traditional. Women go off and get married and have babies, and sure, they can have careers too, but not at the expense of their families. Family first, right? That's the mantra. But I don't see that as being in the cards for me. So I figured if I write a book, then I have a legacy that I leave behind when I die, in much the same way that people have children so they can point to their lives and say, 'There. That's what I did during my time on earth.'"

"So quite literally a book baby."

"I guess so, yeah."

"And what did you say your new manuscript is about?"

"Funny you should ask. It's loosely based on what happened to me in real life—you know, with my sister and my ex."

"He must be the dumbest man in America," Nate says.

The barista calls his name, and Nate holds up a *wait one second* finger before leaving me there to digest that comment while he retrieves our beverages.

"Here you go," he says, setting my coffee down carefully.

"Thanks."

"Can I ask how that thing with your sister happened exactly?" he wonders.

"It was a coincidence. They were both in the right place at the same time, and whatever. I'm over it."

"Of course. You're so over it that you wrote an entire novel about it in three months."

"It's not like that."

"So then, are you dating anyone?"

The question is like a shot in my arm. "Why? Are you propositioning me?"

"No," he replies, his laugh lines on full display. "Just wondering—if you're so over it, I'm sure you're currently seeing someone. Or perhaps multiple someones, given how you're the life of the party."

Unable to come up with a quick one-liner, I take a sip of my latte.

"Okay then. Let me ask you this. Do you go around kissing guys onstage regularly?"

Oof. I did do that.

He's smirking.

"I'm sorry," I say, suddenly swept away with the realization that Nate

Ellis might very well have a girlfriend. "Oh my God," I go on. "I didn't even think of the fact that you might be with someone. Did I just—"

"Relax, CJ. I'm not *with* anyone."

"This is why I don't drink."

"Because you just can't keep your mouth off people? Is that the issue?" He laughs, blowing on his tea.

"No. I just never let loose," I admit. "And to answer your question, no, I am not currently dating multiple someones. Or even one someone. I am single and proud."

"Is that right?"

"Indeed," I nod.

"Well, you're fun. I'm sure you'd make some lucky guy very happy if you ever decided you wanted that in your life."

"You make me sound maudlin. Like some spinster or like I'm half-dead. What about you, Pen? Why are you single?"

He shrugs. "It's been a weird couple of years for me."

"Do you think your success has changed you?"

He swallows, considering the question. "I'm sure it has. I mean, I think underneath it all, I'm still the same guy though. I don't know. It's nice to have money, but nothing comes without a price."

"Like the events."

"Exactly. Readings and signings aside, I will say that tonight was my first and last time doing karaoke."

"At least you got a shirt," I remind him.

"That's true."

"Is everything weird now?" I ask. "Because we made out?"

Nate laughs and shakes his head. "We did not *make out,* CJ. Believe me, if I made out with you, you wouldn't want to be single anymore. But our karaoke exchange didn't mean anything. I mean, of *course* it didn't. We're colleagues, right?"

My pulse is thumping in my neck. *I wonder if he can tell.* "Right."

"Maybe it was your twisted version of research. You know, like the karaoke."

I make a face. "My God. You act like a girl never kissed you before."

"Do I? Truth is I can't keep the ladies off me. I usually carry a baseball bat."

I sip my latte and give him a sideways scowl.

"Can I be honest? Or should I wait until you sober up some more?"

Something grabs my stomach and twists it just a little. "You can be honest." I swallow.

"I'm glad you came out tonight."

I nod. "Me too."

"I don't have a lot of writer friends."

"Really? But you're Nate Ellis."

He emits a deep, gratifying sigh. "That's actually really irrelevant."

"Well, I'm glad I came out tonight too," I say.

"We should do it again sometime."

"The karaoke?"

"No. Just this part."

I nod. "I would really like that."

We continue to chat, and once our beverages are empty, Nate shares an Uber with me to Penn Station and then continues on to his apartment, which, he tells me, is on the Upper West Side. When we say goodbye, he thanks me for a lovely evening and reaches out to give me a hug. It's a tight squeeze in the back seat of the Corolla we're in, but for about ten seconds, our arms are wrapped around each other, and I swear I can hear him inhale my hair.

Not that I notice or anything.

CHAPTER 6

Nate

I'm not really sure what happened between me and Cecily last night. I mean, yes, I was *there.* Obviously. But it's not every day that I hang out with someone unexpectedly like that and enjoy it so much. I'm Nate Ellis, misanthrope, loner. I keep friends and socializing to a minimum.

So you can imagine my surprise when I wake up the next morning and find sixteen missed texts on my cell phone.

Bro! Why am I watching you on Fallon right now?

Honey, we saw you on the Tonight Show! Daddy has it on DVR!

Nate!!! Who's the hot chick eye-banging you on national TV?

Yo, Nate, long time no speak! So, first books, now TV? Let's catch up soon, dude!

And my personal favorite, which makes me want to strangle myself with my phone charger: Hi Nate. 🌚 I saw you doing karaoke on that late night show. Just wanted to tell you that I miss you, and if things don't work out with the girl from karaoke, you know where to find me.

And this is just a *sample.*

I frantically google "The Tonight Show last night" and find Questlove's

Kazoo Karaoke Bomb segment from just hours ago readily available on YouTube. I click on it. It has forty-five thousand views already.

Well.

I suppose objectively, it's not so bad. CJ's on fire—she's really got that whole hot librarian thing down pat—and Questlove looks so damn cool, I'm sure the kazoo will end up trending worldwide. Then there's me. I'm singing. And—*yikes*—attempting to dance.

Breathe, Nate.

And yup, there it is. She lays a fat smooch right on my mouth for the whole world to see.

It's fine. I mean, right? It's *fine.* I'm sure it'll be old news by tomorrow.

In fact, it's so *not* a big deal that I don't even give it a second thought as I shower and get myself dressed for Thanksgiving. I continue to ignore the steady stream of text messages from people I haven't seen or spoken to in forever as I make my way to the NJ Transit train into New Jersey. I switch the phone from vibrate to silent, just because I can't with all the buzzing.

It's only once I'm settled into a seat on the train that I extract the phone from my pocket and see that I've got a mildly disconcerting email.

From Dillon Norway.

On Thanksgiving.

Dear Nate, it reads. I would like to schedule a Zoom meeting with you for this coming Monday at noon. The matter is urgent. The link is below. Please confirm your attendance. Best, Dillon Norway.

I write him back, because I can't *not* respond.

Happy Thanksgiving, Dillon, I write. Can you please tell me what this is in reference to?

I close my eyes and lean my head back into the seat headrest. The ticket agent comes by and scans the ticket on my phone, and I notice that I'm clutching it so hard my knuckles are turning white.

A few stops later, Dillon responds. It has been brought to my attention that you have been intimately involved with a student in the program. Unfortunately, now is not the time or place for me to discuss this further, so I respectfully request that you hold any rebuttal until Monday at noon. Thank you.

Fuuuck.

My knee-jerk reaction is to call CJ, but I realize I don't have her phone number. I do have her email address though, thanks to her being in my workshop. So I forward her the email thread, along with a one-liner: Is your phone blowing up today after our impromptu karaoke session last night?

I hit Send and hope she'll get back to me ASAP.

This is not good, I say over and over in my head as I watch the buildings pass by out the window of the train. It becomes a mantra of sorts. *Not good, not good, not good.*

I rewatch the bit on Fallon a few more times, letting the stress wash over me. Sometimes, when I get really overwhelmed, I just sink into negativity like quicksand. I feel actual weight on my shoulders, as if gravity placed a sumo wrestler on my back and told me to carry it around. It's a new thing for me, dating back only a few years. My doctor has suggested therapy. He says, "Nate, success does not come without an emotional price tag," but so far, I've become very good at avoiding and procrastinating making time for my personal well-being.

What? I'm on deadline.

I'm pulled up momentarily by the arrival of a new email.

Hi!

Happy Thanksgiving.

Yes, my phone's been buzzing off the hook. Shit, I don't like the sound of that email from Dillon Norway at all. I'm sure it'll all blow over if we just explain what happened though, right? I'm around if you want to talk.

My number is (917) 558-0607. Feel free to call or text if that's easier than email.

Sincerely,
Cecily

Panic is a funny thing. It makes my heart beat at the speed of light, makes me sweat, and causes me to be impulsive. I've got her number, so that means I'm calling her. Right. Now.

It rings only once before she picks up. "Hello?" CJ sounds cheerful. I mean, she's always cheerful, but something about even just this single word I find surprisingly soothing.

"Hey. It's Nate."

"Hi. I was wondering what this number was. Good thing you identified yourself right away. I once blocked my doctor when she called me from rounds at the hospital with results from a Pap smear. She spoke so quickly I couldn't understand what she said, and there was noise in the background, so I was like, 'Nope! Must be spam!' and I hung up on her. I mean, not that you need to hear about my Pap smears or anything. Which are fine, by the way. I'm perfectly healthy in my downstairs. Wow. I'm sorry. This call is off to a rocky start, huh? My bad. So…uh…how's it going?" She giggles nervously.

Even with what appears to be thousands of milligrams of caffeine lighting up her voice, I can tell my blood pressure is dropping. *It's fine. Everything will be totally fine,* I reassure myself. "Hi," I reply. "Did you have a hangover today?"

"No, thankfully. I think the latte helped. How about you?"

"I didn't really drink last night," I remind her.

"Oh, right," she says. "Well, have you started drinking yet today? Because that email sounded pretty scary."

She's trying to keep it light, which I appreciate, although I really don't think she understands the gravity of the situation here. "He wasn't exactly writing to wish me a happy Thanksgiving," I say. "And I'm not going to lie, I'm definitely freaking out a little."

"I'm sorry, Nate. I'm sure I can just tell him that it was a mistake. He's my mentor, remember?"

"I remember."

"So I'll just explain what happened. No biggie. Don't even sweat it. Dillon Norway is one of the kindest, most reasonable people I've ever met."

"You sound pretty sure of yourself."

"I'm just saying! I know he'll listen to reason. I'll just explain that it's *his* fault, actually. *He's* the one who told me to get out there into the literary scene and take the world by storm, or whatever his advice was. So I did that! And if it ended up with me drinking a little too much and dragging you up onstage and forcing you to sing with me, then that's on *him*."

"And the kissing? Was that his fault too?"

"I mean, technically? Yeah, I think so. He never told me about wine consumption and book talks. He *assumed* that I would be some kind of connoisseur, which, I mean, I can't *blame* him. I do *look* very posh and chic and all that, but he could have at least *said* something."

"And what would you have had him say exactly? Hey, Cecily, go out and find book events but sip your wine very slowly so you don't end up trying to tongue down your professor?" The guy across from me on the train gives me a look. I shift my body to face the window and lower my voice.

"You're *not* my professor."

"I *was* your professor!"

"For *one* workshop, like, months ago. It's not like you're my mentor or anything."

"Yes, CJ, I know. I wasn't up to your standards for mentorship. Please, kick a man while he's down."

"What? Did you *want* to be my mentor?"

I sigh. So much for my blood pressure. "I wouldn't have been against it," I reply.

"Oh," she says. "Well, I didn't know that."

"I told you I thought your work was good."

"Yeah, but you were sick when you said it. I thought you were just being nice."

"For the record, I'm never nice."

"Okay, Scrooge McDuck. Calm yourself. You're extremely nice. Anyway, mentor stuff aside, it was *one* night. *One* kiss. Onstage with Ahmir 'Questlove' Thompson, so obviously for dramatic effect, right? Dillon Norway is a good and rational human. He will understand. I'll talk to him."

"No, that's okay. I'll just wait until the Zoom thing on Monday."

"Pen, it's fine. I'll shoot him an email and explain what happened. We talk all the time. It's really no sweat."

"I don't know if it's a good idea." My stomach turns a little. I look up; I'm at Rahway. Two stops left.

"Don't try and fight me. He *likes* me. I mean, at least I think he does. He always reads my extra pages."

"Listen, I've got to run. My train is pulling in momentarily, and my dad is picking me up at the station. Bad enough they've got the Fallon bit on DVR. Can we please discuss this tomorrow?"

"Sure thing," she says. "I really am sorry. I can tell you're mad."

"I'm not mad."

"You're worked up."

"A little, but not mad. It's fine."

"I hope this doesn't ruin your Thanksgiving."

"It won't. Don't worry. I'm good."

"Okay. You sure?"

"I'm sure."

"It wasn't even a big deal."

"I know."

"But I'm still sorry."

"Stop. We're fine. We'll talk tomorrow, okay?"

"Okay."

"Happy Thanksgiving, CJ."

"You too, Pen."

It's true what I told her. I'm not mad. I'm upset, but more at the idea that it would be a problem if we had kissed on purpose and people found out, because we're, like, two years apart in age, and we're both consenting adults. The sound of her last sentence reverberates in my brain. *You too, Pen.* I like that stupid nickname, damn it. And I don't like lots of things.

My train pulls into the Woodbridge station, and I walk to the door, steadying myself. The sun is shining, but I can feel the cold trying to push its way through. I get out onto the platform and immediately head toward the front car, knowing exactly where Dad will be waiting. It's like muscle memory; I don't even need to think consciously about the moves I make. My body just knows where to take me.

My parents moved to Woodbridge when I graduated from high school. I grew up in the city, on 88th and Amsterdam, not far from where I live now. Dad worked for Memorial Sloan Kettering in the accounting department, and my mom was a commercial actress—meaning an actress who specialized in commercials. Before I was born, she'd star in advertisements for department stores, mostly Macy's and Nordstrom. Then, after she had me, she really thrived in the laundry circuit. She became "the Tide Lady" for about four years, and that included print ads as well as TV spots, before she moved on to Dreft and, finally, All. She must have really given off that *I can't wait to wash other people's underwear* vibe. When my sister, Katie, and I were teenagers, Mom used to complain that the industry was really shifting to the online market, and the pay wasn't great for the work she was getting, so she wanted to move out of the city and learn how to garden. My dad—a workaholic who swore he'd never retire—agreed that once I graduated from Regis (a pretty big deal Jesuit high school in Manhattan boasting alumni such as SNL writer Colin Jost and COVID master Anthony Fauci), he'd be willing to move to Jersey, land of Wawa gas stations and no left turns.

I was not thrilled.

I decided to go to NYU for my undergrad, and because we were still just a commute away, my father and I took the train into the city together most days. Katie, who's twenty months older than me, was attending school in Philly; my folks' move to Woodbridge gave her a reason to ask for a car, so she was psyched. She ended up moving in with my parents once she graduated. You know, like most kids do, to try and figure out her life now that she had a bachelor's degree in communications, one of the most vague fields out there. She celebrated this degree by working at Applebee's, where she met a guy who promptly knocked her up and then "agreed" to marry her, real romantic-like. They lived in my parents' finished basement with my niece, Lila.

Rent free. For four years.

True to her word, my mother was doing her gardening thing. She excelled at it, really. She joined a gardening club and worked on town beautification projects and at farmers markets on the weekends. My father continued to work in the city—until a few days shy of Lila's fourth birthday, when he had his heart attack. They called it "the big scare," because evidently it could have been much worse. He was fifty-eight but had made more than enough money to retire. So my mom convinced him. Dad liked the warm weather, so they bought a condo in Florida, and they gave their house in Woodbridge to Katie, Johnny, and Lila, with the caveat that if they ever wanted to come back and visit, the basement would be available for them to stay in as a guest space.

And now we have Thanksgiving here every year. Just my parents, my sister, her husband, Lila, and me.

As I'm sure you can imagine, my brother-in-law is not exactly a go-getter. He's an assistant manager at a Dollar General, and Katie runs the after-school program at Tyler Avenue Elementary School. (How'd she get *there* with a communications degree, you wonder? Hell if I know.) Lila's twelve now, and she's becoming a bit of a handful, according to my sister. Don't get me wrong; I love my family, but we just don't have all that much in common. Katie's more concerned with my relationship status than with anything I've done professionally, and Johnny just likes to have another guy around to watch football with (or maybe just someone to drink beer with). When *Work* took off, they didn't come to any of the events or signings—although Katie said that if I did anything in Woodbridge, she'd show up for it (that's right, folks—Woodbridge, New Jersey, a.k.a. the literary capital of the world)—and when the film comes out, they said they'd watch it on Netflix. I never heard another word about it. Family is funny like that, I think. I'm pretty sure Katie and Johnny don't even own a copy of the book.

I'm not bitter about it though. Really. It's actually kind of refreshing to have a handful of people who just see me as Nate, with zero pressure attached.

My parents are a different story. I am definitely a combination of the two of them: creative like my mom, strong work ethic like my dad. We get along well, except now that I'm a name (some) people have heard of, my mom is forever trying to pretend she's my publicist. She was bragging about an interview I did with *Time* magazine while in line at the grocery store, and she made the lady who she was talking to open up her phone and buy my book on Amazon right there on the spot. When she recounted the story to me later that night on FaceTime, she was all giddy and kept saying, "ABC! Always be closing!" while I made a mental note that if any hate mail comes in from a woman in Florida, that's just the fallout from my mother's trip to buy chicken cutlets at Publix.

My father, meanwhile, has found his new passion for life on the golf course. He gets out there at least five days a week, and I think he believes it's his new job. He now likens everything to golf, which is interesting at best and a real stretch at worst.

So when I get to the car (to be clear, this is Johnny's car, a sputtering Camaro from the 1990s with a rust-lined undercarriage that has easily 150,000 miles on it—"I'm *restoring* it," Johnny insists), it's no surprise that the first words out of my dad's mouth are, "Hiya, son. Sorry I had to pick you up in this old thing. Makes my cart look good by comparison."

Because *yes*, of course he owns his own golf cart.

We drive back to the house, and he asks how the new book is coming along. I tell him the truth—it's hard work and I've pushed back the deadline a few times—to which he responds, "Just like the great Lee Trevino once said: 'Putts get real difficult the day they hand out the money.'"

"Yup," I say.

"What about this singing competition on TV? Was it like some new version of *The Voice* or something?"

"God, Dad, no."

"Well, forgive me. Every time your mother looks at it, she cheers so damn loud that I can't hear over her."

I laugh. "That sounds about right. It wasn't a singing competition. It was just a bit where someone from *The Tonight Show* goes out to do stuff among unsuspecting regular people. In this case, karaoke," I add.

"I didn't know you were a big singer," he says.

"I'm not."

"I also didn't know you have a girlfriend. I think that's the part your mother is most excited about."

"Oh. That. Well, she'll have to calm down. That's just CJ. It's complicated."

"Like putting from the rough."

"Yeah, Dad. You took the words right out of my mouth." I shake my head.

Thankfully (or not, depending on how you look at it), we're at the house. Dad opens the front door, and I'm overcome with the scent of home cooking. My mother is in her full glory, with an apron on (I can say with absolute confidence that Katie has *never* worn an apron, as the self-proclaimed queen of Taco Bell), her hair pulled back, and red and gold oven mitts that intentionally resemble the hands in *Iron Man.* She shrieks when she sees me. "Nate the Great!" she yelps, setting down a large Pyrex dish and power walking over to give me a hug.

"Hey, Mom. Smells delish in here."

"Honey, I am *so* sorry. If we had known that you were seeing someone, we would absolutely have invited her to dinner! Why didn't you tell us?"

"Wow, waste no time." I chuckle under my breath. "I'm not, Mom. You're fine."

"But we *saw* you on the television! She is *lovely,* Nathan."

"There's a lot to unpack there, Mom, but the gist is that we are *not* a thing. Very sorry to disappoint you."

"I saw the way she looked at you," my mother insists.

"Hey, little bro," Katie says, wiping her hands on her jeans as she comes out of the bathroom down the hall.

"Thank God," I reply. "What's up, Kay? Good to see you." I give her a hug.

"Mom giving you shit for working those pipes on Fallon?"

"I am *not* giving him shit!" Mom contests.

"Tell us about that chick you were with," Katie continues. "Spicy little number, huh?"

"Sweet Jesus," I reply, rolling my eyes.

"I'd do her!" Johnny calls out from in front of the seventy-inch TV screen in the living room. Not even so much as a *hello* out of him. Heaven forbid he tried a greeting before laying claim to a female who's not my sister.

"Hey, Uncle Nate," Lila says, having emerged from her bedroom. She gives me a weak hug. "Don't listen to them. I thought the whole thing was pretty embarrassing for you. I mean, what even *was* that song?"

This is it, you guys. This delightful scene is my Thanksgiving.

I suffer through it for the next three hours, during which my mother only makes us rewatch the segment on the DVR twice (because once was not enough). I stress eat two overloaded plates of turkey, stuffing, candied yams, homemade applesauce, and green bean casserole, along with a small slice of each of three different pies (apple, pumpkin, and pecan). By the time I'm done gorging myself, I feel so full that there's no space left for anyone's comments inside me. I power nap in my dad's old recliner while Johnny screams at the New York Giants with the gusto of a man who actually believes they can hear him. The screaming makes it so that I can't fully fall asleep, but that's just par for the course (to borrow a term from my dad), when sure enough, on the screen, the camera cuts to none other than—*Seriously? Why?*—Questlove.

"Lots of celebs here today," says the announcer. "There's Questlove and his lovely girlfriend. Oh, did you see his Kazoo Karaoke Bomb last night on *The Tonight Show*? It was classic."

The other sportscaster replies, "Did you know that guy up there was the guy who wrote *Work*?"

"Oh yeah?" announcer number one says.

"True story," announcer number two says. "He should stick to writing, if you know what I mean," he adds with a hearty chortle.

The trio on the couch (Johnny, Dad, and Katie) look at me. "Oh!" Johnny cries. "Sick burn, man!"

And that is my cue to leave.

I pull up the schedule for New Jersey Transit on my phone. Trains are running once an hour, and the next one's in thirty-five minutes. I get up and hit the head, then pop into the kitchen and tell Mom I should get going. She hastily dries her hands off on a dish towel and gives me a big hug. "Next time, you bring her," she whispers in my ear. Then she summons my father to take me to the station. By the time he gets himself together and we arrive, I've got ten minutes to get up on the platform. We shake hands and he wishes me luck with my deadline, telling me to "be the ball," not that I have any idea what he's talking about.

By the time I get back on the train, which is thankfully mostly empty, I sink into a seat and exhale deeply. Something about visiting with my family takes a lot out of me. I pull out my phone and check it. Only a handful of new texts, and it's mostly just more of the same nonsense from earlier, except for one new text from CJ from a little over an hour ago.

Hey, the text reads, just checking on you. I hope your dinner is going okay and that your family didn't upset you even more.

I consider my response, then begin typing. It was fine. On the train home now. Hope your holiday is going well also.

No more than thirty seconds pass when the phone vibrates again.

It's been a crazy evening. I'll be leaving soon. Can I call you when I get out of here?

Sure, I reply.

I proceed to spend the next twenty minutes going through my old emails from back when I was hired by Matthias. I remember receiving a personnel handbook. I never read it, of course. But I think I still have it, so I do a search. After rereading several onboarding emails, I finally find the one from HR. I download the handbook to my phone and comb through the table of contents. Page thirty-three: *Personal Relationships in the Workplace.* I scan through it, as the entire beginning is all about familial relationships and nepotism. Then I get to the section about *Intimate Consensual Relationships.*

It reads as follows:

Intimate consensual relationships between faculty members and students can create an imbalance of power in an academic setting, resulting in an elevated risk for the University's mission of fairness and equality to be undermined. As a result, such relationships are strictly prohibited. (This does not apply to relationships between faculty members. For more information, see page 45.)

There may be instances where a faculty member has a preexisting intimate relationship with a student. While this is a manageable risk throughout the University as a whole, such student may not enroll in the program where the faculty member is employed. (Ex. A student of Theater Arts may not enroll in the Theater Arts program if his/her intimate partner is a Theater Arts faculty member.)

If a faculty member is married to a student, this relationship must be disclosed to the Director of the program in which the faculty member works. The Director may then use his/her discretion to determine if the married student can participate in the program; however, under no circumstances will the student be permitted to be placed in a grade-bearing workshop/class or receive formal mentorship from his/her spouse. These special circumstances are evaluated on a case-by-case basis.

Well, shit.

I get to Penn Station and transfer to the Uptown 1 train, which I take to the 86th Street station. Once I emerge from the city's underbelly, my phone goes off, letting me know I have a voicemail message. I listen to it in the elevator.

"Hi, Nate, it's Cecily. I was just calling, well, because I said I'd call. I guess if you get this and want to call back, you have my number. Okay. Talk to you soon. Maybe. Bye."

Once inside my apartment, I kick off my shoes, go to the bathroom, and then change into sweatpants. I'm reclined on the couch when I call back.

"Hi," she says.

"Hey. Sorry I missed your call. I was on the train and it went underground."

"No worries. How was your dinner?"

"Well, let's see. My mother was upset that I didn't bring *you* to the holiday meal, so there's that."

"Ha!" she exclaims and then begins coughing heavily, as if she just choked on her own spit. When she composes herself, she asks, "Seriously?"

"Yup. And then, not sure if you were watching the Giants game, but the announcers basically said my singing was crap, so that was a fun blow to my ego."

"What?"

"Yeah. Evidently, I did something in a former life to deserve the karma of public humiliation, so Questlove took his lady friend to the Giants game for Thanksgiving, and the announcers commented on my lack of vocal ability. It was great. My brother-in-law thought it was the most hilarious thing he ever heard in his life. This is a man who has been freeloading off my parents and my sister for the past twelve years, so really, an opinion I respect."

"Jeez, Pen. That's rough."

"Just a snapshot of my life at the moment. Ups and downs, right? Just riding this wave until it crashes me headfirst into a brick wall. Which may happen sooner rather than later, it turns out."

"Really? How's that?"

"Oh, I'll tell you in a minute. First, tell me, how was your holiday celebration?"

"Well, you remember how I mentioned in your seminar about my sister marrying my ex-boyfriend?"

"Yeah."

"They're pregnant."

"Ouch."

"With triplets."

"Triplets? Really?"

"Yup. It wasn't enough for them to procreate. They had to do it three times as efficiently."

"Wow."

"They're not the only ones. My older sister Melanie is also pregnant, but only with one. This is also brand-new information. It was really something. So we're all at the table, and Jamie gets up and is all, 'We have some exciting news,' with a smirk on her face. I brace myself, because this is not a surprise. They've been married for a little under a year now, so if they *hadn't* started to procreate, my mother would have staged a fertility intervention."

"What's a fertility intervention?" I wonder.

"Basically, she drops off salmon and avocados at your house every day until you get knocked up. Also, she'll make you wear the necklace."

"Do share."

"She has a gold necklace with a medal on it that has a picture of Aphrodite. It looks sort of like a penny, but with a woman on it instead of Abraham Lincoln. Anyway, Aphrodite is the Greek goddess of fertility. She bought the necklace when my oldest sister, Anna, had a tough time getting pregnant, but to be fair, Anna had only been trying for two months. She wore the necklace throughout the third month and boom—baby central."

"Are you guys Greek?"

"We are not," Cecily laughs.

"Does your mother not believe in mercury poisoning?"

"Apparently, no. And believe me, nothing is more awkward than having a freezer full of salmon you can't figure out what to do with after eating it for a few days in a row. Anna told me she felt like she should be living in Alaska instead of northern Queens."

I snicker. "Okay, so go on with the story."

"Right. So Jamie says she's got big news, and I brace myself, because, I mean, it still stings a little bit, seeing them together, you know? Anyway, she spills the beans, and everyone's really happy and congratulatory, except for Melanie, who bursts into tears and runs to the bathroom. So Jeff—he's Melanie's husband—follows her, and Jamie's all confused, and my mother's about to pass out from the joy of three impending grandchildren. Finally, Jeff and Melanie come back to the table, and Mel says *she's* pregnant too, but there's only one fetus taking up residence in her womb, so now she feels like a failure."

"That's insane."

"Oh, believe me, I know! To recap: Anna and Cody have four kids. Melanie and Jeff are pregnant with their third. Jamie's got triplets in the oven. And my mother, who I'm sure is thinking she'll need a bigger house just for the holiday gatherings alone, gives me a sidelong glance like she's counting my eggs and says that it would have been nice if I told her I had a boyfriend. So I'm like, 'Boyfriend? What's this about?' and she said that I shouldn't go around kissing people on TV if they're not my *boyfriend.*"

"I think your mother and my mother would get along really well," I laugh.

"Sounds that way," she says.

"But other than that, nobody gave you a hard time about the karaoke?" I ask.

"No, but only because they *expect* these types of antics from me. I'll always disappoint them, if for no other reason than I'm not racing down the aisle and popping out grandbabies. I'm pretty sure my mother looks at me and wonders, *Where'd I go wrong with that one?*"

"Well, happy Thanksgiving."

"Seriously. Okay, so now you've heard my saga. Tell me about this brick wall you're about to crash into."

"Fine." I sigh. "Here goes. First of all, we really shouldn't even be talking on the phone."

"What? Why?"

"You know the email from Dillon?"

"Yeah."

"It sounded very much like he was insinuating that I was about to get charged with sexual harassment or something. So I looked in the personnel handbook for Matthias University, just to see if my job is in danger. Unfortunately, it turns out that yes, I am absolutely going to be fired."

"Stop it. No, you're not."

"Hang on. I'm texting you a screenshot." I press a series of buttons and wait for her to respond.

"Got it. Sorry, my phone's taking a sec. I'm opening it. Let me just put you on speaker. What exactly am I looking at here?"

"That's the policy on intimate consensual relationships."

"But we're not *in* an intimate consensual relationship," she argues.

"You're right. Only, according to Dillon, we are. He said in his email, 'It has been brought to my attention that you have been intimately involved with a student in the program.'"

"So I think the real question is *who* brought this to his attention?"

"CJ, it's all over the internet. I'm sure Dillon Norway doesn't live under a rock."

"Fine. I guess that's fair. But it was just a stupid kiss!"

"I know. And I know it wasn't some intentional ploy to destroy my teaching career. But I'm sure Dillon's job is to look out for the university, and if he sees me as a risk in any way, he's definitely going to get rid of me. This has the potential to be a big scandal. Teacher-student interrelations have a terrible connotation attached to them—even if the student is basically the same age as the teacher and they're both in their thirties."

"I'm still twenty-nine," she corrects me. "At least for a few more weeks."

"Still. This is the age of Me Too, and believe me, I'm the *last* person who would intentionally get caught up in anything that could be misperceived. People *know* me. I'm sure there are people out there who would love to see me suffer. You get that, right?"

She sighs, and I find myself feeling bad for *her*, even though I'm the one who's going to get canned come Monday at noon. "Like that awful bitch, Professor Devereaux," she says.

"Exactly."

"So let me get this straight. Not only are we concerned about your job, but we're also concerned about what this could do to your writing career because even just the word *scandal* is basically a quick way to get you canceled."

"Pretty much, yeah."

Here, she stills for a beat. Finally, she whispers, "Damn."

We're both quiet on the line now. Images of Block Island run through my mind. *I enjoyed it there,* I think. *It really jump-started my writing again. I'll be sad to lose it.*

"You still there?" she asks.

"I'm here. Sorry. I was just thinking."

"Thinking what?"

I inhale deeply. "When I took the job at Matthias, it was just so I could hide out, you know? Run from my deadline and all that. But it really helped me, being on the island. I started writing again. It just sucks. I'll have to resign. And I should probably give my agent a call. Figure out how to minimize the fallout from all this."

"Wait."

"My editor is going to be *so* pissed. You know, it's funny. I'm actually kind of surprised I haven't heard from either of them about this yet."

"Nate."

"*Especially* my publicist, Marissa. She's so tapped into social media and anything that could ultimately be turned into a GIF, it's insane."

"Nate!"

I stop. "What?"

"I think I have a solution."

"CJ, I wish there was a solution, but it's pretty obvious that at this point, I need to pivot to damage control."

"No! You're wrong. Hear me out."

"Okay," I say, sensing a combination of urgency, guilt, and sadness in her voice. "Go ahead."

"I think we should get married."

"What? Are you nuts?" *Did she really just say that?*

"I'm serious. Read the thing! It says, 'If a faculty member is married to a student, this relationship must be disclosed to the Director of the program in which the faculty member works. The Director may use his/her discretion to determine if the married student can participate in the program; however, under no circumstances will the student be permitted to be placed in a grade-bearing workshop/class or receive formal mentorship from his/her spouse. These special circumstances are evaluated on a case-by-case basis.' So all we have to do is get married and then beg Dillon Norway to let you stay!"

"Do you hear yourself right now? *All* we have to do is get married?" *She's crazy. I mean, it's sweet, but also definitely not a choice.*

"I mean, I don't know your stance on marriage, but I can tell you that I personally don't really care all that much. My goals include getting an agent and publishing a book. I want to be an author. I'm sure I'll have relationships, and one day I might wind up married, but that's not my number-one priority right now. So it really wouldn't be any skin off my back."

"CJ, I have never met a woman who didn't at least secretly fantasize about a big wedding with a fancy white dress like what you read about in fairy tales."

"Well, now you have," she retorts. "What about you? Are you one of those horse-and-carriage white-knight Cinderella grooms?"

"Um, no. But I'd be lying if I said I've never thought about getting married."

"And?"

"And nothing. I really don't care much about the wedding itself; I care about the woman and the whole idea of, you know, *forever*. But yeah, I'd say it's on my in-my-lifetime to-do list."

"Just not right now."

"Exactly."

"So then it wouldn't massively alter the trajectory of your future either if you think about it. Figure we can at least try. Worse comes to worst, we can get it annulled."

I take a breath. *She's serious. She would actually do this.*

"Okay, let's say we were crazy enough to go down this road. What would be the brilliant story we'd tell? Because once we disclose it to Dillon, we'll have to disclose to the entire school."

"First of all, I don't think the whole school is going to really care about the particulars of the story. But fine. We are creative writers, correct?"

"Mm-hmm."

"So let's create ourselves a story."

"Like *once upon a time*?"

"Exactly. I'll start." She clears her throat. "Once upon a time, there was a girl who wanted to write books. She was a children's librarian and wanted nothing more than to become a real-life author. Your turn."

I can't help but smile. "This is ridiculous."

"I know. But play with me anyway. Go ahead."

"Fine. Let's see." I think for a few seconds. "The girl was fascinated by the literary world, so she…" My voice trails off.

"So she read everything. If it was critically acclaimed, she read it. If it won a Pushcart Prize or a PEN Award, she read it."

"One day, she met this guy in a bar. He said he wrote a book that was going to be published, but—"

"But she thought he was full of it, like, that he had zero game and was just trying to flirt with her—badly."

"Wow. Why does he have to have no game?" I ask.

"Just trust me. It's more believable this way."

"We're only a minute into this exercise, and already it's becoming hurtful," I laugh.

"Focus up. Okay. So even though she doesn't believe that he's got this book coming out or whatever, she still lets him take her on a few dates. They hit it off surprisingly well. But then…"

"Oh! That's easy. Then the book *does* come out, and the girl's eating her words realizing that this guy's the real deal, and then the whole world gets shut down because of COVID."

"Yesss! She comes from this big family in Queens, and they won't let her out of their quarantine pod."

"And he's stuck in Manhattan, where no one wants to be."

"Did you actually live in Manhattan during quarantine?"

"I did," I say. "But that was before I had any money. I was sharing a rental with two other guys in East Harlem. It wasn't terrible, because when COVID hit, one of them went home to live with his parents in

Connecticut, and the other one moved in with his girlfriend in Dumbo. So I was there by myself for the most part. But once the book blew up, I moved to my current apartment on the West Side, which I got for way cheaper than it's worth because everyone wanted to escape the city."

"Weren't you lonely?"

"Yeah, I was. But I worked from home. And I read a lot. Oh! And I taught myself how to cook."

"Really?"

"Uh-huh. I was very taken by the whole bread-baking thing."

"That's funny. I can't picture that."

"Well, maybe someday I'll let you try my rosemary-garlic bread. It's killer." We pause, and I'm dumbfounded by how easy it is to talk to her. *I wonder if she's thinking the same thing.*

"Okay," she continues. "Where were we?"

"COVID quarantines."

"Right. So yeah. They can't see each other because of quarantine."

"He *wants* to see her though."

"Of course he does. She wants to see him too, but her family is overbearing and won't allow someone who lives in Manhattan to come in their house."

"Before too long, he gets really busy because of the book, so they lose touch."

"Yes," she agrees. "And then he gets all famous, so the girl assumes that he'll never want to speak to her again. That ship has sailed, she decides."

"But she's wrong. He's just so busy. And then, too much time passes, and he feels weird reaching back out to her."

"But then she starts her master's program."

"Exactly."

"And they can't help but rekindle what they once had."

"Not right away though," I add. "Because that would get me in trouble."

"Right. So no, not right away. The girl is surprised to see that he's a professor at her school and even more surprised to see that he's *her* professor for workshop."

"Yes, yes. They haven't seen each other in years, and it's weird, them being in the same workshop."

"It's also like fate."

"Ooh. I like that."

"And fate again when they end up stuck in the hallway together at the infirmary," CJ adds.

"Yup," I agree.

There's another break in the action. I can't help but notice my pulse racing. *It must be adrenaline. This is a lot to take in. Also, what if we get caught?* I consider this. The thing is, it doesn't *feel* like we could really get caught. It sounds like an extremely believable story. "So the girl pursues the guy, because she doesn't *know* about the rules as they are clearly stated in the university's personnel handbook—but since *he* knows, he decides to propose to her."

"Why would he propose though? That seems extreme," she says.

"Maybe he doesn't want to risk losing her again."

"Hm. That could be."

"And he knows he's not allowed to just date her."

"And he doesn't want to waste two *more* years waiting."

"That's right," I say. "He loves this job, but he also loves this girl, so he wants to have his cake and eat it too, and this is the only way to do it."

"Assuming his director approves."

"Correct."

"Why wouldn't he just ask first then?"

I toss her question around in my mind. "Because if the pandemic has taught him anything, it's that life is meant to be lived. And she's important to him. Definitely *as* important as the job, but if he's willing to marry her, you'd think *more.*"

"So when do they actually tie the knot?"

"I'm not sure."

"I think maybe they do it over Thanksgiving weekend," she says.

"Seriously?"

"Yeah. Think about it. Maybe he asks on Thanksgiving Eve, which is why they're out celebrating, and then on Thanksgiving Day, they tell their families, and on Black Friday, they get the marriage license, and the wedding is Saturday."

"CJ. Are you listening to yourself?"

"What?"

"That's this weekend."

"I know," she says, only her voice sounds quieter now, as if maybe she *didn't* actually realize what she was suggesting.

"So to be clear, you're saying we should get married this weekend." My chest is pounding saying these words aloud. *I sound like such an idiot right now.*

She says nothing for a beat. Then she clears her throat and speaks. "Uh-huh. There's just one thing."

"What's that?"

"You didn't ask."

"Huh?"

"Well, I think if we both agree to all this, then step one is you have to ask me."

"You mean you want me to propose to you? Right now?" I cough in disbelief. "Over the phone?"

"Only if you think it's a good idea," she posits.

"And if I do, you're saying we should go get a marriage license tomorrow?"

"Mm-hmm."

"Are they even open on Black Friday?"

"Everything's open on Black Friday! Biggest shopping day of the year," she exclaims.

"Who shops for a marriage license?" I ask. My voice sounds hysterical.

"It's a joke, Pen. Relax," she says. "Hang on one sec while I find out." I wait as she types. "Snap," she says. "It's better than you'd think. They do it online now. It's called NYC Project Cupid—and how's this for irony? They're offering it online *because* of the pandemic. It says that the project was created during COVID-19 so that people who still wished to get married could do so without endangering their own health or the health of others."

"So doing it online—what does that entail?"

"You just fill out an application and they meet with you over the internet. Probably Zoom," she says.

"That sounds remarkably simple."

"See? It's fate," she says. "Just like in the story."

"Huh," I say, rendered basically speechless.

"I mean, unless you have other plans this weekend."

"I don't," I admit. "Although getting *married* is not something you do because you don't have other plans."

"Typically," she concedes. "But this is not a typical situation."

"True," I say.

"So…" The sound of CJ's voice lingers in my ear. The muscles in my stomach clench tightly.

"So," I reply. *It's a means to an end, Nate. She's trying to help you, to give you an out. It's really generous of her. And she's owning the fact that the little stunt she pulled could destroy your reputation. She wants to fix it.*

Let her fix it.

It's all just fake anyway.

Plus, it's not like you have any other options.

It's just one little white lie.

Just take a deep breath and do it, Nate. You're fine. You got this.

I inhale. "Are you sure about this?" I ask.

"I think so. I mean, I don't really see any other way to make this whole thing go away. Also, I feel terrible. I never meant to do anything that could potentially hurt you. You and Dillon Norway are the only two people in the program who I actually *like*."

"Okay." I wipe my sweaty hands on my pants and take a deep breath. I blow it out, hard, and the question follows. "CJ Allerton, will you marry me?"

I feel like a complete tool. Those words sound ridiculous coming out of my mouth to this girl who, in reality, I barely even know.

But then she says, "I'd love to, Pen."

And somehow, I instantly feel better.

CHAPTER 7

Cecily

Welp. There you have it. I guess there's more than one way to skin a cat.

Looks like I won't be a total spinster after all.

In fact, one day I'm sure this will all be fuel for a brilliant story. By that time, Nate Ellis will be a distant memory—some (admittedly very attractive) guy who I married once to repent for the sin of letting loose and having a good time one random Wednesday night a million years ago. I mean, if there's a lesson in all this, that would be it, right? Have zero fun in life. Fun only gets you in trouble. I'll be able to check off the *divorced* box on future medical forms instead of the *perpetually single* box.

Talk about a long-term win.

Real talk though? I feel awful. It was a stupid, alcohol-induced transgression, and now poor Nate has to worry about losing his teaching job and sullying his reputation as a result of it. That's not okay, and there's no way I can let it happen on my account. Also, if the roles were reversed, I would be shitting a brick right about now.

So it's simple logic. I screwed it up. I'll go ahead and fix it.

I ask Nate for his personal information so that I can fill out the application, and then I schedule the appointment for us to get the license on Friday at 10:00 a.m. It's better this way—nice and early, so neither one of us has time to back out of it. It's online, so basically just wake up and click a link, answer some questions, and they email you a temporary license while the real one is sent in the mail. Then you have sixty days to actually get hitched, or else the license will expire. (Who knew?) So I think just knowing that even once you have the license, it's not a done deal is maybe a little bit comforting to Nate, who is clearly sweating on the screen when I see him there the following morning.

The lady on the other end of the screen asks us questions confirming our relationship, asks us to take vows that are largely similar to the vows one would take at a wedding, and, at one point, asks why we're not on in the same location for this appointment. "I'm very old school," I reply. "No sex before marriage," I whisper. "He's at his apartment and I'm in mine."

Later, on the phone, Nate tells me, "You know, you could have just said you were at work or something."

"I suppose. But I'm really trying to own my role here. When we're done, I expect an Emmy award. Or at *least* a Golden Globe."

On Monday morning, with our printed license in hand, Nate and I head over to the Queens City Clerk's office in Kew Gardens. Project Cupid doesn't allow virtual marriage ceremonies anymore, but the website *does* still allow you to make an appointment for a live ceremony. The only problem is because they're a government agency, they're only open Monday through Friday. So I make our appointment for Monday at 9:00 a.m., figuring after that, I can drive Nate back to my house in Little Neck, and he can take the Zoom from there, with me. It'll really give credibility to the marriage if Dillon Norway sees that he is in my house—a space we Zoom from every month.

He meets me at the Little Neck train station of the Long Island Rail Road. I live right on the train; it's one of the things I like most about my apartment. Some people would hate all the noise of a rumbling commuter train rolling past your house dozens of times a day, but I just find it to be so convenient that the noise actually comforts me. It's like an old grandfather clock that chimes every time it's a new hour, only instead of a soothing bell sound, the whole house shakes with the violence of an earthquake every thirty minutes.

It's early, and the station is bustling with exhausted post-Thanksgiving-weekend worker bees headed into the city. I've taken a rare personal day off work in order to accommodate this trip to the courthouse, and I'm secretly a little bit grateful that instead of going to work, I am going on an adventure today.

I'm getting *married*.

When he gets off the North Shore Long Island–bound train, I see him right away. He's dressed in khaki pants and brown shoes with what appears to be a shirt and tie on under his olive-green jacket. There's definitely some kind of product in his hair, and he's got that fresh-out-of-the-shower morning look about him. He seems so nervous though. This is a different kind of nervous than he wore at the Book Club Bar before his reading. It's also not the same as the anxiety he experienced when he was stressing out about his seminar when we were infirmed together.

Nate Ellis has several types of apprehension, and I am becoming an expert at recognizing and classifying them.

We walk toward each other on the train platform, and I give him a hug, because he needs it—and because I want him to know this is all going to be just fine. When his arms wrap around me, there's trepidation at first, but then I tightly squeeze his rib cage, and he starts to laugh. "Shit. And I thought your handshake was bad. You're going to squeeze the life out of me."

"Death by hug," I joke. "I'm sure there are worse ways to go."

Once we're in my car, the first stop is 7-Eleven for coffee. It's cold outside; with Thanksgiving a thing of the past, it's officially the Christmas season, and I can feel it on my steering wheel. "Sorry I don't have heated seats or anything," I say when I hear his teeth chatter. "It'll warm up soon though."

"I'm fine," he assures me.

We make small talk for most of the drive. I tell him that the only time I've ever been to the city clerk's office was to fight a ticket in traffic court, but while I was inside the office (after being informed I had come to the wrong location), I came back out to find I had a fresh new fluorescent-orange parking ticket on my windshield.

I am hopeful that today's events will go more smoothly than that.

I find a legal parking spot by the city clerk's office and turn off the car, sliding the key out of the ignition and into my lap.

"You're wearing a dress," Nate says to me, as if he's just realized this.

"Yeah. It's no big deal," I reply. It kind of is though. I'm not much of a dress person, so the only dresses I own are sundresses—and this is now winter. So on Black Friday, after the Zoom session, I went to the mall and bought a dress off the clearance rack at David's Bridal. They suckered me into buying shoes to match, even though I hate heels, and this will be the only time I ever need white ones. Anyway, I waited until just this morning to try the whole getup on. I put on pantyhose, and the knee-length A-line dress fits me, thank goodness. It has long lace sleeves and a lace overlay, and it looks halfway decent. I blew out my hair and used my curling iron to make ringlets that fall down my back. I also put on makeup for a change, and I'm wearing a long black peacoat that I typically save for funerals. After getting dressed, I checked myself in the mirror and said, "Eh. Good enough." You know. Typical bride stuff.

Because the dress was on clearance, I couldn't wear it with the tags on for the hour or two today that I needed it and then return it tomorrow, unfortunately. But I figure I can probably turn it into a Bride of Frankenstein costume next Halloween, so at least that's a win.

So now, in the car, Nate asks, "Is it a wedding dress?" and I'm not sure I can fully detect the tone in his voice.

"I mean, it's all white, and I got it at David's Bridal, so yeah, I think it is."

"Wait—you bought it special for this?" he asks.

I nod. "Indeed I did," I reply. "I'm all in, like I said. Ready to earn myself an award for best actress."

"Shit, Cecily. That must have cost you a decent amount of money."

"It wasn't that bad. It was only a few hundred bucks."

"I feel bad. You shouldn't have done that."

"Well, Pen, I'd say our entire relationship is just a laundry list of things I shouldn't have done, so what's one more?" At this, he smiles, but it's wistful, and I know he's grappling with something. "What's wrong?" I ask.

"It's just—I don't know. Are you sure you want to go through with this?"

"A hundred percent," I say. "You make the mess, you clean the mess. At least that's what I've always believed."

"And none of this is bothering you—like, at all? You're perfectly fine with us just marrying each other, no strings attached?"

I take his hand in mine. His fingers are long, warm, and thick. I've never realized what lovely hands he has until this moment. I can feel his touch run up my arm, down my chest, and straight into my lap, but I make a conscious effort to ignore it. "I promise you. This is totally fine with me. I'm not your typical sentimental girl. I would be way more upset if you lost your job than I am over having to fake-marry you, believe me. I *need* you at the residency. Who else is going to cover for me when I erase the whiteboard with my backpack?" At this, he smiles. I give his hand a gentle squeeze and continue. "Now come on. Let's go."

Nate nods. We step out of the car and walk down the block toward our fate, our hands entwined for dramatic effect. Just before we step inside the building, he says, "You look beautiful, by the way."

I shove my glasses up on the bridge of my nose with my pointer finger. It's been awhile since someone's complimented me like that, and I'm surprised at how welcome the words are. "Thank you," I say, but my voice sounds distant and unrecognizable.

"No, thank *you*—for doing all this," he replies.

I squeeze his fingers, and he gently squeezes mine in return.

We look at the signage on the wall and walk down the hallway to room G-100. Just outside the room, Nate whispers, "Okay. Here goes nothing."

Less than thirty minutes later, we are man and wife.

When we're asked for rings to exchange, Nate procures his grandfather's wedding band and a promise ring Bryce gave me in college from his pocket, like we discussed. When we're asked if we have anything we'd like to read or share before we exchange our vows, I unfold a piece of paper with a reading by Mark Twain on it, titled "A Marriage." It's an excerpt from a letter he wrote to his wife shortly before the pair wed. It is succinct but genuine, and I read it aloud, like we discussed. When Nate is told that he may kiss his bride, he gives me a chaste peck that we hold in place until the count of *three Mississippi*, like we discussed.

If only all weddings were this easy.

We head back to the car, and our collective vibe is momentarily lighter. I try not to notice the fact that our fingers are still interlaced as we barrel through the chilly air, swinging our arms in time with one another. I try to ignore the way my heart is racing. I try not to taste the remnants of Nate Ellis on my lips, try not to memorize the feel of his face against mine or the way his hand felt on my lower back when he pulled me close to him for our intentional matrimonial kiss.

Like we discussed.

"I feel like we should celebrate," he says.

"No time," I respond. "We need to get back for the Zoom at noon. But after, if you want, I'd be happy to have you stick around for lunch."

"Definitely. My treat," he adds.

By the time we're back at my place and I park the car in the driveway, Nate's all stiff again. He notices that my multifamily living situation is directly adjacent to the train he took here this morning. "Welcome to my glorious basement apartment," I announce. "Don't judge me," I go on, smirking.

My rental apartment is approximately 450 square feet, comprised of a kitchen with the basics (fridge, apartment-size oven, microwave, and sink), a small dining area in which I have shoved a table for four against the wall so that it can only seat three, a bedroom, a little bathroom with a stand-up shower, and a living room. In the living room, I have a couch, an upcycled coffee table, a big bookcase overflowing with well-loved books, and a television on an old garage-sale nightstand. The living room boasts a sliding glass door out to a small cement patio with eight steps up to the backyard, but the backyard is not more than a small patch of grass overlooking—that's right—the train tracks.

I live like a bookworm-y college student, and I know it. I don't care, typically, except right now I am perhaps the tiniest bit embarrassed, seeing as how this man probably lives like an actual grown-up in his posh New York City high-rise building.

But that's fine. We're friends.

And, um, spouses.

It's *fine*.

"Can I get you anything? Coffee?" I ask, taking off my coat and hanging it in the front hall closet, like the adult that I am.

Nate drapes his jacket over the back of one of my dining room chairs, and I extend my hand to take it from him. "Coffee would be great, actually."

"No sweat," I say. "Make yourself at home."

I gratefully kick off my fancy white high heels, which were killing my ankles. I pad around on my vinyl sticky-tile floor in my stockings, putting together a fresh pot of coffee for my husband, who is milling about my living room looking at pictures in frames that are scattered about with no real rhyme or reason. He points to one of me and my sisters when we were in elementary school, taken on the first day of my second-grade year. Both of my front teeth are missing. "You were adorable when you were little," he comments.

"Thanks," I reply, adding the water to the coffee maker and hitting the *Start* button. "Seriously, make yourself comfy. Feel free to take off your shoes if you want. We have to make it look like you live here too. I don't know if Dillon Norway would think you'd be all shirt-and-tie in the middle of the day when you don't have a regular job, you know what I mean?"

"That's true," he agrees. "I hadn't thought of that."

"I've got you covered," I say. "Hang on. Just let me change first." I go into my bedroom and close the door. I extract a pair of worn-out jeans from the closet, along with a T-shirt and my favorite snuggly hoodie sweatshirt, a relic from my Bryce days that ironically boasts the New Hampshire Fisher Cats across the front. I dig through my bottom drawer and find an old Bryant Baseball T-shirt in a men's XL. I walk it out to the living room and hand it to Nate. "Here you go; I think this should fit," I say.

"Bryant, huh? Is that where you went for undergrad?"

I shake my head. "My ex went there."

He points at my shirt. "Is this the team he went to? This New Hampshire... What's a Fisher Cat?" he wonders aloud.

"It's like a cross between a squirrel and a cat, I think. And yes, this is his team too."

"So you've got a wardrobe shrine to your ex, and you think *these* are the clothes that will convince Dillon Norway we are a lawfully wedded couple?"

"Dillon Norway isn't going to be reading our shirts," I reply.

"Didn't you just write an entire novel about this guy?" he reminds me. "And as your mentor of choice, didn't he *read* the whole thing?"

"Yes and yes. But all names were changed to protect the innocent."

"Okay, CJ, if you say so. Mind if I change in there?" He points at my bathroom.

"Have at it," I say.

When Nate emerges wearing Bryce's old T-shirt, I find myself experiencing a surprising physical reaction. My chest gets tight like I can't breathe, but only for a second, and my thighs feel momentarily numb. My rational brain knows that this man is very attractive, but I'm triggered seeing him in that shirt. It's like muscle memory: all of a sudden, my body remembers things like desire, lust.

Sex.

"Look okay?" he asks.

"Yup. Looks good," I say, intentionally looking away before I start to stare. I check the time on my microwave clock. It's 11:20 now. I pour a cup of coffee for Nate, move the dining room chairs so we can sit next to each other, and set up the laptop so that we'll be ready when it's time to Zoom. We chat until just shy of noon, him asking me questions about my family and whether I think they'll be mad at me for getting married without them, and me—with an answer for everything—reminding him that it's not a real marriage, not that he necessarily needs any reminders.

I'm not a huge fan of wearing this promise ring though, if we're being honest.

I hate remembering Bryce. I say it that way because when I see him now, it's like he's a completely different person—he's Bryce-Jamie's-husband, not Bryce-who-has-seen-me-in-my-most-scandalous-underthings. We pretend like it's not weird. Like this happens in families all the time.

But I know it's not normal. So I prefer to live in my basement lair and not deal with it.

To be clear, it's not *Bryce* that I miss exactly. It's being someone's *person*. Ever since our split, the whole world exists only on the internet, it seems, and that got, like, ten times worse once COVID hit. I don't know if most people feel this way, but in my opinion, the internet has a way of making you feel like you're not good enough. It's a real bitch that way. I could wear a great outfit, put on makeup, do my hair, even put in contact lenses if I wanted to go balls to the wall, and show up at a restaurant for a date, only to be told that I "don't look like" my profile picture or even worse, be told nothing at all before getting ghosted by a contender on Tinder's top-ten least-likely-to-succeed list. These are men living in the basements of their *parents'* homes (at least I *rent* mine), men with not-always-steady jobs and sometimes extremely steady drug habits, men who are more interested in exchanging bodily fluids than in exchanging basic facts about each other, like, oh I don't know, last names.

I suspect the reason that I was able to be so undramatic about the whole thing now is because, despite taking my virginity, Bryce never once gave me an orgasm. After the newness of it wore off, the sex itself became pretty routine. Nine times out of ten, he would initiate it, and we'd go through all the steps and motions until he was finished. He never asked if I was satisfied—I think his young mind just assumed that because my breathing was heavy, I must have been enjoying myself. Or maybe he didn't want to ask because he was afraid of what the answer would be.

In any case, with the help of *Cosmopolitan* and several articles online,

I figured out how to handle that business on my own. The only thing I couldn't manage was the whole *telling the guy what to do* thing, you know, in order to create results for myself. Of course, I'm a writer, so if you asked me to write down the directions, I probably could, but we all know that men don't ask for directions, right?

So I figured who needs a man when you've got a vibrator?

That's called *options*.

Only, seeing Nate in Bryce's shirt and smelling his cologne—he *definitely* put on cologne today, because I inhaled it greedily when I hugged him—is awakening all the nerve endings deep in my belly. Maybe it's the fact that he's in my apartment. Or maybe it's actual fear, because we're about to get on a Zoom call and basically tell an elaborate lie to his boss and my mentor (a man whose opinion means the world to me). Or maybe it's because he's my *husband,* and I would just really like to see what he's packing in those khakis.

Jesus. I blush. I am an embarrassment even to myself.

I change the subject, and we fill up the time talking about the MFA program and how our expectations of it compare to the reality. Before we know it, the clock strikes 11:57, and I am busily setting us up on the Zoom screen through a login sent to Nate's email address.

Finally, at exactly 12:00 p.m., a bell chimes through the audio, and Professor Dillon Norway's face appears on the screen.

"Oh," he says, caught off guard. "Both of you are here."

"I'm sorry," I begin. "I just wanted to be here with Nate so we could all address this head-on." I remember this is not my meeting and stop talking.

Dillon Norway nods thoughtfully. "Well, okay. I suppose that's fine. I'm assuming that's fine with you as well, Nate?"

Nate nods. "Yes, sir."

"I imagine that you both know why we're here."

"Yes," Nate says. "And I would like to begin by apologizing to you. CJ and I have known each other for several years, and I didn't realize I had to disclose that once I realized she was in this program."

"CJ?"

"Cecily Jane."

Dillon Norway tents his fingertips and leans them to his lips. "The issue is not one of you being acquainted."

"Right. I understand. I assume you saw *The Tonight Show* the other night?"

"I didn't actually," Dillon Norway says. "But one of my colleagues brought it to my attention."

"Well, I'd like to apologize for anything we did that undermines the university in any way."

"Nate. This could turn into a huge scandal, both from a sexual harassment standpoint and a—"

"I know, Dillon, but there's something you don't know."

"What's that?" he sighs.

"CJ and I are married," Nate blurts out. I reach into his lap and thread my fingers through his, even though it's not something Dillon Norway can see on the screen.

"Excuse me?" The look on Dillon Norway's face shifts from being aggravated to confused.

"I'm sorry I didn't tell you," I say. *Shut up, Cecily. Let Nate handle it.*

"So am I," Nate says.

"When did this happen?"

"It's recent," Nate goes on. "Like I said, CJ and I have known each other for a while. We dated for a little while before the pandemic but were separated when the quarantine orders were put in place in March 2020."

"My family's very overbearing," I add. "They wouldn't let me see him because he lived in the city."

"And then my book took off and my life got turned upside down, so I wasn't available to date anyone."

"And you found each other on the island?" Dillon Norway asks.

We both nod. "It was fate," I say.

"Except she was a student, and I was a professor, and I knew the university would frown on that," Nate adds.

"But we didn't want to wait two years to be together," I chime in.

"I couldn't risk losing her again." Here, he looks away from the screen and directly at me.

His gaze is like magic; I freeze and feel a sudden tidal wave of intense sexual energy roil through me, beginning in my throat and burning through my chest, then dropping heavily into my abdomen, and landing squarely in between my legs.

"I love her," Nate says.

Whoa.

All I can do is swallow. I'm stuck in his eyes.

I feel him squeeze my hand, which he's still holding, and it jolts me from my trance. *Now's your chance, girl. Earn that Emmy.* I turn to Dillon Norway. "I've been in love with him for years, and when he proposed, I couldn't say no."

"We knew it was a risk to my job, and I was going to tell you first, but I just felt like it would be a lot more illicit if we weren't married. I planned to discuss it with you before the upcoming residency, but then the television thing happened."

"And here we are," I interrupt.

"Here we are," Nate echoes.

Dillon Norway leans back in his desk chair and folds his hands over his stomach. We wait quietly for him to say something. It feels like an eternity has passed before he finally emits any sound. "Hm." He cracks his knuckles. "We'll have to report this to HR, and there are some particulars we'll need to pay attention to so that we don't end up with any risks of nepotism. You'll be able to produce a copy of the marriage license to HR, right?" He asks this with one eyebrow raised, as if he's not one hundred percent sure he trusts us.

"Of course," Nate responds, while I nod.

Dillon Norway sighs. "Okay. You won't be able to have a mentorship arrangement with Nate at all throughout your time at Matthias, Cecily."

"Of course," I agree.

"And I can't place you in any of his fiction workshops."

"That's fine."

"I wish you had told me about this before the last residency, Nate," he says.

"I didn't know," Nate replies.

"You got the workshop writing samples before the start of the residency," Dillon Norway points out. "I'm sure you don't think there are multiple people named Cecily Jane Allerton."

"That's a fair point," Nate says. "But—and I'm embarrassed to admit this—I didn't read the workshop samples until we were on the island. And by that point, all the assignments had been made. Also, I didn't believe it myself until I saw her. So yes, there was definitely a weird dynamic in our workshop because of it, but I don't think the others noticed."

"Were you intimate during the summer residency?" Dillon Norway asks.

"No," I say. "It was only after we got back from the island."

Dillon Norway exhales. "That's good." He pauses, thinking. "Let me see, what else? Oh. Nate. I'll have to issue a memo to the faculty letting them know about this update."

"Of course," Nate says.

"And I assume you'll want to stay together at the winter residency, so I'll update my room assignments."

My breath catches, and I'm not sure what to do. I didn't consider *that* as an option.

"Naturally," Nate agrees. He looks at me again. "Right, babe?"

Babe. All of a sudden, it feels extremely hot in my apartment. I hope I'm not turning red, but I can feel the temperature notably shift in my face. I pray that Nate—or worse, Dillon Norway—doesn't notice. That *word* just came out of that beautiful mouth when referring to *me.*

Cecily Jane Allerton. Get your shit together, please. This is all just for show, you moron.

Maybe I'm ovulating. I've read that ovulating women get overly horny. "Uh-huh," I reply.

But it won't be fake that we'll be living together for eight days. In the same room. Oh God. What if I snore? My pulse pounds in my ears.

Get your head out of your ass, my rational brain hisses. *Now is not the time for a meltdown.*

"As far as seminars go, Cecily, you can attend Nate's seminar, but we can't count it as one of the five that you have to review for your residency coursework."

"That's fine."

"Other than that, I just respectfully request that you please be discreet about this new development in your lives. I believe the kids call it PDA."

I chuckle and nod.

"None of that, okay? There are people who will be challenged by this development, I'm sure. So I just ask that you not put it on display."

"Not to worry," Nate says.

"I mention it because you just outed yourselves on national TV," Dillon Norway reminds us.

"That's fair," I say. "I'm sorry about that, by the way. It was all my fault. I had been drinking, and neither of us knew that Questlove was going to come perform with us. I just got too excited."

"I believe that's the purpose of the bit," Dillon Norway affirms. "And I understand. Although, Cecily, I have to say, I'm a little bit surprised that you didn't disclose any of this to me during the semester."

My stomach flips over. "I didn't want to get Nate in trouble. We were working out the details, so to speak. I didn't want to incriminate him or put you in an awkward position."

Dillon Norway nods. "Well, thank you for that, I guess."

"Of course. I know it's a weird situation."

"Weird indeed. I believe there will be some form you'll both have to complete. An attestation of sorts. I'll forward that to you as soon I discuss this with the dean."

"Do we need the dean's approval?" Nate asks.

Dillon Norway shakes his head. "No. I'm able to approve it on behalf of the university. I'll be honest, this is the first time in my ten years as director of this program that I've ever had a situation like this come up."

"First time for everything, I guess," Nate says.

He slowly nods his head up and down. "Thank you for meeting with me. Both of you. This isn't how I thought this conversation was going to go. I have to admit, I'm pleasantly surprised. I was preparing to let you go, Nate."

"I'm sorry to have put you through that," Nate says.

"Me too," I add.

"It's okay. I understand. These matters of the heart often don't cooperate with our schedules." Dillon Norway smiles at us. "Cecily, I'm very glad to hear that you've found your happily-ever-after."

Something about that comment assaults me in my gut, and—as if my eyes were just blasted by a puff of cold air—tears spring to fill them. I nod and smile through my now blurry lenses, unable to form words due to the lump in my throat. Nate removes his hand from mine and places it on the back of my head, smoothing my hair just once.

Just once is all it takes.

A tear spills onto my cheek.

Thankfully, Dillon Norway doesn't notice. Nate does though, and he places that same gentle hand on my knee and gives a light squeeze.

"Well, thanks for taking the time to meet with us," Nate says.

"Same to both of you. And congratulations. I'll be in touch." Dillon Norway waves, clicks a button on his mouse, and he's gone.

Just like that.

Nate exhales heavily and swings his whole body to face me. "What happened? Are you okay?" His voice is animated. "We did it," he says. "*You* did it! You saved my job, CJ. I can't thank you enough."

I nod, and more stupid tears fall. I take off my glasses and wipe my eyes with the heels of my hands.

"What is it? Are you totally regretting all of this?" he asks.

I shake my head quickly. "No, it's not that."

"Then what's up? Why are you crying?"

I pull my mouth into a smile. "Just overwhelmed. But I'm good. No worries."

It's a half truth. The whole truth is that I'm not really sure what this feeling is.

But my rational brain is right. Now is not the time.

"I'm starving," Nate admits. "Can I take you out to lunch now?"

I nod. *Yes—now is the time for lunch, not for this emotional breakdown.* I take a rich, cleansing breath. "Can I just wash my face first?"

"Of course. You don't need all that makeup anyway."

Fuck. He's going to need to stop it with the compliments when I'm vulnerable.

I splash cool water on my face, then scrub off the makeup and feel my heart rate come down slowly. *You're fine, Cecily. It's not real. You did a good thing to counteract a mistake. Now your friend can stay in your master's program. You got what you wanted.*

You're just following the rules.

Everything is fine.

I check my face in the mirror after drying it with a hand towel.

None of this is real, I promise myself.

I try like hell to believe it.

CHAPTER 8

Nate

Between our wedding day and the residency, things mostly go back to normal. All around me, it's the busy holiday season. I continue drafting my new book. I had started writing a sequel to *Work,* discussing how the nature of work has evolved since the pandemic ended, but I found that—other than finally being able to find my voice—it wasn't really going anywhere. But something happens at the end of November that gets me all stirred up, and the words can't fly out of my fingers and onto my screen fast enough. It's the story of a man who lets his professional success mute his ability to create success within his personal life until he meets a woman who he sees very much going down the same path. He can only recognize his own mistakes by watching her make them too. Essentially, it's a story about the other struggles that have been magnified by the pandemic, mostly shining a light on our society's inability to form meaningful connections with one another due to the way we view achievement and the rise in technology replacing physical interactions. The working title is *Success.* I don't know for sure, but I feel a fire in the writing and an urgency in the words in a way that I haven't felt since composing the early drafts of my debut.

I don't see CJ again until the winter residency begins on December 27. We speak a lot over the course of the month, mostly via email and sometimes on the phone. Part of me wants to see her, but I don't want to confuse or complicate things any more than they already are. I really enjoy her company, but I'm so excited about the fact that I'm writing again and that this new manuscript finally seems to have some direction, I'm a little afraid that if I pull away from my writing practice (which has become a seven-day-a-week scenario, at least for now), I will somehow jinx myself.

Anyway, she's busy too. CJ works at the Forest Hills branch of the Queens Public Library, and this time of year evidently manifests itself in a variety of craft classes that she puts on for the children called "Snowflake Workshops." Apparently, they used to be called "Santa's Workshops," but she changed it when she stepped into her current role because she wanted it to be more inclusive for the patrons and their children. They paint wooden dreidels while she reads a Hanukkah story. They make patch-work stockings out of old socks while she reads a Christmas story. They dip their own candles for the kinara while she reads a Kwanzaa story. The series keeps her busier than usual, and coupled with holiday shopping and preparing for her first winter residency, she explains that she doesn't have time for much else.

She's also been spending a lot of time researching literary agents and drafting query letters. She sent me her first one—it was all about New Year's resolutions and was quite honestly one of the worst things I've ever read, so I'm trying to coach her away from making the mistake of putting too much of her personal self into the letters. I've been careful not to use words like *desperate* or *pathetic* in her critique, because hurting her feelings is not on my to-do list. But I would love to see her get an agent, which is why I don't think this is the opening she should go with:

Dear <Fill-in-the-blank Agent>,

Some people think New Year's resolutions are stupid. I don't. In fact, every year, I try to make and keep reasonable, attainable resolutions. Unfortunately, like most of the world, life gets in the way, and by February, they are usually a thing of the past.

Not this year.

This year's resolution is the culmination of a dream I have had since I was a child: to become a published author. There's no guarantee that sending you this letter will get me there, but it's a big step in that direction.

Wow…no. Just no. I gently explain that truly nobody gives a shit about her ability to make or keep resolutions and that she should really read several articles written in industry books that reference the idea of "the hook, the book, and the cook." The *hook* is your pitch—your quick line or two that gets someone interested in learning more. The *book* is obviously where you roll out what could eventually become draft jacket copy, and the *cook* is a short bio.

Nowhere in that recipe does it call for one's sad musings on New Year's resolutions.

I also happen to know—since CJ is my *wife* and we have filled out forms to prove it—that her birthday is January 1. And not just any birthday either—her thirtieth. The last thing she needs is an inbox full of rejection as a birthday gift. I've seen her cry twice, and I swear, both times I felt like my heart was being ripped out of my chest by a twisted, violent serial killer. I can't stand by knowing she's about to destroy all hope of literary representation with that sorry attempt at a query opening and not do something to prevent it.

Instead, I guide her through a variety of drafts. By Christmas Eve, we've gone through six different iterations. I almost suggest we get together so we can just bang it out (the *letter*—get your mind out of the gutter, please), but I know her family keeps her busy on holidays, and I don't want to launch an inquisition among her parents and sisters. I mean, sure, we're technically married, but not by the standards they'd want, and I figure we'll see each other in a few days anyway on the island.

By the time we end up with something much more respectable and professional, it's December 26. In the wee hours of the morning that follow, I'm not surprised that when I knock on the door to CJ's apartment, she's clutching Jeff Herman's *Guide to Book Publishers, Editors, and Literary Agents* with Post-it notes sticking out of it in four thousand different directions with a determined look on her face.

I'm not sure why, but my throat gets tight when I see her standing there. She's wearing black leggings, UGG boots, and a cable-knit gray sweater. She looks like a snuggly bubble of hope dressed up as a fuzzy winter owl—because always, the glasses.

"Hey," I say. "It's five a.m. You're reading?"

"No, silly. I'm packing it. And hi! It's so good to see you!" she exclaims. She throws her arms around my neck and hugs me.

I'd like to reciprocate—her hair smells like coconut and sunshine—but my hands are full. When she releases me, we stand there awkwardly, me holding several bags and her with that book.

"Come in! Come in," she says and ushers me inside. "I feel bad I didn't just pick you up at the train. I didn't expect you to be carrying so much stuff."

"Well, this is actually for you," I say, handing her a shiny red shopping bag. I drop the rest of my stuff on the ground by the front door and swing it shut.

"You got me a gift?"

"Yeah. For Christmas."

"Really?" CJ's eyes get wide. "You didn't have to do that."

"I wanted to."

She grins, and it illuminates her whole face. She holds up a single hand. "Wait here," she says and walks into the bedroom. She emerges with a small rectangular box wrapped in silver paper with green ribbon. She extends her hand to me. "For you."

I take the box reflexively, trying not to notice the fact that I still feel like I can't swallow. On the box, there's a gift tag that reads *For my husband* in neat cursive scrawl with a smiley face beneath it.

I try to clear my throat. "Thanks. Go ahead. Open yours." I'm smiling, and I feel like I wouldn't be able to keep a straight face even if I tried.

"Well, wait. Come sit on the couch at least. We can be by the tree," she laughs as she points at the diminutive pre-lit Christmas tree in the corner that stands all of three feet high, tops.

"That's cute. Props to you for even decorating." From my spot on her couch, I look out the sliding glass door into the darkness. All I can see is the reflection of the two of us, sitting on the couch, knees facing each other.

"You don't decorate?"

"Nah. You should see my place. It's very...I don't know. Plain. I haven't done much with it. Furniture's comfy though. It's much warmer here." And it is—not temperature-wise specifically, but from an emotional standpoint. Not that I'm an emotional type of guy, mind you. Her apartment just reminds me a little of warm apple cider. Don't read into it or anything. It's just a metaphor.

"In this basement?" she asks.

"It feels homey. My place might be a lot of things, but homey's not one of them. Anyway," I say, gesturing at the gift. "Open."

She gingerly takes the tissue paper out of the bag and peers inside. Then she pulls out the two things I bought her: a book light with a little owl on it and a pair of earplugs. "Aw," she says, holding the book light. "This guy's cute. And what's this all about?" she asks, palming the earplugs.

"It's really partly an apology gift," I joke. "I've been told that I grind my teeth in my sleep."

"Ex-girlfriend mention that?"

"Dentist," I correct her. "I didn't want to subject you to that for the next eight days. And the book light reminded me of you because of the owl."

"You think I look like an owl?" she asks.

"Not in a bad way. I would say that an owl is probably your spirit animal though."

"I'm choosing to take that as a compliment because it means you think I'm wise. Anyway, thank you. It's a great gift. Very sweet," she says. "Now you. Open yours."

I peel back the paper carefully, like I don't want to rip it. The box is smallish and flat, as if it would fit a bracelet or some other kind of jewelry. *There's no way she got me jewelry though. That would be too weird.*

I pop the top of the box open.

It's a pen.

"I had it engraved," CJ says. "Look." She points at the side of it.

TO PEN, WRITE BRILLIANT STUFF. LOVE, CJ.

"I hope you like it."

I do. I love it. It's sweet and simple and useful.

It's perfect.

Words don't come right away, so I just nod. My palms feel sweaty. Then I cough, clearing a pathway in my throat for a response. "It's great. Thank you."

She claps her hands like a giddy child. "Cool! I'm so glad. I even used that wretched nickname you like."

"It's a good nickname."

"If you say so," she smirks. "Anyway, come on. We better get going. Don't want to miss our boat."

I carefully fold the wrapping paper and put it in the box with my new pen. I pack the box in my laptop bag to keep it from getting tossed around in my luggage.

We carry our stuff to CJ's car out front, and between her bags and mine, it's like playing a game of Tetris to get it all to fit in her trunk. But we manage. We grab Dunkin' at the twenty-four-hour drive-through and then head up to Point Judith, Rhode Island, because the Montauk ferry only runs in the summer. Along the way, we fill each other in about our holidays and family drama. I ask about Bryce, Jamie, and the triplets, and she tells me that Jamie's already showing quite a bit. Her other sister, Melanie, is due a month before her, and Jamie's already bigger than her. I want to ask more, but I decide not to.

The boat ride is rockier than we expect it to be, but we both hold it together—no vomiting today, thank you very much—and when we get to the terminal on Block Island, there's a van there to meet us.

We're early; faculty members are expected to be on the island in the morning so that when the students arrive in the later afternoon, they feel like the professors are already situated. CJ and I are showing up together because, as a married couple, that makes a whole lot more sense than if we were to come separately.

Maggie picks us up at the ferry, wearing a shirt that has a graphic of an open book on it. My eyes are accosted by the text running across her abundant chest—not that I am noticing; it's just impossible *not* to notice. *I like my action between the covers*, it reads.

"That's a cute shirt," CJ says.

"Thank you," Maggie replies, needlessly smoothing her hands over her northern lady parts. She appears amused—or possibly annoyed—that we're obviously traveling together, and as a result, she drives the van as if she's trying out for NASCAR. The roads aren't icy, but it's definitely freezing out, and there's a good chance that patches of black ice could be lurking in the shadows. Maggie evidently does not give a fuck about our safety or her own. She puts her music up loud (today, we're listening to Sisqó's "Thong Song") and ignores us the whole way there.

It's about 10:30 a.m. by the time we arrive at the retreat center. Our van is greeted by Lucy. She barely even looks at me as she hands me my welcome packet and room key. "I heard about your new development," she says to both of us. "But I'm not handing out student packets until after lunch. Also, we only have one copy of the room key. Since all the rooms in the main house are supposed to be singles, the retreat center only gives us one copy of each key."

"You can't make a copy?" Nate asks.

"If you'd like to travel back to the center of town and locate a hardware store, please, be my guest. But I just got here a little while ago and have another seventy-five people to register, so no, I can't do that."

I glance at CJ. "I'm sorry, Lucy. I wasn't trying to imply that you're not busy."

"Not a problem," Lucy says matter-of-factly. "Cecily, your packet will be here after the faculty lunch is served."

"Thanks," CJ replies. "And it's fine. We can just share the key."

"Terrific," Lucy says, although it's clear that nothing in her life has ever matched that description. She walks off, and I'm glad.

"Come on," I say to CJ. "I'll show you where the rooms are."

She follows me up the staircase. Each room is labeled with an index card with a name scrawled across it.

"Here we are," I announce when I see the words *Mr. and Mrs. Nate Ellis* posted on a door. It's just past Alice Devereaux's room, same as last time. (Alphabetical order's a real bitch sometimes.) The single key we have fits the lock, and I open the old oak door.

"Wow," CJ mumbles.

"Is it okay?" I ask, giving the room the once-over. It's the same room I stayed in during the summer residency. There's a queen-size four-poster bed, a small desk, a tall chest of drawers, and an en suite bath. The walls are covered in faded dark-green wallpaper, giving the room a very old-school-bed-and-breakfast vibe. In the corner, there's a small cast-iron gas fireplace perched on a brick slab, opposite a green velvet wingback chair.

"Wow. They treat you guys like royalty here compared to the student quarters. Have you seen those rooms?"

I shake my head.

"It's just bad. I can't describe it. Very prisonlike."

"Oh," I say. "Well, welcome to your upgrade, I guess."

She takes it in, nodding appreciatively. "What do you want to do about…?"

"What?"

"Sleeping?"

"What do you mean?"

"Pen, wake up. One bed. Two people. Living a sham life in a marriage of convenience."

"Jeez, CJ. Lower your voice."

"Sorry. But still. I mean, this channels the vibes of, like, every romance novel written in the past ten years."

"You read romance novels? Really?"

"Not anymore. I used to though. Back when I still believed in happy endings."

"Okay. Well, I just assumed we would *share* the bed. I'm surprised this didn't dawn on you earlier, CJ. You're a smart cookie. Did you think they had the faculty sleeping in bunk beds up here?"

"No, but I sort of thought your accommodations would look a lot more like mine did. How was I supposed to know the room would look all romantic like this?"

Romantic? Really? "You think this is romantic?"

"There's a fireplace."

"It's for warmth. I'm told the heat in this old-ass house sucks."

"Still." She shrugs. "I don't know. It looks nice. It's antique and ornate," she says, tracing her finger along the curvature of the carved bedpost. "It reminds me of something out of *Little Women*."

"I guess we should have talked about this sooner. My bad; that's on me. If you don't feel comfortable sleeping in the same bed, I guess I could sleep on the floor. Or in that chair," I say, pointing at the wingback, imagining the excruciating aches in my lower back that would result from an endeavor like that.

"No, it's fine," she says. "I'm a grown-up. I can handle us being in the same bed. I mean, as long as you can handle it."

"I'm fine. I was expecting it."

"I can be a covers hog."

"Excuse me?"

"I get cold. I like lots of blankets on me."

Through the wall, I hear someone sneeze. "See? I told you," I whisper. "Thin walls in this place. Make sure you don't say anything incriminating. And yes, I'm sure it will get cold what with the wind here. But they had an extra blanket in the closet last time. Let's see." I walk over to the linen closet outside the bathroom door. Sure enough, there's a quilt folded neatly inside. I hold it up to show her.

"They even give you extra linens? I'm telling you, it was just bare bones in the North Wind. I even packed my own towel because the one last time was so small, it hardly covered anything."

I laugh. "I'm pretty sure I was given a stack of towels last time." I pop my head in the bathroom. "Yup. We've got three."

"Unreal," she says, shaking her head. "So what are we supposed to do for the rest of the morning?"

"Nothing really. Unpack. Settle in. There's a faculty meeting over lunch."

"You think they'll let me stay?"

"For lunch?"

"Yeah. I mean, if lunch is during a meeting, I hope they let me eat."

"That's crazy. Of course they'll let you eat."

"I'm not so sure. You didn't get a bitchy vibe from Lucy?" she asks.

"Look who we're talking about, CJ. It's *Lucy*. She's the poster child for resting bitch face."

"You don't think she knows that I was the one behind the whiteboard incident last summer, do you?"

I grin. "Doubtful." I begin to unpack my things into the bottom three drawers of our dresser, leaving the top three available for her to use.

CJ sits down on the bed on the side closest to the door. She reclines her body back, and when her head reaches the pillow, she closes her eyes. "Mm," she says. "Everything is so much nicer up here."

I steal the moment to take in the sight of her. Her brown hair is spilled out all over the white pillowcase, and with her arms up over her head, the tiniest sliver of her belly is on display. The black leggings show off her shapely hips and legs, which are crossed at the knee, boots hanging over the side of the bed. Her lips are deep pink, two plump raspberries shiny with morning dew.

I look away and pretend not to feel what the sight of her is doing to me.

Instead, I talk, willing my chatter to fill the empty space. "I will say, it's been awhile since I've shared a bed with someone. Hopefully it won't be too awful for you."

"You don't starfish, do you?"

I smile. "No. I don't think so."

"So who was she?"

"Who?"

"The last sleepover you had." She rolls over onto her stomach, her legs bent at the knee to keep the boots off the bed, and she shimmies to face me. Now all I can see is the shapeliness of the back side of her... which is not making things any better.

"Last sleepover? Or last girlfriend?"

"Ooh, this just got interesting," she says, her eyebrows going up and down. "Both."

"Well, the last sleepover I had was with my parents, actually. My mom had a colonoscopy scheduled for eight a.m., and the traffic from Jersey is a mess at that time, so my parents slept in my guest room the night before."

"Nate."

"Yeah?"

"That. Is. Not. Hot."

Her disappointment makes me laugh. "I know. I'm messing with you. To be honest with you, I sleep around constantly. I had four ladies over just this past week," I deadpan.

"Well, then we can't sleep in the same bed because I don't want to catch anything from you."

I grin. "I'm kidding, obviously. My last girlfriend was a long time ago. We split up before the pandemic. Her name was Avery. We dated for a couple of years, and she really wanted me to propose to her. You know those women who are just *not* subtle about it?" She nods. "She was like that. I think she just wanted to be married to *someone*. It didn't even have to be me."

"So what happened to her?"

"I got a literary agent. I was so excited, and I took her out to dinner at Mohegan Sun. Told her I had big news. She thought she was getting a ring and was sorely disappointed. We broke up on the ferry ride home."

"Oof. I'm sorry, Pen."

"No, I'm good. I wouldn't want to be with someone like that anyway. The kicker was she got in touch with me once the book got big and was all congratulatory and flirty."

"Ew."

"Exactly."

"How long ago was that?"

"Few years."

"And there's been nobody since then?"

The question makes me uncomfortable. I don't want the truth to be the wrong answer. "There was one girl. She just lasted a few dates. But nobody since before COVID."

"Really? That's a long time to go without…you know."

"Yes, CJ. I know. But it's fine." This is a lie. It hasn't even been in the ballpark of *fine* for a while.

"Do you miss Avery?"

"Never."

"Do you miss the *idea* of her?"

"Not of her, no. But the idea of someone? Sometimes. It can get lonely," I admit. "Do you miss Bryce? Was there anyone important after him?"

She shakes her head.

"I find that hard to believe."

"It's true," she shrugs. "Me and online dating don't mesh well."

"I hear you on that."

"Anyway, then I got married to a super famous novelist, and now I *can't* date anymore."

"Unless he takes you out."

"I suppose that's true." She smiles. "Where do you think he would take me?"

I don't know what comes over me. It could be her angle, how she's sprawled across our bed, or the look on her face of teasing innocence. She's so beautiful, I can't look away. But I'm fixated on her face. So I just stare.

And she stares right back at me.

Her throat bobs up and down as she swallows.

My groin stirs, as if it's waking up from a long, wintry hibernation.

"I think," I say, pausing, "that he would take you anywhere your heart desired."

"Huh," she mumbles, blinking those brown eyes behind her blue glasses.

The silence between us falls heavy and hard, and I begin to understand that maybe the real reason I didn't see CJ over the past month was because I was afraid of what I would want to do to her if I saw her. Realizations crash down around me, but neither she nor I move a muscle.

I want this girl.

I want to do unfathomable things to her.

I think, based on the way she's staring back at me, that she might want me to do unfathomable things to her.

I don't know what to do with this revelation, so I excuse myself to use the bathroom. I close the door behind me and go to use the toilet, taking a few deep breaths to encourage my sudden erection to calm the fuck down. I flush, wash my hands, splash some cold water on my face, and when I emerge from the bathroom, CJ's over by her backpack, extracting her laptop from it and plugging it into the socket near the desk.

"I'm going to work on my query letters," she says. "Since we still have about an hour until lunch."

"Okay," I say. "I guess I'll write."

"You want the desk?"

"No, it's fine. You can take it."

"Thanks," she says.

When she sits down, she's facing away from me. I take out my laptop and set it on my lap in the bed, but looking at her sitting there, I am able to write exactly zero words. Instead, I watch her tap the back of her pen against her lips while she's thinking, crack her knuckles before she types, and flip through that Jeff Herman book studiously.

I don't know how I'm going to be able to handle this for eight days.

CHAPTER 9

Cecily

That night, after Dillon Norway's opening reading, Nate and I head back to our room. I want to make sure I get a good night's sleep before Alice Devereaux's workshop tomorrow morning, and we got up and out so early today, I can only imagine that he's exhausted too. So we skip the first-night open mic and tell folks we just need to turn in.

He's being weird. Or maybe it's me. But earlier, we had a thing. At least I think we did. It was like a staring contest, only every fiber of my being wished he was naked. But then, just as quickly as it started, it was over, leaving me to wonder if I dreamed up the whole thing.

The rest of the day was okay. Okay, maybe a little bit weird. The three youngish girls from last semester (Ashlyn, Kelsey, and Trix) were definitely whispering about me and Nate during dinner, but this time it felt less like they were making fun of me and more like they might be a little jealous—so that was kind of nice. There were other moments too—raised eyebrows and sideways glances at us that came from teachers and students alike. Gurt said hello to me, and I nearly fell over; she must have finally gotten her single because I'd never seen the woman smile before. Trite Tim and Harry Potter both acknowledged me, and Maleficent even sat at our dinner table with us and asked me how my novel was coming. I'm not sure if everyone was just wondering what Nate was thinking for slumming it with the likes of me or if they were giving me credit for leveling up and hitching my wagon to a literal star.

Truth is I didn't care either way. I was just happy to have someone to sit next to in the dining hall who didn't completely ignore me.

It wasn't like we were with each other all the time, of course. He skipped out on Alice Devereaux's afternoon seminar about flashbacks (and I'm not going to lie, I felt her throwing shade at me, although I couldn't tell you why, given that I didn't say a single word throughout the whole thing). He said he needed the time for writing and to prep some stuff for his workshop the next day. And before dinner, there was another hour of downtime, so I holed myself up in a meeting room downstairs in the main house and worked on my query letters some more.

My plan for querying was simple. I created a spreadsheet to track my submissions, and I decided I would schedule them all to send out at midnight on New Year's Day. I would label the subject line Your First Query of the New Year! and this clever approach would pique the interest of the twenty-five agents I selected for my first round when they got back to their offices on January 2. Nate told me this was not necessary, that it was too gimmicky and that I should just let the work speak for itself, but we compromised because he wouldn't let me keep my query letter in its original format, which I thought was charming and he said was *cute at best, unprofessional at worst.*

Rude.

But he also asked me if he could read my manuscript, just to give it another set of eyes before full requests began rolling in. I liked his optimism, so I sent him the PDF, and he said he wanted to spend some time with that as well.

As a result, by the time we get back to our room, it's after 9:00 p.m., and we're both pretty beat.

Nate unlocks the door, letting us inside. He offers me the bathroom first. I grab my pajamas and my towel from home out of my suitcase and head in there, locking the door behind me. I've got my toiletries lined up neatly on the shelf above the sink, and Nate's are beside them. While I change out of my clothes, I scan the shelf, reading the labels of his things. Each one is more than just a product; it's a decision he's made. Old Spice deodorant, Cetaphil face wash, an electric Norelco razor, a nonelectric Gillette razor, Aveeno shaving gel, Nivea for Men aftershave, a bottle of cologne called Byredo Bibliothèque, a strawberry ChapStick, a blue Oral-B toothbrush, and a tube of Arm & Hammer Extreme White toothpaste are neatly lined up on the right half of the single shelf. I lift the cologne from its spot and carefully open it, then bring it to my nose and inhale. He *would* have a cologne that references books in the name.

Mmm. It's just a part of the entire cocktail of products that make up his scent, but I can definitely appreciate it.

Stop being a creeper, Cecily, I admonish myself.

I debate whether or not to leave on my bra. I would typically never sleep in a bra at home, but I'm not home, and I'm not sleeping alone. I vacillate over this detail while I turn on the faucet and let the water heat up.

I wash my face with my CeraVe, brush my teeth with my purple Colgate toothbrush and my Crest whitening toothpaste, then slather on hyaluronic acid serum followed by night moisturizer. I line my lips with balm, dab some eye cream where my puffy bags are, dry my hands on my towel, and take my bra off (because fuck it, I'm allowed to be comfortable), wondering if Nate finds my bathroom products as curious as I find his.

When I step back into the bedroom, he looks up from his laptop at me. "Those are your pajamas?" he asks.

I look down. I'm wearing flannel pants with penguins on them that my mom gave me for Christmas, with a red tank top to match. "What's wrong with them?"

He shakes his head. "I can't with you."

What the hell is that supposed to mean? "I don't get it. Do my penguins offend you?"

"Not at all," he says, grinning. "Not even a little bit. You all set in there?" He nods at the bathroom.

"Uh-huh," I reply, tucking my dirty clothes into a kitchen-size garbage bag.

He excuses himself to wash up, and I notice he took down the extra blanket from the closet for me. I unfold it over the bed, then peel the covers back and hop in on my side. I snuggle up under them and grab the Jeff Herman book off the nightstand. I continue thumbing through it until Nate returns.

In nothing but his boxer shorts.

Oh. My. God.

The man is a fucking *specimen,* to say the least. His chest is broad, his abs defined; he's got a thin layer of that same light-brown, hot cocoa–colored hair that I first noticed in his beard (if you can call it that) the day we met—*that*—on his chest and then leading down from his belly button to south of the underwear border. He's got a few errant drops of water on his chest from having just washed his face, and it's all I've got in me not to lick them off him.

"You forget to put on shorts or something?" I say.

"What?" he asks innocently as if he can't possibly fathom what I could be talking about.

"Nate! You can't sleep here in your underwear!"

"Why not? This is how I sleep."

"No. This is you trying to fuck with me!"

"Fuck with you how?"

I stare at him, crossing my arms just under my chest.

"If it makes you that uncomfortable, I'll put on shorts."

I exhale. "Thank you. Please do."

"But I'm going to have to ask you to put on a bra."

"Wait, what? Why?"

"Because. I can see all of that." He waves at my boobs.

I pull the covers up. "Oh."

"Thank you," he says, pulling a pair of basketball shorts out of the drawer and placing his feet in them, one at a time.

My heart is pounding. I silently go over to my bag and take out a fresh bra. Then, in a maneuver I haven't used since seventh grade gym class, I hook it around my belly and slide it up under my tank top without putting my goodies on display.

"Happy now?" I ask.

"Ecstatic," he says, sliding under the covers. "You?"

"Perfect," I reply. I rejoin him in the bed, trying to focus on staying as close to the edge as possible so that our legs or feet don't touch by accident.

Minutes go by in uncomfortable silence. He goes back to reading on his laptop. Part of me loves that he's reading my manuscript; another part of me hates it for fear of what he might think of me, think of my writing, think of my past.

So Jeff Herman and I busy ourselves finding me the perfect agent. The room settles into a lull and stays that way until the awkwardness disappears and is replaced with coexistence.

"CJ, can I ask you something?" he says.

"Sure."

"Don't take this the wrong way, okay?"

"No promises, since it sounds like it's something bad."

"I'm just wondering… Are you still in love with Bryce?"

"What? No. Why would you ask that?"

"So this is all just fiction that I'm reading here."

"Yeah." I roll over to face him in the bed.

"This is a story about a girl whose first love leaves her to go play professional soccer and then ends up with her sister, leaving the girl heartbroken and struggling to move on."

"So?"

"Well, it just reads a little bit autobiographical is all."

"How so? The narrator's not a writer."

"True, but she's an artist. She works in a museum as a curator, and the story ends with her finding out that she got a scholarship to an arts program. That doesn't feel relatable?"

"Of *course* it's relatable. But it's not autobiographical."

"Here's the thing, CJ. And just please, hear me out. This manuscript is really good. The writing is strong. Great character development. I like how she finds herself over time and how she discovers in an epiphany during her sister's wedding that she doesn't need anyone but herself to find true happiness. Honestly, it's very touching."

"But?" I ask, waiting for the other shoe to drop.

"But are you sure you'll feel comfortable with this story being out there in the world where anyone can read it? Even Bryce?"

"Oh, I'm not worried about that. Bryce doesn't read."

"That's not the point. Your *family* might read it."

"Only if it gets published, which, let's be honest, is pretty unlikely."

"CJ. Do you see yourself? You're over here, at the very start of your second semester of grad school, and you've already completed a manuscript that you're going to start querying agents with. Do you realize there are people in this program who will never finish a whole manuscript? And you finished yours in a semester?"

"So? What difference does that make?"

"It's not just the speed with which you wrote it—although that is incredibly impressive—it's the *manuscript* itself," he says. "It's really good."

"Really?"

"Yes. Really. I think that, despite your silly New Year's email idea, you might actually find an agent to represent this, and if you do, it's going to be out there in the world for everyone to read. So I'm just looking out for you when I ask you if you're still in love with Bryce, because if you are, he's very likely going to find out."

"And if I'm not?"

"Well, if you're not, then you might just want to give him and Jamie a heads-up that you wrote a book based on your time with him but that most of it is purely fiction and that neither of them should worry that you still have eyes for him."

"I don't have eyes for him," I insist.

"If you say so."

"I don't!"

"Okay!" he says.

"What do you care if I do anyway?" I ask.

"I don't," he insists.

"Good."

"Great."

I roll away from him again, frustrated, although I'm not sure what exactly just happened. "You read the whole thing in one day?" I ask.

"Yeah," he says. "Like I said, it was good."

"Well," I say, letting the word hang in the air between us. "Thanks." I reach out and turn off the lamp on my nightstand.

"You, CJ Allerton, are going to be a big deal someday."

I smile into the darkness. "You think so?"

"Yup," Nate says. "I know so."

I say nothing. He closes his laptop and sets it on his nightstand, then turns his light off as well. He settles deeper into our bed. I take off my glasses, fold them, and place them carefully on top of my TBR stack.

I'm not one hundred percent sure if it's in my head or if it's Nate's actual voice speaking, but the last thing I hear before I fall asleep is barely a whisper.

"You already are."

I smile, breathe, and drift away.

CHAPTER 10

Nate

The next morning, I wake up to find CJ's legs entangled with mine. She's cuddling up to one of her two pillows, hugging it tightly, but her legs, with the loose flannel pants pushed up from the bottom, leaving her calves and shins exposed—and God, they're so *smooth*—are all wrapped up in mine.

My dick is extremely hard.

There won't be any way for me to hide *that* in basketball shorts, so I quickly extract myself from her, peel myself out of the bed, and immediately head for the bathroom before she can see any of what I'm experiencing this morning. I'm sure the sudden movement is waking her up, and I would love to just lie there and watch her sleeping so peacefully for a few minutes longer, those full lips pursed as if they're begging to be kissed, but I can't help it. I've got to get out of this bed.

In the bathroom, I decide to just jump right in the shower and handle this business before CJ's any the wiser. It doesn't take me long; I had an extremely hot dream about her, and knowing she's just on the other side of the door makes me feel a little like a deviant, which I'm not entirely against. I'm careful to rinse away the evidence and follow it up with an actual shower for the purpose of hygiene. Then I towel off, brush my teeth, shave, and come out of the bathroom with my towel wrapped around my waist.

"Morning," she says, still lying in bed.

"Hey. I'm sorry if I woke you."

"No worries. How'd you sleep?"

"Like a rock," I lie. It was extremely hard to fall asleep with CJ lightly snoring beside me. Then, when I finally did, I dreamed I was quite successfully seducing her. "You?"

"Really good," she says, stretching.

I wish she would quit it with all that damn stretching.

"Well, bathroom's all yours," I announce, pulling a fresh pair of boxers out of the drawer. "I'll make the bed."

"'Kay," she says, swinging her legs over the edge of the bed and setting her feet on the floor. "Thank you."

I go through the other drawers and pick out the rest of an outfit: jeans, a white T-shirt, a sweater, and warm socks because my feet are freezing. By the time I'm done selecting my clothes, CJ's closing the door to the bathroom.

I get dressed while she showers. I make the bed and review my notes for my workshop this morning. I don't love that CJ's in a workshop with Alice Devereaux beginning today, given how well she did in my workshop last semester. I swear, if Alice upsets her, I'll kill her. It's one thing for her not to like me—and I still have no idea what bug crawled up her ass and laid eggs there—but it'll be quite another if she fucks with my *wife*.

I'm sitting at the desk getting my stuff in order for the day while CJ gets herself ready—hair and makeup take her awhile—but when she emerges from the bathroom, she looks adorable in a pair of form-fitting jeans, a tight black shirt, and a chunky wrap sweater the same shade of blue as her glasses. We don't say much as we put on our shoes and she drapes her name tag lanyard over her head. She packs up her backpack, and I casually mention the fact that I'm heading into town at lunchtime if she needs me to pick anything up for her.

"I'm good," she says. "What did you forget?"

"Oh, um," I begin. "Just deodorant. I'm almost out."

"You could always use mine if it became a dire situation."

"Thanks." I smile, hoping she can't tell that I'm lying to her.

We go to breakfast, walking hand in hand like we often do now that we're here. Her hands are little and soft, and I love the way her fingers wrap around mine with intention. She's never loose or wobbly; everything she does seems very much on purpose. We eat. We drink coffee. She checks the time, and then she leaves. I plant a kiss on her cheek before she goes, because married people do that. She smells like coconut, lime, and sharpened pencils. I smile when my lips touch her face.

I spend my morning leading my workshop, and then an Uber comes to pick me up at the entrance to the retreat center at 12:15 p.m.. I would ask Maggie to drive me to town, but I don't need her trying to shove her goodies in my face with her book-inspired *Wanna get lit?* tank top that leaves nothing to the imagination. Seriously. That's her getup today—that and an unzipped hoodie sweatshirt. In the dead of winter. Anyway, if she drives me to town, she'll try to poke her nose in my (proverbial and also probably literal) business, and I don't need to be the subject of any more gossip than I already am.

Instead, I head to town for the appointment I've scheduled at Gold Diggers. I'm quick about it; I know what I'm looking for, and I find it pretty fast. I tell the Uber driver to wait outside so he can drive me back as soon as I'm done. I pay him a good tip for the inconvenience. I'm back at the retreat center just as lunch is finishing up.

While students and faculty are milling around or filing out of the dining hall and into the brisk December air, I see CJ at the buffet, making a sandwich. I come up behind her.

"You didn't eat with everyone else?" I ask.

"No, I did. I was making this for you. I wasn't sure if you ate in town."

I smile. "I didn't actually. Thank you. What'd you choose?"

"Turkey and cheese?" She lowers her voice. "I wasn't sure what you'd like."

"That's perfect. Come on. Let's go back to our room. I want to hear about your workshop." I take the plate from her.

We head upstairs, her with the massive backpack and me carrying the sandwich and my laptop bag. I let us in and set the sandwich down on the desk. She plops down on the bed.

"So how was Alice Devereaux?" I ask.

"Honestly? She was interesting. She's definitely scary, but my submission didn't go first this time around, so it wasn't as awful as your workshop." She giggles. "No offense."

"None taken. What did she do that was scary?"

"Nothing in particular. She's just so serious, like she is the absolute authority on writing. This is the workshop on publishing, so I think she's expecting next-level work. Naturally, I'm terrified that when she gets to my submission, she'll think it's garbage and humiliate me."

"Well, first of all, your writing is the furthest thing from garbage, so I wouldn't worry about that. But also, that would be extremely unprofessional of her. What did you submit anyway?"

"Pages one hundred seventy-seven through one hundred eighty-eight of my manuscript."

"Is that the part where the sister tells the narrator that she's marrying her ex?"

She nods. "And the downward spiral immediately following that moment."

"That's a good selection. Even though it's not 'literary,' per se, I think it's a strong part of the piece from an emotional standpoint. I think it will move people."

"Even if they haven't read the whole thing up to that point? I feel like that's a big risk to take in workshop."

"It is," I agree. "There's an assumption that every piece begins at chapter one. But I think if you clarified with an opening note explaining to the reader where they're at in the story—"

"I did," she interrupts.

"Then you should be fine," I say. "How was Devereaux's critique of the piece that went today?"

"Not bad. No tears. She kept referencing her own work though."

"Really?"

"Yeah. Have you ever read any of it?"

I shake my head no.

"Well, you guys are with the same publisher. Did you know that?"

"PRH?"

"Further than that. You're both with the same imprint."

"Seriously? She's with Boone Books too?"

She nods and begins fishing through her backpack. "I bought one of her books. I had to, for required reading for the workshop."

"Can I see it?"

"Sure." She pulls the book, a trade paperback titled *Second Fiddle,* from her backpack and hands it to me.

I immediately flip to the acknowledgments. She thanks her agent; then…there it is. Her editor. "I know this name. Georgia Malin. She works for my editor, Dan Brodsky. Dan's the editorial director."

"Small world," CJ says.

My eyebrows knit together as I consider *how* small. "Yeah. I think Georgia's a pretty senior person there too. But Dan runs the show. I wonder if Devereaux knows that we're published by the same imprint."

She shrugs.

"Well, so what's her book about?"

"It's interesting actually. It's about two authors who write books with similar themes. One blows up and the other doesn't. The narrator of the story is the author who didn't blow up. In fact, her manuscript is rejected by the publisher. The other author becomes huge, like a household name. So it chronicles the narrator's descent into madness at the missed opportunity."

"Missed how?"

"It was a timing thing. The narrator submitted her manuscript right after the other author's manuscript was accepted. Like, they were off by just a couple of weeks. But the narrator had spent over a year working on it, and it was the second book in a two-book contract, so she had no choice but to start from scratch because she was on the hook to the publisher."

"That seems unlikely though. Wouldn't the editor have known what the narrator was planning to write about?" I ask.

"Yes, but the narrator changed course after her brother was killed in a plane crash."

"Hmm. That sounds like a decent read."

"It is. I always find books about writers fascinating."

"I'll have to ask Dan if Devereaux is as rude to his team as she is here."

"She wasn't that bad today. I feel like she was more in her element in workshop. She gave pretty good comments to the guy whose stuff we were looking at. And then she did an exercise about pitching your work, which I really appreciated since I'm about to send out my query letters."

"So it went okay?"

"It did."

"And when do you go?" I ask her.

"Tomorrow."

"Okay, so fingers crossed it'll go well." I take a hearty bite of the sandwich she made for me.

"Exactly," she says. "Honestly, Pen, I think maybe she's just rude to you because she's jealous."

I swallow. "Maybe. I mean, she's not the first person I've met who's behaved that way. There were two other writers at Yaddo, and they wanted nothing to do with me. I've just learned to keep my distance."

CJ nods. "I just don't want anyone to be mean to my husband," she says, smiling.

"It's fine. I can handle it. But fuck with my wife…see what happens." I take another bite. "This is delicious, by the way. Is that honey mustard I'm tasting?"

"Yup. It's the only appropriate condiment for a turkey sandwich." I can't tell, but it looks like she might be blushing. "Anyway, you never told me. How was your workshop this morning?"

"It was fine," I reply. "Nothing to write home about. Pretty typical. I've got one woman trying to write romance, so that's sort of entertaining."

"How do you mean?"

"Well, have you ever read a bad love scene?"

"I'm not sure. Actually, no. I don't think I have."

"That's because you typically only read published work. Well, I'm not going to out this person, because that would be wrong, but let's just say she submitted an opening chapter of a novel that begins with a very poor attempt at seduction."

"Why is it a poor attempt?"

"None of the dialogue is convincing. There's not enough interiority, so we have no idea how the main character feels about the love interest. It's written in *omniscient*."

"Is it literary?"

"No, not at all. It's not supposed to be," I explain. "It's one hundred percent genre. But it's just not doing what it's supposed to do."

"Which is?"

"I'm guessing it's supposed to turn the reader on. But—I mean, correct me if I'm wrong—but starting a book with a physical description of a farmhand's erection while baling hay seems a little…I don't know."

"Maybe poorly timed?" she offers.

I grin. "Yeah. Maybe."

"Did you make her cry?"

"God, I hope not. She didn't cry in class though. I tried very hard to take the piece seriously."

"Aw. I'm proud of you. You're growing."

"Maybe I am."

"Have you ever written a scene like that?"

"A sex scene?" I pause to think. "No. Definitely not like that. Why? Have you?"

"Not successfully. I tried to for this manuscript. But I felt weird about it."

"Yeah, I hear that."

"I think I could get by with a lot of internal monologue followed by a fade to black. But even that—the internal monologue, I mean—is certainly not something to sneeze at."

"No. I agree. Sometimes that can actually be a lot more effective than a play-by-play of the mechanics."

"Would you ever write a sex scene?"

"Sure, if the story called for it. Wouldn't you?"

She considers the question. "Yeah. I just would never submit it to a workshop."

"It was bold, to say the least."

"I wonder if she'll read it at the open mic night," CJ laughs.

"God, I hope not," I say. "Hey, are you going to read at the open mic thing?"

"No way." She shakes her head vehemently. "I would be terrified."

"I get that. It's scary, for sure. But didn't Dillon tell you to immerse yourself in the literary world or something like that?"

"He did, but there's no way I'm ready for that amount of immersion yet."

"You'll get there. Just make sure you do it before you graduate. They make a big deal about graduates reading. It's a requirement."

"I know. But I still have a long way to go before I need to worry about that."

"True. Plus, you can always practice with me."

CJ looks at me and smiles. "That's sweet. Thank you, Pen."

"I mean, it's the least I can do. You made me a sandwich." She's doing that thing again—that thing from yesterday where she gives me that look. "What?" I ask.

"Nothing," she says. "I'm just really glad we're friends."

But there's something more behind those words. I can tell. And my body can feel it too. *Dammit. I can't keep getting hard around this girl. This is no way for a man to live.* "Me too," I respond. I cross my legs to try and tamp down the growing situation I'm dealing with in my lap. *Think about the honey mustard. Think about cold cuts.*

Cheese.

Lettuce.

Sensing my discomfort or maybe experiencing some of her own, CJ tells me she wants to give her mom a call before the afternoon seminars begin. She's kind enough to do that downstairs in the main house living room, so I have a moment to breathe once she leaves.

I'm able to calm down physically, but my brain won't shut the hell up.

I think I'm falling in love with my wife.

CHAPTER 11

The rest of the day is pretty much a carbon copy of the one before
it. Seminars, dinner, student readings. Nate and I opt to attend the readings this time just to show our faces, and afterward, when we head up to
our room, it is mutually understood that I will wear a bra to bed and he
will wear more than just his underwear.

As the end of the year draws nearer, so does my impending query
experiment, and I find that I am growing increasingly nervous about it.
I haven't discussed it publicly, but somehow, the next morning, in Alice
Devereaux's workshop, it slips out of me.

We're reviewing my pages. I'm trying not to focus on the sweat pool-
ing under my arms. I've got my notebook open to a clean page and my
pen at the ready. There are three other students in this workshop besides
me: Megan (a first semester student), Drew (a graduating student who
only needs to be here as a final graduation requirement), and Harold,
who was in my workshop last semester. Megan is about forty, and her
workshop submission is a short story about a woman in love with two
best friends. (Spoiler alert: she dies at the end, which seems both extreme
and unnecessary since the depth of these relationships was somehow
missed on the page. There's also a wildly explicit sex scene taking up
six of the eighteen pages, and it's not doing the story any favors.) Drew

submitted the first eighteen pages of his thesis for us to read: it's a historical novella following a family through the early days of the Korean War. It's fine—the writing is competent, and some lines are well put together, evoking a great deal of imagery, but the premise bores me, and I suffer through those eighteen pages in much the same way as I'm sure others in the group feel they've suffered through mine. Harry Potter, who is *not* donning a cloak this time but who *has* grown in an actual goatee to stroke, submits a speculative piece about a man in witness protection who becomes a dog walker in southern Idaho. I have no idea what the point of it is, but I write feedback with thoughtful questions in an attempt to be a good steward of other people's art—in much the same way that I can only hope they will do with my work.

Pages 170 through 188 of my novel were the most gut-wrenching pages I've ever written. They were also the most cathartic. I'm pretty sure that when Bryce and Jamie started dating, innocuous as it may have seemed, there was always a piece of me that wondered if they had eyes for each other back when he was with me. I wanted to ask her if he was as selfish (or maybe just ignorant) in bed with her as he was with me or if he ever talked about me when they were dating—I mean, I *was* his ex, and who else do you talk about when you're dating someone new besides the someones of your past?

Never mind the fact that despite myself, I *missed* him back then. When he left for Vancouver, a tiny piece of me might have broken apart just a little bit. My rational brain understood that he was bound to leave. He was a great ballplayer, and he was going to get drafted. But it definitely stung a little that he disappeared into thin air, literally overnight, without even offering to try to do the long-distance thing, as if all those years together meant nothing. I wasn't even important enough to keep on standby. Even his *let's be friends* suggestion was a thinly veiled attempt at a consolation prize, and then just a few years later, the stars align for him and my sister?

The eighteen pages are not a rant though. Nobody likes a rant. These pages depict the moment my main character, Natalie, receives a phone call from her sister telling her that the thing she's doing with the MC's ex-boyfriend is a whole lot more than casual. Natalie hears this information, holds it together during the conversation, and then unfolds into a flashback of the best day she ever had with him when they were together, which happened to be an outdoor concert they went to at the beach, followed by a make-out session in the sand and a long walk where they discussed their hopes and dreams for the future. It was agonizing to relive that flashback, as it was the only part of the story that wasn't sprinkled with fiction dust. Natalie's optimism is so blissful, and when held in contrast to the news of him seriously pursuing her sister, it evokes the same emotions that one might experience if they watched a kitten get run over by a train.

At least that's what Nate told me.

So when seated in this workshop, I'm reminded that Nate thought these were *good* pages and that his opinion matters more to me than anyone else's here, so I don't need to worry about the feedback I receive. I brace myself, and Alice Devereaux asks me to read the first page of the piece aloud, so I do.

The phone rings, and Natalie notices that the number on the screen, coupled with her sister's photo, immediately turns her stomach now. They usually text one another. There's no reason to be calling, unless...well, unless it's something important.

Natalie knows it's going to be bad from the moment she answers the call. Gina waits too long to respond. Only a beat, but Natalie knows her sister. This is the girl who, at eight years old, thought she was dying when the doctor told her that her swollen nipples were actually breast buds. The very same girl who begged Natalie to come with her to the bathroom the first time she had her period in school. This girl—Natalie's baby sister—shared a bed with her every Christmas Eve until she was twenty-three years old and moved into her own place.

No, Gina would never pause before greeting Natalie unless what she was about to say was going to destroy her.

And then it does.

The words come slow, as if Gina can't even spare Natalie the compassion of ripping the Band-Aid off quickly. "There's, um, something I need to tell you," she begins. Natalie can feel the nervous pops of gas exploding in her belly, filling her with the bloat of a dead fish. "It's just... Ryan and I...well, you know how we've been sort of seeing each other?" she continues.

Natalie swallows suddenly, noticing that her throat is a desert, devoid not only of moisture but also of words. She lets out a guttural sound, which serves to let her sister know that she is still alive, if barely.

"Thank you, Cecily," Alice Devereaux says. "Now who would like to begin?"

Harold raises a hand. "Having read some of Cecily's work before, I have to say, I found this piece to be really well executed. The unfolding of this scene reads very universally. The emotions transcend age. I enjoyed it a lot."

Well, hot damn, I think. *That was such high praise that I suddenly don't even notice the resemblance between Harold and Daniel Radcliffe.*

"I agree," says Megan. "I felt like this sequence was very clean—there's a great balance between the character's inner life and her outer reaction to this news. It's impressive that it's written in third person, but just based on the physical descriptors of how the news hits her, the reader feels the same inner devastation that you might experience if it was written in first person."

This is an interesting note, especially since Dillon Norway and I decided that the entire piece was more effective in first person—a decision we made *after* I submitted this piece several weeks ago.

"Yes." Drew nods. "Even though I've only been given this selection, I already feel for the character. Some of the lines are so vivid. Like this one, on page one hundred seventy-six: *Natalie's chest becomes paralyzed, her lungs threatening a walkout like the one the seniors conducted over gun control last year. Her brain shuts down, and the part of her body responsible for empathy dissolves into a void of empty space, a holding cell for memories and the all-encompassing life force of future possibilities.* It's beautiful writing. You can immediately identify with what the character is going through."

"In the next part, she's thinking to herself, *Sometimes I miss you so much it's hard to remember anything else.* It's so heartbreaking, especially when you realize she's saying that about her sister," Megan adds. "The loss for Natalie is worse than it would be if it were just that they had been killed in a freak accident. Here are these two people who she loves or has loved, who have been two of the most important people in her life, and they're both making a conscious decision to hurt her. It's awful in its relatability."

I scribble down some of the commentary, awash with surprise that these comments are, so far, all positive.

This continues for about ten minutes as they move through the piece. I can't figure out what it is—*Is this only happening because of my association with Nate?* I wonder. Last time I was in this position, I was torn to shreds, but this time, it's like I'm a completely different author. There's no way I got *good* in such a short period of time.

Finally, it's Alice Devereaux's turn to speak. "I'll start by saying that I agree with much of what's been expressed here. I think this is polished prose, and the reader doesn't need to have been on the journey with this character through the first one hundred and seventy pages of the story in order to feel the heartbreak she's enduring. The theme of loss is evident from the first sentence. The use of flashback is powerful, and it moves the story forward, which is exactly what we want to see in flashback placement," she says, referencing her workshop from the previous day. "It's fine work. Really first-rate."

There's no animosity in her tone, no sarcasm in her commentary. I'm shocked. Considering how nasty she's been to Nate, I assumed that she would antagonize me as well, especially since she's in a position of power in the workshop setting.

But I was wrong. She's nothing but kind and supportive.

And this unexpected turn of events feeds my fragile ego in a way I never dreamed possible.

I start to gush, telling my colleagues and Professor Devereaux that I'm done with this manuscript and that I'm planning to start querying it in a few days. I tell them about my research, the work I've put in on my query letters. They nod, smile, and wish me luck as if they really mean it.

They submit their feedback letters to me, and I place them in the *Responses* folder in the back of my binder. I can't wait to go back and tell Nate how completely different it all went this time around. But first, we have a five-minute break, and then Professor Devereaux is conducting a presentation about social media.

I consider a cup of coffee, but my blood is already racing through my veins. Instead, I text Nate. **Workshop went great! Can't wait to tell you all about it!**

Attagirl, he replies. **So glad to hear but not surprised.**

There's not much time to revel, and when the group reconvenes, Alice Devereaux launches into a slideshow about the importance of social media in a publishing career, sharing metrics about case studies of extremely successful commercial authors. She explains how social media has evolved to be a place for book lovers, starting with the launch of Amazon as an online bookseller and moving through platforms such as Instagram and TikTok. She discusses how the influencer culture of these platforms has created the opportunity for new work to go viral. She dissects the genres most affected by these platforms, and then she says—while looking directly at me—that many commercial genres are almost wholly dependent on these types of platforms for the discovery of new talent.

I'm not a social media person. Never have been. I don't even have an old, expired Facebook account or anything close. I could barely handle online dating. The last thing I want to ever have to do is put *more* of my personal information out there on the internet.

I say as much after raising my hand, and Professor Devereaux explains that social media is an unfortunate reality that can potentially mark the difference between being a hobbyist writer versus a professional author. This is a part of the business side of things that many authors don't want to see or perhaps have never been properly prepared for, which is exactly why she's doing this presentation right now.

It's incredible how easily I can be swayed.

For the last eighteen years of my life, since getting my first phone at the age of twelve, I have avoided joining social media platforms. Yet here I am, just days away from turning thirty, being told by a woman who's probably more than twice my age that not having social media could render me DOA when my query letter lands in an agent's mailbox, because they'll look me up online and find me exactly nowhere. Suddenly, I'm downward spiraling into a frantic Google search for "the best social media platforms for authors." Professor Devereaux suggests Instagram for me, and since I am uncomfortable with posting lots of visuals, she recommends that I learn how to use Canva, which will enable me to create imagery without having to actually be in the pictures myself.

While it's an evolving situation, Bookstagram, she says, "is one of several platforms where the writers are expected and encouraged to interact with their readers." But she also suggests TikTok and even YouTube. She tells me that she's responsible for all of the social media accounts for the Matthias University MFA program, and they're extremely useful for sharing news, video reels, events, grants, and such. So by the time I see Nate at lunch, I tell him I need him to take a profile picture of me for Instagram, and he raises an eyebrow.

"Since when do you care about social media?"

"Since Alice Devereaux told me that if I'm not online, no one will ever want to publish my work."

"Okay, CJ. Hear me out. That's a load of bullshit."

"She had *statistics*, Nate."

"So what? I didn't have any social media when I got signed."

"But you do now, so obviously you believe in it."

"My *publicist* believes in it. I'm just saying you don't need to shift your focus to something that's so obviously not who you are. Agents will come for you based on your book, not based on your presence online," he insists. "Trust me. If you were writing nonfiction, it would be another story. You'd need a platform, without a doubt. But for fiction? I could not disagree more."

I sigh. "She had statistics," I say weakly.

He laughs. "I'm sure she did. I'm just looking out for you though. I know how much you hate being online. Having social media is so much more than just putting up a profile. That's what a website is for. With social, you need to *engage* with people. That's a job in and of itself. You need to be active. It's almost worse if you have a social media presence but it's stagnant. I'm telling you—people are paid lots of money to manage social media for celebrities because it's an encumbrance."

"So you think I should wait."

"Sure. I don't see there being any kind of rush. Honestly. Query your manuscript. See how that goes. Then we'll take it one step at a time."

My nerves flutter at hearing him say that *we'll t*ake it one step at a time. I like that we're a *we,* even if we're only faking it.

Unfortunately, Alice Devereaux has planted a seed in my overly fertile gray matter, and it's already taken root.

The next day, I'm excited to be back in her workshop. I feel a little like a traitor; she clearly dislikes my husband, but she also respects me and my work, and I'm so shaken by this development that I'm chasing the high of it. We workshop Megan's piece, and Devereaux rips it to shreds, which makes me feel even more like a big shot, since she was so complimentary of mine by comparison. I feel bad for Megan and look for the redemptive elements of her writing so she doesn't only take away negativity from this moment, especially since she's a new student, and I don't want to see her turn into a pile of mush like I did in my first workshop last semester. But I am bold; I offer up a craft book that helped me refine my dialogue, I mention a great thesaurus I use online, and I suggest a romance author whose work I've enjoyed where the door to the sex scenes is always all the way open.

After the critique portion of the workshop followed by a short break, Professor Devereaux begins a presentation on grants, contests, and prizes. Again, armed with a slideshow, she shares a plethora of intel about different ways to get our work out there, starting from the macro level and working her way down to the micro. She teaches us about a platform called Submittable, which is often used by lit mags for contest entries, and explains how to research different magazines and publications and the importance of building up a publishing résumé so that we have proof positive that we are professional writers whose stuff people think is worthy of reading.

I don't have time to begin writing short pieces for literary magazines (or any kind of magazine or journal) before I begin the querying process for agents though, so I take lots of notes but file them away in my binder under *Next Steps after Querying*, because yes, I have a section for that. I ask if my debut publication in *Seventeen* magazine all those years ago would be good to put on a résumé, and Professor Devereaux smiles politely while shaking her head no. "If you want to be viewed as a professional, don't introduce yourself to the world with your childhood amateur-hour trophies."

Oof, I think. *Noted.*

Professor Devereaux continues her lecture by whittling down all the way to what she calls "hyperlocal" accolades, the most interesting of which is coming up on January 3—the Matthias University MFA Rising Star Program. I read about it in one of my shiny brochures last semester but felt like I was a long way off from applying for it at that time. The application deadline is December 31 (which happens to be tomorrow), and there are prizes for fiction, creative nonfiction, and poetry. The application is available to anyone who is a current or former student at MUMFA, and although the prize money is negligible ($100), it also includes a reading at graduation on the night of the third and publication of the reading selection in Matthias's literary journal, *The Isle.*

If I win it, I could have an accolade to put on my résumé by next week, a speed that is unheard of in the writing community.

I hate to admit it, but Alice Devereaux is becoming a really helpful resource.

I'm eager to discuss the Rising Star Program with Nate, but this afternoon, we have mentor interviews, and since he and I are basically not even allowed to be in the same room during that particular exercise, I figure I'll just have to wait until tonight to talk to him about it.

Nate skips lunch but texts me to let me know so that I won't worry.

Got a sick idea for a plot twist in my MS, he writes. Gonna stay in my workshop room to play with it a little bit. Please eat without me, and don't worry—I'll fend for myself for lunch, wifey. He adds a smiley face emoji, and I respond with a red heart and a Got it, sounds good text. I take the opportunity to sit with Dillon Norway, since I am hoping to keep him as my mentor for the coming semester.

It's as I'm talking to him about his thoughts on social media that Alice Devereaux joins our table.

Small talk ensues, about the weather (a big winter storm is in the forecast) and about the soup choice for this afternoon (tomato basil, which has a little kick to it thanks to the fresh ground pepper on top but is quite good). Then Professor Devereaux asks Dillon Norway if he happened to read the selection I submitted for workshop.

"I did," he says. "Cecily here is quite talented."

"Thanks to your tutelage," I say, smiling.

"Indeed, she is. I was thinking that perhaps she'd consider applying for the Rising Star Program," Professor Devereaux says.

Dillon Norway chews his grilled cheese sandwich thoughtfully, nodding. "You should do it," he says to me.

"I don't know," I reply. "It sounds great, but the deadline is tomorrow at midnight. That's not a lot of time."

"The application's not bad. And you've got the work ethic of a machine. I have no doubt you can complete it without even so much as partially disrupting your New Year's Eve plans."

I grin. "I appreciate your vote of confidence."

"Will you be joining us for the New Year's Eve soiree, Cecily?" Professor Devereaux asks.

"I'm not sure. Maybe?" I respond. "I have to check with Nate. We haven't discussed it yet."

"Not much else to do here on the island," Devereaux says. "I've been on the planning committee for the New Year's Eve festivities since I started here. Gosh, Dillon, can you believe it's been ten years already?"

"Goes by in a flash," he agrees.

"What are the festivities anyway?" I wonder.

"We have the party on the first floor of the main house," she explains. "It opens up quite far in the back, with adjacent meeting rooms and such. There are board games and card games, along with snacks and drinks. Wine and beer. No hard alcohol. It's a fun way to enjoy some camaraderie during the holiday, especially when we don't have our family members to spend it with."

I offer a small smile, unsure of how to reply.

"Although, *you* do, since your husband is here with you, of course," she continues. "And what, may I ask, did the newlyweds do for Christmas?"

I gulp, although I doubt anyone notices. "You know. Normal boring family stuff. How about you?"

"My sister and brother-in-law have been hosting Christmas for years. So I go there. I've got three nephews who are all grown, and they come, along with their girlfriends. Of course, the oldest is engaged now, so it felt like all we spoke about was wedding planning. My sister is very excited."

I nod, saying nothing.

"I don't expect this girl to become a bridezilla or anything, but I think she's already clashing over ideas my sister has."

"That must be challenging," I say. Dillon Norway is of no help to me here. He simply continues to enjoy his sandwich and his soup, occasionally letting out a microscopic moan of appreciation for the way the comfort food lights up his taste buds.

Men.

"It is. I never married, but I know she's really going through it. How about you?" she asks. "Was your mother very involved in your wedding?"

Such a specific question. "Nope. Not really. Our wedding was pretty low-key. I have three sisters, and their weddings were all major productions. I just didn't want that for my own, so Nate and I got married at the courthouse and called it a day."

Devereaux raises an eyebrow. "That sounds…convenient."

I don't love the undertone, but I try to convince myself I'm just nervous because I'm not a good liar. "It was—both from a financial standpoint as well as an emotional one. I didn't want to have to worry about juggling everyone's opinions over dress colors and cake options and all that stuff. Also, who wants to spend that kind of money?"

"I'm quite certain your husband could afford you whatever sort of wedding you wanted," she says.

The comment sounds a little judgmental, but I let it slide, seeing as how she's been so supportive of my work so far this residency. "That's true. I just didn't want anything big."

"Mm. I see," she says. "Well, to each his own. I suppose, based on your workshop sample, that there may have been some unresolved wounds between you and your sister."

Record scratch. I feel my nerve endings stand up on edge. *I do not like this,* they scream. "Oh," I laugh, perhaps too loud. "That's just a story."

Dillon Norway, who knows better from having journeyed with me through the creation of the manuscript, looks up and gives me an eyeful but remains silent. We exchange a glance, my eyes pleading with his not to share what he knows about my writing and his expression silently agreeing to remain mute on the matter.

Meanwhile, Alice Devereaux chews on a bite of salad, studying me with a curious expression. I find myself wishing that Nate were here, because if he was, she likely would never have sat down with us for this meal, seeing as how she hates him.

"Well, nonetheless. I do hope that you and Nate will make an appearance at the party."

"We probably will. It sounds like fun. I love board games," I lie. *Haven't played a board game in years, unless you count Candy Land or Chutes and Ladders with my nieces.*

I successfully manage to change the subject from families, holidays, weddings, and any other thing that she could ask me about that doesn't pertain specifically to writing or reading, ideally, *other* people's work. In the spirit of games, I bring up the hot new word puzzle game that's been all the rage online lately (Bossword, a crossword-type game where the clues all relate to a specific celebrity), and then we reminisce over Wordle and Words with Friends and pontificate on the future of word games for a moment before another student sits down and begins talking to Alice Devereaux about room assignments for mentor interviews.

At which point I shove the rest of my grilled cheese down my throat, ask Dillon Norway if I need to officially interview him if I just want him to remain as my mentor (he says no), and hightail it out of there before I get caught with Devereaux or anyone else who cares about the details of my marriage and family life.

Later that afternoon, after poor Nate has suffered the slings and arrows of outrageous interviewing, he's lying in bed resting—eyes open—while I'm reading over the online application for the MUMFA Rising Star Program.

"So it says here that really all you need is the sample you would want to read, a bio, and a personal statement. They'll pull up your grade report from however many semesters you've been attending, but it doesn't even seem to count for much, according to the rubric."

"Do they care if you've got prior publishing history?" he asks.

"I don't think so," I reply. "It doesn't say."

"Then you should be all set. I'm surprised that you want to read at graduation though, to be honest. I thought you said you were afraid of reading—and that was just for an open mic. This is for a real-deal event, with the whole school plus relatives in attendance."

"Well, I don't *want* to read, but I would love to have an accolade to put on my writing résumé. Alice Devereaux says awards and prizes and things like that are important. I know you don't agree with her about social media, but do you think she's wrong about this too?"

"No. She's right."

"So I'd suck it up as far as my stage fright is concerned."

"I see." He smirks. "That's very convenient."

The word choice reminds me of my discomfort at lunch. "Hey, can I ask you a question?"

"Sure."

"What are we thinking for New Year's Eve tomorrow night?"

"What do you mean?" he asks.

"Well, apparently there's a thing—some party downstairs."

"Then I suppose we'll go to that, unless you have other ideas. Also, I read online that it's supposed to snow. That mid-Atlantic storm is headed this way. So at least whatever they're doing here doesn't require us to travel."

"True."

"You don't sound thrilled."

"Well, a sort of weird thing happened today."

"What?" He sits up a little taller in the bed, then shifts his legs criss-cross applesauce, pulling them toward him by the ankles.

"At lunch. Alice Devereaux sat with Dillon Norway and me, and she started asking me all these questions about us. Like what did we do for the holidays and how was our wedding. Stuff like that."

"Sounds like small talk to me. Did you get a different vibe?"

I shrug. "I guess not. It just made me uncomfortable."

"That's because we're over here pulling off the ruse of the

century. We've got everyone believing our convoluted love story. It's not surprising to me that you would at some point start to feel guilty about it."

"Guilty? Why?"

"Well, because you're *lying*. And you're not a liar. At least I don't think you are."

"No, I'm not."

"So it makes sense. But try not to beat yourself up about it. It's for a good cause."

"I'd say so. I mean, if it hadn't been for this turn of events, I'd still be living in squalor with Gurt and you'd be…well, you'd be fired."

"Accurate."

"I would miss you if you weren't here."

His mouth turns up at the corners. "Is that so?"

"Shut up, Pen. Don't be all weird. You know I would."

Nate goes still for a moment. "I have a confession," he says, and my stomach stirs. I try not to stare too hard.

"Well, out with it. Wait. You're not, like, married to someone else too, are you?"

He smiles. "No. Nothing like that."

"Okay, then go ahead."

"It's kind of embarrassing."

"Please. It's us. This is your fake wife you're talking to, not some real wife who nags you all the time. What is it?"

"Today I realized that I think the manuscript I'm working on is loosely based on you."

My heart stops; I'm sure of it. This is the first stage of a cardiac arrest episode that will define all moments that follow. Only, wait. No. I'm okay. I can still breathe. *Barely.* "Um. I'm not sure how to respond to that," I say, one hundred percent blushing.

"Well, I just thought you should know since I think I'm going to read from it tomorrow."

"Really?"

"Yeah. Tomorrow night, I'm the faculty reader. And then we can go to your New Year's Eve party."

"Okay, so hold on. Back up. What exactly is this new book about?" I ask. Then I laugh to myself. "It's not porn, is it?"

Nate's face becomes animated. "You'd like that, would you? I believe the genre you're referring to is called *erotica,* thank you very much. And no, all of the lurid thoughts I have I'm gentlemanly enough to keep locked up in my brain."

"Wow. I think the lady doth protest too much," I giggle. "Now I'm sure it's porn."

"Wrong you are. And now, because you're out here questioning my character, I will not tell you about the story. You'll just have to hear it for yourself and be surprised like the rest of the student body."

"I'm your muse," I joke.

"You're a pain in my ass is what you are."

It takes all the strength I have not to throw myself on top of him and pin him to the bed.

Not that I want to, of course. I mean, we're just friends.

Right?

CHAPTER 12

Nate

Another day of workshops. Another night of painful blue balls.

To be fair, I'm actually starting not to notice the blue balls so much. They're becoming part of me. Like when a woman gives birth and her stomach changes—and it never quite goes back to what it was before because the muscles tear and stretch. Like that.

Only it's my nut sack.

Today is New Year's Eve. CJ's done with her application to the Rising Star Program; she finished it last night. She's been busy trying to convince me she needs an Instagram account stat, so I caved this morning and took a picture of her sitting in front of the window while the snow fell behind her. She looked peaceful but happy, intelligent as all get-out in those glasses but with a playful gleam in her eye.

I found myself becoming mildly jealous that the whole internet would get to see that photo, especially since I felt like the face she made was one that she saves only for me.

She wants to have the account up and running, along with two hundred followers, by midnight tonight when her query letters are scheduled to send. I don't know what algorithms she's studying (she definitely *is,* because that's CJ), but if anyone can do it, she can.

As for me, I spend the morning leading my workshop. We review one student's attempt at dystopia, only it's set on the sun instead of on any other planet, and the characters' chief complaint is something along the lines of, "Man, it's *hot* here," so I have a very hard time taking it seriously. After the break, I give my lecture on point of view, and we do a generative exercise where the students have to rewrite a scene in a variety of different POVs. While they write, I study my selection for my reading tonight, wondering if I'm about to make a colossal mistake with CJ by reading a piece so intimate.

My saving grace is that she's *married* to me, so even if it turns out to be the wrong move, it's not like she's going anywhere. (At least not until January 4, when we all go home.)

Poor girl is a bundle of nerves today anyway. She's really beating herself up about these query letters going out tonight. I know what that feels like—the rejection one experiences when trying to find a literary agent can make all other forms of rejection in life seem like a cakewalk by comparison—but I don't think that I *cared* as much as she does. I was gainfully employed at the time and was a hobbyist writer, so every step I took down the path to publication was met with *Wow, isn't this cool?* as its response, as opposed to the soul-crushing heartache that I worry will plague CJ every time someone passes on her work.

By dinnertime, CJ looks like she's going to be sick, but of course she now has 312 followers on social media (after a long day of whatever one does to put up such numbers), so that's a win in her book. She followed people until her phone died, evidently, but she plans to throw it back on the charger after my reading when we go back to our room and switch over to the laptop to find more people to follow. The girl has more nervous energy than even me. I don't blame her though. Tomorrow, she will officially be out in the query trenches. I keep reminding her that tomorrow is a federal holiday, so even though the work will be out there in the world for twenty-five sets of privileged eyes to see, it won't truly be under consideration until January 2, so she should allow herself the day to relax. It's her thirtieth birthday tomorrow, and what a way to start her thirtieth year than with a whole shit ton of optimistic possibilities to daydream about.

I too am nervous at dinner. I don't like reading—I don't think any author really *likes* reading aloud—and I'm second- and third-guessing my selection. Unfortunately, I can't come up with a better alternative, so I suffer through a plate of ironic lobster ravioli and leave it up to fate as to whether I will be healthy enough to read this evening. If the lobster does me dirty, as it did the last time I saw fit to consume the delicacy, then CJ will miss the opportunity to hear my literary pontifications via my narrator, Finn. However, if my digestive system does not launch a full assault on this meal and she can focus on something other than her new social media app for about fifteen minutes, it could change the course of our relationship forever.

So yeah. No big deal. No stakes or anything.

After the festive brownie sundae that CJ insists we must partake in, I head straight to the Spiritual Sanctuary to review my pages. The setup goes like this: Finn Stockton is an extremely successful musician. He's traveled the world, played for stadiums of people, and even made the *Forbes* 30 Under 30 List. He's had women—plenty of them, in fact—but with a regularity that has desensitized him to the potential excitement that "normal" people yearn to experience. Finn, like many young stars, is awash with money, power, and fame—the picture of success. But he doesn't recognize all that is missing from his life until he meets Charlie Jones, his new opening act. She is strikingly beautiful, has more raw, natural talent than he could ever dream of having, and has a following that is negligible at best, but Finn's producers at RCA Records believe that she's got what it takes to be the next big thing. Only via his interactions with Charlie does Finn realize everything she'll be giving up in the pursuit of commercial success and how, from the other side of the fence, it feels like maybe the sacrifice isn't worth the reward. The excerpt for my reading begins in her dressing room just before the first time he hears her sing and follows her out to the stage, where Finn watches from the wings as she knocks him sideways with her transcendent voice.

As I look over the pages, sucking bits of brownie out of my molars, CJ walks into the sanctuary. "Mind if I sit?" she asks, pointing to the first pew.

"Please," I say, trying not to notice the snowflakes melting into her hair. "How bad is it out there?"

"Eh. It's really windy, and the snow's coming down. But it looks so pretty that I don't really mind it."

"Maybe no one will come," I say.

"And miss the chance to hear the great Nate Ellis read? In your dreams."

"I guess we'll see. I still have thirty minutes until this thing starts."

"I don't know why you're torturing yourself up there at the podium," she comments.

I shrug. "It's not torture. It's practice." I crack my knuckles and open and close my fingers, stretching them out like a cat.

"You don't need practice. You're the best reader I know."

I try to smile but it's noticeably forced. She furrows her brow. "You seem extra nervous."

"I *feel* extra nervous."

"Maybe you should read to me," she suggests.

"Just you? Here? Alone?"

"Yeah. Get the jitters out. I wouldn't mind hearing your reading twice."

And that does it. My nerves light on fire like a cigarette dropped on the ground at a gas station. "You don't want that, believe me," I say, searching her face, willing her to prove me otherwise.

She steadily holds my gaze, blinking only out of necessity. It's that same look that she gave me the other night in bed, the one that's been haunting my daydreams. All the blood rushes to my groin, but the podium keeps her from seeing it. My hands begin to sweat, and I wonder if my face looks as flushed as it feels. "

Try me," she says.

"Okay," I reply. "Just know one thing though. Words can have intense power, and once they're out there, you can't take them back. Words change things." I pause, swallowing. "*These* words might change things."

She nods. "Sometimes change can be good." There's not even so much as a hint of hilarity in her expression. Her resolute stare bores through my center.

I inhale, nodding, willing myself to read aloud.

I clear my throat. My clammy hands grip the edges of the podium.

Finn opens the door to Charlie's dressing room and sees her standing at the mirror. She's dabbing at her black-rimmed eyes with a tissue. The lashes are obviously fake, and Finn wonders if they're irritating her, causing the tears.

Her body is clad in faux leather, as if she is a dominatrix. It is out of character. Charlie is a sweater-and-blue-jeans girl. But not today. Here, in the lighted mirror, her breasts spill over the top of a black corset, the bodice showing off her luscious curves, and the lines of her hips bend and wind like a rolling country road awash with new asphalt. Her simple beauty is covered by toxic tar. She is fierce and empowered in the getup, but the teardrop threatening to fall tells a different story. She dabs it nervously, turns to Finn, and plasters on a smile. "I didn't hear you come in."

"Sorry to startle you."

Finn is wearing his usual: ripped jeans, a black T-shirt that's tighter than he'd like, and a pair of black Doc Martens. His tattoo artist touched up the black on the tribal scrolling along his collarbone with a Sharpie marker, which peeks out from under the shirt and will have to do for now, seeing as how if he tried to get the ink redone while he's on tour, he'd have to wrap himself in clear plastic under the nightly heat of the myriad stage lights. The rest of the ink cascades down his right arm, and when he sees it in the corner of Charlie's mirror, it reminds him of his grandmother, who once told Finn that only drug dealers and other hooligans have tattoos like that.

It always surprises him that he can hear his grandmother's voice in his head but can't hear the screams of adoring fans while he's onstage. One might say that he is conditioned to the din, which leaves him disquieted at the memory of an interaction as plain as one he might have had on a random Thursday evening over take-out Chinese food and a game of Rummikub no more than ten years ago.

Charlie doesn't know the calloused side of this life yet. In fact, her nerves are still so tender that Finn can almost feel them in his own bloodstream. In her breathing, he can hear the anticipation of the spotlight, the juvenile ignorance of a roaring crowd fueling one's adrenaline like Halloween candy.

"You good?" Finn asks her.

She nods. The doubt is palpable though.

He takes a tentative step closer. "This is what you've always wanted, right?" he asks.

Another nod. "Living the dream."

"Then why the tears? Do the lashes aggravate you? I'm told you get used to them."

"No," she answers. Her voice becomes hollow, the void between them creating an echo chamber. "It's not the lashes," she sighs. He remains still, a silent invitation for her to elaborate. Her shoulders slump forward as she mumbles, "I'm afraid."

"Of?"

Charlie sighs, and she drops her gaze to the floor. "Becoming," she whispers.

It's a single word. Three syllables. They penetrate him in a way that much else hasn't been able to, at least not anymore.

Finn understands the weight of her admission, and he walks up behind her, his steps more certain now. Closing the gap between them, he places both hands on her bare shoulders, watching their reflections echo the movement in the mirror. His touch on her skin is featherlight, but the weight it carries surprises them both. She tilts her chin up and twists around to face him. Finn traces one finger up the side of her neck. The skin is soft, as expected. Here, on this sensitive spot between her jawline and her clavicle, where there is no makeup, she is exposed.

Finn leans his face down to the spot and warms it with the touch of his lips. Charlie's pulse drums beneath the surface, a bass line that intensifies the longer he stands there. He lowers his mouth to her ear and gently licks the lobe, electrified by the intensity of their connection. She gasps faintly at the touch. "It's too late to stop it though," he breathes. "You already are."

"How can you say that?" she murmurs. "They're all here to see you. I'm nobody." Charlie feels the heat emanating from Finn's body onto her own, a tepid blanket akin to the midday sun. "You shine so bright," she continues, quoting the line from his song.

"So do you," he replies, his face buried in her hair now. His free hand slides down her other arm, and when their fingers meet, they interlock like voices in perfect harmony. "This is not something you become. The raw talent is born within you. The will to nurture it is innate." He skims his lips along her cheek, careful not to damage the layers of cosmetic artistry that have dutifully been applied there. When he rests his mouth against hers, he knows not to move or she will smudge. His forehead touches hers, and he exhales through his nose. "Don't you get it? A butterfly doesn't decide to become a butterfly. It doesn't have a choice."

"Then why do I feel so scared?" Charlie asks, squeezing his hand into hers.

"Because you're on the precipice, and now you have to wait. You already are a massive supernova, Charlie Jones. But the speed of light is faster than the speed of sound. That's why when you see lightning, the thunder comes a few seconds later. Look at you," Finn says, pulling his head back from hers to nod at the mirror. "Who couldn't see this? You're so beautiful it hurts my eyes." He leans in and plants a kiss, harder, with intention this time, on her neck. "Being patient is hard, I know. But it will take time for them to hear you, Charlie. You're caught in that very specific moment between light and sound."

Charlie looks up at Finn, searching his stare for reassurance.

"When they finally do hear you, your music will stay with them like a drug, and they'll crave more of it, more of you. They'll want you almost as much as I do."

The door to the Spiritual Sanctuary opens, and I stop reading as Lucy walks in, her loud winter boots depositing tiny chunks of ice down the middle aisle. She's clutching a tote bag, and she stops at the third row to gather herself, but the spell is broken. The words linger in the air between CJ and me.

I feel exposed, like a fresh wound that she's peering directly into. Part of me regrets choosing this selection, but the part that's alive with jitters at watching her watching me wants Lucy to leave so that I can lock the door and see exactly where this moment might lead.

Unfortunately, Lucy is the first person of many to enter. Students begin to wander in, shaking off their jackets, stomping the snow out of their boots, rubbing their hands together for warmth, and helping themselves to a seat. I climb down off the stage, reminding myself that I shouldn't appear embarrassed. After all, CJ is my lawfully wedded spouse. Nothing is illicit when you're married.

When I join CJ on the wooden pew, we remain quiet. The energy between us is so alive, I can feel it sizzle and crackle, like cold bacon in a pan of hot oil. I want to leave with her, to skip the reading, take her back to our room, and—

"I liked it," she whispers in my ear. I smell her, eternal summer here in the barren cold.

I nod silently, unable to act like a normal person and thank her for the compliment. I can't look at her either, so I stare straight ahead at the podium and turn my attention to the intricate detailing along the edges of the archways on the wall behind it.

Dillon Norway enters the space and drops his coat off not far from where we are stationed. He makes some small talk about the storm, confers with Lucy, and before I know it, the pews are filled with bodies, and he's up at the podium, introducing me.

I rise and walk up the three stairs to the altar. I adjust the mic, set my pages on the podium, and take a quick sip of water before placing the bottle on the shelf beneath my papers. I tap the mic once out of habit and thank Dillon for his kind words. "As many of you may know, I've been working on a new novel, which I'll be reading an excerpt from tonight. It's about a man who is the picture of success in American culture; he's a young, attractive, wealthy, famous, and extremely talented musician. He meets a woman who is the picture of striving, which is to say she is everything that he is and more, minus the fame and fortune. This is the part in the story where they begin to examine their relationship with each other, not only personally but from a professional perspective as well. The overall theme of the piece is that often the grass is greener on the other side of the fence, and there are reasons why celebrities are some of the unhappiest people in America. It also explores the notion of how we define accomplishment. I hope you like it."

And then I read. As each word drifts into the airspace between us, I imagine that the audience is blissfully absent, and it's just me, CJ, and this work that she inspired: my deeply private profession of adoration, gratitude, friendship, lust, and yes, love. I lose myself in the words, enjoying their ability to dance along my tongue and pleased at how the sounds call out to each other.

When I'm done, there is applause. I look up as if waking from a dream. I nod at the students and faculty and offer them the chance to ask any questions they might have. There are a few, and they're mostly standard. What's my writing practice like? How long have I been drafting this for? Do I edit as I go, or do I prefer to draft the whole thing and then edit when I'm done? I dutifully answer these and a few others before stepping down off the altar. We dismiss from there. Lucy takes the mic and shares details regarding the party, which is set to begin at 9:30, giving everyone a chance to change into festive clothing should they so choose. People stand and stretch, bundle themselves up against the impending outside air, and trudge across the pathway, which is now completely covered in the thick curtain of heavy wet snow, from the Spiritual Sanctuary to the North Wind or up to the main house. The wind is violent; it shrieks off the sea and makes it impossible to hear. The few trees that dot the grounds sway to the point of snapping in half. The sky is painted in striations of pink, orange, purple, and a deep shade of navy blue that might be peaceful if the ocean below it wasn't a roaring, ominous black. But we can't stay outside long enough to experience it at all. The storm is not the quiet blanket of a Christmas morning snowfall; it's the dangerous *Wizard of Oz* weather that results in insurance claims. We have to get inside and stay there.

CJ and I cut through the North Wind to get back to the main house in an attempt to remain as dry as possible. Still, our coats and boots are soaked through by the time we get to the door of our room. The main house feels cold, but it's still a far cry from outside, because at least there's no wind to contend with. My fingers tremble as I reach into my pocket for the room key. CJ is dance-jogging in place beside me, trying to warm up.

I get the door open just as the lights flicker.

And go out.

"What the—" CJ begins.

"Shit," I say. I look out our window, back toward the North Wind, where all of the windows are dark.

"Do you think it's a breaker or something?" she asks, pulling off her boots.

"I think the power might be out."

"Really? Fuck. That's not good."

I pull back the curtain to show her. "Yeah. The other buildings are dark too." I illuminate the room with the flashlight on my cell phone.

"Do you think there will be any hot water?" she wonders. "I was hoping to have a shower."

"I wouldn't if I were you. There might still be a little hot water, but you don't want to get your hair all wet and then not be able to dry it. Who knows how long this might go on for?" I say. "But I think I can get the fireplace going. Hold this for me?"

I hand her my phone, and I get down on the ground in front of the cast iron hearth in the corner. CJ shines the light so that I can see. On the side of the hearth, there's a knob and a button with the word *pilot* stamped above them. I fiddle with the knob and begin pushing the button. It takes a few tries, but I manage to get the thing lit. I turn the knob to open up the gas line more, and the fire gets bigger, offering both heat as well as a devilish red glow. CJ gives me back my phone, and she hums appreciatively, stripping off her wet socks and hanging her wet coat in the bathroom. When she emerges, she smiles at me. "Thank you for saving us from death by freezing." She wraps her arms around herself and rubs them up and down, searching for warmth.

I remove my own coat, shoes, and socks, following suit with CJ, hanging my coat in the bathroom, placing the wet boots in the bathtub, and laying my socks in front of the fireplace.

"You think they'll cancel the party?" CJ wonders.

I shrug. "Not sure. Maybe."

"Oh my God," she says, her face dropping.

"What is it?"

"If there's no power, we won't have any internet. I won't be able to send out my letters at midnight. And I can't even use the data on my phone because it's dead!"

"Hang on. Calm down. The letters are scheduled, right? Like, off your email?"

She nods.

I'm not a tech guy, so I don't know if you even need to be online in order for scheduled e-mails to go out. But I know CJ. This is going to send her into a tailspin, and she'd rather be safe than sorry. Thinking on my feet, I ask, "Does your laptop have any juice?"

"It should be good, yeah. I always leave it plugged in when I'm not using it."

"Then, no worries. I've got you covered."

Her expression becomes curious. "How?"

"I've got seventy percent battery left in my phone," I say, checking it on the nightstand. "We can run the internet off my hotspot. We'll just configure your laptop to run that way. I'll leave the hotspot on, and the letters will go out as planned."

"Really?"

"Sure. That should work."

CJ sighs with heavy relief, and her eyes light up in a way I've never seen them before. Maybe it's the glow of the fire. Maybe it's my body's residual arousal from reading to her in the sanctuary.

But I don't think so. That look she's giving me, the one that I can't get used to—it's the one from the other day and from just a little while ago, only with added layers of heat, want, purpose.

Intention.

She locks those eyes on me, and I can't speak.

"You're amazing," she says quietly.

I shake my head and swallow.

"I mean it," she says, walking toward me. She stops right in front of me, our bare toes so close that they almost touch.

"It's just a hotspot," I whisper, taking her hands in mine.

"Pen," she says.

"Hm?" I ask, my senses on overload.

"It's more than just the hotspot." The words float, barely vocalized.

I nod, gulping. CJ watches my Adam's apple as it rises and falls, and I can feel her eyes on me until she closes them and breathes in deeply.

I close mine too, and the words rush out of me like a bubbling river. "You're killing me, CJ. I want you so bad that I can't stop writing about it. I know this is just supposed to be an arrangement, but I can't stand here and pretend that I don't have feelings for you. So I'm sorry for this, but—"

Before I can finish, her mouth is on mine, swallowing the rest of my sentence.

CHAPTER 13

Cecily

I didn't plan this.

It's just—between the blizzard and the power being out and Nate's reading and the way he looks at me and the scent of his skin and the fire and the fucking hotspot, I just can't.

I can't *not* kiss him.

I melt into the softness of his lips, the faintest hint of chocolate from dessert still on his breath mixing with the strawberry of his ChapStick to create a taste that will forever be linked to this moment. The weeks of trying to ignore the chemistry between us finally surface, exploding like the first whistle of a boiling teakettle. Exhilarated passion courses through my veins, trailblazing like a pioneer through the wild frontier. I've felt excitement before, but nothing like this. The firsts of my time with Bryce were fraught with the anxiety of potential embarrassment; the firsts of my subsequent Tinder years were marred by disappointment and skepticism, followed up with resignation that maybe love wasn't in the cards for me.

Until Nate.

This—our first kiss fueled by desire and adoration in equal measure—is too much for my fragile ecosystem to handle.

Our first *real* kiss.

Third time's the charm, I guess. The very first kiss was an alcohol-induced mistake. The second kiss (when we were pronounced man and wife) was measured by the metronome of *one Mississippi, two Mississippi*. This unfiltered kiss is feral, tongues lapping at one another greedily, Nate's fingers threading into my hair before tracing down my back and landing on the hem of my shirt, tearing it up and over my head, and then depositing it on the floor.

His hands cover swaths of me with a warmth I've not felt, perhaps ever. It is a combination of certainty and impulse, satisfaction and unhinged yearning. He mumbles my name and audibly gasps when my hands return the favor, stripping him of his sweater and his undershirt, dying to feel the ripples of his muscular torso beneath my palms, and when I peel back the layers and land on his skin, I am overcome with a fresh wave of *Holy shit, how is this man so insanely beautiful?* But just as I feel my senses of touch, taste, smell, and sight overload, he pulls my mouth off his just long enough to mutter, "I've been dreaming about your body since our wedding day," and a flood of longing ignites between my thighs.

Which is when it hits me: this is a man who might actually be able to do something about it.

The realization sends me into a tailspin. Drunk on pheromones, I pull his hands from my waist up to my breasts, and the moan that escapes his lips in response is my undoing. He unclasps my bra, pulling it off me and sending it falling to the floor. His hands work dutifully, cupping me from underneath and rubbing my nipples in slow, gentle circles with his thumbs.

"Good Lord," I purr, leaning my head back and arching my spine into his touch.

"God, CJ," he replies, but then his mouth is gone, having worked its way down my upper chest and landing on my right nipple, where he kisses me as if I am a deity to worship.

This continues for several minutes, as Nate is careful not to favor one side over the other. I'm hungry for more though. As my hands roam impatiently, they land on his belt and begin to tug at the leather and unfasten the buckle. I open the button, pull down the zipper, and his full length springs forward like a clock on daylight savings time. His shaft pushes against the thin fabric of his boxer shorts but doesn't emerge for me to see.

Before I can push his underwear down as well and feast my eyes on what it looks like when Nate Ellis unravels, he lays me down on the bed, removing my pants in much the same way that I just disrobed him. Because I'm on my back now though, he hovers over me, planting kisses on my lips, sucking my swollen nipples, and then sitting up to take in the sight of me in my panties, awash with the burning glow of the hearth.

"Fuck," he says. "Look at you." He runs his thumbs under the black lace that rests on my hip bones. Nate's eyes settle on mine, but all I can feel is those curious thumbs, dipping under the elastic. "Can I take these off?"

I nod, consumed by his earnestness. He slides my panties down and pulls them off my ankles. Then he sits back up and parts my legs with his knee. Looking me over, he says, "You're incredible, Cecily."

"So are you," I whisper in reply.

"One more thing," he says, leaning all the way forward so his face is next to my ear. He pushes his erection, still covered by his boxers, into me, and my senses heighten. *I am ready for you, Nate Ellis,* my body screams. I'm not sure if it's the darkness, the anticipation, or the intimacy of trusting him, but if I have to wait much longer to feel him inside me, I might literally and figuratively explode. "May I take off your glasses?" he asks.

"Sure," I say. The tenderness with which he removes the frames, folds them carefully, and then regards my face is too much to handle.

I need him. Right now.

"Jesus," he breathes. His lips kiss each of my eyelids and then shift down to my lips, where his tongue dances with mine for just a brief moment as he slides a finger inside me. The heel of his hand morphs into a shelf of pressure against me as he hooks his middle digit deeply, then rocks his hand back and forth, creating a sensation that begins to mount. As he does this, all while still in his shorts, he kisses down my belly, lightly biting here and there, until he gets to my navel, and then he works my legs open all the way.

Nate feasts on me like I'm a fucking Thanksgiving turkey.

I grip his hair, unsure of what else to do with my hands, and my hips involuntarily buck up and down against the pushing of his tongue. He continues to work the finger forward, driving me crazy, and I know this won't take very long. As my breath catches, he hums into me, and the vibration tips me over the edge. My body tenses as I careen into a void of pleasure in blissful waves.

I can't believe he did it—and so easily.

Nate made me come.

After my torso relaxes into the covers, he kisses his way back up to my face. "Are you okay?" he whispers in my ear.

I can barely speak. "Uh-huh," I manage to say.

"You taste unbelievable," he replies.

I smile into the darkness and roll over onto my side. "Do you have a condom?"

"I don't," he admits. "I wasn't planning on this."

"It's okay," I say. "I brought some."

"What?" he asks incredulously. "No, you didn't."

I giggle. "I definitely did."

"You knew this was going to happen?"

"Absolutely not," I insist. "But I like to be prepared for the unexpected." I kiss his cheek. "I'll go grab one. Wait right here."

I climb off the bed and then pad, naked, over to my suitcase. It's not easy to dig through luggage by the light of a fire when you have astigmatism, but the heart wants what it wants, and in this case, my heart desperately wants to ride Nate Ellis until he bursts inside my body. Based on his foreplay performance, I can only imagine that sex with him must be truly next level, and nothing will keep me from finding out.

As expected, I am correct.

I bring the condom to the bed, and Nate lifts his hips so that I can pull off his boxers. I slide the latex onto his length before settling down on top of him. I realize once I've already taken him that I wanted to return the favor and feel him in my mouth, but it's too late now. I've never been so selfish in bed before; I can barely even recognize myself. Anyway, it's better than I could have imagined. For someone who I wasn't sure could dance (based on his performance at karaoke), this is a man who knows exactly what to do with his hips. Not only that, he has remarkable upper-body strength, so he effortlessly maneuvers the two of us from one position to the next. I'm on top, then I'm underneath him, then he is behind me, and finally I am straddling him in a seated position, only he's doing the work of lifting me up and down with one large hand on each of my ass cheeks. As his orgasm builds, he buries his face into my neck, kissing and licking my skin, raising my hips faster and faster until finally, he bites down, and I feel him thrust into me hard. He pushes again, again, and once more, until he fades into a series of twitches and trembles, finally able to exhale.

I collapse on top of him, more satiated than I've ever been. I inhale his deliciousness and cannot believe that this extraordinary man, so gorgeous, smart, kind, and driven, has given me the gift of my very first non-self-imposed orgasm.

"You're in trouble, Nate Ellis," I whisper.

"Why's that?" he replies.

"I think you've imprinted on me."

I feel his lips curve into a smile against the side of my face. "Like a wild animal?"

"Exactly."

"Well, I've got bad news for you then."

"Go on. I can take it."

He takes a long cleansing breath. "I want you to be my girlfriend."

I can't help but laugh. "But I'm your wife."

"You're also my muse."

"Maybe I can be all three."

He wraps his arms and legs around me, and I grin under the weight of them. "Yes," he sighs. "Yes to all of it."

CHAPTER 14

Nate

The next morning, we wake up with our limbs intertwined. We are naked but covered by the comforter plus the extra quilt. The fireplace is still on, though I turned it down last night because something about the idea of sleeping with a fire raging just steps away from the bed seemed dangerous.

I check my phone, which I left plugged in just in case the power came back on. It's at twelve percent battery.

I take a moment to regard the angel asleep beside me. She's got her face smushed into the pillow and her mouth open. She's definitely drooling into her hair. Still, she's the prettiest thing I've ever laid eyes on, and I'm overcome with gratitude, arousal, and joy at the fact that I get to wake up next to her, even if our relationship status could technically be labeled as *complicated*.

"Hey, sleepyhead," I whisper into her ear.

She flips onto her side, wiping at her mouth with the back of her hand, smacking her lips together in an attempt to cure an obvious case of dry mouth. "Mmm," she groans.

"I'm sorry to wake you, but it looks like we still have no power, and I want you to check and see if your letters went out before my phone dies."

Yup, that does it. CJ stretches her arms up over her head and takes in the scene that is our shared bedroom. Her panties are on the floor, our socks are laid out by the fireplace, her bra is hanging off one of the posts at the foot of the bed, and my pants are crumpled up by the bathroom door. CJ's laptop is over at the desk by the window with my boxers just sitting beside it, as if I would ever leave my underwear on someone's computer equipment. She reaches for her glasses on the nightstand and sets them on her face. She looks so cute I could just eat her up.

"Hey," I say, reaching for her. "Really quick, before the letters. Happy birthday." I fold her into my arms and give her a hug. "And happy new year. This is going to be your year, CJ."

She gives me a squeeze, and when she pulls back, I push the hair out of her face and kiss her lightly on the mouth. "Thank you," she says and kisses me again, more greedily this time.

"Don't get me all worked up," I say. "Go check your email, please. I'm not going to fight you on engaging in round three or four or whatever number we're up to, but please, just check your email before my hotspot dies." I laugh at how ludicrous I sound, but I know she'll be miserable if she doesn't have the peace of mind of knowing her queries went out.

CJ climbs out of bed and pulls on a pair of sweatpants from her bag. She grabs my undershirt from yesterday off the floor and pulls that on to cover her top. The thin fabric of the T-shirt leaves nothing to the imagination, especially without a bra. I find myself more turned on with that little bit of clothing on her than I was waking up next to her naked.

Eh, maybe not.

She opens the laptop and wakes it up by dragging her finger along the touchpad. Straight to the email she navigates. "Holy crap!" she screeches. "I already have a response!"

"Really? That's great! That means it worked. What does it say?"

"It's from Vision Board Creative Group. It's an auto-reply, saying they're closed until tomorrow."

"That's fine. Good." I nod. "You're officially a querying author. That's a big deal! We should celebrate."

She shrieks and claps her hands. "I'm freaking out! I'm sorry. I just have a lot of adrenaline for first thing in the morning. And then add to it all of *this*"—she waves at the airspace between us—"and I'm pretty much a complete and utter train wreck."

I laugh. "No need to explain. I completely understand. I'm so excited for you. In fact, wait a sec. I have something. Pass me my drawers?"

CJ tosses my boxers over to me. I swing my legs out from under the covers and put on my underwear. Then I turn the heat on the fireplace up higher (because holy hell is it *cold* in here) and open the dresser drawer where all my sweaters are neatly folded. I reach all the way to the back, feeling around for my surprise.

CJ watches me with those beautiful wonder-filled eyes of hers, and I drag her away from the computer and back to the bed with a small black box in my hand. It has a red ribbon around it. I sit her down and hand it to her.

"What's this?" she asks.

"This is your birthday gift. I hope you like it," I reply. My stomach dips, as it might if I were on a roller coaster.

"But you just gave me a gift a few days ago."

"I know. That was for Christmas. It's not my fault your birthday and Christmas are in such close proximity to each other."

She smiles, looking from the box to my face and down at the box again. "It looks like jewelry."

"Why don't you open it and find out?"

CJ nods. Her grin alone is worth the money I spent on this. She unties the ribbon and flips open the box. Inside, there's a wedding band with a dozen diamond chips across the top of it.

She gasps. "Holy shit. Is this real?"

"It's white gold and diamonds. I got it in town. I hope you like it. I just didn't want you to have to suffer forever, walking around with your ex-boyfriend's promise ring on your left hand while your sister incubates his litter of babies. Something about that didn't feel fair. You shouldn't have to endure the emotional turmoil of remembering how much Bryce hurt you every time you look down at your fingers."

"Pen," she says. Her voice is soft, and it sings the nickname sweetly. "This is too much."

"It's really not," I reply. "When you think about everything you've done for me…" My voice trails off.

She looks up from the box into my eyes. Her face gets all scrunchy, and she says, "This is the sweetest, most considerate, most—"

"Good," I say, cutting her off. "I'm glad you like it."

"I love it. It's beautiful."

"Can I put it on you?"

"Of course." She hands me the box, and I take out the ring as she all but rips the old one off her finger. I replace it with my ring, a wedding band for my newly minted girlfriend. The idea of it makes me laugh. *This would make one hell of a story,* I think.

All of a sudden, the lights go on.

"Oh, thank God!" CJ squeals. She peers out the window and points to a truck that reads *Block Island Power* along its side. "That was fast by New York City standards."

"Shit. No wonder we lost power." I nod with my chin. "Look over there," I say, pointing at an ash tree that had split in half, pulling wires down around it. "That tree must have knocked out the grid. I guess from the wind."

"Sheesh," CJ says. "Hopefully no one was hurt."

"Bad news travels fast. I'm sure we would have heard if it got somebody."

"Well, thank goodness the electric is working again," she says. "Now you can join me in the shower."

I don't need convincing. My grin says it all.

One hour and two very satisfying orgasms later (one for each of us), CJ and I are in the dining room, warming our hands on fresh mugs of coffee.

"The charcuterie boards weren't going to keep, so we had no choice but to put them out," Alice Devereaux explains. "I mean, it was *such* a night." She's all wound up with the excitement of regaling anyone who will listen with stories from the party that almost wasn't. "It'll definitely go down in the history books, that's for sure."

Dillon picks at his oatmeal. "Good thing board games can be played by candlelight," he says.

"It's really a shame you two couldn't make it," Devereaux says to me and CJ.

I give CJ a knowing look, but she says, "I know! I was just wiped from the day. Residency takes a lot out of me."

"And now it's the new year," Devereaux continues. "So I take it your queries went out, right?"

CJ grins like the Cheshire cat and nods happily.

"Good for you. Your writing is excellent. I have no doubt you'll get some interest," Devereaux replies.

It *feels* like an honest-to-God compliment, but I trust Alice Devereaux about as far as I can throw her, so I just raise an eyebrow and leave it alone. No need to sully CJ's excitement by shining a light on this woman's personal beef with me. "I'm looking forward to our workshop later today, Cecily. We'll be discussing the process of finding a literary agent, so do feel free to chime in with your thoughts on the research process."

"Oh, I will. It's been super interesting," CJ replies.

"And I was very happy to see that you signed up for Instagram," Devereaux continues. "Thank you for following my account."

"Of course! I'm glad you saw that I did that."

"I post important information regularly, so you'll be able to avail yourself of it. And after you graduate, if you get published, I'll follow your account as well."

"Wait—you didn't follow her back?" I say to Alice. I'm sorry. I can't help myself. That's just obnoxious.

"No, Nate, I didn't. I make it a point not to follow students. Wouldn't want to seem inappropriate, you know," she responds.

Wow, bitch. Just…wow. I choose to let it go, even though the whole table goes silent at the obvious insult.

"Well, I don't know about the rest of you, but I'm glad to have the early part of today off. I'm sure we could all use the extra rest," Dillon chimes in in a sorry attempt to cut through the ever-mounting tension at our breakfast table.

But I *won't* unleash my fury on this second-rate asshole—at least not in public. I'm above that. (Don't get me wrong. At some point, I'll be using pages from her book as toilet paper, just not at this precise moment.) Also, it's CJ's birthday, and I'm not about to ruin it for her by letting my mouth get the best of me. She squeezes my knee under the table though, which reassures me that I'm making the right decision by leaving Alice Devereaux alone. I can't sit here though. "I'm going to head back to the room," I whisper in CJ's ear.

"I'll come with you. I need to check my phone anyway. I'm sure my mom has called me by now."

We politely excuse ourselves, and CJ grabs a banana for the road. Back at the room, CJ hops on her phone right away—she's flooded with text messages to return wishing her a happy birthday, plus a slew of Happy New Year group texts from overnight that she's been included on. And indeed, she's missed a call from her mom. "Is it okay if I call her from here?"

"Of course. Is it okay if I stay here and do some work?"

She smiles. "Yes, Pen. It's fine. You know, at some point, we won't feel like we need to be so polite toward each other."

"Oh, believe me, as soon as you're off the phone, I'll be more than happy to do impolite things to you again," I tease.

"That sounds gross," she giggles.

I shrug. "You asked for it."

She raises her eyebrows as she hits the green *Call* button on her phone. "Shh," she admonishes me. "I don't want my mom to know you're here."

I nod and give her a wink, then pantomime zipping my lips shut and throwing away the key. When her mother answers the phone and launches into an off-key rendition of "Happy Birthday," I stifle a laugh. They chat for almost twenty minutes, talking about all the exciting things going on in CJ's life—the querying and the new Instagram profile (which CJ then proceeds to coach her mother to locate online), followed by a full update on all of her pregnant siblings. Her mom passes the phone to her dad, who talks to her about the importance of joining the library's 403(b) program, especially now that she's thirty. After a brief lecture, he informs her that Jamie and Bryce are home, and would she like to speak to her sister? Of course she would; she's CJ, an endlessly bright ray of sunshine regardless of whose fetuses are in the womb of the person asking. So she makes small talk with Jamie, talks about social media some more (Jamie follows her right on the spot, which makes her eyes light up), and asks how her baby registry is coming along. When she hangs up, I look at her, shaking my head.

"I don't know how you do that," I say.

"Do what?"

"How you can be so nice, considering what Jamie and Bryce put you through."

"It sucked," she agrees. "My mother didn't exactly teach us about 'girl code' though. Her version of success was single-minded and old-fashioned, and I realized from a pretty young age that if I didn't fall in line with it, I'd become an outcast in my own family."

"So you're saying you don't blame Jamie?"

"I did, for a while. I blamed Bryce too. But when I really looked inside myself, I knew that I didn't want the life he would've given me. And if she did, and it made her happy, then I could survive the sting of it."

"You're a better person than I am. If I had a brother and he ended up with Avery, even if I have zero feelings left for her, I'd still be pissed."

CJ sighs. "Well, it helps a lot that I'm super into this new guy I've been seeing."

"Is that so?" I smile.

She nods. "He's the total package. Extremely handsome, funny, smart, generous, and rich and famous to boot."

"Sounds like a dick to me."

"Oh, believe me, he can be. I thought he was a total douche when I first met him."

"Did you?"

"One hundred percent."

"What'd he do to get you to change your mind?"

"He let me humiliate him on national television."

"I'd say it was worth it."

"Me too," she says.

She smirks before tackling me and having her way with me. Again.

CHAPTER 15

Cecily

By the following night, I have stats logged in my notebook.

IG FOLLOWERS: 516

QUERIES SENT OUT: 25

AUTO-REPLIES: 7

REJECTIONS: 4

FULL MANUSCRIPT REQUESTS: 0

I am not doing well.

The social media stats should be providing me with some relief, but really, how hard can it be to get followers? I've posted a few cute things, put up exactly three pictures (one of the snow, one of my TBR stack, and one of the birthday cake that Nate asked the kitchen staff to bake for me last night), reposted a couple of clever things that other people have created, and followed almost two thousand people in small batches of about thirty at a time.

It's not like it's rocket science or anything. A toddler could have the same success as me on Instagram.

The querying, however, is doing bad things to my stomach and my psyche. I know Nate's stats; he told me them. And *Work* was his first manuscript, just like *Hard Pass* is mine.

I thought I'd have at least a few full requests by now.

Yes, I realize it's only been a day, and people are coming off a long holiday break, but still. I am frozen in the desk chair the following night, having skipped an alumni virtual reading on Zoom in favor of staring at my screen, hitting *Refresh* over and over again on my email.

"This is not a good look for you, babe," Nate says.

I smile because I really like the way that word makes me feel. "Keep calling me that. It's way better than CJ."

"Fair enough. But hey, I'm serious. I'm worried about you. This feels a little like a downward spiral you're embarking on here."

"I'm fine," I rebut. "It's just—I mean, I know that our genres are totally different, but you had such incredible stats for your queries. And so fast too."

"First of all, I didn't query immediately following the winter hibernation of the entire publishing industry. And second, I queried different agents than the ones you've reached out to. It's not a one-size-fits-all kind of thing. You know that."

He's right; I *do* know that. It just sucks is all. I hit *Refresh* again.

I have a new message in my inbox. My heart races, but only for a split second. I see it's from Alice Devereaux and assume it has to do with the following day's workshop. Except, *wait a second*. The subject line reads Congratulations.

I click to open it, and my eyes skim the page.

"Holy shit. Pen, you won't believe it."

"What?"

"I won that thing!"

"What thing?"

"The contest thing. Listen to this! 'Dear Cecily Jane Allerton. On behalf of the MUMFA selection committee, I am pleased to inform you that your submission to the Rising Star Program has received the award for

Best New Fiction. We hope you are as excited about this accomplishment as we are. As you know, the award comes with a stipend of one hundred dollars, which will be mailed to you at the address in your application. It also comes with publication in our literary journal, *The Isle*, as well as a special reading at our MUMFA graduation ceremony on January third. More details will follow shortly. In the meantime, congratulations on this esteemed accomplishment. Yours, Professor Alice Devereaux, Selection Committee Chair, MUMFA Rising Star Program.'"

"Babe! That's amazing! I'm so proud of you!"

There's that word again. *Mmm.* It gives me the chills. It's been so long since anyone's called me by a nickname like that. I shake my shoulders. "Oof," I say. "I really needed a win. This is good."

He gives me a hug from behind. I can smell the now familiar ingredients he uses to create a scent that is uniquely Nate, and it warms my insides. He feels like home in the best possible way. "So you'll be reading at graduation tomorrow then. That's awesome. I can't wait."

"Thank you," I say, grinning. "And now I'll have a very particular accolade to put on my next batch of query letters."

"You see? That's why you're supposed to send them out in batches. Because things happen, and you never know when you might want to change them."

"You're so smart. I'm definitely glad that I married a PEN Award winner who's been down this treacherous road before."

He kisses my neck, and I discover I've found an antidote for my querying jitters. Sex with Nate seems to get my mind off things.

Good to know.

The following day, my morning workshop is a lecture covering what to expect when your manuscript goes out on submission—a nice hopeful change from the therapy session Alice Devereaux *should* have led for when we're in the query trenches. Of course, I am the only student at

Matthias who's actively in the process of looking for an agent. Nate says I'm a unicorn. I think maybe I'm just the village idiot, and everyone's having a grand old time watching me flail about like a cartoon character that somebody's inadvertently lit on fire.

People act funny when they're jealous, Nate tells me.

After workshop, we have lunch, and there's an interesting energy in the air. This is our last full day of residency. Tomorrow, we leave the island. Students and faculty are tired; it's a lot to constantly be "on" for twelve-plus hours every day for over a week, but there's also the buzz of excitement about the graduation ceremony. Friends and family members of the grads will be there, and there's a champagne toast afterward in the same area of the main house where the New Year's Eve thing was held. The faculty members are waning from seven days of teaching and lecturing. Everyone is eager to see who will be matched with whom for mentorship this semester. The list will be up on my old friend, *the Whiteboard,* tomorrow morning. The entire lot of us are walking around kind of like a bunch of children on Christmas Eve—all sugared up from too many of Santa's cookies and ready to crash but trying to stay up to catch the big guy coming out of a chimney.

Of course, in my house in Queens, there was no chimney. Mom used to leave a window cracked and told us that Santa knew to just reach in and open it all the way—and that he would close it up on his way out. Not going to lie, between our strange rituals and the annual viewing of *Home Alone,* I used to have recurring nightmares about getting robbed every December.

It's a funny thing that I remember that little tidbit as I'm getting dressed for graduation. No cap and gown for me, of course. I'm not a grad yet. But Nate has to don academic regalia, and I adore how cute he looks in it all.

"You nervous?" he asks me as I straighten my dress in the mirror.

I shrug. "It should be fine. I mean, I'm not psyched about reading, but I have to get used to it, right? Like Dillon Norway said, I have to be willing to immerse myself in this world, and reading my work aloud to strangers is definitely a part of it."

"You're immersing, that's for sure. How many followers are you up to?"

"I haven't checked since lunch. I don't want to become one of those people who's always on my phone. It was very much on purpose that I never had it before this."

"Time suck, right?"

"Yup. I mean, just yesterday alone, I was on there for over three hours when all was said and done."

"How do you know?"

"I logged it."

Pen smiles at me and gives me a soft kiss on my temple. "Of course you did."

"I'm going to try and keep myself to two sessions a day—one in the morning and one at night, no more than twenty minutes per session."

"Whatever works," he says. "Anyway. You have your reading?"

"Yup. I've got two copies printed out in this folder and a backup on my phone."

"Why two copies?"

"I don't know. Just want to be prepared, I guess."

"In case what? A sudden hurricane blows through the Spiritual Sanctuary and sweeps your reading up with it?"

I smirk. "Wise guy."

"You're prepared for anything, I guess."

"You know it."

We finish getting ourselves together and bundle into our coats to walk to the sanctuary at 7:15 p.m. The ceremony begins at 7:30, but they've asked graduates, faculty members, and readers to arrive fifteen minutes early.

In the lobby of the sanctuary, Dillon Norway gives the group a quick reminder of how we ran through the program at rehearsal this afternoon. Of course, I didn't have to read then. It was more Dillon Norway saying, *Okay, Cecily, you'll be seated over here, and then I'll introduce you, and once I'm done, I'll invite you up onstage for your reading.* He showed me which set of steps to use, how to adjust the mic and said that there would be a small bottle of water at the podium for each of the readers labeled with our names on them.

So yeah, the jitters are creeping in.

The other two readers and I are told to take our seats—the front pew on the left side has been labeled *Reserved* for us. I walk carefully in my heels, holding my folder. The sanctuary reminds me of a small church—it's wide but only goes back about a dozen rows. The graduates—all nine of them this semester—will be sitting in the front pew on the right side of the stage, and faculty (of which there are about twenty in total) will be seated all across the front pews. Everything else is open season for family members and other guests.

The space is quite full too. Surprisingly, people have traveled far and wide to be here, despite the residual ice on the roads from the storm the other day. It's warmed up several degrees for the occasion, a balmy thirty-five, but at least the ground isn't completely frozen over. There's a camera set up on a tripod in the middle of the aisle, facing the podium, and a small table, chair, and laptop set up in the back, directly behind it.

I try not to fidget, taking care not to bite my nails or do anything else that could appear juvenile. Finally, the music begins to play, and all heads turn to the back of the room. We onlookers stand as "Pomp and Circumstance" floats in the air around us, causing a swell in my chest (not sure why, but it's one of those songs that has that special power), and the faculty members file into the space, led by Dillon Norway, who looks almost regal in his garb. Nate winks at me as he passes by, and it comforts my nerves a little. It's crazy to think how different this residency has been from my last one. This time around, I feel like I am part of this tapestry of humans, and even though I am maybe somewhat of a zoo animal in that I'm married to Nate and I'm the only one here who's in the process of seeking representation for a manuscript that I completed in just one semester, there's beauty in the striving, and I am part of a journey that we are all on as authors and creators.

Graduations are filled with optimism, just like me.

I watch in awe as Dillon Norway invites us all to be seated, then welcomes everyone to the fifteenth annual commencement ceremony of Matthias University's MFA program. He recognizes the dean, acknowledges the graduates, and shares his own musings on the passage of time, growth, and evolution. He evokes spectacular metaphors, and his language is eloquent in a way that mine will never be. In this moment, I feel particularly privileged to be under his tutelage.

He begins to share the details of the Rising Star Program, and I feel my stomach start to clench. He told us the order would go fiction (me), creative nonfiction, and then poetry. So I'm the opening act.

I try to calm my breathing as I listen to his words.

"It's now my pleasure to introduce Cecily Jane Allerton-Ellis, the winner of our Rising Star award in the fiction category. I've worked with her for the past semester and am privileged to do so again this coming semester. Her high energy, laser-beam ambition, and bright enthusiasm to write and learn have—in a very short time—made her one of my role models."

Wow. My breath catches. *That is one of the highest compliments I've ever been paid.*

"I've been very impressed by both the quality and quantity of her work," Dillon Norway continues, "as well as the voluminous research she's undertaken in just the first semester of her MUMFA career to learn as much as possible about book publishing, with an emphasis on finding an agent. She's figured out early in her MFA career what she wants to accomplish and has since worked single-mindedly toward the goal of writing publishable, popular novels. Her goal is not only to become published but to have a lasting career as an author. She wrote an entire novel this past semester, as she has expressed to me that she plans to do each semester for the duration of her participation in MUMFA. Four semesters, four novels. Her work ethic is unparalleled. She writes crisp commercial fiction, fast paced and lively, with memorable characters and situations and surprising but credible plot twists that reveal what those characters are made of. Her first book, *Hard Pass,* is both entertaining and enlightening and would seldom fail to be interesting to the audience she seeks to enthrall." He pauses to take a sip of water.

"Professionally, Cecily is a children's librarian in one of the branches of the Queens Public Library in New York City; that is, she makes a living by encouraging young people to embrace the vast world of literature. Sometimes, acquaintances or new friends are surprised to learn how deeply informed this bouncy, articulate, hyper-organized, unflappably good young woman is about the world and its conflicts, biases, and many problems. It would be difficult to put into words how enjoyable it's been to work with Cecily this past semester and to see her grow as a writer in such a short time."

He smiles before finishing up this, the loveliest speech I've ever heard. "On a personal note, I encouraged Cecily to dip her toes in the vast pool of the literary world and was unsurprised to find that she cannonballed directly into the deep end, where she inadvertently captured the heart of an esteemed PEN Award winner, our own professor Nate Ellis. Their marriage will keep her treading water out there, sustaining the life of an author just by being in one's constant stead as his wife. However, I have no doubt that Cecily will blaze her own trail with the same rigor and fire as Nate, if not more so. Friends, please welcome Cecily Jane Allerton-Ellis."

Applause follows, and I approach the podium. Dillon Norway hands me a certificate, and we take a picture together. Then he takes a seat. I open my folder and clear my throat.

"Good evening, esteemed colleagues. Thank you, Dillon, for such a lovely introduction."

I look out at the sea of faces. My rational brain knows that it's a hundred—maybe a hundred twenty—people out there, but it feels like the whole world is watching me. Just a normal reading, like an open mic or something, would be nerve-racking enough. But this—well, let's just say Dillon Norway isn't *wrong*. I'm definitely an all-in kind of person. Cannonballing into the deep end, as he put it, is kind of my brand.

I remember Nate's advice and seek out his face in the crowd. *Just make sure you read slow enough,* he told me. *When you think the tempo seems right, slow it down even more.* He smiles at me and gives me a little nod.

"This is the prologue of the manuscript I completed this past semester. It was a labor of love that was borne from personal experiences, which I've dramatized because it's fiction, right? So that's what you do." A low rumble of laughs emanates from the audience. "People like to give new writers advice, and I can't tell you how many times I've heard the saying *Write what you know.* I came to this program as my own personal act of defiance. I was giving up on relationships: a revelation—or epiphany, whatever you want to call it—that came to me during my sister's wedding. I finally had the opportunity to write about it, and the entire story spilled out in just one semester. Anyway, the following—which was my Rising Star submission—was a part of it. I hope you like it."

Audience members shift in their seats, bracing themselves for the ride we're about to go on together. They embody an energy that reminds me of story time on my magic carpet at the library. The only difference is these are grown-ups instead of kids, and I'd be hard-pressed to find a beagle puppy around here looking for a leg to relieve itself on.

I breathe. I smile. Here goes nothing.

If there are two things I know: (1) promises and lies go hand in hand, and (2) Ryan Howland looks damn fine in a tux.

He's got the height, the muscles; he's even got the smile for it. If a guy is tall and has broad shoulders, he *should* be able to pull off a tux, but if he lacks that *je ne sais quoi*—you know, that charisma—he might be able to fill out the thing but could still look like a total dork. In fact, tuxedos were created in 1750 in London by a bunch of dorky men with the intention of taking down the good-looking dudes by making them look dorky too.

It's true. Google it.

Okay, fine. It's a lie. But to be fair, you thought about it. You believed it, even if only for a second.

That's because I've been working on my lying skills.

What is *not* a lie is that Ryan Howland can *get it* in a tux. And it's all because of that damn smile.

I'm looking at him looking at me, and all I can hear is Macklemore's "Can't Hold Us," because that's an anthem and a time capsule all rolled up into a prom song. Our prom song, to be clear. *Can we go back?* it asks.

The answer is no, we can't go back. It was one single night, perhaps the most important night in a young girl's life: the night she loses her virginity to her one true love.

It was prom night. And yes, I know that's cliché. But clichés come from true things that happen over and over again in the real world until they become old, tired stories. And believe me,

I would rather have had my first time be a cliché with the right guy than a truly original scenario with the wrong one.

He booked us a hotel room for after. Prom was at the Marriott Marquis in Times Square. It took me four weeks of paychecks from the bookstore to save up for my ticket. I told Ryan he didn't have to pay for mine since he offered to pick up the tab for the room. A big group of us split the cost of the limo too, so I figured that when all was said and done, Ryan probably laid out close to $1,000 for this one special night.

Macklemore's "Can't Hold Us" was the last song of the night. The DJ was shutting it down afterward. The clock was striking midnight on this fairy tale.

I was ready. I bought new panties for the special occasion. A new bra too, but it had to be strapless because of my dress, so it wasn't as fancy as the panties. They matched though. Black, black, everything black, as if my body was preparing for a funeral. The death of my virginity. I should have chosen white, right? White like angels and purity, or maybe red like the devil, but I chose black and found myself hoping it wasn't an omen.

I purchased and packed my own box of condoms because in tenth grade health class, we learned that safe sex is just as much the responsibility of the girl as it is of the guy, and I took copious notes, not just in health but in life. I also brought a toothbrush and toothpaste, a pair of shorts, flip-flops, and a T-shirt for the day after, along with regular underwear (the kind that actually covers stuff), a sports bra, and my hairbrush. I packed light on purpose. Didn't want to get bogged down by too much stuff. I wouldn't need makeup or anything like that the next day anyway, I figured. Once Ryan had me—all of me—we would be closer than ever, I decided. No makeup necessary.

I loved him. And we were graduating in a few weeks, and then a few weeks after that, we'd be off to college. Thankfully, we both planned to be in the Boston area. He'd be at Northeastern on a soccer scholarship, and I would be at Emerson College in their creative writing program. We did that on purpose. Neither one of us wanted to go to a new school in a new state far from home without knowing that the other was close enough to see on the weekends. So when we made our lists, for every D1 soccer program he looked into, I found a school with some sort of writing program within a thirty-mile radius. It's not exactly how I thought "college shopping" would go, but love doesn't always make rational sense.

We waited to have sex. He'd wanted to for a while, and I'll admit, I was curious, but something about sex just felt so final—like once you did it, you did it, and you would become a different person from that point forward—and, I don't know, the fear always outweighed the curiosity. But during that last dance, it was just like Macklemore said: *This is the moment*. No more waiting.

Also, to be fair, I didn't want to start the next chapter of my life without knowing I had experienced everything I was supposed to experience in the current one first. I couldn't imagine that I would ever love someone the way that I loved Ryan, and I didn't think I would want my first time to be with anyone else. I knew it was unlikely that we would end up getting married one day. I wasn't some stupid kid who thought she'd run off into the sunset with her high-school sweetheart. In fact, I think it was because I was smart and forward-thinking that I believed it was the right time for Ryan and me to do it. I loved him, like I said. And I knew he loved me too. If he didn't love me, I don't think he would have waited as long as he did. We were together for over two years. That's not exactly a short amount of time, especially in high school.

We ran in very different crowds. He tried out for varsity soccer as a freshman and snagged a spot on the team. I played flute in the orchestra. He failed his first three English tests and was told he better fix his grades or risk his spot on the team, and his mother, a gorgeous brunette who reportedly competed in the 1984 Summer Olympics as a gymnast, sought him out a tutor. She figured a peer tutor would help him not only academically but socially as well. The guidance office offered me the gig and said I could count it as community service on my college application, so naturally, I said yes.

Mrs. Howland wasn't wrong about the multifaceted value of peer tutoring. Our relationship was professional through Chinua Achebe's *Things Fall Apart*, Toni Morrison's *Beloved*, and a unit on transcendentalism—he thought that Ralph Waldo Emerson and Henry David Thoreau were really cool, and so did I. Transcendentalism gave us opportunities to talk about something other than school gossip or homework assignments. We talked about life, and that made us feel deeper than other kids, whose musings were limited to such trivial issues as who got the lead in the school play or who was spotted holding hands at the mall.

Of course, he still played soccer and I still played the flute, so nothing major changed in our real lives, but by the time we had to read Stephen Chbosky's *The Perks of Being a Wallflower*, we were definitely in the friend zone. By the spring, when we read the ever-controversial novel *The Lovely Bones* by Alice Sebold, I would battle hyperactive butterflies in my stomach every time we got together for tutoring. He had strong feelings about that book, and it was incredible to see him come alive over a piece of literature.

I made that happen. Talk about a high.

Tenth grade meant British literature, so we worked through Mary Shelley's *Frankenstein* in the fall and Jane Austen's *Pride and Prejudice* in the winter. We had our first kiss when he walked me home in late January of that year, after a heated discussion about Charles Dickens's *Great Expectations*, where Ryan insisted that it made sense for Pip to become obsessed with money and social class, while I argued that he had some nerve begging Estella not to marry Bentley Drummle. We debated the whole way to my doorstep, and when we were done, he looked me in the eyes with great expectations of his own—and then he kissed me.

We were together throughout the rest of high school, each new day adding another small piece to the story of Ryan and me. All those little bits blended together to pave the road that led us to the Macklemore moment in the hotel room after prom.

He stood before me and told me I was the most beautiful thing he'd ever seen.

He pulled the zipper down on my dress and said it again once he got a glimpse of me in those fancy panties.

And before anything else happened, Ryan gave me two things: (1) that gorgeous charming smile of his, and (2) a promise ring. "I swear that I will love you forever," he said, slipping it on my finger as if it were a wedding band.

I believed him, and we made love. It stung, and the pressure hurt far too much to be physically enjoyable. But I curled up in his arms when it was over, gazing at the promise ring, while the tuxedo he wore so well lay crumpled on the floor by the window.

You wouldn't believe me if I told you that the next time he wore a tuxedo was at his own wedding just seven years later, at only twenty-five years old. But it's true. Because like I said, here I am, watching him watching me as I walk down the aisle, Macklemore chanting in my ear. Ryan looks better than ever in that tuxedo.

It's the smile though. I'm telling you.

His groomsmen don't pull off their tuxes the way Ryan does.

I can feel him eyeballing me in my dress. It's floor-length, made of satin. I wonder if he's wondering what I've got on underneath.

My bouquet is a stunner. White calla lilies and deep burgundy roses. The kind that might remind you of bloodshed, of deep wounds that never quite heal all the way.

At the altar, I face him for a split second, just long enough to search his face for any traces of regret, and then I offer him my best, most genuine smile, because like I said, I'm working on becoming a better liar.

It's a split second when we face each other. Something unspoken passes between us. I don't know exactly what it is—whether it's regret, apology, or something entirely different—but I carry it with me as I veer to the left to line up alongside the other bridesmaids.

As my sister glides down that same aisle on my father's arm, the "Wedding March" drowns out the Macklemore in my brain.

Daddy lifts her veil and gives her a kiss on the cheek before sitting down in the front row alongside my mother, who daintily dabs at her happy tears.

My sister weaves her fingers into Ryan's, and there they are, just like I said.

Promises and lies.

Hand in hand.

I look up from my pages, surprised to find my heart pounding but no tears. I no longer feel the pain of this story. Nate beams at me, and the smile I offer him springs directly from my heart.

"Thank you," I whisper, and the room explodes in applause as I retreat back to my space in the front pew, exhaling a cleansing breath.

I did it.

My first accolade is now entirely official, and the hard part's over.

As soon as I get back to my room, I will update my query letters.

My phone buzzes. It's my mom. I shake my head silently. Leave it to her to pick the most inconvenient time to call me. I quickly hit the red button to silence it.

Dillon Norway goes back to his role as emcee. He introduces the winner for creative nonfiction next—a woman who is unironically named Hester. She's about two minutes into her reading when my phone vibrates again. This time, it's my parents' home phone number. The buzzing is *loud,* and I feel like it echoes in this space, so I change the phone setting from vibrate to silent.

I'm tempted to text my mom or dad to make sure everything is okay, but the last thing I want to do is be rude to another reader when I just finished my own reading. Talk about poor taste. I slide my phone under my thigh, and I leave it there until the end of the ceremony, which is only about forty-five minutes later.

The rest of the ceremony is really quite poignant. The graduating class has chosen a student speaker and a faculty speaker, both of whom do a wonderful job reminding all of us that the journey of education doesn't end once you graduate. It's one of those few moments in life when the whole world seems shiny and new, just waiting for you to step out into it like a fresh pair of sneakers. I'm a sucker for this kind of stuff. I love being here, in the world of academia, absorbing information like a sponge, shaping my future. I can't imagine how overcome with emotion I'll feel when it's my turn to wear the flat square hat and the polyester gown.

When everything is said and done, I've choked back tears twice. The graduates disband to find their guests, and I stand up and check my phone.

Holy shit. I've missed five calls and three FaceTimes, all from my family.

My stomach drops, like in that way that it would if you were preparing for your worst nightmare. My mind spirals. *Dad's been killed. They're getting a divorce. Something happened to one of the babies.*

The back of the sanctuary is crowded, between graduates and their families and students trying to file out. The faculty and Dillon Norway are all still toward the front of the room; I guess they're seasoned enough to know that it will take a few minutes to clear out, especially in the dead of winter. Nate approaches me as I type out a quick text. What's up? Is everything okay?

Immediately, a FaceTime call comes in. "Fuck," I mutter under my breath. I turn to Nate. "I have to take it. Something's wrong, but I don't know what."

He nods, but concern weighs down his brow.

"I'll be right out there," I explain, jutting my chin out at the corridor just outside the sanctuary. There are people everywhere, but at least back there, folks are on their way out. I squeeze my way past a family with a baby and a couple walking an elderly woman toward the exit. "Excuse me," I mumble, trying to avoid being rude. The phone in my hand shines with the light of urgency.

I swipe at it, trying to huddle as far away from the grads and guests as possible.

"Cecily?" my mom says. Her face is red, splotchy, and definitely not right. *Has she been crying?*

"Hey, Mom," I say in a hushed tone. "You okay? What's up?"

"I can't believe—"

The phone—theirs, not mine, drops to the ground with a thud.

"Cecily Jane, are you there?" This from my father, whose voice booms extra loud in the reverberation of the cold corridor. Out of the corner of my eye, I see Nate approaching behind me.

"Shh, Dad," I say, because his yelling is causing an echo to bounce off the walls in the cavernous space, and several guests have just turned to look my way. I smile and wave at them weakly in an attempt to show them everything's just fine. *Nothing to see here, folks.*

"Don't you dare shush me, young lady!" he hollers. "Your mother is devastated. How could you *marry* someone and *not tell us?*"

My heart stops, and the moment plays out in slow motion. I look up at Nate, who is now just steps shy of being at my side. He looks at me, horrified. My eyes pop out of my head like a cartoon character, and a faculty lineup that includes Dillon Norway and Alice Devereaux walks through the entryway into the corridor at that exact moment, turning their heads to see what the ruckus is all about. Then, before I can even think to hang up the call, my mother grabs the phone back from my father and screeches, "We heard *all* about it on the livestream, Cecily. You married someone without even telling us, and then you went on to start a smear campaign against your sister and Bryce! My God, Cecily! What the hell is the matter with you?"

"I, um—" I stammer, but nothing else comes out, because all I see is Dillon Norway's eyebrows knit into one, punctuated by a deep crease between his eyes that looks like a stab wound. Beside him, Alice

Devereaux's face does the exact opposite thing, her expression slowly growing jovial at my public scolding. "Mom, I can explain."

I turn, but since I am literally in the corner already, there is nowhere else to go. I can feel Nate behind me, though my camera shows that he is still out of view.

"Do I even want to hear this? Those things you said about your sister—they were abhorrent!"

"I didn't really say anything bad about her other than the fact that she married my first love," I rebut. This is a knee-jerk reaction. An attempt to calm her down.

But naturally it has the opposite effect. My mother clasps her hand over her mouth, and tears spill down her face. My father verbally rushes to her aid, clarifying her prior statement. "I believe it's not *what* you said as much as *how* you said it."

A lump forms in my throat, and I can't speak. My mother wipes her eyes hastily, leaving black lines of mascara that run from her cheekbones to her jawline like skid marks on a highway after a truck blows a tire and careens through the guard rail.

"You married some literary professor—some author—and didn't even think to invite your own parents to your wedding?" she yells at me. "Why, Cecily? What is wrong with you? Why would you keep that from us? Do you hate us all so much? We've never done anything but love you and support you!"

Have you ever had one of those out-of-body experiences where you feel like your life is happening *to* you, and you're just a spectator, watching from the sidelines as if it's happening to somebody else? I feel myself crying. I know tears are bouncing off my cheeks. One hits my chest. The next one splashes on my folder. Everyone is watching me. I can't see them, but I can *feel* them, and I can hear their low murmurs. The din has quieted some, but I know it's not because people have left. I am the modern-day equivalent of a circus freak show. Trapped like a feral wildebeest here in the corner of the corridor. Nowhere to go.

Before I can compose a response, Nate reaches over my shoulder and snatches the phone away from me. He looks into the screen at my mother. Just seeing his unfamiliar face quiets her down.

"Mrs. Allerton," he says, voice composed. "I'm Nate Ellis. It's nice to meet you, although I would have hoped this would happen under very different circumstances. Now, before you say anything else, I'll ask you to please just hear me out. First of all, CJ's writing is incredible. But it's also fiction. Fiction is creative, and many authors use it as a way to process trauma. CJ is not the type of woman to slander her family. However, she is deeply loyal, and once upon a time, Bryce broke her heart, whether you want to hear that or not. What he and Jamie did to her caused no small amount of damage. She used the therapy of writing to move beyond the pain."

Because I've turned around, I can confirm that everyone is watching now—most notably Dillon Norway and Alice Devereaux. I want to steal the phone back from Nate, but he's walked several steps away from me, and my knees are too weak and frozen to make any moves.

"You're that young man from the TV," my mom says.

"Please, let me finish," Nate interrupts. "You have no idea how much your daughter loves you and your family, Mrs. Allerton. She loves you all so much that she held that hurt inside and put Jamie ahead of herself. She came to Matthias so she could start a new chapter in her life, but you can't start a new chapter until you finish the one before it. That's all CJ was trying to do. She was just trying to move on."

No response from my mother.

"As for us," Nate continues. "I would do anything for your daughter. She's a fabulous author with an incredibly bright future, but more than that, she's an incredible person. And I'm pretty sure that I'm in love with her," he says, turning to look at me.

Those words pierce my soul, and I feel my face twist up hearing them come out of his mouth. Shock continues to paralyze my vocal cords. My hands move to wipe the tears from my cheeks.

"And I'm going to lose my job for this, but I can't risk her losing her family for me."

Whoa. No. No, no, no. I snap out of it. "Nate, stop," I say.

He waves me away. "Yes, we're married, but none of it is real," he says.

"Nate! Stop it!" I say again, significantly louder. I lunge at him and try to grab the phone away, but he spins away from me and keeps. Running. His. Mouth.

"It was all a misunderstanding. She married me to save my job after that stupid *Tonight Show* bit. But it was a sham wedding. Legally, it was real, but emotionally, it was fake, all of it. I'm a professor and she's a student, and because we kissed and people found out, the only way for me not to get tossed out on my ass was for us to get married. A marriage of convenience, you understand? She would never walk down the aisle for real without her family there. You have to know that. She's not that person, Mrs. Allerton."

"Goddammit, Nate! Shut up!" I yell. I step toward him again, and this time, I grab the phone successfully. "Mom, I'll call you back." I end the FaceTime, my phone stuck on a picture of my mother in a state of ultimate confusion before reverting back to Blinky, my betta fish from work, who also happens to be my wallpaper. I grab Nate by the wrist and drag him directly into what remains of the crowd, past a visibly agitated Dillon Norway, nearly knocking down several people as I barrel through, pushing my way out the main doors and into the cold.

I drag him several steps toward the parking lot, in the opposite direction of the festivities. "Why would you *do* that?" I scream. The cold night wind howls through the trees as if agreeing with me.

"Do what? I was looking out for you!"

"I could have handled my mother, Nate! You didn't have to butt in!"

"But you weren't handling anything, CJ. You froze. She was screaming at you, and you froze. And to be quite honest, I don't know why you're angry with me!"

"You *outed* us!"

"I didn't out *you*. I outed *myself*. It was never *you* anybody took issue with. It was always me."

"That was totally unnecessary! You ran off at the mouth, and in, like, the *most* public setting possible."

"You *took the call*, CJ! You opened up the can of worms, not me!" He's getting frantic, and it turns my stomach.

Several graduates and their families exit the building, huddled together like a pack of penguins in the chilly air. "Come on. Let's go up to our room. We can't talk here," I say.

"Not so fast," a voice says. We turn in its direction. Alice Devereaux stands several feet away, her arms crossed over her chest, wearing a smirk that looks nothing short of evil. "I *knew* it, Mr. Ellis. I knew you were full of it."

"Please. Not now, Alice," he says, waving her off.

"Oh, yes. *Absolutely* now." She grins. "So what was it? You began cavorting with a student and then bribed her to marry you in order to keep your job? Was it some kind of gag order? Blackmail?" She rubs her hands together. In her graduation robe, she looks like a witch. The tone of voice she's using isn't helping her cause any.

"Professor Devereaux," I say. "Please—"

"No more out of you," she chides me. "You're not the only one who is capable of faking things around here, you know. I had a strong inkling that your relationship wasn't real as soon as I read that piece of yours prior to coming to the island. No one in her right mind could possibly *marry* someone when they're hung up on an ex-lover like that."

I still. I don't like the tone she's using. My face contorts. "I thought you said my writing was good."

"Oh, it's excellent, dear," she seethes. "Very, very convincing."

"I didn't bribe anyone, Alice," Nate says. "CJ and I are a married couple. We have the license to prove it."

"He's right," I say, standing up straighter. "It's true. It's on file with Human Resources."

"That may well be, but you just admitted to the wedding being a sham. Not to mention the fact that on your first day here, I could hear the two of you through the remarkably thin wall separating my bedroom from yours."

"What are you talking about?" I ask.

"You'd both just arrived and were discussing what to do about sleeping arrangements. This was an issue for you because—in your very words, Cecily—you were 'living a sham life in a marriage of convenience.'" Her air quotes stab me in the throat.

I'm stunned into silence. Another group of graduation attendees slips past us, too cold to stop and watch the horror show unfold here in the middle of the walkway.

"I'm not sure what you *thought* you heard," Nate says.

"Please, Mr. Ellis. That's enough. I was lying in my bed, reading. You came hurtling in like two bulls in a china shop. I heard it all. I just needed to find a way to expose you."

"*Expose* us?" I ask.

"Oh, Cecily. It's sad because you really are so naïve," she says. "But I'm sure you've heard of the phrase, *Keep your friends close and your enemies closer?*"

I nod. "But why would I be your enemy?" I ask earnestly. "I never did anything to you."

"Not you. *Him.*"

"Alice," Nate sighs, exasperated. "You've had beef with me since last summer, and I've got to be honest with you, it's a little bit tired. You need to get over yourself and move the fuck on. You're a grown-ass woman. Please behave like one."

She huffs. "Excuse me, Nate. Get over *myself*? How about you get over *yourself*? You sauntered into this program like the goddamn cat's meow, but you're just a fraud, is all that you are. I knew it from the moment they signed you."

"You know nothing about how I got this job."

"Not *Matthias*, you moron. I'm talking about *Boone*."

"Boone? My publisher?"

"Yes, *Boone*, you reckless twit! They signed your stupid book just two weeks before I submitted the manuscript that would have changed my life—and then they told me, *We're so sorry, Alice. We just signed an author whose work has* similar themes. *You'll have to submit something else.* And then your asinine story *took off* because of lucky timing? Only a narcissistic bastard would find a way to turn a pandemic that was killing thousands of innocent people into a *payday*."

The vitriol spits out of her like dragon fire.

Nate nods, his eyes squinting as the puzzle pieces come together. "That's what your book was about. That book you made your students read."

"Well, I had to write something, and *write what you know*, that's what they say. So I knew that it wouldn't be hard to tell a story about a working author who gets bumped by a lucky debut. *That,* I was told, they could publish. They even said I was 'clever' for making lemonade out of the rotten lemons you left me with. Dan finally agreed to publish my original manuscript four years later, after your season had long come and gone. It came out last spring, and though it didn't have quite as much relevance by that point, it still held its own."

"But none of that was my fault. You do realize that, right?" Nate asks.

"And then you show up here, in *my* house, with your dumbass charm and your stupid PEN Award, and everyone falls at your feet while you pour a lovely combination of ignorance and salt right into my wounds."

"I didn't even know who you were," Nate says.

"*Exactly*," Devereaux seethes. "If you had any sense, you would have done your homework and realized that authors do best when they stay in their respective lanes."

"So you set out to—what? Hurt me?"

"I didn't have to try very hard. You dug yourself a fine little hole when you kissed a student on television. All I had to do was chase down that lead."

"You were the one who told Dillon Norway about us," I say. The revelation hits me like a tidal wave.

She smiles, and it's quite reminiscent of what might happen if the Joker from *Batman* crossed with Pennywise from *It*. "I thought for sure I'd be rid of you, Mr. Ellis. But no. You couldn't leave well enough alone. You lied your way back into the heart of Professor Norway, who thought it best to give you a second chance." She laughs. "Only you blew it, not an hour into your time on the island. Fighting about the sleeping arrangements like a bunch of teenagers. You made it all so *easy* for me."

"What does that mean?" I ask.

"You, my dear, are very gullible. One little presentation convinced you that social media was a must. One simple compliment, and you signed up for the Rising Star Program. All I had to do was livestream the graduation and get your family to tune in, and the house of cards crumbled in on itself, now didn't it?"

My heart is racing. The cold air constricts my blood vessels, and I feel a scream rise in my throat. I swallow it down.

"Get her *family* to tune in?" Nate shouts. "What right do you have to speak to her *family*?"

"Well," Devereaux smiles. "Once I saw Dillon's speech in the graduation file, I had no choice. It all happened so *organically*. He felt it necessary to mention your nuptials, which meant I didn't even *have* to find a way to weave that into the comments feed in the livestream. All I had to do was DM your mother and invite her, Cecily. Lovely woman," she smirks.

I'm about to clap back when I see Dillon Norway exit the main doors of the sanctuary. He walks toward us. "You two," he says, looking at me and Nate. "I want to see you right now. Meet me in the library of the main house in five minutes."

"Dillon, she needs to come too," Nate argues, pointing at Alice Devereaux.

Dillon Norway looks at Nate, then at Alice, and back at Nate again. "That won't be necessary," he says. He pulls up the collar on his coat and walks away.

Nate turns back to Devereaux. "You are the ugliest human soul I've ever met. To go after an innocent student like that—"

"Ha!" she cries. "Pot? Meet kettle."

"You're disgusting," he continues. "And you'll get yours. Maybe not today, and maybe not even from me. You know what they say."

"Hell hath no fury?" she snickers.

"Karma's a bitch," Nate corrects her.

He turns to me. "Let's go," he says as the snowflakes gently begin to fall from the ever-darkening pink night sky.

CHAPTER 16

Nate

When we enter the room, he is seated at the head of the dining room table that doubles as a conference space. We are holding hands, even though she's mad at me. She didn't speak a single word to me on the way here—not that it's a long walk—but I tried to apologize, and she just looked straight ahead. I grabbed her hand on the way into the room and was happy she didn't pull away from me. It's like we represent a unified front, even if CJ is quite possibly not speaking to me at this particular moment.

"Sit down," Dillon says. It's not his usual welcoming, almost soft voice. This is a command.

We sit. She takes her hand away from me and places it in her lap, bracing herself for a stern talking-to, like a child about to be grounded.

"Before you start, Dillon—"

"No," he cuts me off. "Not this time. *I* talk first."

I stop. I feel the admonishment in my chest, its growing presence a bubble of unwanted pressure atop my rib cage.

"I don't know what kind of ridiculous little stunt you thought you were pulling, but the charade is over now. You're lying to everyone evidently, to Cecily's parents, to the faculty and students here at Matthias, but I will be *damned* if you're going to lie to me for even one more second. Now, Nate, you're going to remain silent, and, Cecily, you are going to tell me exactly what is going on here."

She looks at her lap, takes a shaky breath, and I do everything in my power to do as I'm told.

"First of all," CJ begins, "I—*we*—are sorry. Like, more than you can possibly imagine. The truth is that back in November, after I finished my manuscript, you told me to get out there and experience the literary scene, and I found a reading that Nate was doing in the city and decided to go to it. I was nervous because I was by myself, so I drank some wine, and I really don't drink, you know? As a result, I got a little buzzed or whatever. Maybe more than just a little bit. Anyway, Nate tried to sober me up, and I dragged him to the karaoke bar and made him sing with me, and we didn't know that Questlove was there or that he was going to kazoo bomb our song, and I was stupid and got all caught up in the moment, and I kissed Nate. Me. Rewatch the footage. You'll see it's very obvious that I threw myself at him. Only then, when *you* found out, he thought he was going to lose his job, so he read through the HR manual and showed me the rules about student-teacher relations, and it basically said that he would be able to keep his job if we were married. So we got married. It was all my idea. I had to beg him to do it, because I didn't want to lose the only friend I had here."

She power breathes. The room becomes so still that I can feel the weight of the silence like concrete blocks tied to my shoes as I go for a leisurely dive off the edge of a cruise ship.

Dillon taps his fingers together and then cracks the knuckles on his right hand. "So all that business about having met before the pandemic and not wanting to miss out on the chance to be together a second time—all of that was a lie?"

She nods. Her face reminds me of how a puppy might look if it just got caught taking a shit in its owner's shoe. "I'm sorry."

"You both just worked out a story and figured I would be dumb enough to buy it."

"Nobody thinks that. I think the world of you, just for the record. But yes, we lied to you. It was the only way for him to have a fighting chance at keeping his job. The whole thing was just a misunderstanding that was all my fault."

"Cecily," Dillon says, tenting his fingertips and placing them in the crease between his eyes while he takes a deep breath. "What is it about me that appears so unreasonable? What makes you think I wouldn't have understood if you just told me the truth?"

"I, um…"

"I have a daughter, you know. She's about your age in fact. We all make mistakes, and I am not some kind of monster who can't understand that sometimes we don't think things through in the moment."

"I don't know what to say," CJ murmurs.

"You'd worked with me for months to that point. I could see how much it pained you to write the manuscript you submitted, and you told me that it was based on true events. I believed you, and I felt for you, and because of that, I was willing to go the extra mile for you as your mentor, because I believed that you were special—that your *writing* was special, and that you were telling a story that you needed to tell in order to seek out your own catharsis. That's why it came as such a shock to me when all of a sudden, you and Nate were kissing on TV, and I was hearing about it from Alice."

She nods, and I follow suit.

"But you lied to me, Cecily. I gave you a safe space to take your truth and turn it into something beautiful, and you took advantage of me. You lied right to my face." He shakes his head in a slow, somber rhythm.

She begins to cry.

"Don't," Dillon says, his voice firmer now. "I will not have you manipulate me twice. You've both done a fine job of convincing me, and I would guess almost everyone else here, that you two are, in fact, a couple. I've seen you holding hands, canoodling. I can't believe the lengths you would go to in order to play me like a fiddle. I'm very disappointed in you, but I'm also unbearably angry. What you did was wrong, and you made me look like a fool. I run this program, and I went to bat for you both. I had to present your case to the dean. You two were so selfish and juvenile that you thought you could just trick us all. Well, game over."

I can't not say something. "It wasn't CJ's idea," I say.

"*More* lies?" he snaps at me. "She just said it was all her idea; now you're saying it wasn't? Would you like me to leave the room so that you two can conspire before you make up your next statement?"

"What I'm trying to say is *yes*, we lied, and *yes*, of course we're sorry, but somewhere along the way, I want you to know that we fell in love—"

"Save it, Nate," he says, slamming his hand down on the table, startling CJ. "That is quite enough."

CJ begins to cry harder.

"You've made the rest of this very easy for me. Effective immediately, you're both terminated from the program."

"What?" she squeals.

"You can't be serious, Dillon," I say.

"You heard me. We're done here. Now, please go."

CJ covers her face with her hands, sobs shaking her whole body.

"Dillon, please don't do this," I beg.

"My mind is made up. Now *go*, before I have to call security to get you out of my sight. I want you both on the first ferry out of here tomorrow morning. Nate, HR will be in touch with you regarding your final paycheck. Cecily, I'll have the bursar contact you about whatever payments you've made for the semester."

She sniffles through her weeping and manages to say, "I have a scholarship."

"Not to Matthias. Not anymore, you don't."

"Dillon!" I yell. "This isn't her fault. You want to get rid of someone? Get rid of me. But leave Cecily out of this. She worships you, Dillon. She thinks the fucking world of you. Please don't do this."

"I'm sorry," CJ says. The makeup is smearing down her face, and she takes off her glasses so that she can swipe at it with the back of her hand. She looks like she's melting, dissolving right in front of me, and it breaks me to know that I am powerless to stop it.

"So am I," Dillon says. "This conversation is over." He pushes back his chair, stands up, and makes for the door. He stops before exiting the room and says, "You've got what it takes, Cecily. I meant every word of what I said in my introduction of you tonight. But I can't let you make an ass of me. You made your bed. And now, the two of you can lie in it."

He turns away from us before I can think of anything else to say.

Once he's gone, I look at CJ, searching her face for something, although I'm not sure what. *Poor girl. She's a total fucking mess.* She won't look at me though.

"Hey," I whisper.

Nothing.

"Sweetheart. Please look at me."

Still nothing. She stares up at the spot where the wall meets the ceiling, far away from my line of sight. Tears continue to stream down her face.

"Come on. Let's get upstairs," I suggest.

She doesn't speak to me. Her jaw is set, eyes glassy. I stand, and she follows. I don't know what she's feeling, but here in the library, while a grad party begins to roar just feet away from us, it's not the proper time or place for the conversation—that much I *do* know. The nerves in my digestive system grip me, threatening to take me hostage. *I did this. This is my fault.*

I fucked everything up.

Once we're upstairs, she heads straight for the bathroom and shuts the door behind her. I sit on the edge of our bed and replay the last hour of events over in my head.

I should never have talked to her parents.

She should never have picked up the phone.

My blood pressure rises.

Fuck.

My job.

I lost my job. After all we went through to save it, I lost my fucking job.

"Hey, CJ?" I call out.

And CJ—the smartest, most hardworking girl I've ever met—just got kicked out of grad school.

What the actual fuck?

I hear the water running. I stand and go over to the bathroom door. I try the knob. It's locked.

"CJ?" I say, louder this time.

She's mad at me.

Not mad—furious.

I just didn't want her parents and her sister to be upset with her.

But no—I was wrong. I shouldn't have touched her phone. I should have let her handle it.

"CJ?" I try once more, just a little louder, in case she couldn't hear me the last two times.

Silence.

"Please leave me alone," she says. Her voice is steady but quiet. She's not yelling. She's just stating her request, matter-of-factly, as if she just asked me to get her a sandwich.

I'm not sure why, but the words sting me worse than everything Dillon said to us downstairs.

My stomach bottoms out, and I fear I might be sick. "Are you sure that's what you want?" I ask through the door. My heart is pounding. *Pounding.*

"If you care about me at all, please, Nate, just give me some space."

The weight of her words crushes my lungs. Suddenly, my body begins moving on autopilot.

I should pack, my brain decides, pulling my luggage out of the closet.

My ears hear her slide open the bathtub curtain and then pull it closed again.

I can't believe this is really happening. I toss the clothes out of my three drawers and into the bag.

I can't stay here, I tell myself. *She said she needs space.*

I look down at my hands. I'm shaking. I rub them on my thighs to get them to stop.

What is this feeling?

Suddenly, I'm overwhelmed by a fury that rolls over me like a snowball down a hill, picking up speed and momentum and gaining in size and strength with each passing second.

I want to put my fist through the bathroom door.

Nothing feels real or right or rational, and the room begins to spin.

I need to go.

Now.

I punch at my phone screen with my thumbs. The nearest Uber is seven minutes away. It takes me less than three minutes to put all my shit in my bag. I don't even bother with the stuff in the bathroom. I'll just buy new stuff when I get home. I put on my coat and take one last look at the room before I go.

I guess not all fairy tales end with a happily-ever-after.

I toss my key on the bed and shut the door quietly behind me.

I don't even say goodbye.

Four minutes later, I'm in a car in the darkness.

Giving her space.

CHAPTER 17

Cecily

I let the shower steam soak into my pores. The firm spray courses into my hair and runs down my back, my legs, and into the drain.

I want to wash this day off me. There's so much to process.

Kicked out of school. If this were a yearbook superlative, I would be the one voted *least likely* to ever have this happen.

It's not who I am.

I follow rules. I study. I work hard.

And I don't fail well.

Case in point: Bryce and Jamie. I know in my rational brain that what happened with them was a timing thing, in much the same way that Alice Devereaux and Nate experienced their "similar themes" issue at Boone. Right place, right time. Or maybe wrong place, wrong time— depending on who you are in the story. In the case of Bryce and Jamie, he was in a bad emotional place, she was a familiar face, and whatever happened after that happened. When Jamie asked me—and to be fair, she *did* ask me first—of course it felt like a major blow to my self-esteem. So I started writing about it. Writing seemed like a safe space to take those feelings. It didn't help that the online dating scene is a cruel manifestation of every reality show that's ever existed. (*Love Island? Double Shot at Love with DJ Pauly D and Vinny?* Or, perhaps my all-time favorite,

Love Is Blind?) There was no way to manifest winning at love out there in cyber-hell.

So I redefined the idea of winning by pursuing the only thing that was making me feel better: words, arranged into sentences, crafted into paragraphs, and woven into stories about girls who don't *need* love in order to live a fulfilling life.

I thought I was one of *those* girls.

Now, I'm not so sure.

I'm mad at Nate. Like, really mad. If he had just kept his mouth shut, I wouldn't have any of these issues. I could have talked my way out of the public FaceTime debacle with a few swift lies and a phone call to my family later on to clarify everything.

Probably.

It didn't have to go this way.

Now, everything we worked for is gone—poof! Out the window like an accidentally erased Microsoft Word document. And for all the *let's snag an agent by adding accolades to my query letter* business, now I'll have even *less* to report on those letters. What am I going to write? *Dear Agent, I was in an MFA program, but I got released after defrauding the program's director. Please sign me though, because my writing's hella strong.* I don't think so.

I'm royally fucked.

It doesn't help that I'm not much of a fighter. Lots of people enjoy a good fight; they like to prove their points and *be right*. But I've always been of the mindset that it's more important to be happy than it is to be right, so I just don't fight with people. I'm an introvert at heart. I don't like to scream and yell my feelings out there to the whole world. Plus, people don't fight fair. They're not genuinely listening to what points you make or what you have to say. In my experience, anything that looks like listening is actually just your opponent grimacing while internally constructing their rebuttal. Some people may find it annoying, but when life gives me lemons, I just ask the lemons to please leave me alone until I can figure out what to do with them. Which is what I am doing with Nate for the moment.

I hear him close the door behind him, and I am grateful for the lack of drama with which he leaves the room. I'm not sure where he'll go—Nate and I have never fought before, so I don't know what his standard operating procedure is for arguments—but I figure maybe he's headed to one of the rooms downstairs to sit and read, or maybe he'll grab a drink at the party (or even from the kitchen staff, who all seem to find him pretty charming) and try to talk Dillon Norway into reducing our sentence. I don't know what his plans are, but it's nice not to have this already embarrassing situation get even worse with the two of us engaging in a useless shouting match.

It's tempting to make a list like I normally would, but right now I know the first thing I need to do is clear the air with my parents.

I wash my hair, and I give myself a much-needed scalp massage, then rinse all the suds off my body and wrap myself up in the towel hanging off the back of the bathroom door. My eyes peruse the shelf of split toiletries and notice our toothbrushes, side by side. Crazy to think that just six months ago, Nate was just a professor at my school, a presumably arrogant award-winning author whose weak stomach would likely never see another lobster again.

Man, how things change.

I dry off, pull on a pair of sweatpants and a T-shirt, and wrap my hair in the towel. Then I park myself at the little desk and brace myself as I swipe through my phone, FaceTiming my mom.

Her tear-streaked face appears on the screen.

"Hey, Mom."

"Hi, Cecily," she replies.

"I owe you an explanation. Where's Dad?" I ask.

"He's right here." My mother shifts the camera angle so that I can see them both.

"Are Jamie and Bryce there too?"

"They're downstairs. Should we get them?"

"Please don't. At least not yet. Did Jamie see the livestream?"

Mom nods.

I exhale, making a mental note to call her next. "Is she okay?"

She shakes her head. "No, she's not."

"That's fair. Don't worry—I'll talk to her."

"She's very pregnant, Cecily," Mom reminds me. "Be kind to her. She's fragile."

"I know."

"So you want to explain," my dad chimes in. "Go ahead. We're listening."

"The man you spoke to—that's Nate Ellis."

"I didn't like how he called you CJ. Your name is beautiful," Mom says.

"He's the author?" Dad asks.

"Yes. He's actually pretty famous." I gulp. "In addition to being an author, he's a professor at my school. Well, *was.* Anyway, remember at Thanksgiving, the whole *Tonight Show* thing?"

My parents nod in unison.

"So I had been drinking that night. We didn't know Questlove would be at the karaoke bar. Needless to say, I screwed up and kissed Nate in a moment of stupidity, and everything just spiraled form there. He was at risk of losing his job as a result of me being an ass, and I didn't want that to happen, so I married him because the university rules said that student-teacher relationships are only okay if the student and teacher are married."

"That's ludicrous," my father says.

"Which part?" I ask for clarification. "The student-teacher part?"

"No. The fact that you decided to *marry* him over a childish indiscretion."

"Well, I hate to break it to you, Dad, but it's not like I was out there killing it in the dating world. Nate was one of the only people in grad school who was nice to me. I'm sorry, but a little bit of kindness goes a long way with me."

"So you actually tied the knot—like, legally," my mother says. It's not a question. It's a statement.

"Yes. At the county clerk's office. Right after Thanksgiving. And everything was going fine. We were just friends, well, until this past week."

"Meaning?" asks Mom.

I sigh. "We came to the residency, and we had to, you know, *fake* being a married couple. They put us in a room together, and let's just say one thing led to another. And now we're—I don't even know what you'd call it. Dating, I guess."

Mom shakes her head, her expression pained with confusion and, I'm guessing, disappointment. "That's backward. So what's your plan now? Just stay married to this man?"

"Well, we can technically have the marriage annulled up to five years after the date of the license. There are rules about that. If it was an arranged marriage or in any way a sham, you're allowed to annul it. So we wouldn't even have to get a divorce. At least I'm pretty sure that's how it works."

"What about when you actually *do* decide to settle down?" Mom asks. "It's not exactly a desirable trait, having been married before."

"Mom, I'm chock-full of undesirable traits. I'm too ambitious, too driven, too nerdy or bookish or whatever you call it; I'm just too extra all around. I would hope that, if I ever do get married, all those things would be reasons why my future husband would want to be with me in the first place, and because of that, he would understand once he knew the whole story. But I don't think I'll ever get married for real. The dating world sucks. Nate's the first guy who I've had any sort of real relationship with since back when I was with Bryce."

"That's ironic, considering the fact that the relationship is actually *not* real, according to what you just explained," Dad clarifies.

"No. It—what we have now—*is* real. It just started under false pretenses," I correct him.

At least I think it's real.

"And so what about the Bryce thing?" Mom asks. "Why did you say all those awful things? You gave Jamie your blessing to be with him. It's unfair to go back on that now. Don't you want *her* to be happy?"

"Listen, Mom. I love Jamie. She's my sister, and of course I want her to be happy. But when she and Bryce first got together, they put me between a rock and a hard place. You can see that, can't you? This boy who I used to be very much in love with decided to date—then marry, then impregnate with a fleet of babies—my sister? Even if years had passed, don't you see how hurtful that could still be?"

My mom sighs. "I guess. But why didn't you say anything back then?"

"Because I didn't want to stand in the way of Jamie being happy. And it wasn't like they were parading it around in front of me. They were miles away in a different state, and since I never had social media—you know, until a few days ago—I didn't have to see any of the pictures they were posting or any of that other early-relationship shove-it-in-your-face kind of stuff. So I wrote about it. And that really helped. And look, my writing was praised to the point where I won an award for it. I never once used his name or hers for that matter. In fact, the only people who will ever know the story is about Jamie, Bryce, and me are those of us who were involved in it directly."

Mom winces. "I didn't know they hurt you, Cecily. I really thought you were over him and had moved on. I'm sorry."

I shrug. "I *am* human."

She rubs her forehead. "I just want all my girls to be happy."

"Can I be honest?" I ask.

"Of course."

I inhale, willing myself to be bold enough to say this thing that's weighed so heavily on me since high school. "You never made me feel like you truly wanted me to be happy. I always felt like all you wanted was for me to become a wife and mother and that unless I achieved those particular milestones, I would always be a disappointment to you."

Her face twists up.

"I'm not trying to hurt you, Mom," I continue. "I'm just telling you how I felt."

She takes a breath and bites her lip, nodding slightly. After an awkward pause, she finally speaks. "I never meant to do that to you, honey."

"But you see it, right? All the excitement you'd pour into Anna, Melanie, and Jamie—their weddings, their pregnancies, their kids? How could I ever really be enough for you if I didn't bring those critical pieces to the table? Like, if all I did was get a good job that I liked and that made me happy, how could that possibly make you proud of me?"

"Sweetheart, I've always been proud of you."

Tears spring to my eyes. "Not as proud as you are of them."

"Oh, Cecily." She rubs her forehead, losing herself in thought. "Did you know that when I was a girl, I wanted to be a veterinarian?"

"What?" I try to think back. *Did she ever tell me that?* I shake my head. "I don't think you ever said anything about that."

"Well, I did. I loved animals. But my parents—your grandparents—drilled it into your aunts and me that our job was to find husbands. It was definitely a different time back then, but I remember being sad about not being able to go to college. I thought I was doing better by my girls by making sure you all got the chance to go to college and study whatever made you happy."

"But a degree is only good if you *use* it. Anna wanted to be an architect. Melanie wanted to produce music. Jamie wanted to be a trainer. Now all they do is raise kids."

"Yes, but, Cecily, they can always go back later and pursue those dreams when their babies are grown up enough not to need them anymore."

"It will be too late then," I argue.

"You don't know that. All I wanted was for you and your sisters to have options. But I'm still the product of my upbringing, and I have three sisters of my own who all were raised the same way. Family first. Kids, holidays, a happy and safe home—that was the job we were raised to do. I'm sorry if I ever made you feel like you weren't enough. I just tried to do better for you girls than my parents did for me."

I let that sink in. It definitely offers a different perspective. I wipe my cheeks.

"I love you, Cecily. I always wanted you to be happy."

I nod. "I love you too."

"And you're happy, right? With the writing and the library?"

My lips form an involuntary smile. "I am."

"Then that's all I could ever ask for."

Huh. It's a revelation, and I'm overwhelmed by a feeling I can't quite describe. But before I can put my finger on it, she continues.

"So you and Nate are dating?"

"We're in a fight at the moment, but yes."

"That's kind of funny, if you think about it."

"What is?"

"You're dating your husband."

"Oh, that. Yeah, I know," I say. "We've joked about it too."

"Are you happy?" Mom asks.

"He's good to you, this Nate guy?" Dad piles on.

"Yes," I say. "Everything is fine." This is obviously a lie, but it appears I've successfully smoothed things over with my parents, so I don't think it's necessary to mention the fact that I've just been booted out of school.

I'm able to wrap it up, and then I make another FaceTime call and have a very similar conversation with my sister, who apologizes profusely.

"I never would have dated him if I knew you were still in love with him!" she gushes.

"I wasn't still in love with him," I explain. "I just felt like it was against girl code, but I love you, and you were so excited, so how could I tell you not to be with him?"

She then cries for about forty-five minutes straight on account of extreme pregnancy hormones. I spend the bulk of our chat calming her down, so that's fun. It's only before I end our call, as I'm pacing the room, that I realize that Nate's dirty laundry bag is gone.

His toiletries are still there, I remember.

But then I check the drawers, and all his clothes are gone too. I check the closet, and so is his suitcase. I hang up the phone with my sister and I call Nate. Straight to voicemail.

Okay. Hm. I'm tempted to panic, but my rational brain comes to the rescue.

I check the time. It's after nine. *He probably just found another room to crash in for the night. Isn't that what married couples do? A husband and wife get in a fight, and the husband sleeps on the couch.*

This is the equivalent of Nate sleeping on the couch.

Maybe he's in one of those awful rooms in the North Wind. God, I hope not, for his sake. But this is on me. I told him to leave me alone, and he respectfully did exactly that. So okay. Don't double down on the crazy,

Cecily. Just take a break from each other for the night. It doesn't need to be a huge deal.

A thought hits my chest: *What if he left the island?*

Nope. He couldn't have left. There's no public transportation off the island after 6:00 p.m. in the winter, unless you're airlifted by an emergency medical helicopter, I remind myself.

We'll reconvene in the morning. If we have to be on the first ferry out of here, that would be the one to Point Judith that leaves at 8:00 a.m. So I'll see him on the 7:30 shuttle van.

It's fine, I decide. *Remain calm.*

Everything's going to be fine.

I pop two melatonin gummies, because there's no way I'll be able to get through the night with all of the thoughts dancing around in my head. And then, because my body is useless when it comes to tolerance, I pass out like a dead person.

The alarm clock on my phone wakes me up at 6:30. I get up, get dressed, make the bed (as if I'm coming back or as if someone else might want to sleep in it), and pack all of my stuff. I pack Nate's bathroom shelf lineup too, trying to push out of my mind the fact that he didn't come back to our room last night.

Once I've lugged all my crap downstairs, I pop into the kitchen to see where Maggie is. At this point, the only people I'm not afraid to run into are the retreat house staff. Of course, as luck would have it, Lucy is there, her resting bitch face in all its glory. She's smirking at me, the look silently shouting, *I told you so.* My response look is one of curiosity, like, *You told me what exactly?*

"Maggie is outside waiting to take you to the eight o'clock boat, Cecily," she says, but the sinister smile on her face tells a different story.

"Thank you," I reply.

"Best of luck to you with your writing endeavors."

"Um, yeah. Thank you."

I turn to leave and notice her smirking toward the kitchen door, where none other than Alice Devereaux is peeking out.

Makes sense that she would be just as shady in my final encounter with her as she was in my initial one, I think as I trudge through the early-morning ice remnants to the running van.

I open the door, expecting to see Nate inside, but it's only Maggie.

"Morning," she says, light-years more cheerful than Lucifer back in the main house. She's wearing a tight black long-sleeve shirt that leaves her whole midsection completely bare. Across the chest, it reads, *This is my (book) clubbing shirt.* Normally, her getup would make me contemplate the Matthias dress code, but right now, it doesn't even register, distraught as I am by the events of the past twelve hours.

"Hi, Maggie. I'm not sure if you heard. Nate and I need a ride to the ferry, please."

"Not Nate. Just you this morning," she corrects me.

"I'm sorry?"

"He's not coming."

"What do you mean? I mean, obviously I can see that he's not here, but won't he be joining us?"

She shakes her head. "Nope."

"Is he staying? Did something change?" I pull my cell phone out of my coat pocket. No missed calls or text messages. I hit the green button next to his name. It goes straight to voicemail.

"I heard he left last night."

"How? There's no way out of here, right?"

Maggie cranks the heat up in the van, then puts it in drive and slowly pulls away from the main house. I try not to notice the lump that forms in my throat as my mind tries to process the idea that this will probably be the last time I ever see this place. She lowers her voice, not that anyone can hear us in here anyway. "When you live here year-round, any kind of news travels fast: bad, good, makes no difference," she explains. "Nate got an Uber last night and chartered a plane back to New York."

"What? Seriously?" I'm stunned. *He just up and left and didn't tell me?*

"Facts. Jared—his Uber driver—posted it on Instagram last night. And everybody here knows the pilot, Frank Fredonia. Nice guy, but more than happy to shuttle disgruntled rich people around for the right price."

That's right. Unlike me, Nate's got money. He doesn't have to live his whole life on scholarship like I do.

"I can't believe he didn't tell me he was leaving."

"Well, you guys aren't *really* married, right? It was all a—ugh, what's the word? Like, a fake-out?"

I shrug, staring out at the quiet of the wintry morning. "I think you mean a ruse," I say with a sigh. "I don't know, Maggie. I'm not sure of anything anymore."

I turn around to see the small campus of the retreat center shrinking farther into the backdrop until finally it disappears entirely as we drive over a hill.

I feel *goodbye* sitting heavy in my gut.

How could he have left without telling me?

CHAPTER 18

Nate

The trip home is not an easy one, but it beats sitting around feeling like shit while people whisper about me.

It begins with Jared, my Uber driver, who evidently knows who I am. He shows up in his Pontiac Vibe with Bob Marley playing and an overwhelming scent of vanilla permeating the car. I drop my luggage in the little space pretending to be the vehicle's trunk, and when I sit down in the back seat, I locate the offending object; the stink is coming from a marijuana leaf-shaped piece of cardboard hanging from his rearview. *Vanilla and weed? Is that a pairing?*

"You're the famous one, right?" he asks me. "They said there was a famous one coming to this Matthias thing for a few days. That you?"

"I guess." I nod. "Mind if I crack this window?"

"You're the boss, superstar. I'm just your lowly horse-and-buggy man." He laughs absurdly, as if he's just made a joke that was coherent and/or funny. "I shall take you to the ferry terminal, no problem, but if you're trying to get back to the mainland tonight, you won't find any boats there."

"Fuck. Seriously?"

"'Fraid so, my dude."

"Is there an airport on the island?"

"Yep. But first flight outta there is also not till morning."

"What airlines fly here?" I pull out my phone to try and book a ticket.

"Just the puddle-jumper express, bro," Jared informs me. "New England Airlines. Only flies to Westerly, Rhode Island, but you can grab an Amtrak from there."

"And that won't leave until tomorrow?" I clarify.

"That is correct, good sir," Jared says. He's driving particularly slowly, and his right eye is bloodshot, like a toddler with a drippy case of conjunctivitis, but only on the right side. *There's an excellent chance he's high.* "Of course, a guy like you has some sick green, right?"

"Weed? No, man, I'm sorry. I'm not your guy for that."

"I mean cash, not kush, bro."

"Oh," I say. *Of course you do.*

But to be fair, he is right. I sometimes forget that I have money. So I let Jared arrange a ride for me on an eight-passenger charter plane with a pilot who seems like he makes a fortune shuttling poor souls like me around—or I suppose I should say *rich* souls with poor circumstances—and is more than happy to capitalize on our grievous situations.

Two thousand dollars. That's how much it costs. "Supply and demand, baby," Jared explains.

Fabulous. Just what I need, I think. *When I envisioned my final moments here, I absolutely hoped they'd include an economics lesson from the drug lord of Block Island, a Gen-Z stoner clearly on a quest to find himself by way of crashing in the guest house of his insanely wealthy parents' summer home.*

It doesn't matter. Jared introduces me to his cousin, a twentysomething with a very intentional mullet who he calls Frank the Stank. Frank is an employee of New England Airlines who side-gigs as a charter pilot. He, thankfully, does not appear intoxicated in any way, so I say a silent prayer, take a seat in his tiny aircraft, fasten my seat belt, put my phone on airplane mode, and politely ask him to take me to JFK in Queens.

Because no way am I going to Venmo two grand out of my checking account to go to Westerly and still have to endure a 4-hour-trek home from there.

In case you're wondering what the ride is like, I'll sum it up by offering you the mental image of a short bus careening down an endless unpaved dirt road. Fifty-seven minutes of white-knuckle-clutching my hands to my armrests as Frank the Stank weaves his way through the frozen clouds. It is a time, to say the least.

I keep my eyes closed, simply out of fear, and spend those minutes in a memory. The very first time I got a royalty statement, I had no idea what to expect. Sure, I could have asked my agent, since it was coming from her office, but because *Work* was a debut, I was a neophyte and still had a day job. I didn't even know *when* a royalty statement would make an appearance in my mailbox.

I was still living in my apartment in East Harlem. My roommates were both gone, having relocated out of our concrete jungle in exchange for greener pastures (assuming one considers Dumbo to be greener than uptown Manhattan). It was COVID times, my rent was frozen, playgrounds were closed indefinitely, and I barely went anywhere, but when I did, I wore a mask: first paper, then cloth, then KN95. I even wore a mask to go downstairs and get my mail, because you never knew who you'd run into in the lobby of the building or who had been breathing the recycled oxygen before you got there.

I opened my gunmetal-gray mailbox with my tiny mail key and shuffled through its contents. Electric bill, internet bill, a postcard advertising grocery delivery, and a plea for donations to St. Vincent de Paul Society. And then, an envelope from Table of Contents Literary Agency. I opened that one first and was shocked to find a check enclosed. According to my contract, I was earning $1.06 per physical book sold and $0.88 per ebook sold. The audio rights and foreign rights in a dozen countries had just been sold, so this was the only royalty statement I would ever receive where one could look at my advance vs. only the physical and e-copies of my book and see how I was doing. My advance was $50,000. This royalty statement arrived ten months later.

The check was for $75,659.64.

Evidently, it covered my first six months of sales, during which time period I'd sold 73,226 physical copies and 54,591 e-copies. Subtract the advance, and this was my first authorly paycheck, so to speak.

It was more money in one check than I'd ever seen in my entire life. I called my dad, the accountant, to ask if he would look it over and help me make heads or tails of the numbers. He did and then offered some investment advice. "The most important shot in golf is the next one, kid," he told me.

I waited six more months until my next royalty statement came (which included foreign sales and was more than five times the amount of my first one) before I decided to make any real moves. The easiest move was the physical one, from my rental in East Harlem to my current digs on the Upper West Side, which I was able to purchase outright. I opened a savings account and deposited the rest in there for the time being.

When the money came in for my film option, I relied on my dad to help me choose some solid pandemic-proof investments to put it in, and after another year of royalty statements, I was comfortably living in millionaire status.

But you know, I still put my pants on one leg at a time. I still take the subway to get around. (I didn't at that time, because nobody took the subway during COVID, but I do now.) I still like a good bacon cheeseburger more than a plate of caviar or whatever it is that rich people eat at one in the morning after a night out with friends at the bar. (Not that I would know. I haven't been out like that in years.)

My point is I don't go around thinking, *I'm a rich guy. Let me buy*

*rich-guy clothes and go on rich-guy vacations and take a private charter plane
to get to JFK when public transportation isn't available.*

Because sometimes I forget that I can do things like that.

But with my eyes shut tightly on the bumpiest plane ride in the
history of airline flights, I realize, *You know what? I am rich. And well
connected. So if I need to make something happen, I can probably find a way
to finagle it.*

Still, I remind myself, there are certain things we all know money
can't buy. I can't change Dillon Norway's mind and *make* him allow CJ
back into Matthias. I wish I could, but I know that's not realistic. I can't
buy creativity; the fact that this girl is my muse and that the perfect
recipe of her beautiful face with those blue-rimmed glasses against the
backdrop of the Atlantic Ocean during a snowstorm will never be a thing
I experience again is not fixable with a fat check. If it was, life would be
a whole lot easier.

But money and fame *can* get you something priceless.

Access.

The eyes-wide-shut insight germinates an idea inside my brain. I jot
it down in the Notes app on my phone so that I don't forget it later on.
It's the kind of idea that can only be borne from a high-stress situation,
such as the flight from hell crossed with a wife who asked you to *please
leave her alone* after you single-handedly destroyed her pursuits in higher
education under the guise of trying to help. The kind of scenario where
you just can't bear to look out the window or at the snake tattoo wrapped
around the fingers on the right hand of Frank the Stank or even at your
own lap, because reality will come crashing down. Or your plane will.
Potato, potahto.

Somehow, we manage to land safely. I don't know how he does it in
that flying tin can, but if I were a more religious person, I would probably
kiss the ground once I set my feet back on it. You know that fun little

icebreaker: *If you could have any superpower, what would it be?* Let me tell you, mine would *not* be flying.

I hop inside one of the long line of yellow cabs at the airport. I give the driver my address and lean back into the black vinyl seat, allowing him to take me home even though I hate the way taxi drivers weave in and out of traffic like they're invincible. I just don't have it in me to navigate the AirTrain through Jamaica and the subway from there with all this luggage. I've had enough stress for one day, thank you very much.

It is only when I have been delivered to my apartment building intact that I am able to breathe again. Because I am shook from the ride, coupled with the events of the past few hours, I make myself a brick of ramen noodles to fill my belly, wash it down with two consecutive double shots of whiskey (a trick I save for only the most dire of circumstances), and go to sleep immediately.

I wake up the following morning at 8:30. Out of habit, I reach for my phone, and when I notice that there are no new notifications, I realize I never turned it off airplane mode. I switch it over to Wi-Fi and see that I have a new voicemail and several new emails.

The voicemail is from CJ. "Hey," she says, in a quieter-than-normal, sad-but-also-nervous tone. "You're not in the van. Maggie says you left last night. Why didn't you tell me? Please give me a call. I hope you're okay. Thanks," she sighs. "Bye."

Out of instinct, I hit the *Call* button. It goes straight to voicemail. "Hi!" chipper CJ sings into the recording. "Sorry I can't make it to the phone right now, but please leave your name, number, the time you called, and a message, and I'll get back to you as soon as I can. Thanks! Wait for the—" and then the phone beeps.

"Hey," I say, somber with hangover undertones. "I'm just calling to let you know that I'm okay, and I'm sorry if I worried you. I was just trying to give you some space, and I knew I wouldn't be able to do that effectively if I stayed on the island. Anyway, I'm home. I imagine you're on your way home now too. I guess, um, call me whenever you feel like you want to."

There's so much more that I want to say, but I don't know how to articulate what I'm feeling, so I hang up instead.

Very mature, I know.

An alcohol-induced night of sleep in my own bed combined with memories from yesterday has resulted in me feeling pretty shitty about the bleak outlook of my foreseeable future.

I put on a pot of coffee and get in the shower, hoping to wash some of the negativity away—and that is where I am when I remember the note I jotted down in my phone during my tailspin through the sky last night.

It's so crazy that it just might work, I think.

After drying off, I grab my phone and call my agent. I don't even bother with her work line. She's probably still trying to get above water with an inbox full of holiday queries and general email catchup. Instead, I call her cell.

Trina went to Bali for Christmas, courtesy of the fifteen percent she earns on my royalties.

Consequently, busy or not, she picks up on the first ring.

"Hey, Nate," she says in a chipper voice. "Happy New Year! What can I do for you?"

A smile turns the corners of my mouth up.

"Actually, I need a favor."

"Anything for you."

I pace my apartment, explaining who I need her to call and for what purpose. I am embodying the phrase, *I'll have my people call your people,* something I never thought I'd need to do.

Alas. Desperate times.

I just pray to God that my idea works.

CHAPTER 19

Cecily

When I get back on land, my phone buzzes with a voicemail.

There was no cell service at sea.

I parked my car in long-term parking at the Point Judith ferry terminal. I schlep my bags off the ship, and by the time I get inside my vehicle, my hands are numb from the cold. I put the key in the ignition and let the car rattle, self-soothing its way to being warmed up.

As I wait, I put the phone on speaker and play the message.

"Hey," Nate says. "I'm just calling to let you know that I'm okay, and I'm sorry if I worried you. I was just trying to give you some space, and I knew I wouldn't be able to do that effectively if I stayed on the island. Anyway, I'm home. I imagine you're on your way home now too. I guess, um, call me whenever you feel like you want to."

Seriously?

After everything we've been through, that message sounds...about as cold as this car. *Just trying to give you some space.* More like just trying to use my words against me to justify dipping out in the middle of the night. Well, fine, early in the night. But still.

To clarify, when I said, *I need some space,* I just meant, *For like an hour.* I didn't think Nate would *leave the state.*

The drive home is long and kind of slippery, thanks to New England weather being a nightmare and I-95 being an endless sea of brake lights. Without Nate to chat with in my passenger seat, I'm left to my own headspace. Not good for business.

My life is falling apart.

I have been expelled from graduate school; how's *that* for an accolade?

My stats this morning included 112 new Instagram followers, but then, out of nowhere, my account got restricted and I couldn't use it. I must have tried to follow too many people. Somehow, I am now officially failing at social media too.

Other pertinent stats included three new rejections and, yes, zero full manuscript requests.

Zero.

My mentor hates me. This man who represented all hope and possibility of hard work paying off, who treated me like the hardworking student I am (well, *was*), who invested his personal time reading all of my extra pages, who told me that I had real, honest-to-God talent and that my scribblings were actually worthy of agency representation—well, I screwed the pooch with him also. By coming up with an elaborate lie so that I could get what I wanted.

And if all of that wasn't bad enough, I went ahead and fell for Nate. Like a fool.

The worst part is, I *know* better. The whole point of going for my MFA in the first place was so that I could become something that *wasn't* defined by having a boyfriend or a soul mate or a husband or life partner or any of that crap. I was supposed to have a *book*. The *book* would complete me.

Because *people* will only let you down.

I could call Nate back, but it's pretty clear he only called in response to my pathetic-sounding voicemail message. Instead, I spend five hours in sporadic traffic trying to get out of my head by blasting my music and hard-tapping on my steering wheel. I grab two Boston cream doughnuts and a chocolate milk from a Connecticut rest-stop Dunkin' because about three hours into the drive, my blood sugar is lower than a gopher hole. So naturally, it spikes back up, getting me back to Queens, and then dips down again the second I walk in the door.

I'm exhausted. Physically, mentally, and emotionally. I don't have the energy to do anything. I need to grocery shop, do the laundry, make a plan, maybe write a new query letter.

First though? I need a nap.

After three well-deserved hours curled up in my bed, I wake up feeling worse.

I can't run from life though, and the clothes won't wash themselves, so I hit the laundromat and put in a load of laundry. While it runs, I head over to Stop & Shop. Then back to the laundromat to switch the clothes into the dryer, home to put away the groceries, and back out to get my clothes. It's as efficient as I can be in my current state. By the time my clothes are folded neatly in the laundry basket, the sun has set. I swing by the Chinese restaurant and grab takeout for dinner. Back at my place, after unpacking all my groceries, I curl up on the couch with my laptop, eating chicken lo mein directly out of the carton.

I check my email first.

One new rejection. Dear Author, it begins. I don't even read the rest. Just the fact that they won't use my name tells me everything I need to know. I put a strikethrough mark over the agent's name in my spreadsheet, crossing my chances of representation off like an Advent calendar leading up to my inevitable demise.

I'm going to end up a single, unfulfilled, old children's librarian.

And I can't stop thinking about Nate.

Shut up, Cecily. Stop being an idiot. He's obviously not into it anymore, now that his job is kaput.

Instead of checking my other pertinent stats, including my follow-to-follow-back ratio on social media, I decide to google "marriage annulment in New York." I remember reading about this back at Thanksgiving, when I first came up with the idea of marrying Nate. I didn't want to have to worry about legal fees later on for a divorce, so I wanted to see if an annulment might be possible.

Of course, the way I read it then seems different from the way I'm reading it now. Google brought me to a website for a law firm called D'Aleo and Strauss—some fancy place in the city, no doubt—and to an article written by one of the partners about marital annulments. Essentially, it said that New York has specific laws about what type of marriage qualifies for an annulment. If you're married to more than one person (like you got married a second time, but your first marriage hadn't been dissolved yet), you qualify. If one of the two partners is not physically able to have sex, you qualify. If someone was forced into the marriage, you qualify. If one of the parties was underage at the time of the marriage, you qualify.

And then there's the bit about fraud. It says, If the marriage was fraudulent, you may qualify for an annulment. Okay, so back when I read that at Thanksgiving, I thought we'd be able to simply file for an annulment when I was done with school. I didn't think about, oh, I don't know, reading the remainder of the paragraph at that time.

But now I do.

And I realize that we're probably fucked.

It goes on to say, An action to annul a marriage whereby the consent of one of the parties involved was obtained by fraud will be granted provided it is within the time frame for enforcing a civil remedy of the civil practice law and rules. However, if the spouses voluntarily cohabitated as husband and wife, and both gave consent to the fraudulent marriage, an annulment will more than likely no longer remain an option.

And so, ladies and gentlemen, consider this a book-length PSA about the importance of reading the fine print.

The fact that I won't even be able to annul my own fake marriage is sadly on-brand for me at the moment.

I navigate away from the D'Aleo and Strauss website and open up another window in Google. There, I open QueryTracker.net, because I'm going to need to figure out a new query letter and begin to develop a new list of agents to send it out to.

Because I am a glutton for punishment, I spend the next six hours on the sofa, attempting and reattempting to pull together a reasonable-sounding letter. It takes several tries before I land on this:

Dear <Agent>,

Art imitates life imitates art. No one knows this better than me.

I'm sure I'm not the only girl who has ever had to watch her first love marry her sister, but I'm definitely the only one who's ever written a full-length manuscript about it. My novel, *Hard Pass*, is ironically about what can happen to someone after they come face-to-face with deeply personal rejection.

Read this carefully, <Agent>, since you are a rejection-master, aren't you?

Natalie Green is the perfect high schooler. She's polite, has good grades, respects her family, serves her community, and is exactly the opposite of the kind of girl you'd want to read about in a coming-of-age story. You're looking for redemption: the troubled girl who finds her way, the orphaned girl who finds a family, the ugly duckling who becomes the swan. Well, my story turns those tropes upside down, because Natalie Green is none of those things. She's likable and easygoing, in love with her first real boyfriend, heading off to college, about to spread her wings and fly.

But Natalie is about to become a human game of Jenga. Knocked down, built back up, knocked down again. Just like me.

I'm Cecily Jane Allerton. I just got kicked out of Matthias University's MFA program for defrauding its director, my former mentor. I married a professor after kissing him on national television just to try and save his job. I wrote this manuscript in my first semester at Matthias and won the Rising Star Award for Best New Fiction. Of course, I can't put that on a résumé anymore. It's too dramatic.

That's attempt number five, and I don't need to be a Matthias University graduate to know that it's a trash safari.

It's late now, and my computer battery is dying.

I can't believe Nate hasn't called me. I realize he *did* call me last and that technically, it's my turn to call him back, but I'm a stubborn asshat.

So forgive me for being a little bit surprised when my phone lights up with his name on the screen.

I brace myself. I'm not sure what I'm expecting, but my stomach contracts quickly, tying itself up like a garlic knot.

"Hello?" I say.

"Hey. I'm glad you answered."

I relax a little, even though he sounds kind of weird. *Maybe he's been drinking.* I could understand that. A little social lubricant might be a nice assist to help me work through my current state of mental constipation. "How are you?" I ask.

"Good, fine. I need you to do me a favor."

Excuse me? You're good? You're fine? I'm over her, miserable, and you're just totally copacetic, living your best life in your city apartment with—

"You still there?" he asks.

"Yeah, I'm here. What's the favor?"

"Can you turn on the TV, please? Put it on NBC."

"Um, okay." *Why the cryptic request? What's going on here?* Still, I grab the remote and hit the button for channel four. "What am I—" My voice drops off. I'm looking at the flat screen of my modest thirty-two-inch LG HDTV, and I can't process the picture looking back at me.

"Just watch, please," Nate says.

It's Questlove.

"So I had a very strange and special request today," he begins. He's sitting on the couch next to Jimmy Fallon's *Tonight Show* desk. "Y'all know my Kazoo Karaoke Bomb bit that I do, right?" The Roots Crew rattles off the jingle that marks the bit. Quest smiles. "Thanks, guys," he laughs.

Even his laugh is smooth like butter. *How can someone always be so chill?* I wonder.

"So anyway, a few months ago, we did an epic Kazoo Karaoke Bomb at Sing Sing in Alphabet City. Let's run a quick clip."

He cuts to the viral worst moment of my life. I'm belting it all out while Questlove kills it on his red and yellow kazoo, and then I swirl around and plant a huge kiss right on Nate's lips.

The beginning of the end.

The video clip pauses there, and a digital marker draws a circle around me kissing Nate. Right there on the screen, like a meteorologist marking up a map with weather pattern predictions or a child playing with a painting app on an iPad.

"See that? Well, we didn't know it at the time, but this was the beginning of a real big scandal for these two. The guy in the picture is Nate Ellis, the famous writer who everyone was calling the 'Literary Nostradamus' after his book, *Work,* took off and became an overnight sensation. And the girl, well, that was a student in the master's program where he was teaching. Scan-duh-luss." A knowing smile from Quest.

No big deal, huh, Ahmir? Just the end of my life, on full display for the late-night-viewing world. It's very apropos for *The Tonight Show* to feast on the humiliation of poor souls like me to later turn it into fuel for America's viewing pleasure. But I thought Questlove and I had something special, so I'm a little peeved to see him reminding the world of my alcohol-induced transgressions.

"Now, now, let's just clarify—these are two almost-same-age consenting adults here. But because they kissed on TV, he could have lost his job. So here's a real fairy tale for you—she cares so much about him that she *marries* him, just to save his job. Only, because he's a man, somehow he finds a way to mess it up." Questlove shakes his head. "Shameful. I mean, right?"

"Just like a man," Black Thought sings.

A crowd of voices cheer and laugh.

"Anyway, he contacted my agent today and relayed this extremely sad tale to me—you know, boy meets girl, boy fake-marries girl, boy becomes unemployed, boy loses girl—just your typical romance story, right? I could write up this stuff—maybe for my next book. Yo, you guys know how it ends, right?" The camera cuts to The Roots crew, and Black Thought nods his head affably, running his hand along his beard. "Boy gets girl back, am I right?"

The audience cheers.

"So—I'll have y'all know Jimmy had to move the whole schedule around for this, but without further ado, I present to you *The Tonight Show*'s first installment of Defusing the Kazoo Karaoke Bomb!"

The crowd applauds again, and the camera cuts to a dark stage. "Here goes nothing," Nate says to me through the phone, which I am still holding up to my now-slack jawline.

The lights fade on, and Kamal Gray from The Roots plays a slow, sad yet familiar piano melody in the background. Captain Kirk Douglas joins in on an acoustic guitar. Questlove emerges from behind them all and takes a seat at the drum set. I recognize the tune, but it's slower and softer than I recall, so I can't immediately place it.

Then the camera cuts to a spotlight shining on Nate Ellis, in the middle of the stage, holding a microphone.

"Holy shit," I whisper.

He takes a deep breath and puts the mic to his lips, his soulful eyes looking down at his feet, then up into the camera. "Ooh it's somethin' about, just somethin' about the way she moves," he sings.

Tears spring to my eyes. It's a totally different rendition.

"I can't figure it out, it's somethin' about her," he sings. His voice drips like honey, thick and sweet into the microphone. "Said, ooh, it's somethin' about the kind of woman that want you but don't need you," he croons. "I can't figure it out; it's somethin' about her."

Nate is swaying with the melody, and absent the synthesizer, the song sounds completely different, like a ballad, an epic composition of love and adoration for the object of the singer's desire. He works it, pouring himself into the lyrics in a way that seems almost surreal, and I can't be sure if I'm dreaming. I have to consciously work to hold the phone up to my face, as my jaw is slack with disbelief at the scene unfolding on my television.

As the chords build up the crescendo of the chorus, Nate's voice stays light, a huge contrast to the screaming and yelling we did at Sing Sing not six weeks ago.

"She's got her own thing," he goes on. "That's why I love her. Miss Independent, won't you come and spend a little time?"

As The Roots add more people and instruments for the second verse, Nate says into the phone, "Please let me in, CJ."

I can barely answer, as my eyes are transfixed on the TV screen. "What do you mean?" I manage to ask.

There's a knock at my door.

"Wait—you're here?" I hop to my feet, almost dropping my dead laptop on the floor, and slide across the vinyl sticky tile floor to open it. I don't let my gaze leave the screen. The second verse begins. I take Nate by the hand and drag him back to the couch. "Isn't this live? What did you do?" I ask him, feeling his fingers lace into mine. I squeeze them tight.

"Ow," he whispers.

"Sorry." I smile. Tears stream down my face, but I don't wipe them away.

"We filmed it this afternoon," he explains.

I can't speak. This is indescribable.

"Ooh, there's somethin' about the kind of woman that can do for herself," TV Nate sings. "I look at her and it makes me proud; there's somethin' about her."

The camera cuts to Questlove on the drums, notably absent his plastic kazoo, looking classy-casual in his black sweater with a matching pick in his hair. He raps on the drums as his upper body rocks with the slow sexy beat.

"There's somethin' oh-so-sexy about the kind of woman that don't even need my help…"

I shake my head, my grin swallowing my whole face. I can't stop staring at the screen. I know he's sitting right next to me, but since this version of the song is laced in minor chords, it's haunting. Nate's voice isn't singing-contest-winner status, but it doesn't matter. It's still the best sound I've ever heard.

I will never love someone as much as I love this man.

"She's got her own thing; that's why I love her," he sings in stereo with himself—next to me live and prerecorded on the television.

I don't even want to join him. I want to remember this moment forever as a spectator of the world's best private—or hugely public (depending on how you look at it)—serenade.

"Ooh, the way we shine," he whispers in my ear, pulling me close to him. He smells like Nate, like clean sheets and spearmint and cedar.

Like home.

When the song is over, the audience goes crazy. TV Nate smiles and blushes, and Questlove emerges from behind his drum set and heads up to the front of the stage.

"CJ, I'm sorry for everything," TV Nate says. "But nothing else matters as long as I have you. I hope you'll forgive me."

"C'mon, CJ! You *have* to forgive him. I mean, it takes a real special kind of dude to go all out like this," Quest says.

The audience cheers.

"Well, you'll have to call me and let me know what happens, man," Questlove says to Nate.

"I will," Nate promises. They shake hands.

"Okay, folks, we'll find out on tomorrow's show if the karaoke bomb was defused!"

The segment ends, and the show cuts to commercial. I hit *mute* on the remote.

He pulls his phone out of his pocket and sets it up for a video recording. Then he holds it out like as if we're going to take a selfie.

"What are you doing?" I ask.

"We need to tell Questlove if you forgive me," he says. The video's rolling. He raises his eyebrows. "So do you?"

I laugh. "I do," I say, nodding.

"And do you love me?"

"I do. I love you, Nate Ellis."

"Good. That's all I need. Well, that, and this." He cups my face with his free hand and pulls my face in to his. He drops the cell phone. It records the ceiling as his tongue slips into my mouth, erasing all the mistakes we made.

When we stop to take a breath, he reaches for the ground and stops the video. Then he texts it to someone.

"You have Questlove's number?" I ask.

He shrugs.

"Stop it. You do not."

"Don't worry about it." He reaches up and takes off my glasses. I close my eyes, and he wipes my tears away with his thumbs. "Hey," he whispers.

"Hm?"

"I love you more."

Nate

Okay, fine.

I'll tell you how I made that magic happen.

It was simple, really. My agent, Trina, knows someone at Questlove's agency, and Trina owed me a Bali-trip, new-car, and down-payment-on-her-house-size favor. So she made a few calls for me, and Quest talked to the producers, who said that if I could make it into the studio by 2:00 p.m. for rehearsal and stay through a 4:00 p.m. taping, then he would help me out. Thank God the publishing world is small.

It just so happens that Questlove's a really good dude. He even gave me a signed copy of *The Rhythm of Time* for CJ's autographed collection at the library.

The rest goes like this:

CJ's manuscript got two full requests, but they both said the same thing: it wasn't high-concept enough, meaning that for a debut, it didn't offer anything fresh and new to the literary scene. Strong writing though. Good voice. Lots of potential. We reworked her query letter so it didn't come off quite as threatening (not a look that will endear an author to a potential agent), but after a few more rounds of querying, we decided to put that manuscript in the drawer, and I suggested we try something new.

It was really fine. Bryce was old news by then. Jamie had the triplets, adorable preemies they named after famous baseball players: Mikey (Trout), Aaron (Judge), and Ruthie (as in Babe). Jamie and the babies moved upstairs in CJ's parents' house because her mom insisted the basement was too cold. Jamie struggled to adjust to motherhood, while Bryce went off to Florida for six weeks of spring training. Melanie had a sweet little girl named Scarlet, her third kid. Everyone was healthy, and CJ's mom was in her full grandmotherly glory.

We talked about our marriage and what we should do about it. I told her that if she wanted to get divorced, I would be fine with handling the legal fees. I also wanted to get her back in school, but CJ's a pain in the ass who wasn't about to let me pay for anything. Ultimately, we decided that we might as well stay married while enjoying the early stages of traditional coupledom. She lived in her apartment in Queens, and I stayed at my place in Manhattan. She slept over my place on the weekends, so I had ample opportunities to take her out on fun city dates until Sunday evening, when we'd head back to Bayside so we could attend the weekly family dinner, and then I'd sleep at her place on Sunday night. She did her library thing during the week, and I worked, first with Trina and then with my editor, Dan, to make edits on my second novel, *Success*.

I brought CJ to New Jersey to meet my sister—but only once, because once is enough outside of mandatory holiday obligations. (I blame Johnny for that; Lila's almost old enough to make her way into the city by herself, and once that happens, I'll be the coolest uncle she could ever ask for.) When my parents came up for Easter, CJ and I had brunch with them so we'd be free to have dinner with her family. We took more Advil in that single day than ever on account of all the maternal screeching.

Around Valentine's Day, I emailed Dillon Norway to petition him to forgive CJ. She wasn't going back to Matthias; he'd made up his mind about that, and we both respected it, but she was sad about how their relationship ended. So I just told him how much she regretted the fact that in order to save my job, she had to lie to him. He wrote back and said that he hoped I knew what a special girl I had on my hands and told me that I'd be a fool to lose her. He said that I should alpha read for her. *She doesn't trust herself,* he wrote, *but she should. And she will, with encouragement.* He also said that when CJ inevitably cut her teeth in the publishing world—when, not if—he wanted a signed copy of her first novel, and he would be more than happy to pay for it.

Class act, that Dillon Norway. I printed out the email exchange and gave it to her as part of her Valentine's Day gift.

The other part? A two-week couples writing retreat I found through *Writer's Digest* magazine.

Because I had an idea.

"Let's write our story," I suggested. "We can do it in alternating POVs, where you write your side and I'll write mine. And then we can pitch it to my agent. There are other awesome agents at Table of Contents Literary Agency. I'm sure someone would love to represent you there."

She scrunched up her nose. "I don't want to get an agent by riding your coattails."

"Of course not. I'm not suggesting that you can't do this on your own. I'm just saying it's a great story. We could be a husband-and-wife writing team."

She folded her arms. "That's not a thing."

"I knew you'd say that." I handed her a gift, neatly wrapped in brown craft paper with a red bow stuck to the top. "Open it."

"It's a book," CJ guessed.

"Naturally," I laughed.

"Emily Wibberley and Austin Siegemund-Broka. Who are they?" She flipped over the book, titled *The Roughest Draft,* and skimmed the back.

"They write mostly teen romance. But this book is for adults. Read it. I think you'll really like it."

"You actually think we could write a book *together?*"

"Absolutely. At the very least, we could give it a shot."

So that's what we did. By Christmas, the manuscript was done, and CJ, stubborn bull that she is, insisted that she wanted to query it.

But Trina and I had other plans.

For her thirty-first birthday, Trina set her up on a phone call with Evan Dresner, an agent at Table of Contents who reps Karlie London, a super-famous romance writer. He was trying to blaze trails throughout the romance space, and Trina and I thought he'd be a great long-term fit for her.

We were right.

Publishing a novel takes a long time. Most people don't realize exactly how long the process takes. For CJ and me, it was about ten months of writing, then another four months of editing with Trina and Evan, another month on submission (since our story wasn't appropriate for Boone, we had to go out on sub, a great experience for CJ to have firsthand), and eighteen more months from signing to publication.

Almost three years in total.

By that time, we'd bought a house in Little Neck, a few blocks away from CJ's rental. I kept my apartment in the city to use as an office and commuted there every weekday on the Long Island Rail Road. We wrote as a team in the early morning, and then I'd work on my solo projects in the afternoons so we would be together in the evenings.

Our writing team's debut novel was called *A Storybook Wedding.*

On release day, we drove down Northern Boulevard to the Barnes & Noble in Manhasset and found our book baby on a table display in the middle of the store. We snapped a picture and posted it on social media, where CJ's twenty-five thousand followers liked and reposted it. Then I got down on one knee and proposed to her—for real this time—right in the middle of the bookstore.

"I know we're technically married," I said as she looked at me with a combination of amusement and shock. "And to be honest, I'm really nervous right now, because I don't know what your answer will be. But I'm typically a pretty traditional guy, and I would really like to marry you the *right* way. I want the big party. I want a thick photo album full of pictures that collects dust on our coffee table. I want the silly favors and the line dancing and the fancy cake. And not just for me. I want it for you, sweetheart. For us. Because our love deserves to be celebrated." I took a deep breath and pulled a velvet box out of my pocket. When I opened it, a 2.5-carat diamond glimmered up at her, and I smiled as her jaw dropped. "So, Cecily Jane Allerton, for the second time—will you marry me?"

She said yes.

Our wedding was planned for the third week in July on Block Island at New Beginnings Retreat Center. It was two days after Matthias University had finished up their residency week, so the dormitories were available for people to stay in. Block Island is gorgeous in the height of summer, and it just seemed fitting to put a nice bow on our story in the place where we met. CJ got really into the planning process (what can I tell you; my girl's a planner), and I added my own little touches—things that would only really make sense on the island. For example, I made sure we had a whiteboard outlining all the activities for our guests to participate in: welcome cocktails, rehearsal dinner, ceremony, reception, after-party, and farewell brunch, all in permanent marker so no one could erase anything by accident. I arranged for Maggie to pick up our guests from the ferry and shuttle them to and from the retreat center as needed, and she didn't fail to disappoint, with a tiny T-shirt that read, *I'm just here for the happy ending.* I also had a signature cocktail called The Infirmary, which was a reddish-pink rum punch with a lobster gummy pierced by a toothpick umbrella sticking out of the top.

CJ added her special touches too. She ordered a cake for us that was made to look like a stack of books, with our title as the top layer, and a little man-and-wife statue perched in the frosting. She named each table at the reception after a famous children's story, with titles including *Cinderella, Sleeping Beauty, The Frog Prince,* and more. And in predictable wedding fashion, she gathered up something old (her grandmother's pearl earrings), something new (a frilly white garter), something borrowed (Jamie's veil), and she opted to wear her adorable glasses for something blue.

CJ's whole family was there, and I'm pretty sure we had as many flower girls and ring bearers as we did guests at the thing. (Her family has a *lot* of little ones.) Her mom wept happy tears, and Jamie was her matron of honor. My family came up as well, along with about fifty of our closest friends and colleagues. CJ was radiant in a stunning white gown, and my breath caught in my throat as she walked down the aisle of the Spiritual Sanctuary on the arm of her father.

Perhaps my best surprise was the officiant though.

I contacted Dillon Norway right after our engagement in the bookstore and explained to him that it would mean absolutely everything to both of us if he would not only attend but officiate our wedding. Time heals all wounds, and Dillon was going to be on the island anyway for residency. It would only mean sticking around for a couple of extra days, so *sure,* he said, with his usual laid-back tenor, he could marry us. It was a breeze to get ordained online. Took him less than fifteen minutes.

The look on her face when she walked down the aisle was something I wish I could bottle up and keep with me at all times. She stared at me first, smiling, then looked around and acknowledged various guests who were standing in the aisle seats. She has generally bad vision, which was exacerbated by the tears in her eyes, so only when she actually approached the altar did she realize it was Dillon standing there.

CJ's face melted then. She broke down crying and gave him a huge unfiltered hug.

"It's you!" she exclaimed into his shoulder.

"Surprise," he replied.

When she pulled back, she grabbed my hand and pulled me in for an embrace.

"Uh, uh, uh," Dillon said, wagging a finger at us. "Not yet, please. There are rules about these sorts of things."

She laughed, and we took our respective places on the altar.

We wrote our own vows, of course. Dillon gracefully led us through the ceremonial rituals, and then we each took a turn to speak. I wish I could remember exactly what was said. Weddings go by in a blur, so I'm glad I have the video to revisit. The major plot points included how lucky we both felt, how funny life can be, and a laundry list of promises I knew we would both keep forever.

We honeymooned in Fiji, and it was as glorious as you'd imagine it to be. Then we came home and settled back into our day-to-day life. We get caught up in the little stuff now, like what to bring to the Sunday dinners at CJ's parents' house or what color couch to put in CJ's new writing room at our home in Little Neck.

We live happily ever after, just like we're supposed to.

Because if anyone deserves a fairy-tale ending, it's CJ.

Acknowledgments

I could never have written this story had it not been for my own MFA experience. I went to Fairfield University, to a low-residency program held on Enders Island just off the coast of Mystic, Connecticut. While my experiences there did not include falling in love with a professor, I *did* fall in love with the world of writing and publishing as a result of my time in graduate school. Because of that, I would be remiss if I did not begin by thanking Sonya Huber, the director who accepted me into the program. Also to Valerie, Dane, Sam, Stuart, Ivan, Jerri, Meg, Brad, and anyone else who tried to make me feel comfortable on the island and, later, on Zoom, a million thanks. I am the worst at navigating social situations.

To Alan Davis: You were the perfect mentor for me, and I cannot sing your praises enough. Your comments gave me the courage I needed to keep learning, keep writing, keep pushing myself. Without you, I would never have been bold enough to start querying agents after that first manuscript. I am more grateful to you than words can express, and I'm proud to call you my friend. Also, I'd like to extend my gratitude to Eugenia Kim, Rachel Basch, Bill Patrick, Dinty W. Moore, and Phil Klay for the part each of you played in teaching me the craft of putting together a novel. And to Chris Belden and Katie

Schneider, for everything you do for the FUMFA Alumni community, I think I speak for all of us when I say thank you. (I hope to one day be as cool as both of you!)

To Elizabeth Copps, my soul sister and the best agent on the planet, how did I get so lucky? Cheers to the drink options at my house, especially Basic Bitch Chardonnay and Lactaid. I hope there are many more sleepovers to come.

To Alyssa Garcia and the marketing team at Sourcebooks, thank you for embracing my hustle and working with me to leverage it. Our partnership means more to me than you know, and I'm grateful beyond words.

To Deb Werksman, Susie Benton, Jocelyn Travis, Aimee Alker, Sabrina Baskey, Farjana Yasmin, Stephanie Gafron, India Hunter, Stephanie Rocha, Rosie Gaynor, Tara Jaggers, and anyone else who helped pull this book together behind the scenes, thank you. I hope you are as proud as I am of what we've created.

To Questlove: You are cool as hell. Thank you for letting me put you in my story and for making the permissions process so easy. I hope you feel like I did your character justice.

To Kristan Higgins, for being an unexpected little ray of sunshine in my life. You are who I aspire to be.

To Emily Wibberley and Austin Siegemund-Broka: thank you for inspiring the ending of this story with your own happily-ever-after. You guys are amazing.

To Cam Eden, for sharing your grind with me so that I could write about it and for being a highlight of every summer, thank you. We will always cheer the loudest for you!

To my author friends Lee Matthew Goldberg, Stephanie Eding, Lauren H. Mae, Anastasia Ryan, KL Cerra, Lisa Roe, Shauna Robinson, Terah Shelton Harris, Kristyn J. Miller, Nancy Crochiere, Jenny L. Howe, MA Wardell, Mia Heintzelman, Jessica Payne, and Sara Read—each and every one of you has brought valuable insight and good vibes to my new life as an author, and I am thankful to know you! Similarly, to Kelli Tager and Nick Mondelli, for lending me your incredible talents on TBP, *spasibo* (which means thank you in Russian, lol).

To the bookstores and libraries that have welcomed me with open arms and the beautiful people who work there, you have my unwavering appreciation. Thank you for welcoming me into your spaces and making my work available to your patrons.

To the Bookstagrammers and BookTok influencers who have embraced my books and posted about them, I am indebted to you. What you offer authors by way of free advertising is truly priceless. Thank you for taking a chance on my books and for the generous, kind messages you've shared with your audiences.

To my launch team, thank you for early reading and posting about this book and for your contagious excitement. Working with you makes the process of launching a book a whole lot more fun than if I was doing it alone!

To the Literacy Nassau team, including my staff, my board (past and present), and John and Janet Kornreich: thank you for making my day job a calling instead of a chore. Kate, Anne-Marie, Renae, Izzy—you guys are the best coworkers I could ask for. I'm grateful for you every single day.

To my dear friends the Chauvins, the Cruz familia, the Meccas, Sue Flecker, Melissa Golfo, Rosie Cook, Jessica Cardinali, Valerie Polakovich, Chris Fields, Mike Torem, Holly Dorrance, and Maria Kata—thank you for your endless encouragement and for being champions of my work!

To my mom, thanks for being my first cheerleader. I hope you enjoy this book as much as you liked *The Book Proposal!* I love you.

To my family—the Wares/Judges and the Micciche clan—thank you for your support and excitement about this new phase of my life. It's been so wonderful having all of you join me on this journey.

To Haley, my sweet girl, I hope you're as proud of me as I am of you. You're growing into a sparkling young lady, and every day, you amaze me. And to my darling Julie, you are the coolest horseback rider I know. May your passion for animals be as strong as my passion for books. I love the two of you more than you will ever understand—plus one anything you say. (And my cubit is bigger than yours.)

To Chris—thank you for our storybook wedding, our beautiful family, and our happily ever after. I could not do this without you. You're a hell of a coauthor, babers. I love you forever and ever (and ever).

And finally, to my readers. It is the honor of my life to share my stories and my characters with you. Thank you for choosing to spend your precious time with me.

About the Author

KJ Micciche is a novelist who hails from Queens, New York, where she spent countless hours curled up under the covers, reading the Baby-Sitters Club as a kid by flashlight way past her bedtime. KJ runs a nonprofit organization that teaches kids with dyslexia how to read. Proud mom of two little girls, she and her family live on Long Island and summer in Cape Cod.

Website: kjmicciche.net
Instagram: kjmicciche